TIBETAN SKY

NING KEN

Translated by

Thomas Moran

SINOIST

Published by Sinoist Books (an imprint of ACA Publishing Ltd)
London - Beijing

info@alaincharlesasia.com ☎ +44 20 3289 3885
www.sinoistbooks.com

This edition is published by arrangement with ACA Publishing Ltd through the agency of China National Publications Import & Export (Group) Co., Ltd.

Author: Ning Ken **Translator:** Thomas Moran
Editor: Susan Trapp **Cover Art:** A. Bodrenkova

 A catalogue record for *Tibetan Sky* is available from the National Bibliographic Service of the British Library.

Paperback ISBN: 978-1-83890-591-0
Hardback ISBN:978-1-83890-593-4
eBook ISBN: 978-1-83890-592-7

Supported using public funding by
ARTS COUNCIL ENGLAND

Sinoist Books is honoured to be supported using public funding by Arts Council England.

The translation of this novel was funded by the China National Publications Import & Export (Group) Co., Ltd.

Additional support for the production of this volume was provided by the Middlebury College Greenberg-Starr Department of Chinese.

Tibetan Sky

Ning Ken

translated by
Thomas Moran

Sinoist Books

Can a soul in pieces
come back together in the Tibetan sky?

Can a mind unmoored
find its mooring by a Tibetan river?

Table of Characters

Main Characters

(Mr) Wang Mojie (Wang Mo, Wang Wei) – Chinese philosopher from Beijing, teacher at the middle school near Drepung monastery outside Lhasa
(Ms) Ukyi Lhamo (Shen Jiayuan) – Tibetan/Chinese, colleague of Wang Mojie's at the middle school, French speaker
Mrs Ukyi Lhamo – Tibetan, Ukyi Lhamo's mother
Ma Dingge (Matthias Robert) – Ukyi Lhamo's guru, at Drepung monastery, from France
Jean-Philippe Robert – French philosopher, father of Ma Dingge, visits from France
(Ms) Yu Youyan – Chinese, minor court official, S&M partner of Wang Mojie
The Mathematician-Poet – Chinese, maths lecturer/poet at Tibet University, ex-lover of Ukyi Lhamo
The Mountaineer – Tibetan/Chinese climbing instructor at Tibet University, lover of Ukyi Lhamo

Ukyi Lhamo's Tibetan Relatives

Madame Ukyi Lhamo – Ukyi Lhamo's maternal grandmother
Lungshar (Lungsharwa Dorje Tsegyal) – Ukyi Lhamo's maternal grandfather
Lhalu (Lhalu Tsewang Dorje) – Ukyi Lhamo's uncle and brother of Mrs Ukyi Lhamo
Lady Lhalu (Yangdzom Tsering) – Lhalu's adoptive mother and later wife
Thonpa Sonam Dekyi – Lhalu's second wife

Wang Mojie's Tibetan Students and Their Families

Kalsang Dekyi – Schoolgirl and class monitor
Sangnyi – Very poor school girl with a little brother
Penpa Dolma – Schoolgirl whose mother dies
Lhadron, Chokyi, Dechen Dolkar, Tsedon – Schoolgirls
Penpa Tsering – Difficult boy, expelled from school for a time
Dolma – Penpa Tsering's mother
Tenpa Nyima – Schoolboy and class monitor
Tenpa Nyima's grandfather
Wangchuk – Schoolboy
Wangchuk's father – Cement factory boss
Lhakpa, Nyima Tsering – Schoolboys

Tibetan Buddhists

Khanor Rinpoche – Ukyi Lhamo's first Buddhist teacher, at Nechung monastery
Nyima Tsering – Mandarin-speaking monk at Nechung monastery
Kangyur Rinpoche – Ma Dingge's teacher in Darjeeling
Tenzin Sangmo – Nun at Tsamkhung nunnery

0. Snow

White. Afternoon. The Thinker. Adhisthana.
The valley. The river settled into winter. Grass. Sandbars. The other side of the river.
Long hair. Blue jeans. A cigarette. Prayer beads on a wrist.
The cigarette didn't go with the prayer beads very well.
A juxtaposition. Memories.

By the time my friend Wang Mo laid eyes on Ma Dingge, snow had been falling all day and into the afternoon. The mountains were white, everything in sight was pristine, empty. On the plateau, Wang Mo said, you can never tell how large an area a snowstorm covers. Snow might have been falling all along the Lhasa River, maybe even along part of the Yarlung Tsangpo too but no farther away than that. No storm can blanket the entire plateau, Wang Mo said, just like sunlight can't. Maybe Ma Dingge was seeing distant sunlight in his mind's eye, perhaps he was seeing sunlight from beyond the far mountains. To look at him you would have thought so. Snow covered his robe of red *pulu* wool, and even though the snow had filled the folds in the fabric, he seemed untouched by it. Depending on how you looked at him, he was a snowman, he was a sculpture, he was *The Thinker*. Behind him was the white expanse of the monastery, and the snow seemed to be pouring down from that direction. The monastery was ancient, it had once flourished. The active monastery complex was enormous, and it was surrounded by an equally enormous expanse of abandoned, ruined buildings. The monastery and its ruins were a pale hue in the background, which is not a metaphor. I don't mean the historical background, it was literally in the background as Wang Mo looked at Ma Dingge, like a mountain might be in the background as birds fly by in the foreground.

Ma Dingge was meditating, he was in the moment with no thought of any past or any future. He was motionless, still to the point of stopping time. He never held on to time, which is why he had all the time in the world. He was sitting on a huge boulder – Wang Mo had once sat there himself – that rested on an otherwise barren slope. Ma Dingge was facing the snow below the mountain, the river valley, the river settled into winter, grass, sandbars, the mountains on the far side of the river and sunlight beyond the mountains and into the distance. Ma Dingge was in all of these places at once.

Ma Dingge's hood was pulled over his head and covered in snow. All you could see of him was part of his face, just visible under his hood, like he was looking out from a window. If it weren't for the glint from the frames of his wire-rimmed glasses and the light reflected in the lenses, he would have looked exactly like a snowman. You could see his eyes through his glasses. They were extraordinarily pale. Whatever the weather, it always seemed to be snowing in his eyes. His gaze seemed to take everything in but also turn everything away.

Wang Mo and Ma Dingge knew each other, but at that moment Ma Dingge saw no one, and so Wang Mo was able to walk back and forth in front of him as if Ma Dingge were a statue. Wang Mo was wearing a leather jacket and a grey checked scarf. The scarf looked somehow wrong, like the external manifestation of Wang Mo's troubled soul. Wang Mo stood near Ma Dingge for a long time, and the snow soon covered him too. He and Ma Dingge were objects occupying adjacent points in space. Like one statue in juxtaposition to another, Wang Mo said. He was pleased by his simile and thought that by standing perfectly still he could experience the mysterious realm where Ma Dingge had gone.

As the author of this novel, I will interrupt the narrative from time to time with thoughts and comments, and the first thing I have to say is that Wang Mo's simile was in fact inapt. Wang Mo had a rich inner life, he was a man of sensibility, but he was infatuated with his inner life, and his sensibility was often too delicate.

I say his simile was inapt because usually – or at least much of the time – a statue captures some timeless emotion, attitude or expression, and therefore if one were to say that Ma Dingge in meditation was like a statue, it would be understandable, if a bit forced. Wang Mo was standing stock still, but his mind was racing and his expression was changing constantly, so no matter how still he stood, he could not be compared to a statue. To put it another way, in Wang Mo's face you could see time passing, you could see impermanence and change. So, while Ma Dingge and Wang Mo were indeed in the same space and adjacent to each other, it was nothing like one statue in juxtaposition to a second statue.

Yes, you are right, Wang Mo was a friend of mine, as was Ma Dingge. Several other characters who will make their appearance in this novel were also friends of mine. I understand them. I know them well. I lived among them for a long time. I lived in Tibet for many years, off and on, and I have written about a few of the people I knew there, but there are even more I have never written about. It is not easy to tell their stories. They are set in Tibet, which gives them an inherent interest, but still they are not easy to tell. Actually, because they take place in Tibet it makes them more difficult to tell. There is something about Tibet that cannot be captured in language. Tibet works on the emotions the way music does. Tibet is abstract. It is something you feel. It escapes narrative. You cannot describe in words what is special about Tibet (those characteristics that are like music) or what is special about the people there. We relate to Tibet the way we relate to music. For years I have tried to write about Tibet but to little avail. I have not succeeded, and this time may be no different I'm afraid. I'm not trying to tell the story of what happened in people's lives. I'm trying to write about existential being. It is relatively easy to tell someone's story, but to capture existential being in language is almost impossible, especially when that existential being has the qualities of music.

Wang Mo went by Wang Mojie, but his real name, the name on his National Identification Card, was Wang Wei. He didn't use the name Wang Wei, but the people who knew him in Tibet didn't call him Wang Mojie. They shortened it to Wang Mo, which was a bit sarcastic and teasing but also, of course, a gesture of a little respect. We are often fascinated by people we find both ridiculous and admirable. Wang Mo shared his real name with the Tang dynasty poet Wang Wei. The Tang poet's literary name was Wang Mojie, which is where my friend got the name he used. He did, in some ways, pretend to be like the Tang dynasty Wang Wei, who was a Buddhist who wrote about the peace and beauty of the countryside, but actually my Wang Mojie or Wang Mo was the opposite of everything the poet had been, and he admitted as much himself. It is impossible for times like ours to produce people as free, natural and unrestrained as the Tang dynasty Wang Wei. At best, all our age can produce is people like Wang Mo. For several reasons, including the demands of fiction, from now on I will refer to Wang Mo as Wang Mojie, which will have its significance.

Everything begins to change in the moment of its becoming, and precisely at the moment that the idea of the statues came to Wang Mo's mind, he was surprised to discover that Ma Dingge was not, in fact, motionless. The snow on Ma Dingge's robe and hood was melting and falling from him. This was happening slowly, like the imperceptible change in the shape of a cloud. When we perceive a change, it is always at the moment that the change accelerates. Change begins before we are aware of it, and we perceive it only as its pace increases. This is true of many phenomena; we notice them only after they have begun to change and as the change accelerates. This is the experience of existing in time. Wang Mo saw that Ma Dingge's red robe was quickly free of the snow, its colour now particularly vivid because it was damp. The falling snow had retreated from Ma Dingge. It seemed to stop at a distance from his body, forming an oval around him. Ma Dingge sat in the middle of this oval like a lamp or like its flame, glowing, transparent. From a distance, it was like seeing lamplight in a window on a snowy night. Nearby, Wang Mo's students were yelling and laughing as they chased one another. It was just noise to Wang Mo, but when the sound reached Ma Dingge's ears it might have sounded to him like birdsong in heaven for all one knew.

We left him alone, we let him listen to the birdsong, Wang Mo said. Some of my students came running over towards the boulder, he said, but I held up my hand, stopped them and made them turn around. They were just running around, without any thought of disturbing anybody, like birds in flight. They had noticed Ma Dingge right away, but they were used to him and found nothing unusual about the sight of him sitting out on a boulder in the snow. The birds had seen him before, the children had as well. A pack of dogs ran after the children, the children wrestled and tumbled in the snow, and the dogs imitated them. Now and again, the dogs dashed in and out of the woods just below the barren slope, kicking up plumes of snow. The dogs played even harder than the children. Typically, the dogs followed the children to school every morning and followed them back home every afternoon. They never entered the school compound. They lay outside the gate.

In any field of phenomena, however, there are exceptions to the rule, and one day I was in the middle of a lecture about Guo Moruo's poem "Celestial Market Street" when all of a sudden, the door opened and a big grey dog swaggered in. I knew the dog well, just like I knew the student he belonged to. I called him Grey, in Mandarin, not Tibetan, but he understood me. Grey had obviously forgotten the rule against dogs coming into the school. As far as Grey was concerned, there might as well never have been such a rule. He came in, walked up to the lectern and stood next to me. Things like this didn't happen often but when they did, none of the students found it surprising. It was surprising to me that the students didn't react. They didn't stir, nobody said anything. Grey was calm, serene even, as if he was the instructor and I was the assistant, but maybe the reverse. In any case, the relationship between us was collegial. I continued to discuss the poem and got the students to read it aloud in unison, their voices strong. It was a happy classroom moment. Grey stood there for a while and then, perhaps disappointed to find that this was all there was to school, he lifted his head, yawned, turned and walked away from the lectern, ambling out of the room like someone with nothing much to do and nowhere in particular to go. He was bored. He rejected me.

Later the snow seemed to ease slightly or it might have been just that it was getting darker, and so it appeared that the snow wasn't falling as heavily as it had been. A change was happening to Ma Dingge. The sphere around him where the snow didn't fall seemed to be getting smaller. Well, no, it didn't seem to be, Wang Mo said, it *was* getting smaller. This is how things always are: change begins before we can perceive it, and we perceive it only as its pace accelerates. Indeed, very quickly the air around Ma Dingge was filled with falling snow. Snow settled on his shoulders. Ma Dingge could no longer keep the snow from touching him. Not even the most accomplished Buddhist adept can do that. Buddhist spiritual practice is an inner-directed activity. It is about self-regulation, self-control. Imagine that within the body of the practitioner there are dozens of lamps. One by one, they are lighted until they are all burning, all shining as brightly as they can. Then, one by one, they are extinguished until they are all out. Then the process begins again. There is nothing unchanging, not even for an instant. Buddhist practice is an endlessly repeating, inner-directed activity. This is why the space around Ma Dingge where snow was not falling shrank and then disappeared. Ma Dingge again became a man of snow. There was nothing in any of this to be considered miraculous.

The snow was actually falling harder than ever, but because it was dark you couldn't see it. Often what our eyes tell us is quite contrary to the truth. Misperception is common. What we think is true often is not true. This is why the Buddhist practitioner accepts the existence of many truths. What is truth, anyway? If there are many truths, can we then say there is no such thing as the one truth? As he was thinking about all of this, Wang Mo looked up at the sky and then off into the distance.

It was time to send the students home. They had played themselves into a frenzy. They were still running around, still rampaging, still yelling. The big April snowstorm had driven everything from their heads, and they had spent the whole afternoon playing. They were supposed to have had a Chinese lesson and then private study, but because of the snow they couldn't sit still. Children have an innately strong bond with nature, and it was impossible to keep them in their seats. The school was part of the surrounding natural world, just as the monastery was, just as the village was. The school was by a road at the foot of Mount Gephel where the ground begins to slope upward, and so the school grounds weren't entirely level, not even the playground was level. Wang Mo's stone house faced uphill towards the playground and beyond it the school buildings. When he opened his door, he could see the sky. At night he could see the stars and the lights of the monastery that stood tall and imposing farther up the mountain. Taking in the whole area at once, the school seemed to be part of the monastery complex.

But that particular night after that snowy afternoon, Wang Mo could see no stars, and the lights from the monastery were hidden by the silently falling snow. Wang Mo couldn't stop thinking about Ma Dingge. He stood in front of the door to his stone house. There was no wind, but snow drifted in with a whisper. Wang Mo let the door stand open. He looked out into the night and the snow he could not see, his mind on Ma Dingge sitting out there in the storm. Ukyi Lhamo claimed that Ma Dingge once sat in meditation in the snow for days and nights on end until the snow stopped, and he was perfectly fine.

But she was just repeating what she had heard. She hadn't seen it with her own eyes. If Wang Mo wanted to have another look at Ma Dingge, it would mean a long walk in the dark. He would have to go through the village with its barking dogs and then cross through the woods, which would be nearly impassable because of the deep snow.

Ukyi Lhamo was home, of course, as he could smell the cigarette smoke from where he stood in front of his house. Her place was dimly lit and full of cigarette smoke as always, and this night the smoke seemed thicker than usual. Obviously there was more than one person in there. Ukyi Lhamo was dressed as usual: jeans, a loose-fitting blouse with a pattern of Buddhist symbols, a cigarette in her hand and prayer beads around her wrist. The cigarette didn't go with the prayer beads very well. She seemed to float out from the smoke. She said nothing to Wang Mo, I mean Wang Mojie – I said I would call him Wang Mojie, and I will from now on – about having company, and Wang Mojie didn't say hello to her guest. He pretended not to see him. Wang Mojie asked Ukyi Lhamo to come with him. She quietly said something to the man who was sitting, legs tucked under him, at one end of her sofa, smoking a cigar. She draped a white shawl, like a Tibetan monk's, over her shoulders and followed Wang Mojie out of the door.

—Want to put on a little more? Wang Mojie asked.

—No, it's not cold, Ukyi Lhamo said, holding the ends of her shawl.

—You should at least put on a hat.

—When have you ever seen me wear a hat just because it's snowing? Ukyi Lhamo asked disdainfully, turning her face to the snow in welcome.

Wang Mojie looked her over.

—Long hair in the snow. Very pretty, he said.

—Don't be stupid. Snow is *adhisthana*.

Ukyi Lhamo believed snow to be a blessing from the Buddha, but still from time to time she shook her head, as if she were humbly declining to be blessed, and snowflakes flurried from her hair like so many diamonds. They didn't say much as they crossed the sloping, snow-covered playground, left the school compound through the back gate and walked into the village that lay just on the other side of the school wall. The village was called Danba and like the school, it seemed to be an organic part of Mount Gephel. They walked steadily uphill. It was slippery, and they almost fell several times. They kept having to hold each other up. The snow blotted out the lights from the village, but Wang Mojie had a torch, and they could follow the footsteps of others who had gone before them. When they had to cross ditches or step over rocks, Wang Mojie considerately took Ukyi Lhamo's hand. Her hands weren't cold. Indeed, they seemed to generate a steady warmth, but it was hard to understand where that warmth could be coming from.

They left the village behind but still had the woods to cross. The village dogs barked from all around. The barking followed them, now and again, all the way to the edge of the woods. The trees were a type of poplar, the bark not white but mottled. For poplars to grow at all at this elevation was something, and in the autumn, the most vibrant season of the year, they were beautiful, turning a rich golden colour that stood out against the white of the monastery walls. The footpath through the woods forked. Taking either path at the fork would lead them to the boulder on which Ma Dingge sat, but Wang Mojie decided to take the path on which he could see faint footprints in the snow. This was the path he had brought his students along when they had returned to the school that afternoon.

There was no wind, not a breath. Snow was draped on the trees, silently, layer upon layer. The grove of trees was a white palace. It really wasn't that cold but still, Wang Mojie thought, Ukyi Lhamo was wearing too little. The stranger on the sofa had kept a chilly silence, and certainly it wasn't the thought of him, with his cold reserve, that was making her hands so warm. It had to be Ma Dingge. Obviously, it was Ma Dingge. He was Ukyi Lhamo's guru. Maybe as you got nearer to your guru, your heart grew warmer, and your hands did too. With Ukyi Lhamo this was entirely possible. She said she once sat in meditation in the snow. When she was at her most despairing, she had sat in meditation in the snow for a long time, until finally her body slowly started to feel warmer and warmer, so warm that the snow that had fallen on her almost started to melt. Wang Mojie didn't really believe her, he didn't think you could call that meditation, it was more a fit of madness but, he mused, madness can give you power. They dropped the subject and talked instead about Ma Dingge's father. Ukyi Lhamo regarded Ma Dingge with the greatest esteem, but she was surprisingly cool when it came to his father.

—So it looks like his father is really coming this time, Wang Mojie said.

—The philosophical sceptic, Jean-Philippe Robert.

Ukyi Lhamo said the name, in its proper French pronunciation, with indifference.

—He's a big deal, a member of the French Academy, very influential in the West, Wang Mojie said.

—Did Ma Dingge tell you that? Ukyi Lhamo asked. She didn't believe Ma Dingge would say such boastful things.

—He didn't have to tell me. I read a book by him a decade ago, from the Commercial Press. I've seen photographs of him too. He must be nearly eighty by now.

—Why is he coming? He still wants to have that conversation with Ma Dingge?

—Of course. Why else would he come to Tibet? And Ma Dingge has agreed to it. He will welcome a visit from his father, a philosophical sceptic.

—At his age he's risking his life, Ukyi Lhamo said.

—That's what seekers after truth do, especially intellectual titans in the West.

—You shouldn't worship foreigners. You're encouraging Ma Dingge in this, aren't you? Ukyi Lhamo asked.

—I admire, I don't worship. You have to make the distinction. Think about it. A philosophical sceptic in conversation with a believer in Tibetan Buddhism. And they are father and son. That's going to be interesting. How are they going to engage? How will they frame their discussion? And not a single scholar in all of the interior is going to have any idea that such an important conversation is taking place. It's all too incredible.

—You're hoping to join the conversation?

—Unfortunately my French isn't very good. I'm going to have to rely on you.

—I'll look after the old gentleman, but I have zero interest in what he has to say.

—Don't you worry about Ma Dingge. He'll be fine.

—Why would I worry about Ma Dingge? Don't be foolish. The last thing I am is worried about Ma Dingge.

Wang Mojie knew that Ukyi Lhamo's coolness towards Robert was not unconnected to her faith, but he also thought she was being typically female. She was reacting emotionally, not rationally, which is something about her that Wang Mojie thought he understood only too well. Talking off and on, they walked out of the woods and into a world that was so completely white it seemed unreal. They walked up to the boulder on which Ma Dingge had been sitting. He was gone. There was nothing there except snow, a thick blanket of snow.

—That's weird. He was sitting right there, on this rock, Wang Mojie said.

Wang Mojie shone his torch all around but there was nothing to be seen. Ukyi Lhamo said nothing. There was nothing to say. The beam settled on the boulder.

—If he was here and then left, why isn't there any sign? Even if where he was sitting and his footprints got covered by snow, you should still see some trace. It's weird. No way I'm wrong. He was right here.

Not too far away was where Wang Mojie's students had played in the snow that afternoon. You could still make out their footprints. They were faint because of the new snow but clearly visible. The dogs had been running around there, too, and you could see their prints. But the snow on the big rock was untouched. Not a mark.

—That's not possible, right? Wang Mojie asked Ukyi Lhamo in a serious tone.

—Why are you asking me? Ukyi Lhamo answered, folding her arms and squeezing. She seemed to be shivering. She looked cold.

—So Ma Dingge can fly? Even if he could fly, there would still be some trace of where he was, right?

—Maybe he was never here in the first place.

—Are you implying that I hallucinated it?

—Who knows what goes on in your head? What do you mean by all this, anyway? Why drag me out in the middle of a snowstorm?

—Are you saying I just wanted to see you?

Ukyi Lhamo glanced at Wang Mojie, then turned and walked away without a word. Wang Mojie stood, immobile, his torch on Ukyi Lhamo. It shone on her feet as they moved through the snow. It shone on her long hair, glittering with snowflakes, as it swung side to side. It shone on the small of her back, then right on her backside, then on the ground ahead of her. Ukyi Lhamo was walking quickly, and she sped up as she went. Soon she disappeared into the quiet, white woods. Wang Mojie lowered his torch. Then, as if having dismissed Ukyi Lhamo from his mind, he turned the torch back on the big rock.

Each of the myriad snowflakes was remarkably distinct in the torch's beam. There didn't seem to be a mark on the blanket of snow on the boulder, Wang Mojie thought. The snow kept getting thicker. It felt like a dream. The students had run up near the boulder. They were like birds. And like birds, they had no thought to disturb anybody. They had noticed Ma Dingge right away, but they were used to his presence and so ignored him. He was nothing that the birds hadn't seen before and nothing the children hadn't seen before. They ran and played, the dogs ran after them, the children wrestled and tumbled in the snow, and the dogs imitated them and did so too. Now and again the dogs dashed into the woods and dashed back out. That particular dog was called Grey. I called him that in Mandarin, but he understood.

As you will have noticed, Wang Mojie at times likes to repeat things and revisit events.

Grey was calm, serene even, as if he was the instructor and I was the assistant or the reverse. I continued to discuss the poem, and the students read it aloud, nicely, their voices strong, in unison. It was a happy classroom moment. Grey stood there calmly, pretending to be interested in the lecture. Then, perhaps disappointed to find that this was all there was to school, he lifted his head, yawned, turned and walked away from the lectern, ambling out of the room like someone with nothing much to do and nowhere in particular to go. He didn't even close the door behind him.

He was bored. He rejected me.

Did I care?

No. Yes...

1. Shadows

Everything was creating its shadow.
Including me. I was motionless. The village was motionless.
Everything was motionless. Light. Water.
A three-year-old boy put his shoe into the water. Lifted it out. Put it back in.
Like his older sister Sangnyi drawing water for the family.

The snows of eternal winter lay across the mountain tops but summer was approaching. These were days of melting snow, and bright little streams flowed through the village. You could have easily followed any of the streams back to its source. You only needed to walk upstream to the ridge. In contrast, it would be difficult to follow any big river upstream back to its source, and it would have been just as difficult to follow one of the little streams not to its source but to its destination. Where did all the streams flow to? Into what river? Which tributary to what river? Where did the water finally reach the ocean? Searching for the final destination of something can be more baffling than searching for its origin. The destination often remains hidden, but the source is always there for you to find.

It was afternoon. The sun was strong, and the village was quiet. Dogs slept at the foot of walls. The tractors were like objects in a still life. The yak dung stacked for fuel looked ready to combust. The stone buildings cast short shadows. The stacked yak dung cast shadows. The prayer flags cast shadows. Window lintels did, the livestock folds did.

Everything cast its shadow. I did too. Under my feet, a short shadow was growing. I was motionless. The village was motionless. Everything was motionless. I stood against the backdrop of the village, my body covered in points of light. Because I could hear the water flowing past the village, I had the sensation that the entire village was filled with light shining off water. Everything was bright, dazzling, dizzying. It was dizzying, but dizziness can be a source of art. I'm no artist, but I know a little about Georges Seurat. I know why you would use pointillism to paint sunlight. It makes sense.

I had been living in the village for some time but still didn't know much about it. For example, how old was it? Were the stone buildings the first ones ever built there? Why did the place get so quiet in the afternoon sun? I presumed the establishment of the village had something to do with the monastery up on the mountain, the village belonged to the monastery, I imagined. But when had the monastery been founded? Where did the monks come from? Everything is entangled with everything else, and when you learn a little about something, it just makes you realise how much you don't know.

But I don't think it is necessary to know exactly how things are connected. Everything has its reason to exist in and of itself. The village was connected to the monastery, but once the village was established, it existed for itself. For example, you couldn't say the tractors had any connection to the monastery, and the same was true of the post office, general store, school and the roads.

I had my reasons for coming to the village, and once I moved there, reasons for me to stay presented themselves, and I began to forget why I had moved there to begin with [Wang Mojie came to the village in 1996 as a "Teach for China" volunteer]. It felt like something was growing. Sometimes it even felt as if I had been grafted onto one of the village trees and was inextricably linked to the very warmth of the air.

Morning, noon and night, I existed there in the village but remained a stranger to it. When one is a stranger to something, that thing retains its relative independence. Over time, I also became another unknowable part of the village. You would have seen me set off against the flora, me set off against the rocks, me and the village reflecting each other. Actually, given my academic training [Wang Mojie had two academic degrees, he had begun as a student of biology but later switched to philosophy], I can accept that it is possible for a person to be taken up into a tree or converted to rock. In my memory, I was in the trees and rocks. Every day when I walked through the village, I discovered new streams, brand new, no fish in them yet. Some of the village children knew me, some of the adults knew me too. They saw me when they were standing in their courtyard gates, sitting by a wall or going to draw water from the river, but they rarely invited me into their homes. They were respectful of me, but we were strangers.

Sometimes I invited myself into their homes, and I was always warmly welcomed, everybody in the family gathered around me. Often, I couldn't figure out who was related to whom or how, and so I was completely unsure about etiquette. I didn't know who was the father, the mother, the aunt or the uncle. I couldn't tell from their faces how old they were, and so I couldn't tell who was who. After I had met the parents of my students, I couldn't remember them. I couldn't recall their faces, and so I didn't recognise them when I saw them again. When I went to their homes, I usually didn't have anything in particular I wanted to say, I just sat awhile with them. I knew the children, so I would chat a bit with them. Or I would get them to translate so I could talk to the parents, talk about how the children were doing, say something about their study, their deportment. Nothing special. When the adults (that is all I knew about them, they were adults and somehow related to my students) understood me, they looked moved and grateful. They would say something to me in Tibetan, which I couldn't understand. All I knew was, "*Thuk je che, thuk je che*", which means, "Thank you, thank you!" Tibetan has a delicate sound, like flowing water. I would drink tea with them. An older woman, a grandmother I imagine, would bring over a brass kettle of tea, and every time I took a sip, she would refill my cup. If they gave me tea, it meant, of course, they were relatively well off and usually had a room where they could receive guests, with big cabinets and Tibetan mats they call *khaden* or sometimes even carpeting.

More often my visits just put my hosts out. Most people in the village were not well off, their houses were crudely built and had poor sanitation. They lived above their livestock, so it smelt. It took me a while before I realised that this was why they didn't invite me into their homes. Once I rather rashly walked into somebody's courtyard. This was on the edge of the village, a place exposed to the wind and facing the valley. The courtyard walls were in disrepair. Prayer flags cracked in the wind from the roof of the house. It was Sangnyi's house. My arrival surprised her, and she got flustered. She said something to her family, and they invited me in. I climbed the stairs to the front door, and the yaks in the dark pen below didn't move. Maybe they were watching me, maybe not. They were just yaks but seemed divine. Sangnyi led me through hallways and rooms, too ramshackle to describe, to a room where there was a niche with a statue of the Buddha. As a rule, no matter how poor a family is, they will still have a niche for a statue of the Buddha, and by custom, guests don't enter this shrine room. The room was different from the rest of the house. It had windows and was bright. The construction was crude but the room was clean. The niche with the Buddha was above a cabinet, and in front of the Buddha was an offering of barley, a *khata*, a butter lamp and a bowl of water – water is a standard offering because it is readily available, even to the poor. The wooden niche that housed the Buddha was painted with gold-coloured inlay. There wasn't a speck of dust on any of it. They obviously cleaned it every day. My hosts wore expressions of reverence but also fear as if my presence violated a taboo. An older woman – the grandmother I suppose – gave me some newly-made butter tea. She cleaned a wooden bowl for the tea and handed it to me with two hands. It wasn't polite for me to let an elder serve me, so I tried to decline, but she insisted. I took the tea, thinking that I shouldn't have come. My hands were shaking slightly.

Tibet, needless to say, is the abode of the spiritual. It is a land where the Buddha is venerated. But this aside, where else but Tibet is human dignity so constantly on display? They were not generous and hospitable only because I was a guest, it was simply in their nature to be so. The room was clean and plain, the *khata* as white as snow, the water offering sparkled, and the sheen on the wood of the niche was like a mirror. A beam of sunlight was shining in, and in it you could see no dust, not a speck. They valued cleanliness. The *khata* proved it, the barley proved it, the water, the butter lamp and the sunlight proved it. The snow on the peaks proved it.

I enjoyed my status in the village as a respected stranger, and I tried to never take it upon myself to visit a home without good reason. Sometimes when I came across my students on my walks, they ran away, but for all I know they stopped somewhere, hid and watched me. During the summer, the village women went to the river to wash clothing and clean their *khaden*. Their singing was loud and clear, like the sound of the river. When they saw me, most of them would stop singing, but there was always at least one exception. When I walked by, I could hear them laughing and whispering as they waited for me to move off, and after doing so, I usually heard them break out in loud laughter. I assumed they were laughing at me, including those among them who were my students. More than once I asked them what they were laughing at, but they never would say. It was their secret.

I think I probably was laughable. Always by myself, me and my shadow, wandering aimlessly. When I reached the foot of the mountain, where was I going to go? I could go up to the monastery, but I didn't believe in Buddhism.

I like this long-winded interior monologue of Wang Mojie's. It gets across what I can't get across in any other fashion, and so I will often allow Wang Mojie to tell his own story, including in his interior monologue.

Once when I was wandering aimlessly like I did, like I was dreaming, I suddenly saw a boy in the fierce sunlight. I say it was like a dream because I had found myself standing at the gate to Sangnyi's home, but I had had no intention of going there. The sun was shining straight down. The gate to the courtyard creaked open slowly and in the growing gap of the opening gate, a little head appeared. When I say that my walks were like dreams, I am thinking of times like this wonderful moment when I first saw the boy.

At most, he was three years old. He was a little Hercules, the way he pushed open the big, creaking gate and then, after he came out, the way he leaned into it and pushed it closed. I felt I was outside of time or the boy was outside of time. To put it another way, if I wasn't an extraterrestrial, then the boy was.

No adult was with him. He was alone. But he was so young, and he didn't seem to know where to go. He didn't know what lay ahead in any direction. He stood there awhile, looking up at the sun with a serious expression. The sun didn't scare him. He squinted his little eyes and stared right at it. I was worried for him. He was only three, but his face already showed signs of being burned by the sun, and now his eyes would be burned. But he was not afraid. He was stubbornly curious about the sun. He looked at the sun for a while, then lowered his eyes and started to walk downhill, which was natural. Of course he went downhill, gravity led him downhill. But even gravity's pull couldn't take him far because the streams blocked his way. The snow was melting, and water flowed everywhere in an interlacing braid. No matter where he turned, running water stopped him from going any farther.

The streams were narrow, not even a metre across, an adult could step over easily, but to a three-year-old child they might have seemed like raging rivers. The boy stopped instinctively when he came up to the water, but it wasn't all instinct. In the moment he seemed to have a thought. Had he paused to think about what instinct was telling him to do? What was on his mind? Was he thinking about water he had encountered before? Thinking about the last time he walked up to running water? He would have been even younger, so would he have dared to walk up to the water? Did he approach one more step closer this time? He squatted and looked intently at the water, studying it. There is no light quite like the light in eyes still innocent of the world.

He wasn't wearing much. Well, it wasn't how much he was wearing, it was that what he was wearing was little more than rags. His clothes were so tattered he looked underdressed. He was wearing what any boy in the interior would wear, but the buttons were missing. His trousers were in a similar state, so worn you couldn't tell what material they were made of. The left trouser leg was longer than the right, which exposed his calf. But it didn't matter. He could have been naked and it wouldn't have mattered. We should not judge children who live in poverty by the clothes they wear. All that matters is the innocence in their eyes. There is no poverty in their eyes. Quite the opposite. Their gaze is penetrating. In their eyes you can see their essence. It is like looking into a river at its source. But what was the boy looking at, his head turned down like that? It couldn't have been fish, it was too early in the year for fish. Was he watching a piece of amber tumbling in the water? Or the glint of golden sand? How could he stand there so stock-still?

As I expected, after standing there watching for a while, he slowly put a hand down to try to dam the flow. The water eddied for a second and then swirled up his arm, splashing him. It was a small stream but fast. This might not have been his first experience with running water, but he was still unfamiliar with the nature of water. He plopped down on his bottom, frightened. But he recovered quickly. He had just grown up a little. He was different now. He got up and tried again. This time he kept to his feet. He quickly learned to control the flow of the water. He was happy. He had no toys. He had nothing. His tattered clothing made it obvious that he had nothing. His sister Sangnyi had no toys to share with him. She had never had any herself. But he wanted to play. He wanted a tool to play with. This is innate to humans and makes us different from animals. He had to find a tool. A rock, a stick, anything. But rocks and sticks were too primitive, and anyway, he had played with them often and was bored with them. Children like novelty. He kept putting his hands into the water. Then he noticed his shoes, which was inevitable because when the water splashed him, his shoes got wet, and that was uncomfortable. Instinctively, he sat down and took off his shoes. He was captivated by his shoes. He picked one up and looked at it. He slowly lowered the shoe into the stream, and it quickly filled with water. He lifted it out, put it back in, lifted it out, put it back in. This is what his sister Sangnyi did when she drew water for the family. The boy couldn't have been happier. After this beginning, he soon came up with different games to play.

By now the sunlight no longer vibrated as it had in the morning. The village looked especially lovely, lovely as the sound of a flute in a valley. Yes, the sound of a flute in a valley in the afternoon when the sun is warm and the birds are at rest. At this time of day, how great would it be for a boy to have a green plastic bucket? The kind you buy in a set with a spade, a scoop and a second, smaller bucket. How great would it be to have a bucket to play with in the stream? But it didn't matter that he didn't have one. His shoe would serve just as well.

I had moved closer to the boy, but he hadn't noticed me. Why would he notice anybody? The boy was one with the water the way humans were one with nature at the beginning of time. I thought I might whistle at him to get his attention but suspected he would probably just glance up and then go back to playing in the water, imitating what he had seen others do and making up things himself. Which is just what happened. I waited briefly and whistled softly. He jerked his head up, a look in his eyes that was unfamiliar to me. It wasn't a look of alertness to danger, that wasn't it. All I can say is that it was just different, not like anything you see in a child's eyes but not like an adult's eyes either. I can't describe the strange look in his eyes as he looked at me. Maybe I had scared him, but to him I was just some man, even though I wasn't like all the other village men.

He went back to playing in the water but a little more cautiously, which was because of me, to be sure. There was now one more person in his world, a pair of eyes watching him, and there had been a whistle too. Well, was my whistle a type of arche-violence? What Jacques Derrida called "the transcendental origin of an irreducible violence"? I don't mean the boy thought of it that way, of course, but some sort of shadow had fallen on him. Sure enough, precisely because of some intangible interference in his world, he was heedless of his shoe for just a second, and he dropped it into the water. I don't think my presence was determinative. This was merely coincidence. Perhaps if I hadn't whistled, there would have been some other sound to distract him, and he would have dropped the shoe anyway. It was inevitable. I simply happened to be present at this occurrence.

The shoe stayed on the water's surface and slipped downstream like a boat. The boy was stunned but showed no sign of feeling a loss. He didn't chase after the shoe, he was fascinated by the novelty, and a little smile at the new sensation came to his lips. He had forgotten about my existence. He had his world to himself again. He lifted his head and watched the shoe. When it disappeared from view, his smile faded. He still felt no loss. Indeed, with excitement he picked up his other shoe, looked it over, then carefully but without hesitation, quite deliberately put the shoe into the jubilant, rushing water. This had nothing to do with my whistle. It had nothing to do with me. But what was it all about?

The shoe sailed away on the current. This time he had acted with volition, and he ran alongside the shoe as it floated away. It is difficult to say why he chased after it. Clearly the psychological process in his little head was not simple. We can make the following two inferences at least: he chased it because he wanted to make his delight last longer, and he had finally felt some vague sense of loss. He ran, but the water was faster, and he tripped and fell. He slowly got to his feet. The shoe was gone. As he got up, he looked into the distance where the shoe had gone. He didn't start running again. He stood there motionless, looking for what had disappeared. There in the afternoon sunlight, he looked like a little statue. His shoes were gone, the stream still flowed, and his expression of happy curiosity had vanished completely. His eyes didn't look so innocent any more, there was insight in them. The shoes weren't on the ground by him any more, they were lost to him. Now he was required to think about the notion of "being without". He had lost his shoes and now had to go barefoot. He had nothing to his name, nothing at all.

If he was too young to reason, then I must reason for him. Let's assume the first shoe was an accident, and let's assume that I caused it. But why did he do it a second time? Why deliberately repeat an accident? What did that mean? If we repeat an accident, the second time surely is no accident, correct? His joy the second time was obviously of a different sort from his first joy. He got something extra out of the second time. He was like Isaac Newton, who was inspired by an accident that he then repeated. But there was a difference between the boy and Newton. Different environment, different circumstances. Newton's apple could be tossed up and down over and over, but when the boy's shoes were gone, they were gone. Is that why his happiness was gone in that moment too? Of course that's why. He was left with nothing to his name. Would he put his shoes into the water the next time he came out to play? His behaviour betrayed a fundamental secret about all of us. As he grows up, he will learn to live as we all do, and the choices he makes will be constrained by the need to survive. His animal intelligence, his vitality, will have to yield to his need for survival and to the rules and discipline the world imposes upon us. There will be a limit to his freedom to act as he wishes. Moreover, every wilful act will carry a cost.

Perhaps, I thought, I should make him a gift of a new pair of shoes. Or give him cash. Twenty yuan? Fifty? One hundred? But I checked this strong impulse. The boy was in for a spanking from his mother and maybe from his sister Sangnyi too. I imagined what would happen if this three-year-old boy came home with a handful of cash. It would no doubt be taken as a sign from the gods. It would be a new text. It would become folklore. I was not going to do that. No. I would not. I had no way of knowing what sort of sign from the gods it might be taken as. I can believe in the miracles of others, but I don't believe in any miracles for myself. I am just made that way. When I get profoundly moved by something, I feel an even more profound doubt.

With regard to the "new text" that I have mentioned, I believe that the archetypes of the world have been obscured or even replaced by all sorts of variant "texts", and so the archetypes have disappeared. After the structuralist Claude Lévi-Strauss pioneered the fieldwork approach to anthropology and sociology, many anthropologists and sociologists went out among the people to research and write about folkways and customs, and they now speak of "popular culture as text" or "the village as text" or even "ethnicity as text". In a world obscured by so many "texts", our former archetypes have vanished, and we are misled by fragmented, false impressions. The false impressions we get from the many "texts" are endlessly produced by, for example, commercialised performances of folk music, which are used in advertising and in ethnic tourism to boost local economies. All this is packaged for our consumption, and, compared with the original archetypes, it is meaningless post-card culture, tourist culture. The disappearance of the archetypes is one of the greatest tragedies of our age.

That is the opinion of Wang Mojie in the above paragraph, and I agree with it, but I don't think that setting up a binary opposition between archetype and text solves the problem. We have to acknowledge that the creation of a text is an effort to understand an archetype, even though it is true that the text very likely obscures the archetype. But any object comes into being for us only as we engage it. There is no archetype that is elemental and exists in and of itself, just as there is no ultimate reality or truth, and so we can't dispense with our texts. Wang Mojie didn't accept my dialectical logic. He believed it was simplistic. We argued about it.

2. Ma Dingge

The environment has nothing to do with philosophy – different philosophies are not the result of different environments.
Robert distrusted the anti-rationalist philosophers who followed Nietzsche; he was consistently critical of structuralism and deconstruction and had a low opinion of the way Foucault and Derrida used linguistic theory.

Jean-Philippe Robert was a man of more than seventy years of age and had a head of striking white hair. He wasn't tall but stood straight. He liked to chew on the bit of his unlighted pipe. This wasn't to help him think, it was just an enduring habit. Who knows how long he had been a pipe smoker, but to look at him, you would have guessed he had picked it up as a young man. It must be said that the way he chewed the end of his pipe made him look more like a retired police detective than a philosopher. His eyes were old, cool and heavily bagged, but his gaze was still sharp. He could give you a humourless, withering look, like an older Sherlock Holmes, but his snow-white hair softened this Holmesian intensity and reflected how influential a thinker he had been.

Robert had charisma, but because he was short, he looked unimpressive standing next to his son, who was a tall man. Although they were father and son, you would not have guessed that they were related. Ma Dingge was French, and his name was Matthias, but we always called him by his Chinese name. He was physically imposing, solemn of demeanour and moved with deliberation. In his crimson *kasaya,* he was like a temple with red walls. Next to his son, Robert looked like just another tourist. There was nothing unusual about him, except perhaps for the pipe and shock of white hair.

Robert and his son were different in terms of physical appearance and temperament. Perhaps because they hadn't seen each other in over twenty years, perhaps because they might as well have been living in different eras and perhaps because faith and doubt are incompatible, when they met there was no display of affection, no hugging. They acted as if they had seen each other just the day before. It didn't seem like a father and son reunion. More like the first encounter of creatures from different planets. Ma Dingge, following Tibetan custom, held up a *khata* with two hands and placed it around his father's neck. Robert took it off almost immediately. It obviously made him uncomfortable, so he took it off, but to show respect, he folded it carefully and placed it in his expensive-looking briefcase.

Robert didn't seem particularly interested in seeing the sights of Lhasa. Its rivers were unlike any to be seen in the West and the Himalayas towered over the Alps, but the environment has nothing to do with philosophy. Different philosophies are not the result of different environments. This was Robert's consistent position, and so he didn't have much to say about the landmarks of any place he visited. Robert owned a seventeenth-century house in the Alps near the French border with Switzerland, and there he kept some photographs of Tibet that his son had sent to him years ago. He spent some time each year at his home in the Alps, doing research and writing. To Robert, the Himalayas were just mountains, no different from his familiar Alps, and he might as well have been in his own house looking at their snow-covered peaks, especially after the dialogue with his son had begun.

Robert belonged to a school of philosophical scepticism characteristic of older French liberal philosophers. He was different from post-structuralist thinkers such as Roland Barthes, Jacques Lacan, Michel Foucault and Derrida. Robert was classically conservative. His beliefs had their origin in the work of David Hume, Michel de Montaigne, René Descartes and Blaise Pascal. He came from this line of philosophical sceptics. Because he distrusted the anti-rationalist philosophers who followed Friedrich Nietzsche, he was consistently critical of structuralism and deconstruction and had a low opinion of the way Foucault and Derrida used linguistic theory. He argued that the contemporary impoverishment of philosophy and the narrowness of science were the reasons Buddhism had become so enormously attractive to people in the West. But, he wished to know, can Buddhism really answer the ancient question, "How should I live?" And in what ways can Buddhism be considered a philosophy? When we get right down to it, is Buddhism a philosophy or a religion?

Robert was not in Tibet for a family visit. He had come in search of debate. Twenty years before, his son had decided to abandon his study of biology at the University of Paris to devote himself to the study of Tibetan Buddhism, and while Robert had always respected this decision, he had never approved of it. Respect was one thing, approval another. Robert had never asked his son why he had made his decision. He had always assumed that it had been nothing more than an impulse prompted by the emotions of a moment, and he didn't discuss emotions. But two decades had passed, and with time, Robert had come to understand that what he had taken as his son's emotional decision had its rationality; Buddhist philosophy had appealed to his son. At the time, Ma Dingge's decision seemed to his father to have been driven by some fad that mystified him, and twenty years later it all remained a mystery to him. He still did not understand what the appeal of Buddhism was.

Robert wanted to ask his son how he could have turned to Buddhism after doing top-level research in biology at the University of Paris. When and how had the idea of becoming a Buddhist begun to take shape in his son's mind? Robert should have asked this question twenty years ago, and now while the question was the same, the context was not. Twenty years ago, it would have been a father's question to his son, but now both men had been imbued with gravitas by the passage of time. Had anyone else asked Ma Dingge why he believed in Buddhism, he would have answered promptly, as he did quite often. People asked out of curiosity but also with respect, and so Ma Dingge always gave a patient, straightforward answer. I asked him myself once, and he gave me a thorough answer. Ma Dingge had heard from Ukyi Lhamo about the circumstances that had brought me to Tibet as a volunteer teacher and about the way I lived my life. He encouraged me in what he called my spiritual journey. He often praised me in front of Ukyi Lhamo, which rather annoyed her.

Despite Wang Mojie's constant inner monologue, he always had a firm grasp on what went on around him. For example, his description of Robert's personality and his account of Robert's philosophical heritage are precise and clear. And so I will, in the main, leave the telling of the encounter of Robert and his son to Wang Mojie. If Wang Mojie wrote novels, while I'm not saying he would be better than me, I am sure he would be better than many fine writers. Perhaps because I have said this, some readers are going to suspect that Wang Mojie is me. I don't deny that novelists do this sort of thing all the time – they either give their story to a character or take a character's story as their own – but I want to make it very plain: I am not that type of novelist.

As everybody who knows me is aware, I have published several novels, and in my novels the protagonists are not me. Given my established practice as a writer of fiction, simple logic should tell you that Wang Mojie is not me. Moreover, Wang Mojie's academic expertise is in philosophy, including the philosophy of religion, and he also studied biology, and I know nothing about either subject. The reason I am leaving the telling of most of the conversation between Robert and his son to Wang Mojie is because I am not an academic. I will say it again, Wang Mojie is not me, there really is a Wang Mojie.

Wang Mojie and Ukyi Lhamo were friends of mine. I observed them over many years. A novelist needs as many such friends as he can find. I no longer live in Tibet, but I go back every year to see my friends. I like getting together with them, I like the engaging, deep conversations we have. You may have already noticed that this novel bears the rather obvious traces of relying on material from my journal. You may also have noticed that my narrator simply observes and reports. He relates stories he has heard. As I was nearing completion of the first draft of this book, I increasingly warmed to the device of having the story told by a narrator who simply reports what he observes and relates what he has heard. I don't have the patience to make it any more complicated than that. I like that the novel often seems like a mere record of observations. In the first place, I like it because it is more proof that Wang Mojie is not me – let me say it again, I am not Wang Mojie. And don't think that because I'm denying it so strongly, I must be Wang Mojie. In the second place, I like it because it is a very old and venerable narrative technique.

The classics of Axial Age civilisation, such as the Analects *of Confucius and the Buddhist* Tripitaka, *use this narrative convention. The* Analects *is famous for its phrase, "The Master said", which makes it obvious that what we have in the* Analects *is the students of Confucius relating what their master said. In the* Tripitaka, *the Buddhist canon, the phrase is "Thus I have heard". All the texts in the Buddhist canon begin, "Thus I have heard". It is true that there are two different explanations of how we should understand this phrase, but both accept that what is going on in the text is that someone is reporting or relating what they heard. The first explanation is that the phrase means "That which I have heard I will now relate for everyone else to hear". The second explanation is that it means "Hear what I say as if you are hearing it directly from Sakyamuni". The words are Sakyamuni's, but they are conveyed to us by someone else. To me, the second explanation is the better one. It says we are hearing the words of the Buddha in the voice of someone else. It addresses us in the second person (you listen), but in its reference to Sakyamuni, it has the character of third person narration (he said), and this doubled voice makes it a worthy subject of study for students of narratology. In sum, whether it's "The Master said" or "Thus I have heard", what we have is a linguistic form that dates to the Axial Age, and I would be pleased if the relating and retelling in this book are taken as my homage to it. I even thought about titling this novel* Thus I Have Heard *but decided that one shouldn't take anything too far. Going too far is as bad as not going far enough, they say, and I think it best that I follow this advice.*

This time, of course, it wasn't just anybody asking Ma Dingge the question, it was his father. Ma Dingge was quiet for a long time. This bothered his father, the nonbeliever. It bothered him because, in his silence, Ma Dingge seemed to be like one of those many statues of the Buddha that Robert had seen in the monastery. Ma Dingge kept his gaze lowered, his imposing frame leaning forwards slightly. He wasn't looking at his father, but he was a large man, and he loomed over his father as he sat there, pipe in hand. Good thing for Robert that at this moment he could start to chew on his pipe because that gave him something to do while he waited for an answer, which let him keep something of his usual arrogant demeanour.

It wouldn't do, of course, for Ma Dingge to give his father a straightforward answer such as, "It is a rare and precious thing to be born as a human being, but this existence is *anitya*, impermanent, there is only reincarnation, the cycle of rebirth, so if you seek the path towards liberation from the six rebirth destinies, from *samsara*, it is to be found in the *buddhadharma*." He couldn't say this to his father. Besides, he was cognisant of the fact that his father had given him life. They hadn't seen each other for twenty years, and Buddhists are not given to dwelling on the past. For Ma Dingge, thinking about the events of decades ago was like remembering a former life, like remembering a person he no longer was. Had there been some seed of spirituality in the person he once had been that had come down to the person he was now as though by transmigration? If so, no matter what, according to biology this seed was connected to his father. The life given to him by his father had carried by chance a seed of Eastern spirituality. It had not originated with his father, of course, it was merely transmitted through his father. Was this what he should say to his father? Well then, what had first awakened that seed of spirituality? The University of Paris? Or was it before then? Was it even earlier that the germination of that seed was triggered by his reading?

Robert asked his son when "even earlier" was. This might be considered an odd question for a father to ask his son. That he didn't know how old his son was when he read the esoteric books that Ma Dingge mentioned might mean Robert had been an indifferent father. But it wasn't odd that he didn't know because Robert and Ma Dingge's mother had divorced, and the boy had grown up with his mother. Robert had been a responsible father. He fulfilled his legal obligations, but more than this he arranged for Ma Dingge to stay with him on a regular basis. Being raised in a divided family certainly left its impact on Ma Dingge. This is not to say the experience scarred him, but life with his father was separate from life with his mother, which impressed upon him that a family is not an indivisible unit. It is difficult to say whether he reached this conclusion out of rational objectivity or indifference. Not really indifference, I suppose, but in any case, growing up as he did exposed Ma Dingge to more of the world. He met both his father's friends and his mother's friends, he met his father's women and his mother's men, and most were well known in society. Ma Dingge was raised in elevated company, but he never wanted to become part of it. Ma Dingge wanted for nothing and received the best education possible. Everything seemed to go smoothly and according to plan right up to his matriculation at the University of Paris.

But not everything was as it seemed, of course. Ma Dingge told his father that through his microscope he could see every minute detail of a bacterium, but it was easy to lose track of what connection this had with the human organism, much less its connection to the human soul. Science can teach us about matter, but it cannot teach us about the soul. Ma Dingge was only fifteen when he first read Arthur Schopenhauer, but it wasn't his reading that kindled his interest in Buddhism, it was his trip to the Himalayas in 1966.

—You were only twenty!

That Robert was able to come up with his son's age at the time so quickly showed how vivid his memories of his son were. Despite his father's interruption, Ma Dingge remained engaged in his recollection.

—In the Himalayas, Ma Dingge said slowly and deliberately, I met people who in their very being embodied what they taught. Even though I couldn't fully understand what they had to teach, it was obvious to me that they were living sages, philosophers, the sort of people you would have found everywhere in ancient Greece but can't be found anywhere in the modern West. I am convinced that the Tibetan masters living in the Himalayas are the last great philosophers, they are exemplars of the spiritual life. During that vacation, I had planned to go to Japan but changed my mind and went to the Himalayas.

—Is the corporal important? I mean is it important for a student to be in the physical presence of those great masters?

—Of course it's important.

The mountain range of the Himalayas is the highest in the world, of course, but were it not for the crimson-robed Buddhist masters who live in these mountains, their height would be a mere geographic feature. Despite the presence of these great masters, Western philosophical sceptics such as Jean-Philippe Robert deny that the Himalayas have spiritual loftiness, and because they deny it, they are not interested in the mountains' physical height. Unlike Ma Dingge, Wang Mojie had come to the Himalayas for reasons that had nothing to do with religion, but he agreed that Ma Dingge's father was too Western and too much a positivist. As a foundation for science, positivism can defeat superstition, but it cannot defeat symbolism, allusion, metaphor, association or any of the other rhetorical resources we have for expressing the spiritual. Positivism is not an answer to mysticism, and Wang Mojie believed that no matter what anyone might say, there was something transcendent about the

Himalayas that directed one's attention to the sky and the spiritual. Their physical height aside, the natural beauty of the Himalayas moved one, making one forget oneself and rendering one speechless. Wang Mojie was of the East, and this belief was in his genes, even if the habit of doubt was also rooted deep within him.

---

3. A Mute Tongue

Of the liberation of Auschwitz in 1945,
Aharon Appelfeld wrote, "The few people left alive
describe the prevailing silence as the silence of death...
Nobody was happy. The survivors stood at the fences in amazement.
Human language, with all its nuances, turned into a mute tongue."

"Always, Darkness Visible", by Aharon Appelfeld, translated by Barbara Harshav from the Hebrew. The New York Times, *27 January 2005.*

I made a small garden for myself in front of my house, thinking I would grow some vegetables. I wasn't pretending to be a traditional literatus. I wasn't trying to be Tao Yuanming, even though Ukyi Lhamo and her self-satisfied friends mocked me for just that. They were mistaken. That wasn't what I was doing. It had nothing to do with Tao Yuanming. I just wanted vegetables in my diet, and when I wanted vegetables, I had to ride my bike for an hour to a market in Lhasa. I did it constantly, and it was a chore. The climate in Lhasa is good for gardening. It is always sunny. In the winter it can get up to 18 degrees Celsius. I had studied biology, and that gave me a particular feeling for plants, so I decided to go ahead and grow some vegetables for myself. It isn't hard. All you have to do is prepare your ground, put down plastic to kill the weeds and then plant your seeds and water. Easy. It wasn't about getting back to nature, for real or for show.

Wang Mojie's vegetable garden wasn't large, but it had variety. He planted rape, cucumber, beans and tomatoes. As he says, Wang Mojie had studied biology at university and so, in a way, growing vegetables was part of his trade. Even so, when the rape poked above the ground, green and slender, Wang Mojie was truly quite excited. With a little exaggeration, he said it still amazed him how a tiny seed that came wrapped in paper could gradually transform itself and become a green, living thing. At first, whenever he had a moment, he went to look at the miracle of his garden. Sometimes he would look at it for minutes or hours at a time. He studied the changes to the soil after he had watered, he studied how tiny cracks slowly opened and how the soil domed as tiny sprouts, still a bit yellow, pushed up, until one day they broke through, slender and pretty. They were beautiful. Everything is beautiful at its beginning. One morning, however, half of them had disappeared.

Ukyi Lhamo stole my vegetables! She admitted she stole them. She said she fed them to those awful friends of hers from Lhasa. She said she did it alone and I shouldn't suspect anybody else or blame the innocent. I could tell from her face that she had no more regard for me than she did those rape plants just out of the ground. She offered me money, but I didn't take it. I said, forget the money, Ukyi Lhamo, I just want to know how you could pull up those little plants that were barely out of the ground. Guess what she said. She said, with no trace of shame, that's when they taste best, they aren't as good later. Ukyi Lhamo had a Beijing accent and spoke fast. As soon as she opened her mouth you could tell she grew up in Beijing. I was all too familiar with Beijing Mandarin. I said, Ukyi Lhamo you are not Tibetan, you are Han, you'll eat anything, you'll stoop to anything. Ukyi Lhamo just said, You're funny, you're too funny. I take a few rape plants, and because of that you say I will stoop to anything? She hadn't reacted to being accused of not being Tibetan. So I repeated it. Ukyi Lhamo, listen, you are not Tibetan, you're Han. She said sarcastically, So I'm Han, aren't you Han yourself? Don't go around pretending to be one of us Tibetans because it amuses you. You just keep an eye on your garden.

My garden was just about ruined. But the vegetables weren't the issue. If Ukyi Lhamo had wanted to eat them, I would have given them to her gladly. The issue was she gave them to her friends. And what sort of people were they, you ask? I knew only too well. They had their clique. They were smug, arrogant, they didn't give a damn about anything. They had brought to Tibet the punk attitude that was so popular in the interior in the 1990s, and even the ones who weren't really so punk pretended to be. I had been a bit like them myself once. I had had a cynical punk attitude, even towards marriage, but I had left all that behind when I came to Lhasa. My marriage, which I can't bear to think back on, had ended, and I had left my position at my university in Beijing [after graduating with his two degrees in 1993, Wang Mojie's university had employed him as a lecturer]. I was offered a position at Tibet University, and I looked into it but wasn't keen. First, it is right in the busy centre of the city, and if I had wanted to be in a city, I would have stayed in my home town of Beijing. Second, it seemed to me that the atmosphere at the university was not very different from that in the interior, and there was a lot in the air on campus that was familiar, all that "please don't call me human" and "I'm a tough guy, I don't fear anyone" sort of stuff.

Regarding the 1990s, let me say this: as the author of the necessarily somewhat cryptic novel Gate of Silence, *I have been called on to answer questions from reporters and critics about the meaning of the argot of that decade. I think that compared with the eighties, as we moved into the nineties something had changed. We thought we had turned cynical, but in fact we were still innocent and naive. Take the title of Wang Shuo's novel* Please Don't Call Me Human *and a comment he supposedly once made, "I'm a tough guy, I don't fear anyone". Those phrases now sound very innocent, very naive. They sound like a child running up a tiny hill but yelling and making a big fuss about it. No matter how famous those phrases were as a response to the times, looking back on them, it is impossible to take them seriously. I once asked some questions of my own. What was behind that kind of language? It is hard to say, isn't it? Do they sound innocent, even childish, to us now because we know their little devilry seems naive given our knowledge of great evil? Li Man, the protagonist of* Gate of Silence, *sometimes wonders if the reason Chinese jugglers win such acclaim abroad is because they get so much practice juggling everything that life throws at you in China. This is a bizarre way of putting it, of course, but it is rhetorical irony. I told reporters that what was happening in the nineties produced such rich supply of rhetorical resources, including the phrases "I'm a tough guy, I don't fear anyone" and "please don't call me human". Poetry, including so-called "lower body poetry", led the way in the rhetorical response to reality. Fiction did its part too. But in the end, it was all just rhetoric, which is the tragedy. Wang Mojie agreed with me. On this question, our point of view is essentially the same.*

I was disappointed in Tibet University. Nothing about the institution seemed elevated, not literally, much less figuratively, even less in a spiritual sense. I didn't care whether I taught in a university, a middle school or a primary school. I had come all the way to Tibet. Why should I care where I was teaching? Besides, there is a precedent of a university professor teaching in a primary school. Ludwig Wittgenstein left his position at Cambridge and taught for many years at a primary school in the Austrian mountains. It didn't stop him from writing his great works. I wasn't trying to be Wittgenstein, of course. I wasn't trying to be anybody but me. My situation was my own. I picked a middle school on the outskirts of Lhasa. The school was in a beautiful spot. It was in a mountain village, below a monastery, above a river, by the road. The living conditions were difficult, but it was a perfect place for introspection and self-improvement. There was nothing fancy about the school. It took me in as a monastery takes in a monk. They gave me a classroom, some teaching materials and a stone house by the sloping playground.

My life was rather monastic. I just watched nature all day, my heart at peace. I was at my lectern or among the children, surrounded by them, like Sakyamuni under the Bodhi tree, full of inspiration, my words coming easily. I liked my house, the look of the stone. I liked the way the mica glittered in the sunlight. I liked the sunlight and the village. I liked to stare at the mountains, at the night sky, at nebulae, at dark matter. I spent hours thinking, I read for hours. When I wasn't teaching or out for a walk, I spent most of my time reading. Reading in Tibet is really reading. You feel as if no one else exists, you are outside of time, away from the world. It is a peaceful, dreamlike state. This dreamlike reading, the dreamlike thoughts that came to me while I was reading, made me feel as if I were floating in air, everything around me filled with my own soaring thoughts. I liked the winter and how long it was. I liked the snow and the quiet. I could feel something latent. The sunlight reached all the way to the ground under the trees in the woods. I liked the greyish-white of the trees. I liked the clarity of everything. In winter the woods were reminiscent of a philosopher's prose late in his career, direct and unadorned. The paths through the woods were obvious in winter, the contours of the land stood out below the high sky.

Wang Mojie thought that he and Ukyi Lhamo would have got along just fine if it wasn't for that motley crowd of hers, all of them with the bad habits of people from the interior. When he considered her the way normal men would, Wang Mojie agreed that Ukyi Lhamo was one of the more pleasing sights to be seen on the remote campus. What made her striking was her bearing. She was tall and stood straight. And she was always wearing something new and interesting. Her clothes were Tibetan, but they were fashionable, and the combination looked good on her. For example, her long slender legs might be clad in pressed jeans, but she paired that with a loose blouse with a pattern of Tibetan Buddhist symbols. The jeans were tight and sexy, but the blouse gestured at the spiritual. If she was wearing a white jacket, say a snug-fitting, white leather jacket, then she would be sure to also wear a heavy string of turquoise prayer beads on her wrist or around her neck. Her hair was braided and full of jewellery, like Tibetan herdswomen wear their hair, and she wore high Tibetan boots. In summary, Ukyi Lhamo wasn't fashionable in the ordinary way, but she didn't dress like a local either. On anybody else it might have looked a mess, but Ukyi Lhamo brought it all together, she transformed it. The effect was singular, showy. Wang Mojie thought that Ukyi Lhamo when by herself was one of the best things about that school out in the middle of nowhere, but just as a flower isn't left alone by bees and butterflies, Ukyi Lhamo wasn't left alone by men.

Men constantly came to the school looking for her, especially at the weekend when there was always a party at her place, with drinking, laughter and loud music, sometimes Western symphonic, sometimes Indian. Often there were so many Jeeps, motorcycles and bicycles parked in front of Ukyi Lhamo's house that the school didn't seem quiet and remote at all. It was like she was running a private nightclub. When Wang Mojie first arrived, Ukyi Lhamo invited him to her parties, but he always declined. Not only did he turn down her invitations, but several times he bluntly asked Ukyi Lhamo to have a thought for others and keep the noise down. He was serious about it, sanctimonious even, but he came across as rather a bogus hermit. Ukyi Lhamo was easy-going and Wang Mojie's aloofness didn't bother her. The affair of the vegetable garden, however, taught her not to underestimate Wang Mojie. It wasn't Ukyi Lhamo, of course, who had sneaked into the garden at night and stolen the vegetables. It was her friends, and Wang Mojie imagined them laughing at him behind his back. Ukyi Lhamo had warned him to keep an eye on his garden, which he had to take seriously. He decided to put a fence around the garden and set up plastic row covers too. This would guard against any repetition of what had happened. He decided his garden had looked a little too temporary and ramshackle, which invited disdain and disregard.

Wang Mojie made a trip to a market in Lhasa's western suburbs and bought a saw, an axe, paint, wooden posts and plastic sheeting. Then, over several days, he carefully built a fine-looking fence around his garden, with plastic sheeting running from post to post. He made a gate and put a big padlock on it. He had almost bought a smaller padlock because it was just for show and wasn't going to keep out anybody who really wanted to get in. Still, in the end he decided to get a lock big enough to attract attention. He had his reasons for doing so. It was an Ironman brand lock, the biggest he could find. Whether it kept anybody out was beside the point, it would get attention, and that was important. When he finished, several of his students and colleagues came to have a look. They said the work looked good and solid. It was art, they said. As for Ukyi Lhamo, when he began to build the fence, she had kept laughing at him for being so defensive, and when she saw the big lock, she couldn't help raising her voice.

—Wang Mo, is that lock for me? Now you're going too far!

Wang Mojie ignored her for a moment. He waited before turning and staring at her intently.

—I haven't gone too far. I haven't put in an alarm system.

—You're trying to shame me. Over a few vegetables? Seriously?

—If you can feel shame, that's a good thing. The lock puts you on notice.

—You mean that, Wang Mo?

—Take it as a joke if you want.

—You think a lock is going to stop me?

—It will, unless you rip the plastic. If you... or if they do that, then I'll put in an alarm.

—You! OK, here. Here's some money for what we took. Take it.

—Hold on. That's not enough to cover what they took, is it?

—It's ten times what it would cost!

—Those plants were priceless. Just stay away from the garden from now on.

Wang Mojie had been only half serious when this conversation with Ukyi Lhamo started, and he was surprised to find himself growing more and more intense, his words more and more cutting, until finally he sounded like a policeman giving somebody a talking-to. Only when Ukyi Lhamo walked away did Wang Mojie realise what a contemptible show he had been putting on. It wasn't like him at all. Then again, speaking so harshly had given him an unfamiliar but strong feeling of pleasure. Wang Mojie had to admit to himself that while he tried to ignore the beautiful spectacle that was Ukyi Lhamo, she had settled deep in his consciousness, like sediment, getting thicker and thicker, becoming rock that finally heaved up, breaking to the surface. Wang Mojie lived an ascetic life, but he wasn't a real monk, and even a monk would be unsettled next to the fascinating, seductive Ukyi Lhamo. In other words, Wang Mojie's thoughts about Ukyi Lhamo weren't exactly pure, he wanted her, but he hadn't admitted this to himself yet.

Wang Mojie and Ukyi Lhamo lived in the same row of stone houses that belonged to the school. One house separated them, which was good because if she had been next door, Wang Mojie would have been able to hear everything going on at her place. Even so, every now and again at night, the sound of music, laughter and partying would drift over to Wang Mojie's ears. These were happy sounds of normal life, but they disturbed him. He could always hear Ukyi Lhamo's voice, and he could hear her laughter more clearly than anything else. He liked her voice. It was husky and resonant, and Wang Mojie thought it was like the call of a crane, a black-necked crane. Had it just been Ukyi Lhamo talking and laughing, it would have been fine. What annoyed Wang Mojie, and sometimes made him angry, was the sound of Ukyi Lhamo getting out of control among those friends of hers. When he heard this, Wang Mojie couldn't stop picturing what was going on at her place. He imagined her as the centre of attention in a crowd of men and revelling in it. If Ukyi Lhamo's parties had been like anybody else's, just people talking, drinking and getting up to dance when a good song came on, Wang Mojie could have handled it. The problem was things didn't stop there. Sometimes, after the music stopped and guests had left, he could tell someone had stayed behind. On those nights, Wang Mojie could hear Ukyi Lhamo moaning low, which upset him and was more than he could bear. It just made it worse that she wasn't loud, she didn't cry out. It wasn't loud, wild sex, which Wang Mojie might have enjoyed hearing.

But that wasn't Ukyi Lhamo.

The only sound she made was a low, muffled moaning, holding herself back. To Wang Mojie it sounded like the cries of cranes carried on a chilly breeze. No other sound could have brought such vivid pictures to his mind. Sometimes the sound made Wang Mojie leap out of bed. He stood trembling in the cool moonlight that also felt hot, his body convulsing as if in seizure. He couldn't stop himself from whipping himself with a towel, whipping himself down there. He saw himself in all his desire and was revolted. When this started, Wang Mojie thought about leaving his job at the school, but in the end he stayed. He could endure Ukyi Lhamo or maybe it was himself he could endure. He craved that low moaning sound, he craved the sting of the towel, but that did not mean he was thinking of crossing any boundaries.

He never did take the money that Ukyi Lhamo offered him. It wasn't about money. It was about getting back at her, getting back at them. That's what the padlock meant. One morning about two weeks later, however, he had a shock. His garden was simply gone as if blown away by a cyclone. There was nothing left but debris. But there hadn't been any wind the night before, and of course no storm had done it. It was human violence. His garden was beautiful but also a provocation, things had escalated, and they had levelled the garden. The wood was broken and scattered, the plastic ripped to shreds, the plants pulled up by their roots. Broken beer and spirit bottles were littered about. You could smell the alcohol. It was obviously the work of more than just a couple of people. It was mob violence. They had enjoyed it.

Acts of violence like this can defy comprehension. That they dared do this was a demonstration of their power and proof of the vulnerability of his garden and his powerlessness. He felt stupefied. Stupefied into helplessness. His mind was a blank. Wang Mojie was an intellectual, he enjoyed the life of the mind, and nothing defeats such a person as much as violence that exceeds the power of their imagination. He was too stunned to feel anger. He felt only surprise, shock and disbelief. He couldn't begin to understand them. All he could do was withdraw and question himself. Was the lock a mistake? Too much of a challenge? Had he gone too far with it? Would it have been more reasonable to have bought a smaller one? Would that have served just as well to signal his protest without inciting them to violence? Wang Mojie thought hard about himself, turning his mind away from the people who had brought violence upon him, just as when we think back to that ruthless violence of years ago, we find that our only choice is to think about our own mistakes. This is the only memory of that event that is permitted, but it is also the only way to free yourself from that past, the only way to make yourself feel a little better about it. (When violence defies our comprehension, or when we are not permitted even to discuss violence as an effort to comprehend it, all we can do is withdraw and consider our own faults.)

Many of the other teachers came around to see, and they asked, "What happened? What's going on?" You might say that something big was happening that morning on the remote campus. People gasped, sighed and assigned blame. Nobody could figure out who Wang Mojie had offended. Wang Mojie wasn't close enough to anybody to offend them. They couldn't understand it, so they decided it must just have been somebody who was drunk. When Principal Tsering Wangdu heard what had happened, he came to inspect things personally. Like many of the others, he instinctively looked over at Ukyi Lhamo's house, which was quiet that morning. He shrugged, shook his head and asked Wang Mojie if he wanted to make an official report. He meant well, but you could tell by his tone that he wasn't sure what to do. Wang Mojie shook his head woodenly, he didn't think a report was necessary, he said, it was a matter internal to the school and wasn't worth reporting. The principal was happy to hear Wang Mojie say this, so he volunteered that the school would do something to help compensate him for his loss. Wang Mojie thanked him but declined.

At a faculty meeting at the end of school that day, the principal talked about the incident. He said he himself was to blame. He blamed his own mismanagement for poor security at the school, and he instructed the dean to redouble efforts in the area of safety and security, stressing that they had to ensure that all visitors registered at the gate. The principal made a point of praising Wang Mojie for thinking of the good of the group and for valuing the school's reputation, and he spoke highly of the contribution Wang Mojie was making as a volunteer teacher. The principal meant this, and Wang Mojie was indeed everything the principal said he was. By habit, whenever the principal praised Wang Mojie, he was sure to mention Ukyi Lhamo, and whenever he praised Ukyi Lhamo, he was sure to mention Wang Mojie. Today was no exception. He added a word about Ukyi Lhamo, but it sounded a bit forced. She was at the meeting, and while the principal was describing what had happened, a lot of people automatically turned to look at her. She finally stood up and walked out, back straight, head high, eyes forward, the sound of each step reverberating in the room. This amounted to her confession.

Days passed, and while Wang Mojie might have been expected to clean things up or somebody might have been expected to do it for him, neither he nor anyone else did so. The ruins lay there in the strong sunlight. One day, in between lessons, his students started to clean up, but Wang Mojie stopped them.

Wang Mojie hadn't experienced anything you would call pain, he felt numb, helpless, but these were familiar feelings for him. It was an empty feeling he knew well, the feeling that unimaginable violence on a historical scale leaves you with, violence you can't think your way through. When he wasn't teaching, Wang Mojie usually sat quietly by himself in the blinding sunlight. He wasn't daydreaming. He seemed to be simply soaking up the sun's energy. He had his grey checked scarf around his neck, which he didn't seem to wear either for warmth or for appearance. It just looked odd, to be honest. It might have appeared a bit gallant had his expression not looked so violated. Mahatma Gandhi, the champion of nonviolent resistance, liked to sit under the blazing sun, absorbing its energy. Why else would he have gone around naked from the waist up? But, Wang Mojie wondered, what was it that he was soaking up? What could he draw on for strength? He couldn't go around shirtless like Gandhi, could he? That wouldn't work for him, he was sorry to say. He ran his hand down the folds in his scarf, his eyes straight ahead.

His thoughts turned back to the sacred Gandhi. Just like Gandhi's bare shoulder, Wang Mojie's grey checked scarf was a sign of resolve. Wang Mojie was thinking that Gandhi did not respond to violence with violence, but this did not mean he was powerless. Gandhi was able to make those who used violence feel ashamed and uncertain. He never stopped resisting, he was never helpless. Gandhi's marches and sit-ins and his philosophy of nonviolence shamed those who used violence, and they abandoned it. Gandhi's greatness lay in the fact that he overcame fear and hatred. It pained Wang Mojie to realise, however, that Gandhi's philosophy was tied to a specific place, time and culture. Facing the Nazis, for example, facing tanks rumbling down the middle of a city's streets, even Gandhi would have no solution, regardless of how much of the sun's power he had soaked up. No solution. It had been so many years and there had been no solution.

There was nothing left to do but stage a sit-in. Just sit. In silence. Wang Mojie later quoted a scholar named Chen-kuo Lin, who wrote, "At the heart of violence, however, language always loses its voice." Of the liberation of Auschwitz in 1945, Aharon Appelfeld wrote,

> The few people left alive describe the prevailing silence as the silence of death. Those who came out of hiding after the war – out of the forests and monasteries – also describe the shock of

liberation as freezing, crippling silence. Nobody was happy. The survivors stood at the fences in amazement. Human language, with all its nuances, turned into a mute tongue.

After quoting Appelfeld's New York Times *editorial, Wang Mojie read more to me from Chen-kuo Lin. He read, "Nevertheless, the limitation of language shall not completely prevent us from meditating on this problem... Following Nietzsche and Heidegger, Derrida (1978) treats violence as a metaphysical act that attempts to reduce the irreducible to something more essential. Beings are made intelligible within a system of metaphysics structured by the categories of duality and hierarchy. For instance, with the ontological distinction of 'transcendental' and 'empirical', beings are often explained in terms of a reduction from the 'empirical' to the 'transcendental'. A typical example is Platonism, in which the 'transcendent' is considered more fundamental than the 'empirical' in terms of truth and value. However, such metaphysical differentiation and reduction finds no deeper ground other than itself for justification. Moreover, metaphysical reduction has always been done in a conspiracy of suppression and domination. For Derrida, violence is always already immanent in all forms of metaphysics, such as logocentrism, ethnocentrism, phallologocentrism, and so forth."*

At this point, Wang Mojie stopped and said that for "phallologocentrism" he would substitute a word he made up: "authoritarianocentrism". Then he continued. He said, Derrida places violence in the context of writing-slash-naming, and then he read to me something that Lin quoted from Derrida: "The structure of violence is complex and its possibility – writing – no less so... There was in fact a first violence to be named. To name, to give names that it will on occasion be forbidden to pronounce, such is the originary violence of language which consists in inscribing within a difference, in classifying, in suspending the vocative absolute. To think the unique within the system, to inscribe it there, such is the gesture of the arche-writing: arche-violence, loss of the proper, of absolute proximity, of self-presence, in truth the loss of what has never taken place, of a self-presence which has never been given but only dreamed of and always already split, repeated, incapable of appearing to itself except in its own disappearance" (Chen-kuo Lin, "Emptiness and Violence: An Unexpected Encounter of Nagarjuna with Derrida and Levinas," in Liu, JeeLoo and Douglas L. Berger, editors, Nothingness in Asian Philosophy, *New York: Routledge, 2014, pages 78, 82-3). I listened to Wang Mojie, but he had lost me. Derrida is incomprehensible to me, and I know that I'm not alone in this. Derrida is for people like Wang Mojie, people afflicted with the disease of over-intellectualisation. The average reader may ignore the Derrida, you may skip it. In fact, I suggest you skip it.*

While he sat out in the sun, nothing was compelling Wang Mojie to think about these things, but in any event, thinking was all he could do. Sometimes he sat because he was waiting for Ukyi Lhamo to return from teaching. As she walked to her house, she would see Wang Mojie and his ruined garden. He wanted to see how she reacted. But he seldom saw her. In the morning there were few chances to see her between lessons, and most afternoons she didn't teach. Ukyi Lhamo, who often wore her white leather jacket, floated by like a cloud, like part of the landscape, well, like part of the landscape if it was liable to suddenly duck out of sight. Her behaviour proved she wasn't as indifferent as she pretended to be. At the very least she felt awkward, which was some consolation to Wang Mojie. Throughout this time, Wang Mojie was stuck, either musing over random stuff, World War II, writing poetry after Auschwitz being barbaric, the Square, that sort of thing, or indulging his habit of observing Ukyi Lhamo. He was looking for a weakness, however slight, in she who had brought violence upon him. He wanted to find a weakness and learn from it.

At night Ukyi Lhamo's house was usually ablaze with light and loud with music, but lately, Wang Mojie noticed, it was dark and quiet. Clearly, to avoid seeing Wang Mojie she was staying in Lhasa. Once, very, very late at night, as Wang Mojie walked back from the public toilet on the far side of the playground, he saw lights on at Ukyi Lhamo's place. Her house had been dark when he had walked to the toilet, but the lights were on as he came back. Ukyi Lhamo must have just returned from Lhasa. He couldn't tell, however, if she had come back alone or if somebody had driven her. As he walked past her door, he listened but didn't hear anything. He assumed that Ukyi Lhamo would go right to bed, but later, before going to sleep, he went to the toilet again and saw that her lights were still on. He wasn't that surprised, he had half expected it. He stopped by her window and turned an ear to listen but heard nothing. Ukyi Lhamo must have come back by herself, he decided, if not it wouldn't have been so quiet. Her curtains were closed tight, and he couldn't see anything through her windows. He wondered what Ukyi Lhamo was doing. He assumed she was reading or maybe had fallen asleep with the lights on. Maybe she was just sitting there thinking, just as he sat outside in the sun and thought? As he asked himself these questions, he found himself looking up at the sky. Orion, the Plough, Vega, the Weaving Maid's star, Capricornus, all were spread brightly across the sky, which was like the most ancient geometric shape, Archimedes' sphere. It was Immanuel Kant's sky: the starry heavens above, the moral law within. If there is a universal human moral law, its basis is in the heavens. Wang Mojie wondered if Ukyi Lhamo could see the starry heavens through her window, but even if she couldn't, she would not be able to ignore the moral law within her heart, especially because the ruins of his garden still lay there, untouched, not far from her door. Wang Mojie wondered if things would be a little better if he cleaned it all up, maybe a lot better. The ruins had become installation art, a didactic piece that Ukyi Lhamo saw every day. The question was who should clean it up? Well, fine, he thought, he would leave the ruins there, as a lesson to her.

Wang Mojie was waiting for something to happen. He rarely saw Ukyi Lhamo. To be sure to catch her between lessons, Wang Mojie went to the English department offices and studied her teaching timetable. He decided he would wait passively no longer. He would act. One day, he shifted his lessons around so he could wait in front of his house for Ukyi Lhamo. Eventually the bell sounded and shortly afterwards she came walking quickly across the playground, just as he expected. Wang Mojie was sitting posed like *The Thinker*. He looked up at Ukyi Lhamo. She saw him and stopped. This was unconscious, she caught herself and quickly started walking again. As she got closer to him, she pretended to look for something in her bag. She took something out and looked at it as she walked. After a few steps, she put it back in and walked on, lengthening her stride, as if she regretted the pretence. She walked with head high and back straight. She didn't look directly at Wang Mojie, but she had to see him there in front of her like *The Thinker*. She was trying to look tough but in fact she didn't want to face Wang Mojie. These conflicting emotions might be why she tripped and almost fell as she started up the steps to her door. She put a hand down to catch herself and her hair fell across her face. This was amusing. It was as if Wang Mojie had made her fall. But he didn't laugh. He had to keep a straight face. He had to be impassive. Otherwise the tension between them would disappear and Ukyi Lhamo would be absolved. He couldn't let her be absolved. He would wait to make her face him. That's all he could do, other than brood about what had happened.

If Wang Mojie had known when enough was enough, if he had ended things at the right time, when Ukyi Lhamo was feeling vulnerable, like when she stumbled, for example, and if he had cleaned away the ruins of the garden and taken down the installation art, then Ukyi Lhamo might have felt ashamed and maybe Kant's starry heavens would have shone within her. Maybe she wouldn't have taken revenge by inviting her friends over for a party more spectacular than any she had thrown before. It isn't always the case that with time the truth will out, and time did not work in Wang Mojie's favour. The destruction of his garden ceased to be news. People ceased to care. It was over, forgotten, done with. Now it was just a pile of junk that didn't symbolise justice denied or anything else for that matter. The dead plants, wind-blown plastic and broken wood and glass just got dirtier, more depressing and more ignored with each passing day.

The school was quiet for a long time, but one weekend it came to life as music blared across campus. Symphonic music, Shostakovich's Symphony No. 7, which had played when Stalin reviewed troops on Red Square. This was incredible, no one at the school had experienced anything like it. Ukyi Lhamo came out that day wearing a red leather jacket and a black beret. Her long hair spilled from under the hat, and she kept shaking her head to toss it back. She had been feeling the prick of the moral law within, but today she was shaking it off. She was in high spirits, back to her old self. Wang Mojie could sit by his door if he wanted, he could sit by the ruins of his garden if he wanted and he could pose like Rodin's *The Thinker* if he wanted, but in reality he sat by a junk heap and looked like a rubbish picker. The Shostakovich was deafening, the volume loud enough to make Wang Mojie as irrelevant as the junk that surrounded him.

Time can be cruel to people who stick to their principles and stand their ground. Time leaves us isolated and forgotten. Our hopes don't come true. The Shostakovich gave way to disco, and Wang Mojie knew then that it was over, a page had turned. Wang Mojie got out the broom, shovel and wheelbarrow that he had long since prepared and went to work clearing away the rubble, one shovelful at a time, underneath the sun, to the accompaniment of the blaring music. From just before noon, through the afternoon, right up until dusk, Wang Mojie worked quietly and without attracting attention. He cleared the rubble away, restoring the ground to what it had been. He found some plants that had survived and were still growing well, but he dug them up, turning all the soil over. He put Ukyi Lhamo and her music out of his mind, but his scarf fluttered from his neck as if keeping time. The wet dirt gave off its distinctive aroma, and Wang Mojie sensed that essential something in the world that never changed.

The next day was Sunday, and Wang Mojie went back to the store on the western outskirts of Lhasa and bought more wood, plastic, paint and nails. This time he bought better wood, not the rough, unfinished boards he bought the first time but darkly stained wood like you might use for interior work. This time he spent a lot more money. For many days after, whenever he had the time, Wang Mojie went out under the sun and tinkered away at his garden. He didn't ask anyone to help, not even his students, he did it all himself, methodically, spending more time on it this time around. Sometimes as he worked, he caught sight of Ukyi Lhamo walking across the playground and turned his back to her. He could feel her eyes on him. Once he heard her boots walk up behind him and stop. The sound of the boots seemed to be an invitation to a conversation. But he didn't turn around, and after a while the boots walked away. Work done slowly is work done well. It took three weeks before the garden was finished. It was nicer than before. This time Wang Mojie built a moon gate for the garden, and he didn't put a lock on it. He even tied prayer flags to the gate, draped a *khata* over it and hung up a *thangka* with an image of Sakyamuni. The prayer flags and the *khata* waved in the wind, and the *thangka* was resplendent. Maybe, Wang Mojie thought, these things could accomplish what the padlock could not.

4. Cataracts and Moonlight

Simple scenery can still be pretty, and besides,
there is no such thing as simple scenery.
Different languages give rise to different ways of life,
the limits of a language are the limits of a world.

It was seven in the evening, but the sun was still high. The barley was doing poorly, and though it was harvest time, no one had come to bring it in. Would it stand there through the autumn and winter and into the following spring? Would they then turn the soil and hoe it all under? This happens. Often.

There were trees ahead. A row of short trees. Simple scenery but pretty. Simple scenery is still scenery. Was there a stream running hidden through the trees? Maybe the tributary to a big river.

Sure enough. Before I reached the trees, the simple scenery, I could just make out the glint of light on water and the quietly winding line of a stream. Just another stream in another wood, like another stranger on a street. Its source couldn't be far, right nearby probably, somewhere on the ridge. There was a bridge, well, not really a bridge, just a row of stepping stones. After crossing the bridge of stones, I walked into the autumn woods. Under the trees, the stream divided, one branch narrow, the other wider. The narrow branch flowed through a ditch.

The ditch was a sluice someone had dug. A mill house was situated downstream, and the sluice diverted water to the mill house. The sluice and the stream were close in places, elsewhere far apart. There was a raised bank of earth between them, and trees, which you could see from a distance, grew on the bank. A footpath followed the bank, but you could barely make it out. Few people walked it, so it was overgrown and looked abandoned, not like a proper path. In the afternoon and at dusk, when you walked the path in the shade, it was always quiet, and were it not for the pyramidal snow peaks that you could sometimes see through the trees and the prayer flags, the scenery would have seemed like the river country of southeastern China. Everything was still, no movement to catch the eye, except for the shorebirds flying up from the Lhasa River and the ducks and geese, plump and white, that paddled on the water. There was nothing else to catch your eye. But you might catch their eye. Very often, herring gulls flashed up from the river through the trees like arrows, drawing your gaze to the river, where the ducks and geese, all white as snow, would bob their heads and quack at you as if they were put out and wanted to know just what it was you thought you were looking at, while you had no intent to offend.

This happened often as I walked with no particular destination. I went for strolls, and because I walked the same routes I took to visit the homes of my students, there was no way to keep leisure and my work responsibilities separate. There were students of mine living in any direction I might walk. Some lived at the foot of the mountain, some down on flatter ground where their families farmed, others by the streams that fed into the Lhasa River. Some were living on the First of July State Farm, or right next door to the school in Danba, and others lived on the grounds of the Lhasa Cement Factory with its clouds of dust. The only way to avoid running into a student was to keep my eyes on the ground as I walked. But walking along the path by the sluice, even with my eyes down, I knew when I was coming up to the mill house because I would hear the water wheel turning and would feel the spray. If I looked up, then through the spray I would see the mill house there among the trees, its big water wheel turning, turning endlessly, water splashing and spraying.

The mill house looked ancient. It was a rectangular structure that straddled the water. It was simple, pleasing to look at, built all of wood, once brightly painted obviously, but the colour, like all its carved decoration, like its contour, had been burnished and softened by weather and time. You could imagine how beautiful it must have once looked, which made you think about time. It was one of those buildings that convey a sense of history, making you realise there isn't a people on the planet that isn't ancient, every people has its way of life and history. If every child is the future, then every older person is our past. The lady of the mill house seemed to me as old as the building. I never wanted to bother her, I truly didn't, but some things were not in my control.

She wasn't old, I learned, only forty, but she looked older. It was the effect of living under that fierce sun and because of other things too. Her middle age had gone by even more quickly than her youth as if she went directly from being young to being a white-haired old woman. The grass in Tibet is like that too, it is barely green before it starts to fade and yellow. Her name was Dolma, which means "goddess", and maybe she had been as beautiful as a goddess when she was young, but when I met her, she was old, and her braided hair was white.

She kept her eyes down as she walked, always. Her white hair was a sign of her difficult life and humble status. At first, she was to me just a shadow at twilight that I seemed to see over and over again. At first, I had no idea she was Penpa Tsering's mother. She was a stooped, fleeting shadow, a little scary, and I sort of avoided her. There are always shadows at dusk in Tibet, shadows of trees, shadows of walls, of clouds, of ghosts, shadows of folklore. Never speak to a shadow, I was warned. Unless the shadow speaks to you first, then you have to talk to it, or to them as sometimes there is more than one. This is what my students and colleagues told me. If the shadows invite you to have a seat, you must sit. If they want to have a drink with you, you must have that drink. If they want you to... Because of all these stories, when I saw certain shadows, I turned my eyes away and walked on as if I hadn't seen them. I knew there were some warnings I should always heed. I knew I should at least respect the discourse, respect the narrative. I agree with Wittgenstein that to imagine a language is to imagine a form of life. I agree with him that the limits of a language are the limits of a world, that the world exists in language, and that nothing is more real than language.

I had just started with a new class and didn't know any of the students. On the first day of term, Penpa Tsering walked in with a swagger and took his seat, but he had been expelled, for good, the term before. Tenpa Nyima told me this after the lesson. He said, Penpa Tsering isn't in school any more, he was expelled last term because he punched a teacher. Tenpa Nyima was class monitor, he had the responsibility to tell me this. He said, Penpa Tsering going after the teacher was to do with him, Tenpa Nyima. Penpa Tsering was supposed to obey Tenpa Nyima. He didn't, they got into an argument, and the teacher took the class monitor's side as he always did. Penpa Tsering started throwing punches, the teacher got involved, and he ended up with a black eye and a bloodied mouth. Clearly, according to one discourse, Penpa Tsering was a dangerous student. The next day I went up to the swaggering Penpa Tsering and asked him if it was true he had been expelled. He turned red and his classmates started to laugh. He frowned, cocked his head, shrugged his shoulders and, taking his sweet time, got his things together and walked out. I had no idea what he was thinking. Did he think he could get away with it because I was new to the class and wouldn't find out? At least he didn't take a swing at me, that much was good. He left as soon as I spoke to him, which gave me a good impression.

Penpa Tsering left my classroom, but he didn't leave the school. Every day he was among the crowd of students walking to the school, trailed by their dogs. Before school and between lessons, he joined the other students in their horseplay, their joking and rough and tumble, or he would get into fights. After the bell rang and quiet fell on the campus like a spell, he sat outside by himself. Sometimes he would disappear for a while and then return. Sometimes he sat under the classroom window in the sunlight with a book bag slung across his shoulder. If he got bored, he would take a book out of the bag, its cover bent and curled, flip through a few pages as he sat in the bright sunlight and then put the book back in the bag. Sometimes he would then take out a different book, glance at it, and put it back. Sometimes he would draw on the ground, sometimes he would do nothing, he would just sit looking up at the sun. Whenever there was commotion in the classroom, he would leap up and look in the window, his gaunt, freckled face pressed against the metal grate, with the undulating ridge of the snow peaks in the distance pressing in behind him. The school was below Mount Gephel and from the classroom, when you looked in the opposite direction away from the mountain, you saw the Lhasa River down below and mountains on the far side of the river. So, when Penpa Tsering pressed his face against the window, we saw him against the backdrop of those distant mountains. His face would be there as if he were in the room with us, and if we were singing, Penpa Tsering, his face against the grate, would sing along with his former classmates.

It wasn't long after this that I saw Dolma's shadow, and because of her shadow, I was able to see many other shadows as well. Dolma's shadow and Penpa Tsering's shadow fell together, one darting around the other, one hurrying on, the other hanging back. When I saw their shadows it was afternoon, lessons were over and the school was quiet. As twilight neared, all sorts of shadows fell, and more than once the shadows of Dolma and Penpa Tsering approached quickly through all the other shadows but then vanished. They came up to me, then slipped away, which made me a bit nervous and disinclined to investigate. If somebody had told me that Penpa Tsering had left the school but his shadow had stayed, I would have accepted it. It would be like a departed soul leaving a shade of itself behind. But who was the stooped, white-haired older woman with him? Was Penpa Tsering projecting some second shadow? Did he cast a doubled shadow?

It never occurred to me that she could be Penpa Tsering's mother. I thought she looked old enough to be a grandmother. To me she was an ancient shadow, but not a shade from hell, her white hair meant she must be from heaven, so I wasn't really afraid of her. I decided Penpa Tsering's shadow must have refused to leave the school (I was feeling guilty about him) and was playing tricks on me, making it appear to me that the old woman's eyes were like prisms, that the walls around me bent, that the sky was filled with inverted shadows. I realised that my consciousness was experiencing the world in four dimensions, even if I didn't accept the theoretical possibility of a fourth dimension. I knew that a particular discourse was changing what I perceived, so I kept my eyes straight ahead and down as I walked from the classroom to my house. If a fourth dimension was forming in my mind, I would deal with it in my mind, as I would deal with a dream.

But one day, to my surprise, a shadow blocked my way, and I almost tripped. I heard the shadow speak to me, "Mr Wang!" The sound seemed to come from Penpa Tsering's shadow. Penpa Tsering's voice brought me back into the world of three dimensions. I saw Penpa Tsering and Dolma standing there struggling with each other. It seemed he wanted to leave, but she wouldn't let him. They were by the end of a wall, and they kept disappearing behind it, then reappearing. Finally, with a last effort, Penpa Tsering shoved the old woman up towards me and ducked out of sight behind the wall.

—Mr Wang, my mum wants to talk to you, Penpa Tsering said from behind the wall.

I looked at Dolma, at her long white plait, her stooped shoulders, her lowered head, her palms pressed together in salutation. She spoke to me without looking at me.

—I'm begging you, I'm begging, let our boy come back to school, I'm begging you, let our boy back into school.

As Wang Mojie and I and others who have lived in Tibet know, when Tibetans speak Mandarin, they sometimes don't distin-

guish between first-person singular and first-person plural, between "I" and "we". So, for example, for "My mum and my dad", they often say, "Our mum and our dad". That might not be standard but when you get used to it, it starts to make sense and even sounds endearing. They don't seem to think of themselves as a singular "I", it is always the plural "us", "we", "our". This is wonderful. I don't know if this reflexive "selflessness" is the influence of Buddhism. Wang Mojie thinks not. He thinks it comes from living in such a difficult environment, but I don't necessarily agree. "Our dad". "Our mum". What a beautiful way of putting it. There is something metaphysical in it, for sure.

I explained that Penpa Tsering had been expelled the previous term and that I hadn't been involved. I said she would have to talk to the dean of students or the principal. But she didn't pay attention, she just kept repeating her appeal, like a mantra. At first, her eyes were closed and her hands, palms together, were held up to me, but slowly, slowly, she lifted her head, she lifted her eyes towards my face, and then she kept looking higher and higher, over my head up into the heavens. That's when I could see that her eyes, those eyes lifted to the heavens, were clouded over in white because she had cataracts.

—Let our boy come back to school, she said.

Then she started repeating something in Tibetan that I could not understand. Maybe she was saying the same thing she had said in Mandarin. Her eyes slowly brimmed with tears. The day was still bright, but I had the sense that I was seeing moonlight, moonlight behind clouds, the moonlight white of her cataracts. I couldn't say no to her. I said yes. But she didn't seem to understand or she hadn't heard me. She stood there, eyes to the heavens, listening, her palms pressed together and held before her. Penpa Tsering, the little coward who had made his mother handle everything for him, came up and tugged at her, stopping Dolma in her prayer. But she stopped only for a second, then continued, tears running down her face turned up towards the heavens.

I never went down the mill house path without cause. I couldn't bear the way she looked at me, her eyes full of gratitude, like she was looking at her saviour. But I kept finding myself stepping onto that particular path. When I did, I always tried to avoid going near the mill house, I would stop at a distance. But more than once there was a sudden shout from across the stream, and I would see Dolma and

Penpa Tsering standing in the mill house door calling to me. They had seen me coming and were out to welcome me. Penpa Tsering would run over and take my hand and not let it go. Dolma would stand to one side in the doorway, bowing slightly. She couldn't see me too clearly, she could just make me out, and she kept her white, moonlit eyes fixed on me.

They lived in the right half of the mill house as you faced it. It was unlike any other home I have ever seen. They lived with the constant sound of the water wheel and water. Attached to the water wheel were six prayer wheels, all hung with many *khata*, and they never stopped spinning. Inside they had, as everyone did, a shrine room with an image of Sakyamuni, barley and water offerings, and a butter lamp. But I had seen these things before only in ordinary stone houses. Here in a house built over running water, everything felt different. It was charming in a very moving, timeless sort of way. The sweet tea that Dolma made was delicious, and she also offered me butter tea, dried fruit and milk-skin cheese. Butter tea was still too much for me, but I liked Tibetan sweet tea. Dolma always had a thermos of it, and every time I took a sip, she refilled my glass. She brought out every treat they had in the house and put it all in front of me. And that wasn't the end of it, what truly made me uncomfortable was that when I left, she always gave me a basket of eggs and a thermos of the sweet tea to take with me. The tea I didn't mind taking, but eggs were worth too much. They sold eggs and needed the money, but she always wanted to give me one or two dozen, and that was the main reason I tried to avoid the path along the stream in the woods. Then Penpa Tsering started leaving a basket of eggs by my door every so often. I always gave him money, I made him take it. I knew, though, he wouldn't give it to Dolma. He probably spent it on cigarettes or in a teahouse.

Penpa Tsering came back to school. This wasn't any credit to me, I simply did the right thing. I told his other teachers and the principal that I vouched for the boy, which was not noble, it was nothing special. Penpa Tsering still misbehaved, he still couldn't control himself, his grades were poor, he got into fights, he picked on the girls, and he tied Sangnyi's and Lhadron's plaits to the back of their chairs. He still didn't do what the class monitor, Tenpa Nyima, said, and he still tried to fight Tenpa Nyima after school (he was completely outclassed, Tenpa Nyima was much bigger). But he regarded me as a god. I always backed up Tenpa Nyima and scolded Penpa Tsering. He would give me an embarrassed smile, then set upon Tenpa Nyima again, fists flying. Still, I could not imagine him ever attacking a teacher.

5. Venus

As Venus rises, a colourful scene unfolds along the Lhasa River.
People walk to the river, embrace the sky and dance with the water.
The khata *didn't cover Ukyi Lhamo's body as much as describe its contours.*
No one had ever gone into the river draped only in a khata, *ever.*

There are a few days late in each summer in Lhasa when day seems to linger into night. The stars come out while the sun is still setting, light and darkness meet at a balance point and stop there, as if they will forever. When Venus appears in the sky for the first time each year, rising over Bumpa Ri, the holy peak southwest of the city, a week-long festival commences. These are the days and nights of Karma Rishi, special days for the cleansing of the body and the cleansing of the soul, days of renewal.

Because of the festival, I learned the Tibetan names for the days of the week. Monday is *Dawa*, the Moon. Then comes *Migmar* or Mars; *Lhakpa*, Mercury; *Phurbu*, Jupiter; *Pasang*, Venus; *Penpa*, Saturn and finally *Nyima*, the Sun. At dusk on each of the seven days of Karma Rishi, everyone – the elderly, teenagers, married couples with children – everyone comes down to the river, where they set up blue-and-white-striped tents and put out colourful *khaden*. They shed their heavy robes, turn to face Venus as it rises over the beautiful Bumpa Ri that is shaped like an eight-petalled lotus, and they wade into the variegated waters of the Lhasa River. Bonfires blaze along the riverside, flames rising against the sunset glow and the oncoming night. It is a magnificent, dazzling sight. At their campfires, people brew strong tea and boil meat. They drink spirits from bowls. The delicate aroma of tea and the mouth-watering smell of the meat drift through the willows on the banks. When they have had enough to eat and drink, they strike up the *dramyin*, playing ancient Buddhist songs as wild as the wildest love songs, and they dance the Toeshey and Nangma around bonfires. It is a wonderful scene. Of course, it goes without saying that the attack on old customs that took place in the rest of China happened in Tibet too. Tibetan ritual practices, including those of Karma Rishi, were halted for a time by what we may call, euphemistically, the "intervention of history".

The ancient customs have been revived, but something just isn't the same any more. Some of the traditional instruments are no longer played, and the Toeshey and Nangma are now danced to music that blares from boomboxes, which isn't quite right. Tibet hasn't been spared the arrival of the things that are popular throughout the world, either, and it's all there on days of the festival of Karma Rishi, the "Bathing Festival" as the tourists call it: disco, beer, karaoke, Coca-Cola, denim jeans, fancy tents, souvenir stands, food stalls, open-air bars, prostitutes, hordes of tourists with their camera lenses and flashes and so on. The nights of Karma Rishi are still wonderful, it's still a celebration, but it is starting to be like any other showy, commercialised holiday.

When the transmission of a tradition is severed and when this tradition is then resurrected for tourists, when it exists to be photographed, it will never be pure again, it will never be the original "archetype" again, it can only be a "text". In the past, you might have seen a young woman turn the miracle of her naked, moonlit body towards the slowly rising planet Venus. Now, during Karma Rishi, Tibetans follow some of the old customs only out of the sight of tourists. Now, if anyone goes into the water naked, it is probably somebody showing off for the cameras on a dare. At best, it might be a complex modern expression of a traditional cultural practice, as it was when Ukyi Lhamo went into the water. She was being provocative. She wasn't entirely naked, she was wearing a thong and had a long *khata* draped around her neck and falling over her breasts. The *khata* kept catching the breeze, and the motion of the *khata* kept drawing your eyes to her breasts. A *khata* is a ritual object, and there is no tradition of wearing a *khata* as you go into the river. I don't know if this was Ukyi Lhamo's own inspiration or if some clever artist in Lhasa dreamed it up to join the ancient and modern. If so, he must have been there on the riverbank with the others like him, men and women who stayed aloof and apart from the ordinary folk. Wang Mojie knew some of them, some he didn't. If they had done a live television broadcast of Ukyi Lhamo going into the river, it would have truly connected the ancient to the modern. It would have been taken as a simple act but richly meaningful, a traditional rite performed in fashionable, sexy underwear and the whole thing brought off well. Ukyi Lhamo could have been an exotic Tibetan lingerie model. Ukyi Lhamo was fashionable, but she was also a Tibetan woman undergoing the ritual of cleansing, as Tibetan women have done forever. At the moment she walked into the water, the past did open, and the sight of her made you think of Sarasvati, the Goddess of Wisdom and Learning, as she is painted on *thangka*.

Ukyi Lhamo's background was complex. She was a graduate of the Beijing Foreign Languages Institute, where she had studied French. Her father was Han Chinese, her mother was Tibetan. She grew up in Beijing. Both of her parents worked at the Central Academy for Nationalities, where her father taught English and her mother worked in the library. Her Chinese name was Shen Jiayuan, which was the name she used throughout her childhood. After graduating from university, she went to France. She told Wang Mojie that it was only after arriving in France that she felt a strong identification as a Tibetan. After she came back from France, she moved to Tibet, just like her mother had. And she renamed herself. She began to use her Tibetan name, Ukyi Lhamo, but a lot of her friends continued to call her Shen Jiayuan and she didn't mind. She still sometimes thought of it as her name out of long habit. Instead of settling in Lhasa, she took a job teaching English, her second foreign language, at the school in the village west of the city. She did this because Lhasa wasn't like the old city of her imagination, life in Lhasa was just like life in the interior or overseas. Also, the village was near the Lhalu Wetlands, and the Lhalu Wetlands had a special meaning for her. It was where she had her roots and where her mother lived before she left Tibet for Beijing. Wang Mojie and Ukyi Lhamo were colleagues at the school, but she didn't live like a hermit the way he did. At weekends, she went to her mother's home off Barkhor Street in Lhasa. She couldn't live without at least some city life and her group of friends.

A veil of mystery surrounded Ukyi Lhamo that made her an object of fascination when she showed up at any social function in Lhasa. It was because her background was so complex. Born and raised in Beijing, half Chinese and half Tibetan, a returned student from France, living in a remote spot at the foot of the sacred Drepung Monastery, a believer in Buddhism and a student of many masters. Half the mystery surrounding her came from the association with Drepung. She was happy with this state of affairs, it was exactly what she wanted. At the weekend, she would put on Tibetan clothing and go with her mother to spin prayer wheels at the Jokhang, then at night she would show up at a party or bar she had been invited to, and she would be wearing something that looked Tibetan but fashionable. She was always surrounded by ardent admirers. She was used to it.

In Wang Mojie's opinion, even if you granted that Ukyi Lhamo, as a type, represented the trend towards cultural hybridity, she herself was just a muddle. A *khata* is a symbol of piety and purity, but she was making associations between the *khata*, her naked body and the planet and river. What did the *khata* have to do with ritual cleansing? Was it just a provocation or was it a symbol of homecoming to her? What she did wasn't a real ritual cleanse. The *khata* then was just a sign, a symbol, and any sign can become separated from what it originally signified. Fortunately, there was no live television broadcast and so it was a one-off event, otherwise we might have seen a fad for wearing *khata*, just like we have a frivolous fad for wearing clothing modelled on the Tang dynasty. You had to admit, though, that as a one-off it worked. The *khata*, at least superficially, signified Tibet, and it looked beautiful on Ukyi Lhamo, startlingly so. She was always very aware of her body, even while fully dressed, and she knew that wearing almost nothing except the *khata* she would make a striking sight. It wouldn't have been beyond her to have practised in front of a mirror or rehearsed in front of her fashion industry friends – an "undress rehearsal". In any event, she was prepared. She walked slowly towards the river, head high, heart full, eyes on the planet rising over the mountain, arms stretched upward. The wind caught the *khata* now and again and lifted it, her long hair floated on the breeze, and the flash from cameras sparkled on her skin. She was oblivious, she was like Tara or a "wisdom consort". And who was she, really? Shen Jiayuan or Ukyi Lhamo? The *khata* would suggest the latter, but the thong made you think of the former at a beach resort.

Wang Mojie was the only person in the crowd in whom Ukyi Lhamo inspired these sorts of thoughts, but as he looked at her and saw her as Shen Jiayuan, rather than Ukyi Lhamo, he admitted to himself that he was staring at her breasts just like all the other men. He understood why men fell so hard for her, went crazy over her and did outrageous things to get her attention. She could have stepped out of a fairy tale, she was so beautiful and sexy too, and the combination was very alluring. This wasn't about ritual cleansing, Ukyi Lhamo was putting herself on display, a flower in bloom, nothing to hide, a woman in the fullness of her power.

Beauty is a problem for women, and when women are sexy as well as beautiful it is a problem on top of a problem. Beautiful women have to decide how they will carry their beauty. Should they play it up or play it down? If they play it up, they lose that part of themselves they might keep to themselves, and they lose a little charm. And it is a reserved charm that can be the most stirring quality of a beautiful woman. But if a beautiful woman is too reserved, too cool and aloof, she ends up lonely, and isn't that a waste of her beauty, like throwing away money? In spring, the blooming flowers can make a beautiful but lonely woman feel heartache. The flowers will seem to her to bloom in such profusion because they are terrified of being alone. This is always the way with beauty, whether shared with the world or kept to oneself, the denouement is always such. There is no nirvana for a beautiful woman. Ukyi Lhamo, however, brought together as one her beauty, her Buddhism and her sexual allure, and so can we not say that this was movement in the direction of nirvana? That is what Wang Mojie said about Ukyi Lhamo. It didn't lack sarcasm.

Wang Mojie got to the river a little late. He had been hesitant about going ever since Ukyi Lhamo told him of her plan, but in the end he turned up. He arrived quietly and escaped notice. By the time he arrived, Ukyi Lhamo had gone somewhere and changed, she had the *khata* around her neck, and cameras with their flashbulbs crowded by the bonfire as if by a fashion show runway. Ukyi Lhamo was ready to walk into the river. Someone was making a short film of it: *Tibet: Yesterday, Today, Tomorrow*. Wang Mojie didn't have his camera with him because he thought of himself as a person who didn't need to filter everything he saw through a lens. When the breeze lifted the *khata* and her breasts touched the water, however, Wang Mojie reproached himself for always taking everything so seriously. If Ukyi Lhamo had been completely nude, then he wouldn't have wanted a photograph, but she had the *khata* on, which was not something to be seen every day. When the wind lifted the *khata* it was *sui generis*, a moment never to be repeated. In the river Ukyi Lhamo went through the ritual, she looked up at Venus, flicked water from her thumbs with her ring fingers, took water in her cupped hands and poured it over her head, and put her hands in her long hair and spread it before the sky. The water glistened like diamonds down her breasts, the *khata* moved in the breeze, she lowered herself into the water and slowly stood back up, and then she took off the *khata* and put it on the water. It drifted away, gracefully, an offering, taken away by the river, returning to its origin. Ukyi Lhamo glistened, baring everything to the river, giving everything to the river. Slowly, she turned and walked out of the water up onto the bank and past a bonfire, wearing nothing now, her thong gone, as naked as when she was born, everything down to its natural essence. If not for the flashbulbs, if the only light had been from the bonfire, it would have been the Tibet of yesterday, not the Tibet of today. Flashbulbs assassinate tradition, they kill the past. But very likely it was precisely because of the flashbulbs that Ukyi Lhamo walked so proudly, head high, an arrogant look in her eye. In the light from the camera flashes, her face was pale, white as wax even, her eyes expressionless, like those of a manikin, she saw no one, she saw no man, no lover, she didn't even see the light from the fires. And she didn't walk towards her friends or the bonfire where the crowd of onlookers had gathered, she walked instead towards her mother's small tent, which was a short way off. Incense was burning in a small brazier in front of the tent. Her mother came to greet her, put a towel around her and hugged her. Her mother was reciting something to herself. Ukyi Lhamo seemed to be crying. Her mother wrapped the towel more tightly around her daughter and took her into the tent.

Ukyi Lhamo's mother had worked her entire career in a library, but although she had spent her life surrounded by books, now in her old age there was nothing about her that suggested she had any attachment to books. In fact, she looked as if she had no attachment to anything. She had left Tibet for the interior when she was in her twenties and enrolled in a training course at the Central Academy for Nationalities. Later she married a young English teacher, Ukyi Lhamo's father, and they remained at the academy. In the 1950s, this was a success story for a member of a minority. She gave birth to five children, and she gave her own name, Ukyi Lhamo, to her youngest daughter. Her own mother had the same name, and her maternal grandmother had also been named Ukyi Lhamo, and before her there had been generations of Ukyi Lhamos. After returning to Lhasa, she lived off Barkhor Street in an old house that had long belonged to her family. Every day, three times a day, morning, midday and evening, she walked the Barkhor circuit around Jokhang Temple and then went into the temple to make offerings of incense and butter for the lamps and to pray, her right hand on her forehead and her left hand placed gently over her right, as she stood with head bowed before the image of the Buddha for a long time. Except on days of major festivals, she did not put her entire body on the ground in prostration and touch her forehead to the earth the way Tibetan herdsmen did. She had, after all, spent decades living in Beijing. But be that as it may, she seemed to grow more pious with each day. Usually, she spent her days venerating the Buddha and chanting sutras, even when she was knitting something for her children or her husband far off in Beijing. She chanted sutras as she knitted, often endlessly repeating om mani padme hum, *and it was as if she was making up for all the lost time when she had not chanted. On the evening by the river, she was wearing traditional Tibetan dress, had prayer beads in her hand and was sitting peacefully on a* khaden *in front of her tent. The tent was blue and white and decorated with auspicious symbols, and it seemed to radiate an aura of ancient history.*

Ukyi Lhamo's mother hadn't done a ritual cleanse. Her daughter, who was as she had once been, had gone into the river for her. Ukyi Lhamo's mother certainly didn't look like someone who had worked in a university library for decades, but she didn't look entirely like a local either. She resembled an ethnic Tibetan who had returned after a life lived overseas. Her tent was only a few metres away from the bonfire where her daughter's friends were gathered but was a world unto itself. She did not, however, feel isolated.

Wang Mojie was the one feeling isolated. He was sitting by himself on the side of the bonfire opposite everybody else. He had nothing in his hands, not even a bottle of water. Ukyi Lhamo's mother had her prayer beads and incense and the planet above the mountain. Wang Mojie had nothing. He just sat there, interminably.

Ukyi Lhamo dressed, came out of the tent and joined her friends by the bonfire. She was greeted with cheers. A man with a big beard spread his arms and with a flourish sang *O Sole Mio*. He sang as he walked towards Ukyi Lhamo, "*Che bella cosa na jurnata 'e sole*". Ukyi Lhamo gave the bearded singer a light hug, then took the glass of red wine handed to her by a friend. Her female friends were lavish in their praise for her as if to show how close they were to her, how they best understood her, and how proud of her they were. They raised their glasses and drank a toast to her. Music started to play, and someone yelled, "Let's dance! Let's dance!" They could hold back no longer.

Wine, a bonfire, dancing. None of this had any connection to Karma Rishi. Or the Lhasa River. Or Venus or even Ukyi Lhamo. They were done with the sacred, it was time for the secular. They danced. Turning together, close, intimate and fevered, whispering. These were teachers, journalists and government employees, also artists, business owners, tourists and so on and so on.

Ukyi Lhamo walked over to Wang Mojie. She was bound to. Wang Mojie had been expecting her to. They looked at each other for a moment. Ukyi Lhamo was wearing a dress now, the glass of red wine in her hand.

—Either come over or move farther away. Don't you feel ridiculous over here by yourself?

Ukyi Lhamo looked down at Wang Mojie sitting on the ground. Wang Mojie gestured to Ukyi Lhamo to sit. She didn't, of course.

—You think there's something ridiculous about being alone? The materfamilias is alone, too, if I'm not mistaken.

—She's not alone. She has her god. Who do you have?

—Surely you mean the Buddha, not God, I assume?

—Same difference.

—Well, I think there is a difference. One belongs to a deistic philosophy and the other to a philosophy that is not deistic. Anyone can become a Buddha. Can anyone become God?

—Thanks so much for the lesson. You still look ridiculous.

—I don't feel ridiculous.

—It wouldn't be so ridiculous if we didn't know each other.

—I see. We know each other, so there's an implicit association in play. I take your meaning, very well put.

—I regret that we know each other. Some of my friends know you, too, and they would like you to join us.

—They would like me to or you would like me to?

—They would, Ukyi Lhamo said and pointed to her friends.

—There is no connection between me and them, Wang Mojie said.

—You're bothering them.

—I can go. I was getting ready to leave anyway.

—You do what you want, Ukyi Lhamo said before walking away.

Wang Mojie stood up, hesitated and, rather despite himself, followed Ukyi Lhamo. From a distance, he was able to observe her crowd of friends quite clearly, he saw them as a relief sculpture but moving. As he drew nearer, quite contradictorily, he saw them less and less clearly. Wang Mojie was not accustomed to being near so many faces at once, he wasn't accustomed to the scene by the bonfire. With some formality, Ukyi Lhamo introduced Wang Mojie to those friends of hers who had yet to meet him. She told them where he had gone to university, what he had studied and why he had come to Tibet. She expressed her admiration for volunteer teachers like Wang Mojie and said that she had "always held him in great respect", but as she spoke, Ukyi Lhamo's formality seemed more and more tinged with sarcasm.

—Excuse me, can I have something to drink? Wang Mojie said before Ukyi Lhamo had finished.

Somebody passed Wang Mojie a can of beer. Wang Mojie asked if there was any bottled water because he didn't drink alcohol.

—Ha! Get a load of him, an ascetic! someone yelled in response.

—There's no bottled water, Ukyi Lhamo said. Do you want sweet tea?

—No, Wang Mojie said.

Out of politeness, someone offered Wang Mojie a cigarette, but Wang Mojie said he didn't smoke. The man who had offered the cigarette looked at Wang Mojie and then spoke.

—You don't smoke, you don't drink, so I'm sure you don't go...

He didn't say "whoring", instead he paused and let his coarse implication sink in, then with the offered cigarette still in his hand, he asked Wang Mojie a question.

—So what do you do?

—Not much. Hang out, Wang Mojie said.

—Hang out?

—Yes.

—Fuck. You are too fucking much, the man said.

The man with the cigarette suddenly turned towards his friends and spoke with affected seriousness.

—I've never heard that before. This guy is honest, he tells it like it is. He is fucking honest. People from the interior always ask me what I do in Tibet, like it's all so mysterious here. I'm always too embarrassed to admit that life here is boring, so I always go on about how great it is. We've got snow peaks, grasslands, beautiful temples. I say we live among the celestials, but that's all bullshit. There's not enough oxygen, there's nothing to do, we just hang out! Comrades, comrades, did you hear him? From now on, anybody asks me what I do in Tibet, I'll say, "I hang out!" That is so fucking great. What are you doing? Nothing, hanging out! You are the best, my man, I drink to you!

This sort of gathering, with its sarcastic banter, was something that Wang Mojie was not unfamiliar with from his time in Beijing. But heard here, this particular idiom sounded intimidatingly aggressive. Not like criminal aggression, more like political aggression. A woman handed Wang Mojie a can of something. Her smile was impossible to read.

—Black-bone chicken soup. It's a tonic, she said, speaking softly but clearly enough for everyone to hear, though someone pretended not to have heard.

—What? What? Yu Youyan, say again? What's it a tonic for? What part of the body does it help?

—Ignore them. Shall I open it?

—Thank you, Wang Mojie said.

—Here. Allow me.

As she opened the can, she asked Wang Mojie if he was always on his own like this. Her voice was sweet, full of caring, as if she were speaking to a child, but there was something creepily possessive about her tone.

—So, Ukyi Lhamo was saying you studied biology?

—And philosophy.

She was being very affected, while Wang Mojie was being utterly straightforward. Who admits to studying philosophy these days?

—Oh? Philosophy? I like philosophy. What I really need in my life at the moment is philosophy. Would it be OK if I paid you a visit?

—Ha ha! Youyan, you trying to put an end to his religious vows? someone yelled.

—Shut up. Mind your own business. Such an annoying person.

She spoke to Wang Mojie again, still just as softly.

—Can I? Would it upset your routine?

—I think it would.

—Ha ha. Too much! someone yelled. Everyone laughed at what Wang Mojie said, Ukyi Lhamo included. Wang Mojie didn't as much as smile.

—Ignore them, Yu Youyan said and slapped Wang Mojie's hand flirtatiously. She said, I really do have a lot of questions for you about philosophy, and I want you to teach me to garden. Those greens you grew were delicious. Will you show me how to garden? OK, you're saying yes, that's great! Will you dance with me? Come on, come on. There is no such thing as being unable to dance. Anybody can dance. Get up, come on, I'll teach you.

Wang Mojie let himself be pulled to his feet. It had been a long time since he had touched a woman, but he felt no rush of pleasure. Yu Youyan pressed close to him, and Wang Mojie's body tensed. Yu Youyan told him to relax, she whispered in his ear, she said he was entirely too strait-laced, there was something holy about him, something Daoist about him to be specific, and she asked Wang Mojie if he had been to Mount Qingcheng or Mount Lao or other places sacred to Daoists. At this point, Wang Mojie took his first real look at Yu Youyan. He had a feeling she was just pretending to have some culture. She was wearing a long slip dress and a white cashmere sweater with a low neckline, her hair was neatly bobbed to her ears. She looked like a Japanese schoolgirl, but she had on sexy red lipstick, and up close the fragrance of her perfume mixed with the equally strong smell of wine. She had large breasts, strikingly large, there was something maternal about this but alluring too because she had the lively demeanour of a young woman. He couldn't decide if she looked like a girl or a woman, but either way something was just not right about her. A few times she seemed to press her breasts against him deliberately, they didn't feel soft, they felt firm, solid. Years ago, when he was still very young, Wang Mojie had a girlfriend, his first, who liked bras with thick, pointed cups. Wang Mojie asked her, quite seriously, if she would please not wear that sort of bra when she was alone with him. That sort of bra, he said, was for when you went out in public, it was not made to wear with your boyfriend in private. He told her that small breasts had their own beauty, and he said that beauty still developing and ready to burst forth was even more captivating than beauty in its full maturity.

As Wang Mojie thought about this, he began to move with a little more ease, falling into step with Yu Youyan. He held her hand with his left hand and put his right hand on her waist as they turned together, dancing something like a rumba.

Indeed, it was a rumba. Wang Mojie had forgotten that he knew how.

—Hey, you can dance! Yu Youyan said happily.

—I forgot I could. But I don't dance well, Wang Mojie said.

—Stop it. Look how good you are!

—Really?

—Really, she answered, dropping her affectation and looking at Wang Mojie with ardour.

—I haven't been to this sort of party in a very long time, Wang Mojie said with a sigh.

—I'm sure you were popular back in the day.

—I wouldn't really say that.

They danced, seeming to have found an understanding, but Wang Mojie still kept looking up to find Ukyi Lhamo. She was in the arms of the man with the big beard who had sung *O Sole Mio*. She looked over at Wang Mojie now and again too. Ukyi Lhamo held her head high, her expression blank. There in the light of the bonfire with the darkness all around, Wang Mojie felt her gaze rest on him for a moment, a moment he easily could have missed. She smiled at him, just for the briefest second, then it was gone, and he couldn't catch her eye again.

—She is why you came? Yu Youyan asked softly, in a matter-of-fact tone, no hint of jealousy.

—Yes. She invited me, Wang Mojie said, his eyes searching for Ukyi Lhamo.

—She's taken. That guy over there. The one not dancing.

—I know, Wang Mojie said, his eyes finding Ukyi Lhamo as she danced.

—You know? Really? Then I am definitely coming to pay you a visit, for real.

Wang Mojie looked at Yu Youyan.

—It wasn't for real the first time you said it? he asked.

Yu Youyan pretended to be angry, and she pinched Wang Mojie on the small of the back, which startled him, but he didn't let it show.

—We all know who you are. We ate your greens.

—And destroyed my garden.

She pinched him again, a little harder, as if to mean that the garden was just the beginning.

It felt good. It excited him. It had been a long time.

—You rebuilt it, made it even nicer, and you put up the Buddhist stuff too.

—I took those things down.

—Why? I know you did, but why? I wanted to ask you about that.

—Someone said it was disrespectful.

—Who said?

—A Buddhist, of course.

—Ukyi Lhamo? Why listen to her?

—I can't help it with her.

She pinched him again, hard, and pressed her breasts against him. It was a seduction.

But Wang Mojie had his eyes on "that guy over there", the one not dancing. He and some other man were talking, heads together. He was wearing a red scarf that was just visible tucked inside his black leather jacket, its collar upturned. His bearing was calm, solid. Maybe they were talking about poetry and poetics. They spoke in low tones, intently, pausing to smoke. They were oblivious to the music, the bonfire and the river. They could have been in any smoke-filled office. Wang Mojie knew the man taught in the mathematics department at Tibet University and that he wrote poetry. He was a school of poetry unto himself. A critic once wrote that he tried to create geometric structures in his poetry and that he wrote by running dream imagery through mathematical formulae.

Ukyi Lhamo had a new dance partner. Now she was dancing with a lithe, rugged-looking man in a Tibetan herdsman's felt hat. Maybe because the music had changed to a fast tune, Ukyi Lhamo and the cowboy-looking guy were dancing fast and passionately, whooping and hollering. The maths professor-poet paused briefly in his conversation and looked with great calm over at Ukyi Lhamo, who was so graceful and so provocative. Maybe he was thinking that the curves of Ukyi Lhamo's body escaped what his geometry could contain, her form beyond mathematical or geometric measure. The rugged-looking man was a climbing instructor with the Mountain Club at Tibet University. He was almost forty but sinewy as a racehorse, muscled head to foot, looking stronger and fitter than much younger men. They said that more than once he had defied the odds by walking away unscathed from an avalanche. He was known to be fearless. Ukyi Lhamo was obviously aroused by this rugged man, this was clearly not their first dance. They turned together, embraced and fell apart, communicating wordlessly, so sexy, so in tune with each other, the two of them oblivious to everyone else. The sight of the two of them got your blood going, but it didn't make you jealous. It was beyond that, beyond anybody's sense of propriety, they were a natural pair, they belonged together, and it would have been right for them to make love, right there, they were just incredible. Dance is all about sex, everybody knows this. Everyone else stopped dancing and stepped back from the bonfire into the shadows to watch them dance.

They were like fire, primal and wild, and the fire metaphor worked to describe their relationship in more ways than I can describe. The song ended, and the poet started clapping, cigarette in his mouth, but only a few people joined him, and the man who had been in conversation with him did not. There was a lot of drinking, a growing heap of empty beer cans, and the ground became strewn with rubbish. After some more drinking, Ukyi Lhamo and her mountaineer danced again. They hadn't had enough, they wanted to feel all those emotions of sunset again. They danced a waltz. They danced together, so close, a narrative, a lullaby. He kissed her a few times, there in public, Ukyi Lhamo pulled back but only slightly, she didn't really mind.

The rest of them resumed dancing, even more out of control than before. Yu Youyan asked Wang Mojie to dance again, but Wang Mojie thought it was time for him to go. He said goodbye, he said that would about do it for him tonight, but just as Wang Mojie was about to leave, the mathematician-poet crossed in front of the bonfire and walked over.

—Don't leave. It's you I want to talk to, he said as he handed one of the two cans of beer he was carrying to Wang Mojie. He continued to speak to Wang Mojie.

—I know, I know, you don't drink. I know, but it's not like you've never had a drink, right? You take one when you visit Tibetans' homes, right? You must. Come on, have a drink. You don't have to finish it. No pressure.

Wang Mojie took the beer. The man banged his can against Wang Mojie's and invited him to drain it.

—Bottoms up?

Wang Mojie didn't react. He just stared at the man intently. The two of them, both wearing scarves, had something very similar about them but very different too. Wang Mojie's grey checked scarf was wrinkled and lent him an air of quiet introversion and otherworldliness. The poet's red scarf was straightforward, striking and uncomplicated. But no matter how similar or how different they looked, either would have done well to lose the scarf.

—Youyan, Youyan, can you get a couple more beers for us, please? I should have grabbed more.

—Wait, I don't drink, Wang Mojie said and held up his hand.

—Tonight you have to have a drink with me. I'm treating you as if you were Tibetan.

—Too much honour. I wouldn't presume.

—I am never this polite to anybody.

—I'm alcohol intolerant, actually, Wang Mojie said.

—OK, OK, I believe you, I should believe you, the poet said and then took a long drink from his beer before continuing.

—You and I have seen each other many times, but we've only crossed paths, we've never spoken. I've been wanting to talk to you about that unfortunate incident with your garden, it was just supposed to be a joke, but I was drunk. I've been drinking a lot lately, for about six months now. Youyan knows I've been drinking all the time, don't you, Youyan?

—How would I know? Leave me out of it, Youyan said with a tone that made it clear she wanted nothing to do with the poet, as if he were objectionable to her.

—OK, OK. Sure, you don't know, sure. Nobody dares be truthful, it's a pity.

He turned back to Wang Mojie.

—I told her to invite you, he said, gesturing in Ukyi Lhamo's direction. You can ask her yourself if you don't believe me. You're a smart guy, I know. I've got some things I want to say to you, but not now of course. Here's my phone number. Come and see me at the university, I'd like that. Come over anytime. Tomorrow. Next week. Next year. Well, perhaps not that long. Just don't forget.

—OK, thanks, Wang Mojie said.

—Bottoms up?

—Sorry.

—Good luck to you.

—And to you.

6. Two Banks of One River

Not only do they believe in the soul, they can see it.
They say it is like the way we wear clothing, the soul has its clothing too.
The body is the soul's clothing. They say it's like the way we
take off our clothing to sleep. The soul removes the body and departs.

Penpa Dolma had a birthmark on her face that ran from her temple across her cheekbone to her eye. It looked like her ear had been put in the wrong place and then moved, leaving a mark. It was dark and made her eye appear very white when she opened it wide. She was tall and skinny, with a long, thin face. She had a lively, spirited laugh, and the birthmark added something complex and animated to her expression. She wasn't self-conscious about the birthmark at all, she was always talking and giggling, she liked flirting with the boys, and she liked making goofy, scary faces with the birthmark. Since she had the birthmark, why hide it, why not show it off? She liked it when people were startled by the birthmark, it made her happy. The other students called her "Goofy Ghost", which I didn't understand because I didn't think of ghosts as goofy, but I learned that Tibetans didn't think ghosts were anything to be afraid of. They believed that ghosts or spirits could be goofy, happy, sad, angry, anything, and they could communicate with the living. Penpa Dolma once disappeared from school for a time, and it was a while before I found out that it was because her mother had suddenly passed away. During this time, the atmosphere among my students was charged with something that puzzled me. They kept whispering to one another, even when I was talking. They were secretive, as if they were talking about something very mysterious and interesting. Finally, a few of the girls explained everything to me with great seriousness, but I found it hard to believe them. They claimed that two days after Penpa Dolma's mother died, she communicated to the family that she would visit them at home at twilight on the seventh day after her death, and she did. That's absurd, I said. She's dead. She can't come back home for any visit. That's impossible.

The girls asked why it was impossible. They said that after we die we become ghosts, and they had all seen Penpa Dolma's mother's ghost with their own eyes. They told me the exact route her mother had taken to get back home, whose houses she had walked by and exactly when. They said the reason Penpa Dolma's mother had sent word ahead of time was so that people could avoid running into her, because if she encountered a stranger, she would not be reincarnated, she would be a homeless ghost forever. Everybody knew this already, but she wanted to remind them, especially the children, just like the way a teacher repeats the rules even though all the students know them already.

They were able to tell me everything that happened in great detail. They said that on that day on the cement factory campus, where Penpa Dolma lived, it was very quiet along all the streets, and as the sun was going down Penpa Dolma's mother appeared, exactly as she said she would. She came home safe and sound, travelling with the shadows of twilight. Kalsang Dekyi told me this. She was a class monitor, a great student, a good girl and completely trustworthy. She said that as soon as Penpa Dolma's mother got home, she opened their cabinet with the lotus and white elephants on it and took out a silver bracelet. She polished it with a cloth and handed it to Penpa Dolma. She ate dinner with the family and then had a talk with Penpa Dolma. She told her to study hard and listen to the teacher. [At this point in his story, Wang Mojie made what is for him a rare expression of helplessness, meaning that all this was utterly beyond his comprehension, it was a reality other than his own.] Kalsang Dekyi said that Penpa Dolma's mother drank some freshly made butter tea and some sweet tea too, then she put a *khata* around her neck and, travelling with the twilight shadows, returned the same way she had come. Kalsang Dekyi said that while all this was happening everybody was on their best behaviour, everybody was very quiet, and nobody moved around. At such times you are not allowed to speak loudly and you are not allowed to bang dishes or chopsticks around, and you can't have any of the usual drinking and laughing.

That's impossible, I said loudly. Impossible! Kalsang Dekyi argued right back. She had never argued with me before. She kept saying that she had seen everything with her own eyes. She said Penpa Dolma's mother was like the shadow of something cast on water, she wore all black but with a green headscarf like she always wears, and she had on black earrings. Dechen Dolkar agreed with Kalsang Dekyi, she had seen it too. Tsedon said the same thing. Even Tenpa Nyima, whom I never knew to say anything that wasn't the truth, said he had seen it. They had all seen it. They all said they saw it. So I was the only one who didn't see it? You didn't know it was happening, they said. We didn't tell you. Why didn't you tell me, I asked. We just couldn't tell you, they said. Why, I asked. Why? No one answered. Finally, Tenpa Nyima said, You're a stranger, you're not like us. He almost said, You are Han. I said, So the dead are afraid of the living? That was a new one on me. I said if something like this happens again, you have to tell me. Kalsang Dekyi said, Even if we tell you, you still won't see it. I asked her why. She didn't answer. Maybe there was no answer. To them I was just different and that was that. If I die, can I come back? I asked. If I die, can I come back to school and give you lot homework? They gasped, they had not expected me to say that.

Penpa Dolma returned to school. She didn't seem any different, but she had a new bracelet on her wrist. Kalsang Dekyi held up Penpa Dolma's arm and said, Look. Penpa Dolma just nodded her head to mean that everything Kalsang Dekyi and the others had told me was the truth and the bracelet was proof. I didn't doubt for a minute that they believed everything they were telling me. I even seemed to see Penpa Dolma's mother, all in black, in their innocent eyes. I had met the woman. As Penpa Dolma's teacher, I had come to her house, and I had met her mother. Now I could see her in my students' eyes.

I am quick, Wang Mojie said, to learn to find my way within any given "linguistic field". He said that after enough exposure to that particular discourse, he could see in his mind's eye shadows walking down the road at twilight just as described in the local folklore. He said it is difficult to explain the phenomenon of Penpa Dolma's mother's ghost, but many phenomena vanish as soon as you try to explain them. He said that at the time he had not yet read Jung's commentary on The Tibetan Book of the Dead, *but he knew about theories of the "linguistic field". He knew that while we assume language arises from phenomena, in reality phenomena can be created by language. Different languages give rise to different ways of life; different ways of life exist within different languages. Wang Mojie said he was aware that Wittgenstein believed that nothing existed outside of language and that philosophy was simply a use of language that could not tell us anything about the world. Each person and all communities exist within a particular language and this language is their world, their home, their identity. Whether something has happened or has not depends on language. In one language and the world it creates it has happened, but in another it has not. We can't get beyond language. Science can't help us explain the phenomenon of Penpa Dolma's mother's ghost. Science is not omnipotent; science does not reveal absolute truths.*

How do we establish that an event has really taken place? Where do the limits of the real lie? We believe in the existence of the table in front of us because we can see it and touch it. There are many ways to prove that a table or a similar object exists, unlimited ways. But have we ever proved the reliability of these proofs we find so convincing? How do we know that what we know is true? Is there a philosophical proof of a table's existence?

We place strict limits on what we think is possible and impossible, but Tibetans do not acknowledge these limits. They don't accept, or one might say their language does not accept, that death exists. As they understand it, life exists on both banks of a river that we can cross repeatedly. There is no absolute separation between the living and the dead. We do not see only with our eyes, we see with our consciousness, and the nature of consciousness is determined by language. Tibetans don't just believe in the soul, they can see it. They can see a person's soul as it walks around like a living person. My students explained it to me using clothing as an analogy. They said we wear clothing, and in a way the soul does too. A living body is like a coat worn by the soul. The soul does not stay in the same body forever. Just as we take off our clothes at night before bed, the soul can take off a body. Later I heard the father of one of my students use the analogy of dreaming. When we dream, we enter a different form of existence in which we are only a soul, we have no body. When we dream, our souls leave our bodies. He was an educated man. Going back to the clothing analogy, he said just as we discard clothing when it becomes worn out, the soul will leave a body when that body no longer functions. If this happens suddenly, because of something like a heart attack, then the soul leaves the body and wanders awhile. If the living person has left anything unfinished, then the soul will return to the person's home, put his things in order and say farewell to the family. This was why they had the custom of not making a lot of noise in fields or mountain gullies or by abandoned buildings because the wandering ghosts, the wandering souls, like to go to these places to rest. They are easily frightened, and if frightened, they are transformed into hungry ghosts and become trapped in rivers from which they can never escape. This is the only sort of permanent death they believed in.

This is one explanation, one particular language. It is the language of the Tibetans, the language of their lives as they have been for generation after generation. Except for this language, there was no real difference between them and me. Our lives weren't all that different. The people I knew in Tibet liked to laugh, they liked to drink, they loved life. They made plans, suffered, felt sadness and had hopes for the future. They just didn't believe there was such a thing as death. They had an extra dimension in their universe, a dimension I do not believe exists. But how could I explain Penpa Dolma's bracelet? That wasn't a matter of language or consciousness, it was a concrete physical object, so how did it end up on Penpa Dolma's arm?

When all this about her mother was over, everything returned to how it had been. The bracelet was on Penpa Dolma's wrist, it would stay there, and eventually it would be passed on to the next generation. I taught my students, I imparted knowledge to them, and I was often the object of their fun. I didn't change them, and they didn't change me, it was a two-way exchange between us, between different habits of the heart.

That's it. Different habits of the heart.

7. The Monastery

"Elder one, hear what I am saying, walk the path of ease.
Your feet are growing colder, the life is leaving your legs.
The cold is moving up your body. Be at peace.
Let go of this life, enter the Bardo of Dharmata."

Sometimes, often at dusk and dawn, it was like a summons and as you walked into the sound of drums and horns, you entered the white expanse of the monastery. As you ascended the mountain, you wouldn't have even noticed the quiet village, the woods with their old snow, the barking dogs or the rocks and gullies and the sound of water. To the sound of drums and horns, the white monastery complex opened up before you. The monastery climbed like a staircase up the side of the mountain. The magnificent assembly hall seemed to have been carved right out of the rock. The monastery was like the remnant of a glacier from the Cretaceous Period. The monastery had innumerable windows, stone steps, courtyards, alleys and prayer wheels.

There was no way to know when the monastery was built or how many pairs of wise old eyes watched from the windows of all those hidden rooms. You lost track of time in there, and it was even harder to keep track of where you were in space. It was hard to orient yourself. There was no obvious exit, but then again there were exits everywhere and every exit was an entrance. Sunlight poured into some places but was blocked out in others, and there were hidden spots down high-walled alleys where you might find a grand hall or a secluded courtyard with walkways roofed with double eaves on all four sides. Shafts of sunlight reached the courtyards deep within the monastery and there was the sound of water dripping on stone, but not from nearby, coming from above it seemed. Troughs channelled water from above, they ran below the eaves, in and out of the sunlight, but the sound of the water always seemed to come from even higher up. It was a sound from a different place, a different time. When you entered a courtyard, you could leave in a different direction, and you would find yourself taking some different route, down a different winding alley, through a different world. You might find yourself standing on broken stone steps, standing in the sound of a sutra being chanted. You might feel a breeze, and if there was no breeze, when you looked up you might see a tall wall cutting off your way ahead. Or a huge double door. A door to history. Not an exit, but maybe the true exit. You could not go in. If you did, time would flood in after you, and something that would otherwise be eternal would come to an end.

But I did enter, even though I remained outside the door. The door was ajar, and through the crack I saw a brilliant, hidden scene of juniper and cedar smoke gently rising in the light from three thousand lamps, light that danced and flickered on the many red-robed figures who swayed gracefully in front of a giant golden statue of the Buddha. A drum boom, boom, boomed. It was a rare and secret drum made with human skin. Its origins lie in some form of ancient torture and it was borrowed into Buddhist ritual, and it is said that it was made from the skin of a beautiful pure young maid. That is the source of the mysterious sound of the Tibetan drum, the origin of the vibrations in the air that rippled the water in the offering bowls. The old monks in their red robes sat in rows facing each other. Banners hung down from the ceiling between the rows. Way up above, a narrow walkway circled the room and there was a skylight, angled, so the sunlight didn't fall to the floor, it fell instead on the carved beams and wall paintings. Shadows of the banners fell across the paintings. In the middle of the hall, an old man lay on his back on a bed covered in yellow satin. He was dying. Some part of him was taking leave of its corporeal form. The monks, at least three hundred of them, intoned a sutra to send him on his journey to the *bardo*. The final exit. He was only a moment away from entering the sunlight of the heavenly realms. An old monk with an air of the divine about him held the dying man's hand lightly in his, and he spoke with a voice that came from his diaphragm, low and rhythmic.

—Elder one, hear what I am saying, it will help you walk the path of ease. Your feet are growing colder, the life is leaving your legs, the cold is moving up your body. Be at peace, let go of this life, enter the Bardo of Dharmata. There is nothing to fear. Elder one, you are falling, the dark shadows of the coming long night are falling across your eyes, you are drawing nearer and nearer to your final release from this life.

As he spoke, guiding the dying man on his way, the monk tapped the man lightly and repeatedly from his collarbones to the top of his head to help his soul leave his body without suffering. The monk swayed and gestured, each movement meaningful, guiding the soul to safety.

—Elder one, the mountains point to the heavens in silence, the wind stirs the waters, flowers blossom, your approach does not frighten birds into flight, they cannot see you, they cannot hear you. Elder one, you can no longer see anything, your breath has stopped, you are freed from this existence, go your way, and we will go ours, continue on your way.

The dying man's body was making a sound, it had a cadence, it followed the rhythm of the mysterious, grand ceremony taking place around him, the sound melded with the drums. I knew Tibetans believed this to be the sound of the soul leaving the body and following the sunlight into the heavens.

Had I heard the sound of a soul leaving a body? Ma Dingge thought for a time that I had, but he said that not just anyone could hear the sound. Once, as we sat in Ma Dingge's sunny courtyard, I asked him to explain it to me. He said that only men who have been through years of Buddhist training could hear the sound, and only they can help a soul on its way. He also said that without Buddhist training we remain blind to our own existence, we cannot perceive our own selves, which I found to be a truly fascinating thought. Ma Dingge said that the essence of Buddhist training is to realise one's own spiritual nature. He said in Buddhist training we study ourselves over a very long period of time, and only after this observation are we able to perceive the soul within us and perceive the souls of others. Ma Dingge said that this life is not all there is. We have past lives and we will have future lives. The soul has permanence and is not limited to existence within a single body. After the soul leaves a body, its passage to a new life takes a period of time, and during this time the soul must be protected, comforted and guided. Otherwise, the soul will wander aimlessly and become lost, with no abode, no home to return to.

I could accept none of this. In fact, my belief is quite the contrary. I believe that when we die, it is our consciousness, our soul, that dies immediately, while it takes time for our bodies to decompose and disappear. Indeed, even with cremation, according to the law of the conservation of matter, the stuff that makes up cells and our DNA can never disappear. So, what is a "soul"? If the soul has no physical existence, if it isn't made of molecules, atoms or quarks, then in what form can it be said to exist? Descartes claimed that the soul is located in the pineal gland. That was his intuition or else the product of his imagination, and he couldn't demonstrate it, of course. A man's philosophy can be immortal, but I don't believe in an immortal soul that is able to leave the body. I don't believe that after I die, I will go on a journey and then be reborn in a new body, and I said so to Ma Dingge. He pointed out how many times I had used the word "I", and he asked what the meaning of "I" was. He asked if "I" was a body or a soul?

I asked Ma Dingge, How can body and soul be separated? My thinking on this question was clear, and I was confident my position was correct. Ma Dingge looked at me with his pale eyes and said, When we say "I", we first mean our physical selves, but Buddhism teaches that "I am not my body". Buddhism teaches us to recognise that the "I" or "me" we are so accustomed to speaking of has no real existence. He said the self is a stream of consciousness. Many times Ma Dingge and I became so engrossed in our conversation on our walks together that we would suddenly discover that we had crossed from one end of the monastery to the other, all the while accompanied by the sound of the monastery drums. At these times the monastery seemed no longer to be something foreign to me, and for a while I considered making an effort at Buddhist contemplation, to try to see if I could stop my thoughts entirely. Once Ma Dingge and I stood together on the terrace high up in the monastery complex, and oh yes, Ukyi Lhamo was there too. The three of us stood together on the terrace. Behind us were the ruins of the abandoned buildings that covered a greater area than the monastery complex still in use and behind that the snow-covered mountain top. This was the highest spot in the monastery, it looked out over the Lhasa River, which was not far away. It was twilight, of course, it was always twilight when we went up there, always when the sun was setting. The light at that hour was inspiring but also brought a feeling of peace, a peaceful thrill, you might say.

Twilight comes and goes suddenly in Tibet, but to get a good sense of this suddenness you have to be at a high spot from which to watch the huge shadows racing past. Below, at the foot of the monastery, were the woods, then the village, a small hill, then more buildings and fields, and all of this fell into the shadows as we watched. Just before the shadows descended on the Lhasa River, the water and its far bank glimmered in gold, then turned a beautiful fire red, the river flowing in the direction of the setting sun. The Lhasa is a large river and it flows into an even larger one, but from our vantage point the view of the Lhasa was cut off by a low ridge, and so it seemed to vanish into the shadows, but if we turned our gaze farther to the right, we could see the river again, running broader now across a plain. This, I knew, was the confluence of the Lhasa and the Yarlung Tsangpo. The water reflected the light, and the combined river seemed to meet the horizon as it opened like a fan, spreading out in marshes and golden mudflats. Spread across the mudflats were countless pools of water, bright like mirrors, like horse hoofprints seen in a dream, and the light of the setting sun turned the ground the same colour as the orange sky. The sky looked as if it had just been patched up by the goddess Nüwa and was still trembling. We looked far into the distance, Ma Dingge, Ukyi Lhamo and me, our faces lit up red by the sun, our bodies almost translucent in the light.

Ukyi Lhamo introduced Ma Dingge to Wang Mojie, but in some ways the relationship between Wang Mojie and Ma Dingge was closer than that of Ma Dingge and Ukyi Lhamo. By no stretch of the imagination could one say that Wang Mojie was a religious person, but Ma Dingge respected him and treated him as an equal. Usually Wang Mojie and Ukyi Lhamo went to see Ma Dingge together but even so, over time Ukyi Lhamo found herself increasingly excluded from the conversation between the men. It was as if she wasn't there, as if they were asserting some sort of masculine superiority. This impressed upon Ukyi Lhamo that feminism was also needed in religious life. She wasn't wrong about this, but she also fully understood that because she was Ma Dingge's student she could not interact with him as an equal, while Wang Mojie could, and so while she tried hard to shore up her confidence, it was difficult for her not to feel inferior. At first, she was angry that she did not have the same sort of relationship with Ma Dingge that Wang Mojie had, but she could not tell him this, and she had no good reason to refuse to allow Wang Mojie to come with her when she went to see Ma Dingge.

But then, in an instant, in a fleeting instant, our bodies turned a blue-green, or almost grey, a silvery grey. It was a bright, transient moment, the world was still, but our spirits quivered, more alive than ever, even though we could not have told you what we were thinking. That one time on the terrace, I could not help but say to Ma Dingge that even in such a moment as that, not only had my sense of having a "self" not disappeared, it was stronger than ever. It did not seem to me that my thoughts ever ceased racing, even when I wasn't quite conscious of them.

8. Darjeeling

Darjeeling lies on the southern edge of the Himalayas. It is beautiful, the climate is cool, dry and refreshing. On clear days you can see three of the world's highest peaks, Lhotse, Chomolungma and Kangchenjunga, and the three peaks are lit with an ever-changing kaleidoscope of colour.

The name Darjeeling is from the Tibetan "*dorje ling*", which means land of the "*dorje*", Tibetan for the Sanskrit "*vajra*", meaning "thunderbolt". Darjeeling, then, means "land of the thunderbolt". Darjeeling reflects the mixed influences of Chinese Tibet, Nepal, Bhutan, Sikkim and Bangladesh. There have been long periods in its history when it has been unclear what political entity it belonged to, and it was only in 1861 that it became part of India, due to the action of the British colonial administration. Darjeeling is culturally complex. Hinduism, Islam and Sikhism all are found there, but Buddhism dominates. The Buddhist temples are, for the most part, in the hills and mountains, as if snow peaks are the natural habitat for crimson-robed lamas. Below enormous Mount Kangchenjunga, Bhutia Busty monastery looks insignificant, but it possesses one of the most complete copies of the *Bardo Thodol*. This Tibetan Buddhist classic, translated as *The Tibetan Book of Living and Dying*, has fascinated many in the West and has had a great influence there because it teaches us that death is not the end of everything but is rather the beginning of our awakening. In the moment that our breath stops, we see a light, a pure light, and this light shows us the path that leads our soul beyond life and death. At the moment of dying, we enter this light, and once within it we no longer know if we are alive or dead. Within this light we can see our families and we can hear them if they cry, which is why the bereaved do not cry because the sound of crying will only disturb the spirit of the departed. The bereaved want the spirit of the departed to remain in light until it is reborn as a new life.

Ma Dingge had first learned something about all this while still young, and he knew that American scientists claimed to have found experimental evidence of something very much like the Radiance of the Clear Light of Pure Reality mentioned in the *Bardo Thodol*. They acknowledged that their research entered the realm of the metaphysical and that the Clear Light of Pure Reality did not exist as matter. But it existed all the same. Ma Dingge went to Bhutia Busty monastery and saw its copy of the *Bardo Thodol*. He became interested in the Clear Light of Pure Reality, which kept him in Darjeeling longer than he had planned.

Darjeeling lies on the southern edge of the Himalayas. It is beautiful, the climate is cool, dry and refreshing. On clear days you can see three of the world's highest peaks: Lhotse, the fourth highest, Chomolungma or Everest, the highest, and Kangchenjunga, the third highest. At sunrise and sunset, these three peaks, lined up in this order, are lit with a kaleidoscope of colour. As you look at them you find yourself imagining climbing to the top of the world. One afternoon in 1953, Tenzin Norgay set out from Darjeeling and became the first person to reach the summit of Chomolungma. After reaching the top of the mountain, he said that as a boy, when he was herding yaks for his father, he used to imagine that being on the summit would be like being in the sky. He said he was certain the summit was the abode of deities. He said that the summit of Chomolungma was rocky and icy, but he could feel a warm spirituality in everything. Tenzin Norgay liked to spend time at Darjeeling's Himalayan Mountaineering Institute, founded in 1954. There is a memorial to him at the Institute and a statue, and since his death in 1986, people come from all over to leave flowers in his honour. In 1966, Ma Dingge made a trip to the Himalayan Mountaineering Institute. Who knows, maybe he and Tenzin Norgay walked right by each other. While there, Ma Dingge sat and looked at the Himalayas for a long time. He liked looking at the mountains. He liked their vast contentment and the imposing nature of the landscape. It moved him and was impossible to describe, which he appreciated. In this, he was utterly unlike his father the philosopher, who was openly sceptical about everything.

Ma Dingge stayed in Darjeeling for three weeks. He went out for the occasional walk, but he spent almost all his time simply sitting in the presence of Buddhist master Kangyur Rinpoche. Since the time of Socrates, there have been no philosophers in the West who live their teaching, but in Kangyur Rinpoche's company, Ma Dingge felt as if he had travelled back to ancient Greece. The culture of antiquity survived in Kangyur Rinpoche's body, and in his presence the two thousand years between past and present collapsed into one moment. If our hearts can be inspired by the sight of a man-made image in a Buddhist temple, then our hearts and bodies can be pierced all the way through when we are in the presence of a living spiritual master. If body and mind are inseparable, then the "body" is also the source of philosophy.

Inquiry into what we may call a philosophy of the body proceeded without interruption from Descartes to Baruch Spinoza. In Wang Mojie's opinion, Descartes' proposition that "I think, therefore I am" asked one to consider not just the mind of the thinker but also his body, his physical form. Moreover, Wang Mojie said that Maurice Merleau-Ponty had taken this inquiry to the next step. Merleau-Ponty argued that it is impossible to conceive of a body without consciousness. Having consciousness or, more properly, having experiences is how a mind establishes its connection to its world, to its body and to others. Merleau-Ponty, who died in 1961, was strongly influenced by Edmund Husserl, but he broke with Husserl's phenomenology and established his own philosophy, which is known as the phenomenology of perception. Merleau-Ponty argued that there can be no separation between body and consciousness. Wang Mojie called Merleau-Ponty's philosophy the phenomenology of the body-subject. When Ma Dingge came to India in 1966, he had never met Merleau-Ponty, but he knew of his theories and accepted them. When he became a Buddhist, he naturally abandoned his belief in Merleau-Ponty's phenomenology. For Ma Dingge, the Buddhist teaching that the body is not the self replaced the phenomenology of the body-subject. He still accepted, however, that the body was a vehicle in which the spiritual could have its beginnings, and this was an idea he never abandoned.

Ma Dingge spent three weeks in the company of Kangyur Rinpoche. When sitting with the master, Ma Dingge could hear the voice of his own heart, and it was as if this voice was in dialogue with the master. In Merleau-Ponty's terms, Ma Dingge was engaging in sensing, rather than knowing. He was directly perceiving Kangyur

Rinpoche. He established a connection to Kangyur Rinpoche that could not be broken. Even after he had passed away, Kangyur Rinpoche remained with Ma Dingge. Ma Dingge left Darjeeling and continued his travels. He went to Kashmir and then Damascus. But nothing could compare to the three weeks he spent with Kangyur Rinpoche in Darjeeling.

9. A Phenomenology of the Body-Subject

He held the high-heeled shoe as if it were sacred.
He turned his body around, eyes fixed on the shoe, entranced,
moving as if in a ballet. He kissed the shoe and said,
You know, there is a difference between theory and philosophy.
The key to philosophy is logic, the key to theory is rhetoric.

The day of Wang Mojie's first visit to Ma Dingge happened to coincide with Yu Youyan's third visit to Wang Mojie. It was a quiet, sunlit day, a workday, and so it surprised Wang Mojie when Yu Youyan appeared. He and Ukyi Lhamo had arranged to see Ma Dingge that afternoon, but as he was heading out, Yu Youyan showed up uninvited.

Since they first met, Yu Youyan had visited Wang Mojie twice, but neither visit had been particularly pleasant. The first time, she stayed only briefly, no more than a few minutes. She had come from Ukyi Lhamo's and said she was just stopping by to say hello. She gave Wang Mojie a package of cured meat, a commodity hard to come by. It had been rationed out at her workplace. Yu Youyan said she had brought some for Ukyi Lhamo and so Wang Mojie's thanks were owed to Ukyi Lhamo. But he knew this was just an excuse for dropping by to see him. They talked, and Wang Mojie learned she worked at the Lhasa municipal courthouse. That Yu Youyan had brought him meat she had been given at work struck Wang Mojie as bizarre. Later, Wang Mojie would recall that he had a hard time believing Yu Youyan was a judicial officer. During their brief conversation during her first visit, he let slip that he found judicial officers imposing. In response, Yu Youyan pushed her chest out, something she did often, and rather crossly asked Wang Mojie if he was saying she failed to look imposing. Precisely, Wang Mojie said.

For an officer of the court in Tibet, Yu Youyan wasn't very imposing. At the very least, you could tell she hadn't been on the job long, either that or she was too young. Not long after graduating from university, she was assigned to work for the judiciary in Tibet, which she accepted readily, reasoning that it wouldn't be a hardship and might even be a good thing. Her time in Tibet would be something to savour in an otherwise dull career. It would be a romantic memory for her after she returned to the same boring city where she had gone to school. She often swore to her friends that when she returned to the interior, she would stop working for the judiciary and find a job with some company.

The second time Yu Youyan came to see Wang Mojie, she was wearing her court officer's uniform. Perhaps she wanted to prove how imposing she could be. The uniform was new, crisply ironed and impressive, the dark necktie lending her an air of dignity. She wasn't wearing a stiff-brimmed cap, her straight bobbed hair fell a little longer on one side, and she sported four-inch high heels, but still, in her uniform, she did look imposing. Her epaulettes, badge, metal buttons and tie were particularly striking. Yu Youyan was unaware that in uniform she was more sexy than when she dressed like a Japanese schoolgirl. Everything about her, the overall look and each of the details, made a deep impression on Wang Mojie. It was difficult for him to keep his excitement in check. Yu Youyan didn't realise what sort of pleasure her uniform was giving Wang Mojie. She said she had come hoping to be taught how to garden, and so Wang Mojie took her to his little fenced-in piece of ground. Perhaps because she was in uniform, Yu Youyan dropped her customary giggling, flirting, artificial bashfulness and affected air of mystery. She asked a lot of questions as if she actually did care about gardening, and Wang Mojie answered them all earnestly. Wang Mojie was, for him, unusually solicitous and amiable, obsequious even, enough to make Yu Youyan slip into talking to Wang Mojie like a policewoman, ordering him about, telling him, for example, that he should dig a garden for her. Wang Mojie readily agreed. It was hot and humid, and Yu Youyan took off her jacket and stood in her white shirt and tie, looking even more attractive.

Wang Mojie cordially invited Yu Youyan to stay and eat with him, and he picked some greens. Yu Youyan delayed before accepting the invitation, specifying that she couldn't cook, and he shouldn't expect any help from her. Wang Mojie said he would do the cooking and wouldn't think of letting her help. He said this more than once. He said, This is not a job for you, you don't have to do anything. Find something to read, I have lots of books, including legal books, read whatever you want. Wang Mojie doubled down on his solicitousness. He seemed to be somebody completely other than himself. In fact, had Wang Mojie not invited Yu Youyan to stay for dinner, she would have asked to stay. Once he had invited her, she acted more and more like an officer of the court, which Wang Mojie enjoyed. He liked her in her shirt and tie, but it wasn't quite as pleasing to him as when she had been wearing her uniform jacket. Wang Mojie made his specialities of sausage and rice, scrambled egg and tomato, stir-fried aubergine and cold cucumber salad. The last two were luxuries in Tibet. Wang Mojie never served his guests alcohol, it rarely even occurred to him to do so, but this time he said he would go to the store near the school's gate to buy a bottle of red wine. He had an ulterior motive, but Yu Youyan surprised him by telling him he didn't need to. Wang Mojie knew that Yu Youyan drank. That night by the river during Karma Rishi, she drank enough to get a bit floaty. When they had danced, Wang Mojie could smell the alcohol on her breath, and the only reason he had put up with her in that state was the way she kept pinching him in the back. When Wang Mojie said he would go to get wine, Yu Youyan asked Wang Mojie if he was going to have something to drink with the meal. She said she would only do so if he did. Wang Mojie said he didn't drink but if she wanted to have wine, he would have a glass with her. At this, Yu Youyan said, Then let's forget it. This rebuff was embarrassing to Wang Mojie but he was still happy.

After they ate, Yu Youyan volunteered to clean up. She said she would do the dishes, but Wang Mojie told her to stay put, and he served her tea with great politeness and servility, just as he used to do for his policewoman wife. When he was married, he had always cleared the table, washed the dishes, wiped everything down, made the tea and served it. He never let his wife do any of this.

During his married life, he did all the housework, he was a model husband, too much so. When his wife came home from work, he took her shoes off for her and washed her feet. He kissed her feet, kissed her shoes. When he pulled her square-toed work shoes from her feet, he did so not with his hands but with his teeth. He inhaled the smell of her shoes, like a drug, and he licked their broad heels, licked the toes. He made his wife put the shoes back on, and then he made her put her feet, in the shoes he had licked, on his chest, his lips, his nipples, then his stomach, his thick bush of pubic hair and even his penis.

She put her foot on it, toyed with it, abused it and pointed her service revolver at it, then she pointed the gun at his head. Such was his unconventional marriage. Then she handcuffed him and put him in shackles. The gun, handcuffs and shackles were real, not props from some fetish shop (her work had its advantages). She tied him up on the floor, knotting the rope elaborately. She was wearing her uniform blouse and hat, but she had taken off her trousers and was wearing just a thong. Her arse wiggled in the thong as she picked up her belt and whipped him, again and again, across his back, shoulders and buttocks, the belt thwacking loudly and crisply. He lay on the floor tied up deep into the night, being whipped and kicked, until he got that feeling deep in his bones and felt release; only then did he pull his wife on top of him. He was still tied up, and he made his wife keep her uniform blouse on so that, for him, it was like being raped by a policewoman. Every time they finished, his wife cried hard and swore she would never do it again. She had had enough, she felt she was going crazy. And every time, he promised it was the last time, but after a while he always came to her again, begging her to do it just once more. And when they finished, she said he was filthy, a pervert, disgusting. She said he should surrender to the police and get it over with, stop this fooling around. But he said he was guilty of no crime he could turn himself in for. She said he was the most degraded person on earth. The most disgusting. Her angry condemnation did not make him feel ashamed, it only excited him, it excited in him a profound sexual desire and made him erect again. She ducked away from him, spat at him, leapt off the bed. But finally, amid her curses and screams, he achieved his death-like orgasm. He always thought of orgasm as a kind of death.

All these crazy memories were running through Wang Mojie's head as he talked to Yu Youyan. Yu Youyan was telling him he gave her many different impressions and seemed to be several completely different people at once. She asked him if this had anything to do with his degree in philosophy. She found him difficult to understand but fascinating. He gave her a straight answer. It has nothing to do with philosophy, he said (his mind on his memories as he spoke), any person is the same from moment to moment but also different. Everybody was like that, he said, not just me, no human had ever been a single unified being... Finally, his wife couldn't take him any more and asked for a divorce. He refused, he was steadfast, and so she had no choice but to take him to court, where things did not go in his favour... Yu Youyan said, Any person is the same moment to moment but also different, that's philosophy, right? It's very theoretical, right? Yu Youyan was, after all, educated and was discerning, to a point. Wang Mojie raised his opinion of her a bit. She was sitting upright and looking straight ahead, in part because her uniform made it difficult for her to sit any other way, and in part because she had discovered that her stern seriousness was getting a great reaction. You can think of it as philosophy, of course, Wang Mojie said, but actually it has nothing to do with philosophy. You know, there is a difference between theory and philosophy. The key to philosophy is logic, the key to theory is rhetoric.

Suddenly, Wang Mojie turned the conversation to Yu Youyan's high heels. He said he was astonished at how high they were. The heels were both high and narrow, delicious to look at. Wang Mojie had always wanted his wife to wear high, thin, spiky heels like that, but she was tall to begin with and so always insisted on wearing flats. She never wore shoes with heels any higher than those on her work shoes.

—Your shoes are very pretty, they're lovely. Are you allowed to wear heels like that at work? he asked, his mind still on the past.

Reacting to the compliment, Yu Youyan unconsciously lifted a foot, forgetting what they had been talking about. In truth, she didn't enjoy talking about philosophy, the subject made her uncomfortable, as uncomfortable as her uniform jacket made her feel. As she lifted a shoe into the air, some sort of signal, some sort of provocation passed between them.

—Those are designer, expensive. Can you take one off so I can have a look?

—Yes, of course, Yu Youyan said.

Yu Youyan looked up, her demeanour transformed, as if she had shed her sober uniform and felt freed. The high heels were the only thing she was wearing that day that expressed her individuality. She had been secretly proud of them, and it surprised her that Wang Mojie had noticed them. She was astounded to find that he had his hand cupped over one of her shoes. No man had ever reacted to her pretty shoes this way! She bent to take off a shoe, but Wang Mojie stopped her, which she did not expect.

—Wait, let me. Here, like this.

He removed her shoe and held it as if it were sacred. He lifted it high, as if he were a ballet dancer lifting his partner. He studied it unselfconsciously. Yu Youyan didn't understand what Wang Mojie was doing, but her confusion was overcome by an unexpected delight because she took what was happening as merely a man's singular way of expressing his appreciation of a woman. Everybody knew that Wang Mojie was different. He was clearly hinting at something to her. But no, she decided, he wasn't hinting at anything. He was openly enjoying it, it was the expression of a romantic feeling. But what Wang Mojie did next shocked Yu Youyan. He slowly brought the shoe to his face, put his nose into it, and inhaled deeply, twice, three times.

—Nice, really nice. Your body smells better than any perfume, much better.

Wang Mojie held the shoe against his cheek, and as if embracing a person. He kissed the shoe's upper, instep, toe and heel, and then he took the tip of the heel in his mouth! Yu Youyan cried out shrilly.

—What are you doing? That's filthy!

—You haven't answered my question, Wang Mojie said. Do you wear these shoes to work?

—Of course not. I wear leather uniform shoes.

—Like the shoes police wear?

—Don't know. I never noticed. Why ask me that? You're weird!

—I'm not weird at all, Wang Mojie said, looking at the shoe, then kissing it again. I'll put it back on for you.

—No, don't.

—I took it off, I should put it back on.

Wang Mojie knelt like an actor on stage, took Yu Youyan's foot in his hand and lifted it. She was wearing see-through stockings, new and pretty. If this had been an expression of love, he should have looked happy, rapt, but Yu Youyan saw that he appeared emotionless, like a statue. He looked so calm, she wondered if he wasn't making fun of her. Yu Youyan didn't know what to do, and she couldn't make Wang Mojie listen to her. Wang Mojie put her shoe back on, but this wasn't the end of it. He kissed her heels again. She yanked her feet back as if from flames.

—Why are you so into shoes? It's perverted.

—There's a lot I'm into. Shall I tell you? You remind me of my wife.

—Your wife? Yu Youyan's eyes widened.

—You and she have similar professions. She is a policewoman. She might have studied law like you did. She graduated from the People's Public Security University of China. There is a law course there, I think, but I'm not sure.

—Of course there is, Yu Youyan said with professional confidence. Some people at the courthouse graduated from there.

—My wife didn't do a law degree. She studied criminology, that much I know.

—Criminologists have to study law. Our chief justice was a criminology graduate.

—Of course, that would be only reasonable.

—I wouldn't have guessed you're married. You feel comfortable leaving her all alone?

—She divorced me.

—Why did she want a divorce?

—I liked her shoes, her belt and her handcuffs and shackles.

—What? What do you mean you liked them?

—I like to be punished. Understand?

Yu Youyan's expression was that of a sleeper waking from a dream, then it hardened.

—So... you really are... a pervert?

—Don't use such prejudicial language. It's just a game. Role playing.

—I, well, I have heard something about this, but I never met anybody!

—It's a fun game, if you're interested.

—No, I'm not interested.

—Everybody has a predilection for violence. You would be dominant. You can do whatever you want. If you have some new ideas for inflicting pain, so much the better. A sadist needs imagination. Can you think of something new to do to somebody?

—No, no, Yu Youyan said, then she stood up and shuddered.

—You like to pinch people. You pinch pretty well.

—Oh, I'm sorry, I have to go. I had no idea you were like this. Are you really?

—Would you like to have a try?

—No. Thank you for dinner.

Yu Youyan hesitated, but Wang Mojie didn't try to make her stay. He had said all that to her quite deliberately. He was very clear about what he wanted. He felt pent-up physical desire. He had spoken to Yu Youyan in a very nonchalant, matter-of-fact tone. He had hoped she would run away from him if he talked casually about his shocking predilections. His desire was, of course, stronger than his hope that she would flee, but nevertheless he was relieved when she left. He might have taken things more slowly, but instead he had been quick and direct, which was the right approach with Yu Youyan he felt. She was a woman anyone could sleep with. Even when she was on the job, there was something quite sexy about her. He knew she would either play along or steer clear of him. She couldn't compare to his former wife. His wife was from a long line of policemen. Her grandfather had been with the police during the Republic, her father was a policeman for New China, and she had done the rigorous training at the police academy herself. Yu Youyan could bring him nothing but a bunch of nonsense that messed with his head, precisely the kind of thing he was hoping to escape by coming to Tibet. Of course, he knew that just because he had come to Tibet, a completely new environment for him, it didn't mean he was a new person. The new is always layered over the old, it doesn't replace it. But if Yu Youyan hadn't appeared, if her imposing uniform hadn't come into his life, he would have gone on seeming to be a new person, even if the old Wang Mojie was there under the surface.

In many ways, however, he was a new person, albeit layered over his old self. He was living like a monk, away from society, cut off from the outside world, in touch with nature, everything bringing him new feelings, new convictions and new ideas. You could say he had remade himself. The first time he heard about Ma Dingge from Ukyi Lhamo, he found what she said about him hard to believe, and yet he sensed a light as if suddenly he could see everything more clearly. He was surprised that Ukyi Lhamo knew somebody like Ma Dingge and surprised to hear her refer to him as one of her Buddhist teachers. It was the morning after a night of rain when Ukyi Lhamo mentioned Ma Dingge to Wang Mojie for the first time. It seemed offhand, but maybe she had long planned to say something, Wang Mojie didn't know.

One morning Ukyi Lhamo's mother came to Ukyi Lhamo's house to get her daughter so the two of them could go up to the monastery to listen to a lecture. A monk who had recently finished a three-year retreat was going to talk about scripture and the *buddhadharma*. Ukyi Lhamo wanted to make her mother something to eat, and Wang Mojie told Ukyi Lhamo she could get something from his garden. Ukyi Lhamo thanked him and that she would also help herself to something for a friend. Wang Mojie couldn't stand his vegetables going to Ukyi Lhamo's friends. She could have as much as she wanted for herself and her mother but not for her friends. Ukyi Lhamo was quick to explain that it wasn't for anyone in her Lhasa crowd but for a very special lama at the monastery. That is when she mentioned Ma Dingge to Wang Mojie for the first time, and even her few brief words about him were enough to surprise Wang Mojie. He couldn't quite believe what he was hearing. He had studied biology? He was a scientist? Wang Mojie turned each of Ukyi Lhamo's statements into a question. Yes, Ukyi Lhamo answered, he is a biologist, you and he have something in common in that.

As soon as she uttered the words "in common", Ukyi Lhamo stopped as if she were guilty of a terrible indiscretion. She said, No, no, no, I don't mean that, you have nothing at all in common with him. You can't be compared to him at all, that's much too flattering to you. Ukyi Lhamo let loose a barrage of criticism, belittling Wang Mojie, speaking rapidly, sounding just like the sharp-tongued Beijing girl she was. I mean, your academic degrees were the same, she said. You studied biology, too, but you aren't in the same league as Ma Dingge. What sort of scientist are you? You just garden. And you are so stingy. Look how uptight you got when I said I wanted to give something to a friend. What a miser. Ukyi Lhamo enumerated Wang Mojie's faults as if to cancel her indiscretion, and as she spoke, she never stopped harvesting from the garden. She picked a bag of green beans, four aubergines, five cucumbers, then why not a sixth for an even half dozen, and she kept going, working quickly, picking the garden clean. She was taking advantage of Wang Mojie's generosity, and he felt punched in the stomach. He regretted telling Ukyi Lhamo to pick the vegetables, he should have picked them himself. He sighed. Give some people an inch!

Wang Mojie and Ukyi Lhamo later agreed to go together to visit Ma Dingge. It was on the day of their planned trip up to the monastery that Yu Youyan came back for the third time, which surprised Wang Mojie, as he hadn't expected to see her again. She was dressed simply, wearing nothing of her uniform, but she didn't resemble a schoolgirl any more either. She was wearing clean pressed denim. Clearly, she had thought about what Wang Mojie liked and had decided that denim might do almost as much for him as uniforms did. Her denim top was open at the neck and underneath she had on a tight black T-shirt, displaying her full breasts. It was obvious she was wearing a padded bra, you could see its seams under the T-shirt. She had thought carefully about what to wear, and the effect was not bad, at least it was a bit better than her customary schoolgirl's dress. The tight black T-shirt looked nice paired with the rougher texture of the denim. There was something a little wild about it, while on the other hand, her straight, neatly bobbed hair, a little longer on one side, had something of a fair maiden touch. Of course, her high heels just drew attention to her arse in her tight trousers, a look that made her seem slightly wanton. Wang Mojie took it all in, but he wasn't interested. He looked her over, head to foot, but with detachment. She lifted her chin a little, stuck out her chest and stared right at Wang Mojie.

—What are you looking at? You don't recognise me?

—Not bad. But how is anybody going to know you work for the court?

—If they don't, so what? I'm sick of the court.

—I'm busy. I can't ask you to stay.

—You have to teach? That's fine, go to your lesson. I'll stay here and read.

Yu Youyan turned, her body bursting from her tight clothing, her arse firm, nothing artificial there. She turned towards the bookshelf, her back to Wang Mojie, and walked back and forth in front of him, showing off her body. She pulled down a book and asked Wang Mojie what he thought of it. Wang Mojie was picturing Yu Youyan in her uniform, but he patiently gave her his opinion of the book. They stood in front of the shelf of books, looking at the volume she had taken down, talking in low voices, heads together like sweethearts in an old love story. That's what they looked like from the waist up, but if you turned your gaze down, down to Yu Youyan's arse in her tight jeans, you would know this wasn't some old-fashioned courtly love romance but naked desire. The way Yu Youyan was dressed and was acting should have been enough to seduce any man, but it wasn't working on Wang Mojie. He recommended several books to her, but she said one was enough and asked Wang Mojie to pick one. He patiently did so, but when Yu Youyan took a look at it, she wasn't satisfied and told him to pick a different one. Wang Mojie was thinking about his appointment with Ukyi Lhamo and finally couldn't deal with Yu Youyan any longer. He looked at his watch, knowing he had to send Yu Youyan on her way. When she expressed interest in yet another book, Wang Mojie spoke very bluntly.

—I don't have to teach. I have to go somewhere. Apologies.

Even being suddenly shown the door didn't seem to faze Yu Youyan. She casually asked Wang Mojie where he was going and if she could come along. Wang Mojie had to tell her he and another person (he wanted to tell her it was Ukyi Lhamo, but he decided not to) had plans to go up to Drepung Monastery to pay their respects to a monk. Yu Youyan was insistent, pressing Wang Mojie to tell her who it was that he was going with and explain why she couldn't join them. Wang Mojie didn't answer. He began to gather some things, not that he needed to, he was just making a show of getting ready to depart as a way of telling Yu Youyan to please leave him alone. Finally, she stood up, as if to leave, but she suddenly asked Wang Mojie a question.

—Is Ukyi Lhamo home? I'm going to go see her.

Wang Mojie stared at Yu Youyan, knowing exactly what she was getting at.

—She's at home. She's the one I'm going with. She's waiting for me.

—Wang Mojie, I guessed that right away. Are you really a pervert or are you just pretending?

Wang Mojie gave her a puzzled look, speaking only after a pause.

—I'm only a pervert with policewomen or women who work for the court. Otherwise, I'm normal.

Suddenly tears welled in Yu Youyan's eyes. She looked at Wang Mojie uncomprehendingly, angrily. She looked at him for a long moment, then turned and walked out resolutely. Wang Mojie watched her go. What exactly did she want? He had been hoping, in a way, for that show of anger. But could she really be that obtuse? He couldn't figure her out.

10. Ma Dingge's Quarters

In everything we do, we should value the spiritual, not the material.
What comes from the heart is more permanent and dependable than any object.
Our history of the heart-to-heart transmission of ideas is ages old.
The accelerated pace of the circulation of material things has thrown life out of balance,
and we are now surrounded by nothing but fakes and fragments.
Who could have imagined that the tantric Buddhist rite of abhiseka *would become*
a spectacle you can pay to watch? Just like those heritage villages for tourists where
for a hundred yuan you can dress up like an ethnic bridegroom in a pretend wedding.

Wang Mojie was worried Ukyi Lhamo might leave for the monastery without him, and she did. Her house was empty, she was gone. Wang Mojie looked at the lock on her door and regretted not acting more decisively with Yu Youyan. Why was he drawing things out with Yu Youyan? Why was he still fantasising about her? It all just proved two things, he thought. One, a man is merely the sum of his various desires and two, time waits for no one. Wang Mojie kept looking at his watch, kept trying to will time to slow, but he told himself that it was probably fine and Ukyi Lhamo couldn't have got far. He was right not to worry. When he went out through the wall at the back of the school compound, a wall with too many gaps to serve any real function, and had just entered the village, he saw, very clearly, the figure of Ukyi Lhamo up ahead on the small, winding path. He saw only her silhouette from the back, but he could tell it was Ukyi Lhamo, even in the unfamiliar long Tibetan dress of black wool. At a glance, Wang Mojie could tell it wasn't any woman from the village, it was Ukyi Lhamo. Under the sunlight, the village was motionless like a painting, the midday shadows were short. On the path through the village with its white walls and black window frames, Ukyi Lhamo's black wool dress looked like an extraordinary shadow, sombre and unadorned. When he could see her better, he decided she looked like a typical Tibetan woman, except that her hair was in a long ponytail. How lovely it would be if she dressed like this all the time, Wang Mojie thought. He raised his camera and took a picture of her in profile as she rounded a corner of a wall, composing it like a painting.

Wang Mojie caught up to Ukyi Lhamo.

—What are you doing here? she asked.

—Why did you leave?

—You ditched her?

—We agreed we'd go to see Ma Dingge together.

—We can see him anytime. Go back.

—She's already left.

—You should be a little nicer to her, Ukyi Lhamo said softly.

If she hadn't been wearing the sombre Tibetan robe, Wang Mojie would have found this remark of Ukyi Lhamo's ridiculous. But the comment suited her attire. She was completely different from usual, she didn't seem like herself, not at all. A change of attire can be a reflection or manifestation of a change in mindset, sometimes clothes do make the woman. Ukyi Lhamo wore Tibetan dress from time to time at school, usually for festivals or at someone's request, and there was always something of a public show about it, something theatrical as if she were in costume. But today, on this particular afternoon, things were different. Ukyi Lhamo was, it seemed, under the sway of the village, under the sway of the white walls, the black windows, the alleys, the stacks of yak dung drying for burning, under the sway of the prayer flags flying from roofs, under the sway of the monastery up the hill and under the sway of her woollen Tibetan robe. Mixed-race Ukyi Lhamo was not split in two today, her Tibetan blood was running pure, and the words she spoke seemed to usher not from her lips but from her soul.

It was autumn, everything was bright and clear. They walked into the grove of trees. There were few leaves on the ground, most of the golden leaves remained on the trees, their colour vibrant and glowing. The autumn colours in Tibet are more intense than anywhere else, purer, because of the great change in temperature from night to day, because of the fierce sun, the air, the snow peaks, the water and the solar wind. In this season, the trees in Tibet are as transparent as fire in a dream. If autumn trees exist on some other planet in the universe, they could not surpass what you see in Tibet. But Wang Mojie and Ukyi Lhamo weren't paying much attention to the colours around them. They were so used to the scenery they didn't notice it. They were talking about Yu Youyan, her relationships with men, and her emotional needs. Things were as Wang Mojie suspected, no aspect of Yu Youyan's behaviour with him was anything unusual for her.

—She's actually a simple girl, she just can't take being hurt again, Ukyi Lhamo said.

This remark surprised Wang Mojie. She couldn't take being hurt again? What did that mean? Ukyi Lhamo was now talking about things that had nothing to do with the village, things completely disconnected from her Tibetan dress. Wang Mojie thought it over seriously for a moment and then spoke.

—I think I know what you mean. She's always getting used, right? That's what I understand you to be saying, even though you didn't say it directly. That's what I think has been happening with her. Even if you don't say so, I can tell. But if you really want to talk about using people, don't you think it's probably her that's doing the using?

—You don't know her, Ukyi Lhamo said.

She wasn't angry, which surprised Wang Mojie, her voice remained soft and calm.

—She tells me everything, and she is always falling for men I know. But I don't know them that well, and so I can't help her with them. Of all the men I know, you're probably the least likely to hurt her, that's the only reason I'm telling you.

Wang Mojie's response was blunt.

—The real question is, who are you to judge her? You think you're different from her?

—I feel sorry for myself too, Ukyi Lhamo said softly, surprising Wang Mojie by tacitly admitting that what he had implied was true.

—Has she been involved with your poet friend, that maths professor poet bloke, or any of those other men?

—Yes, she has...

Ukyi Lhamo looked directly at Wang Mojie, the stern look in her eyes shattering the mood that her Tibetan attire created.

Wang Mojie fell silent. It might have been best for them to turn around and go back, rather than walk on towards a Buddhist monastery talking about love affairs and using people and getting used. Even though they had stopped talking, Wang Mojie was continuing the discussion in his head, and Ukyi Lhamo seemed to be doing the same. Wang Mojie found something a bit ridiculous about Ukyi Lhamo's logic, no, not a bit ridiculous, completely ridiculous. Ukyi Lhamo believed that Yu Youyan was always being used in her relationships with men because they were never honest with her, and she was always the passive partner in a relationship. Wasn't Ukyi Lhamo precisely the opposite in her relationships with men? What was the difference when it came down to it? Somebody was always getting used if you wanted to think about relationships in those terms. So, Wang Mojie reasoned, what logical reason was there for Ukyi Lhamo to feel sorry for Yu Youyan? Because Ukyi Lhamo was stronger than Yu Youyan? Because Ukyi Lhamo was pursued by so many men?

Ukyi Lhamo sympathised with Yu Youyan, she absolutely did, but apparently not completely. Wang Mojie believed the reason people can be so hard to understand is often not because they are complicated but because they are confused. He believed that this is especially true of women. He thought that women don't always know exactly what they are trying to say and often when they are saying one thing, they get caught up in another thing, some emotion (pity or something like that, for example). The emotion, which is sincere, takes over, and they get worked up and forget what it was they were going to say. Wang Mojie thought that maybe what Ukyi Lhamo wanted to say was that he (a man of a type similar to Ma Dingge) should not get tangled up with somebody who slept around like Yu Youyan did, as this wasn't good for either of them, especially not Wang Mojie. If so, and even if Ukyi Lhamo was right, it still wasn't very egalitarian of her because it implied both that Ukyi Lhamo had something to teach Wang Mojie and that Yu Youyan was deserving of disdain. And it was what Ukyi Lhamo was implying rather than saying that mattered to Wang Mojie. So who did she think she was? What right did she have to make these implications? Was she better than everybody else? All this, Wang Mojie believed, deserved analysis and discussion.

They walked out of the woods, and Drepung Monastery loomed impressively above them. The monastery always stunned you at first sight, made you forget yourself, drew you into it. All religious architecture has this power, and it was particularly true of Drepung Monastery. From a distance, it was a massive, tightly constructed totality, but once you were inside, it was a maze of many independent parts, like someone's scattered thoughts. There was no symmetry to it, no apparent coherent layout, no way to get a perspective on it. It was buildings piled on buildings, monks' quarters, the assembly hall, temples, gold roofs, prayer wheels, banners hanging everywhere, each space connected to all others. There were innumerable alleys, a network of them, and the layout always seemed unfamiliar. No matter how many times you walked the alleys or climbed the stone stairs, it never became familiar. It had no main exit, but there were exits everywhere, and every exit was an entrance. You walked from light into shadow and back. Courtyards sat behind the high walls of the alleys, quiet courtyards surrounded by verandas. Shafts of sunlight reached down into the courtyards. You could hear the sound of water dripping from somewhere above, just as Wang Mojie said when he described his experience in the monastery. You might walk one way into a small courtyard, with its small square of sky, and take a different way out, walk out into a different passageway, into a different world. There was no main route to follow but no route was the wrong route. In a sacred place, there is no right path or wrong path.

Ukyi Lhamo came here once a week and knew the place, but she couldn't say for sure if she took the same route through the monastery every time. She said it didn't matter, that any route they took would get them to where they were going. Wang Mojie followed Ukyi Lhamo as they climbed, turned, went left, right, down, up. He tried to memorise this route to Ma Dingge's quarters, but when he asked Ukyi Lhamo if they were on the western side of the monastery, Ukyi Lhamo said he was exactly wrong, they were on the eastern side, Wang Mojie had got completely turned around. Also, although there was no water to be seen anywhere, there was the constant sound of running water. The sunlight was bright, shadows were scattered everywhere, the sunlight and shadow folded together, everything now bright, now dark, *yin* and *yang* impossible to separate. After climbing a set of steep, narrow stairs they looked up and saw a line of crimson-robed monks, like red clouds floating down from the sky. They floated into the narrow alley, and Ukyi Lhamo respectfully turned sideways to let them pass, acknowledging them with her eyes. Wang Mojie didn't know the etiquette, and Ukyi Lhamo tugged at him to get him to move to the side. Ukyi Lhamo's deference was unaffected, it was natural, and it spoke to Wang Mojie of the Tibetan blood that was half of Ukyi Lhamo's heritage. Ukyi Lhamo stood respectfully, and for an instant, Wang Mojie could picture her with her hair shorn like a nun's. He was thinking that if she took vows and put on a crimson robe, she would make half the congregation swoon. Maybe that could be considered a real option for her, Wang Mojie mused.

They stopped in front of a simple wooden door in the shadows. The door was closed tightly but opened with a slight push. It opened to sunlight, brilliance, to another world. The door led onto a small courtyard, about thirty metres square. There were two trees in the courtyard and beneath them a few stone tables and stone stools on a patch of grass. Ma Dingge's rooms were in a stone building that caught the sunlight on one side of the courtyard. Its door, door curtain and windows were plain and unpretentious. This was the most intimate of spaces in the monastery. It was neat and tidy, very simple and pretty as a picture. Ma Dingge came out from the room, the stone lintel was low and so he stooped, which made the tall man seem modest, shy even. His face was gaunt and pale as if he had been cloistered for years. He didn't look like a foreigner, not at all; looking at a serene man in a crimson robe, it doesn't occur to you to make the distinction between east and west. He was part of the ancient monastery. His inner being was expressed in his outward appearance, his outward appearance reflected his inner being, they were unified. He was one with the scriptures, the votive lamps and the stone walls, his body was a Buddhist temple.

Wang Mojie said that in the presence of Ma Dingge, it is possible to believe that Tibetan Buddhism is, almost first and foremost, a kind of body art, and only next is it a philosophy, ideology or religion. No other religious body is quite like the Buddhist body. In the presence of such a body, there is no need to speak, all you need do is observe quietly and you will begin to sense the flow of time in the depths of your soul. You will feel like the body before you is pouring time into you, and time becomes like water from a spring or like the light and shadows of twilight that fall everywhere.

For the most part, I agree with Wang Mojie, even if he does exaggerate. The Ma Dingge I knew was an ordinary Buddhist monk of the academic type, not an eminent monk and not a Living Buddha. He didn't wear a yellow robe of distinction, just an ordinary red Tibetan wool kasaya*, one shoulder bare like any other monk, very ordinary. Still, all in all, there was something profound about him. I too could feel the power that Wang Mojie said you could feel coming from Ma Dingge. I met Ma Dingge* *before I met Wang Mojie, actually, just like I knew Ukyi Lhamo before I knew Wang Mojie. Without a doubt, Ma Dingge was not an ordinary man, and from the day I met him, I knew that sooner or later he would find a way into my fiction. Indeed, I have always wanted to tell his story, but I have never known how to frame the story. I knew he could never be the main character in a novel, because too much about him was predetermined. Yes, he was wise and learned, like the Buddha himself, but the path he walked was far too set, there was no room for a novelist's unbridled imagination. How to write about Ma Dingge became clear to me only after Wang Mojie showed up, and Ma Dingge found a place in my novel about Wang Mojie.*

It is often like this with fiction, you want to include a particular person in your life, but it turns out not to be the best time to write about him, but then someone else makes an unexpected appearance in your writing, and the person you wanted to write about in the first place suddenly fits into your story in the precisely appropriate way. I have written a few novels that failed, meaning I never finished them; the manuscripts are buried in a drawer, and I will never take them out because as they are, they can never be made into true novels, they would be dead on the page. It is much better to leave them waiting to be rescued, waiting for a new lease of life, waiting to be used in a different novel. The appearance of Wang Mojie in my life suddenly made apparent the connections among characters who had been previously disconnected, and it revealed other characters who had been concealed to me. This gave birth to an entire world.

Ma Dingge's room was simple, nothing in it but books, *thangkas*, a photograph of his teacher and, of course, the requisite butter lamps, bowls of offering water and *khaden*. You could sit on the *khaden* or use it as a bed, there was a quilt rolled up at one end. But if you wanted to talk simplicity, Wang Mojie thought, Ma Dingge's place was not as austere as his home at the school. Wang Mojie had no shrine, no niche with a statue of the Buddha in it, and so no butter lamp or bowl of offering water either, no *thangka*, no bells, no *vajra*, no whisk or any other sort of Buddhist ritual implement. But what were the things that propped up Wang Mojie? Could his learning inform not only rationality but also some sort of faith? Did he need something to believe in? He had always been convinced that the pursuit of truth was all he needed, but the truth could leave you lonely, the truth was often frightening. Ma Dingge's simple lifestyle was grounded in his Buddhism. Wang Mojie wondered what his own simple lifestyle was grounded in. A particular philosophy? Some sort of minimalism? He believed in simplifying life, not complicating it. He had the conviction that adding things to your life only took you backwards. In this, he and Ma Dingge were similar.

Ma Dingge said thank you in Tibetan to Wang Mojie for bringing the fresh produce, he expressed admiration for Wang Mojie keeping a garden, and he praised him for volunteering to come to Tibet to teach. Ma Dingge obviously already knew about Wang Mojie. Ukyi Lhamo had spoken about him to Ma Dingge on more than one occasion.

Wang Mojie knew only a little Tibetan, he could understand a bit but could hardly speak it at all. He had expected Ma Dingge and Ukyi Lhamo to speak French and that he would join in by speaking English or his rudimentary French, so it surprised him that they spoke in Tibetan, the language filling the air between them. Wang Mojie had always assumed that part of the reason Ukyi Lhamo visited Ma Dingge so often was to practise her French, but this idea was now dispelled. To Wang Mojie, Tibetan sounded like the natural language for religion, it sounded pure. He could tell, however, that Ukyi Lhamo's Tibetan was nowhere near as good as Ma Dingge's, and from time to time she switched to French to ask Ma Dingge something.

Ukyi Lhamo had told Wang Mojie that today she was there for a lesson in Buddhist precepts and that he should just listen and keep quiet. Wang Mojie told Ukyi Lhamo not to worry, he enjoyed being a third wheel. The red-robed Ma Dingge sat in front of a table beneath a butter lamp on a shelf. He held a sutra that he recited from and then explained to Ukyi Lhamo. He didn't seem like her tutor, he was well beyond that, not like her professor either, he was beyond that too. Ma Dingge's Tibetan sounded native, without any French accent. He didn't stumble at all, but of course Wang Mojie's Tibetan wasn't good enough for him to know if Ma Dingge made any mistakes. If Ma Dingge were speaking Mandarin, maybe Wang Mojie would have been able to detect a French accent. Wang Mojie knew only that Ma Dingge's fluent-sounding Tibetan made him feel ashamed of himself. Because from time to time she had to ask Ma Dingge for an explanation in French, Ukyi Lhamo should have been even more ashamed of herself, Wang Mojie thought. But except for when she did occasionally break into French, Ukyi Lhamo seemed like a complete stranger today. Her black robe, white sleeves underneath it, her hair in a ponytail, the look in her eyes, all of this was nothing like the Ukyi Lhamo that Wang Mojie was accustomed to. It was good for a woman to have religious faith, women with faith are beautiful.

This last thought sent Wang Mojie into a reverie, he found his mind drifting to paintings from the Renaissance. He imagined a painting of a woman's beautiful face, she was looking up, lit by warm candlelight. He thought of Raphael, Botticelli and Titian, and time seemed to flow backwards. It wasn't the late twentieth century any more, it was the Middle Ages or the time of Dante, people were becoming enlightened, but the light of faith was still shining. Wang Mojie lifted his camera and took a photograph of Ukyi Lhamo looking up reverentially at Ma Dingge as he taught her the sutra. The sudden ugly light of the flash broke in on Ma Dingge and Ukyi Lhamo, who had been outside of time, and their expressions changed for a second as if they suddenly had come back to the twentieth century. Modern technology is too powerful, there seems to be nothing it does not destroy. Wang Mojie quickly put his camera away and took no more photographs. He wanted to take more, but the thought of it made him feel like some modern monster rushing back through the corridors of time, wreaking havoc. Wang Mojie decided to just listen carefully and concentrate on appreciating this rare tableau, this moment outside of time. Ukyi Lhamo was talking to Ma Dingge about something that perplexed her. She said she often lacked the willpower to persist in her practice. Each time she undertook *prayoga* she felt unable to complete the required three hundred thousand repetitions of the mantra, and she always gave up. The most prostrations in prayer she had been able to manage was thirty thousand, and even the Manjusri Mantra, which she revered, she had only recited fifty thousand times. She had managed to recite the Mantra of Padmasambhava one hundred thousand times, but she did so for selfish reasons as she recited it only when she was travelling or in some peril.

One hundred thousand times, fifty thousand times, three hundred thousand times, these numbers shocked Wang Mojie, he couldn't believe them. That is just mechanical repetition, he thought, the ticking of a clock. How could a person count on endlessly like some clock ticking away? Wang Mojie remembered that Ukyi Lhamo telling him that the prayer beads she wore around her wrist were given to her by Ma Dingge, who had used them to count one million recitations of the Manjusri Mantra. This hadn't meant much to Wang Mojie at the time, but now he found it hard to imagine. Wang Mojie doubted he could force himself to count to ten thousand, much less count that high while reciting a mantra. This was not a religion he could understand. Was he to think that Buddhism was just an endless string of astronomical numbers? Or even some sort of numerical compulsion? But that compulsion and those astronomical numbers were what Ukyi Lhamo needed because lost in them she was calm, beautiful, ancient and unconscious of any boundary between herself and the world. The power of religion often lies in repetition. A million repetitions changes a person, you become part of what you are repeating, you and the universe become one.

At the end of Ukyi Lhamo's lesson (finally it's over, thank goodness, Wang Mojie thought), Wang Mojie said to Ma Dingge in English that if it was OK, he would like to come to see Ma Dingge often. He was interested in Buddhism, but there was a lot that confused him and it would please him to have the benefit of Ma Dingge's instruction. Ma Dingge's English was, as expected, just as excellent as his Tibetan. Merely based on his mastery of languages, Ma Dingge deserved the title master. In English, Ma Dingge told Wang Mojie that the quest for knowledge and enlightenment began with confusion. The Buddha was twenty-nine before his awakening, and before then he too was lost in confusion. The Buddha exists because there is confusion in the world. Wang Mojie asked Ma Dingge if there were still things that left him perplexed but as soon as he did, he regretted it, because it was an impolite question and shallow. But with a great teacher such as Ma Dingge, Wang Mojie needn't have worried. Ma Dingge remained composed, and he said to Wang Mojie that all people live with confusion. There are none who do not, this includes men who have meditated for years in monasteries. If you are looking for the path of liberation, you have found it in Buddhism, he said. With great sincerity Ma Dingge added that although Wang Mojie was still young, his heart had been moved to seek liberation, which was a precious beginning.

Ma Dingge was so amiable and unassuming that Wang Mojie forgot they were speaking in English. Ma Dingge was a puzzle, his Buddhist practice, his knowledge, his understanding of Buddhist teachings and his crystal-clear logic, which was the legacy of his scientific training, were all beyond anything Wang Mojie could have imagined, and he was full of admiration. Of course, this didn't mean Wang Mojie had dropped his scepticism about the mechanical repetition of mantras fifty thousand or one hundred thousand times, which he even found risible. But he didn't let Ukyi Lhamo know he felt that way. Wang Mojie felt that he could express his doubt to Ma Dingge but not to Ukyi Lhamo, just as you can doubt God but you cannot doubt his believers. Wang Mojie knew that believers who, for various reasons, surrendered themselves to

God or the Buddha usually got some benefit from it. Ukyi Lhamo did, he knew.

When they left Ma Dingge's courtyard, the sunlight was still strong. They stood on the steep, narrow flight of steps, and below them they could see the Nechung Monastery like a mandala at the foot of the mountain, with fields, cranes or maybe storks flying over the Lhalu Wetlands, the blue Lhasa River streaked with light and on its far bank a grove of trees in their autumn colours. There was some snow on the mountainsides, which outlined the peaks. The monastery looked down on this every day.

—It's hard to believe you've been studying sutras, but clearly you have, Wang Mojie said to Ukyi Lhamo in praise as they walked.

—I'm not very good at it, they are difficult, Ukyi Lhamo said softly.

—Maybe if you took the vows, here at Drepung for example, they would be easier.

Wang Mojie hadn't meant to tease Ukyi Lhamo, but he couldn't help himself.

—They wouldn't take me, Ukyi Lhamo said, I'm not sincere enough.

—Well, you looked beautiful in there, that was you at your most beautiful maybe. I took a picture of you, it should come out looking like an oil painting from the Middle Ages. It's too bad I didn't take more.

—You haven't seen the photograph of me getting *abhiseka,* me getting initiated. That's true beauty.

—*Abhiseka*? That's Sanskrit for "pouring water on the head", right? I saw you do that, during Karma Rishi...

—You're an idiot, Ukyi Lhamo said, sounding like herself again. Who performs *abhiseka* on themself?

—I do it all the time, and I use soap, Wang Mojie joked.

—You like the water, do you? What's your sign? Cancer the Crab?

—No, Pisces, Wang Mojie said, deadpan.

Wang Mojie paused and sighed before continuing.

—It would be best to take fewer photographs or none, there's too much media in our lives. Sometimes I ask myself why we don't let Tibet keep its mystery. Attention from the media ruins everything. How much do we have left that is still original? Cultures are going extinct as fast as animals are, faster even. Subjectivity has overwhelmed the objectivity that is necessary for survival, the object no longer restricts the subject, which is dangerous, and the excessive development of technology is a road to ruin.

Wang Mojie knew that what was typically called "subjectivity" in Chinese was usually referred to as "agency" in academic English, but in any event, his point was that technology was driving the homogenising forces of globalisation and allowing people to change the world at their subjective whim.

—Well, you still took the photograph, didn't you? Ukyi Lhamo retorted.

—I regretted it a little bit right away. I could tell I was spoiling something. Actually, in everything we should value the spiritual, not the material. What comes from the heart is more permanent and dependable than any object. Human beings have a history of several thousand years of the heart-to-heart transmission of ideas. The circulation of material things just produces excess, and in the end, everything becomes nothing but a single-use fragment of some lost whole. Who could have imagined that the tantric Buddhist rite of *abhiseka* would become a spectacle you can pay to watch? Just like those heritage villages for tourists where for a hundred yuan you can dress up like an ethnic bridegroom in a pretend wedding. There is a flood of cultural rubbish out there. We ruin everything that has value.

—You seem to like to think about religion from a perspective that stands outside religion.

—Those aren't my original ideas, they belong to the philosophers of the past. Søren Kierkegaard thought about these things, for example.

—Oh, you were just quoting. I thought you were being brilliant.

—Just quoting? There is nothing wrong with quoting.

They were walking along a stretch of cobblestones. This was not the way they had come. They were on the path that leads to Nechung Monastery, which sits above the Lhalu Wetlands.

11. Mandala

Khanor Rinpoche gazed down at her with a smile.
The smile reached her heart and a lotus blossom opened within it.
She was enveloped by his gaze. As if enchanted by his smile,
she could not stop herself from slowly lifting her bowed head up to him.
Would she have dared lift her head, if not spellbound? Ah, the youthful
Khanor Rinpoche.
The vastness in his eyes made her dizzy.

A mandala is a complicated, profound symbol. In Sanskrit, "mandala" means "circle". The Tibetan word for mandala means "centre and surrounding environment". A mandala can be round, square, two dimensional or three dimensional but always follows the principle of "centre and surrounding environment". In a rectangular mandala, the four sides represent the four cardinal directions of north, south, east and west, and the centre and four sides constitute a space that collects the energy of the universe. According to Tibetan Buddhist belief, the universe itself has the shape of a mandala, and so we should value mandalas, we should make them and consecrate them because in them is the essence of the universe and the *buddhadharma*. For example, at the centre of a mandala might be the palace of the male and female deities of time, Kalacakra and Visvamata. In addition, there might be as many as 721 other deities depicted, and in this particular case, many of them might have something to do with time, for example, the deities of the seasons or of the sun and the moon. Other deities depicted might be those of the elements, the senses and the constellations. In our example, in the centre next to Kalacakra and Visvamata are four meditating Buddhas and also *dakinis*, along with many bodhisattvas and protector deities of Buddhism. The closer to the centre of the mandala, the greater the efficacy of the deity. A mandala's structure can be seen as the universe in miniature, it is a visualisation of the universe. Mandalas can be painted on *thangka* or walls, or made with sand on the ground, and sometimes a temple is built in the shape of a mandala, as Nechung Monastery is, for example.

Nechung Monastery is at the edge of the Lhalu Wetlands. It is of a standard rectangular construction, built around a central courtyard, on all four sides of which there is a covered corridor, a feature required to complete the mandala. Colourful paintings line the corridor, more of Kalacakra and Visvamata than any other deities. The corridor and the open space it encloses make up about two-thirds of the monastery grounds, with the main hall comprising the other third. When you come in through the east gate, you enter a courtyard enclosed by the surrounding covered corridor. The courtyard is paved with grey stone, in its centre is a stone pillar, a dozen metres high, and from its top, prayer flags and pennants always snap and flutter in the wind. Every year on the last day of the Saga Dawa Festival, the day of Sakyamuni's birth, enlightenment and *parinirvana,* a religious celebration is held at all the major monasteries in Lhasa, Nechung Monastery included. Nechung Monastery is much smaller than the three great monasteries of Lhasa, but because its construction is most closely modelled on a mandala, there is something majestic about its festivals that hints at the mysteries of the universe. Nechung does not belong to any particular sect, neither to the Gelug school of Tibetan Buddhism (which tourists call the Yellow Hat Sect) nor to the Kagyupa (known also as the Red Hat Sect or White Hat Sect). All orders may hold scripture-reading festivals there. If during the festival a *thangka* of Padmasambhava is hung in the middle of the monastery and the day is devoted to his teachings, it means that among the several orders of Tibetan Buddhism, it is the Nyingma school, the oldest of the schools of Tibetan Buddhism, that is holding the festival.

Ukyi Lhamo met her first teacher at a Nyingma school scripture-reading festival. On that unforgettable day, Ukyi Lhamo told Wang Mojie, the Nyingma pennants snapped in the wind and caught the sunlight, which blazed down like coloured rain, while the young and handsome Khanor Rinpoche walked at the head of a group of monks who entered the courtyard through the east gate, bringing with them all the red of the rainbow, as horns and beautiful conch shells sounded. They carried in the middle of their procession a *thangka* of the Eight Manifestations of Padmasambhava, which they slowly raised upright, and they carried a variety of ritual implements that reflected the sunlight in a variety of hues. The light and the sound of the horns and shells came together in this variegated time, under the colourful sunlight falling like rain and dew, like grace. Amid the sound, light and colour, below the *thangka* of the Eight Manifestations of Padmasambhava, a monk, young but eminent, sat elegant and radiant on his ceremonial throne. He was so young it startled Ukyi Lhamo. He accepted the *khata* offered to him by the worshippers. He sat above them, a beneficent presence, and reached down to touch each bowed head in blessing. He was the renowned Khanor Rinpoche, and the queue of believers there to see him stretched beyond the monastery gates, winding down into the village, like a prayer flag fluttering along the path through the village.

Ukyi Lhamo was in the queue. She was wearing a new black robe of Tibetan wool and almost no jewellery. Unlike the others waiting, she wasn't counting prayer beads with the fingers of one hand while spinning a prayer wheel with the other. And she wasn't draped with silver jewellery the way the Tibetan herders from the grasslands were. They wore sacred mirrors and turquoise that jangled when they walked. It wasn't the first time she had worn her new robe, but it was one of the first. It was so new that it still gave off the smell of the Indian incense that burned in the Nepalese shop on Barkhor Street where she had bought it. On the day of the festival, she had only recently arrived in Lhasa, and she was very unsure about everything. She should have hung prayer beads around her neck or wrist but she had none. Instead, she was wearing a necklace of dark blue beads, not Tibetan but something she used to wear in Paris. In Paris, the necklace seemed Tibetan, in Tibet it looked Parisian, which is how Ukyi Lhamo felt about herself.

She was towards the end of the queue, moving slowly forwards in the rainbow sunlight, over the shadows the pilgrims cast upon the ground. During the previous few days, she had been to Jokhang Temple, Ganden Monastery, Drepung Monastery and Sera Monastery and had learned something about the rituals, so today she had brought a *khata*. It was almost noon when she entered the mandala of Nechung Monastery, and it all felt brand new and strange to her. She had heard that the fabled Living Buddha of the Nyingma school would be teaching that day, and now she would see him. She didn't know the first thing about the Nyingma teachings, all she knew was that they were supposed to be mysterious and possessed some miraculous power, which made her a little nervous. She got closer and closer to the Living Buddha, unconsciously bowing her head lower and lower. There was a whole line of people with bowed heads, and she followed suit. She could not see the Living Buddha's face, even though she was right in front of where he sat. She could see his feet, and as she lifted the pure white *khata* to place it over his bent head, she expected it would be like what happened at Sera Monastery and Ganden, she would feel a light touch on her head, and then she would silently withdraw.

She did not intend to raise her head, she was going to back away, then leave, but unlike her previous experience, this time she felt some power envelop her. Something formless but very strong. She sensed a flash of light, an instant of elevation, and a flame seemed to ignite in her heart. She very clearly heard him speak to her, and she found the courage to raise her head. She never forgot that moment. Khanor Rinpoche was smiling down at her, and when she saw his smile, the flame in her heart turned into a lotus blossom. She was enveloped by his gaze. As if enchanted by his smile, she could not stop herself from slowly lifting her bowed head up to him. Would she have dared lift her head, if not spellbound? She hadn't expected him to look so young, it was a marvel how young he was. And his eyes were like water in a mountain lake, pure, bright and calm.

He touched her on the head. In the hand with which he touched her, he held black pebbles. He opened his hand to her, meaning she was to take the pebbles. Her hands opened of their own accord and as the pebbles, like black pearls, fell one by one into her hands, suddenly her tears started to fall like white pearls, a tear for each pebble. She could do nothing to stop them. She raised her hands with the pebbles and turned her face and tears to Khanor Rinpoche, and he touched her again on the head. She kept her head up, gazing through the sparkling, gold light of her tears at the young, almost still a boy, Living Buddha.

Thanks! she said and, surprisingly, she smiled at Khanor Rinpoche. It was her voice and her smile, she was aware of what she was doing. She was no longer only a worshipper, she was also acting from a woman's instinct. She couldn't say exactly why she had been compelled to challenge the etiquette, but she had, she had raised her head and smiled at him, and even given him rather a flirty look. She shouldn't have done these things, but they were spontaneous. Her heart surged, and she felt joyful. But as she looked at him in her joy, she did not see Khanor Rinpoche's expression change at all. He remained untouched, as still and calm as the surface of a lake. The change had been to her, not to Khanor Rinpoche, and the change in her was caused by him. She felt cool and transparent as if her clothing were made of water. She felt as if she was being pulled into the lake of his eyes.

—Everything about that day seemed like a dream, a dream that has always stayed with me and will never go away. Khanor Rinpoche and I are joined forever, his heart imprinted on mine. Do you know what I mean? The imprinting of one heart on another is like two lights coming together, it happened so fast, like a flash. I think it was what we mean by a light year, do you know the meaning of a light year?

—As time, a light year is a year, light travels for a year, simple, Wang Mojie said with a straight face.

—No, that's definitely wrong, Ukyi Lhamo said.

—It's common knowledge from physics, Wang Mojie said, still teasing her.

—I think it's different. A light year is about space. Does an ordinary year have anything to do with space?

—OK, it is to do with space, but as a measure of time it's the same, he said, not letting go of his joke.

—That's what I'm saying, what's different is the idea about space. But no, time is different too.

Wang Mojie thought that perhaps Ukyi Lhamo truly did experience a different sort of time while in the mandala of the monastery. Einstein's theory of relativity allows us to imagine that as the mind of Khanor Rinpoche imprinted on the mind of Ukyi Lhamo, maybe it did create some sort of distanced psychological space. And in the moment, time soared and space spun. Time can be accelerated by the eyes at the centre of a mandala, and at any instant time can be suspended by those eyes. When Ukyi Lhamo felt as if she was wearing clothes of water, maybe time had been suspended for her, it was a freeze frame, there was something on the brink of happening. It was, there could be no doubt, a mystical moment of one heart imprinting on another.

No matter how long or how brief a moment it was, when it was over Ukyi Lhamo had to depart from Khanor Rinpoche because, she told Wang Mojie, many people were waiting behind her. She backed away slowly, she didn't lower her head as the others did, she kept her eyes on Khanor Rinpoche, her eyes meeting his, his eyes like a lake of cool water. Her clothing felt made of water, then it slowly transformed into fine gauze, she felt herself stepping into one of the wall paintings, she felt herself stepping into eternity. Khanor Rinpoche continued to deliver blessings. His hands, holding a ceremonial bell and drum, were beautiful, just like the hands depicted in the ancient wall paintings. As he gently shook the bell and slowly banged the drum, he was Kalacakra, he was the deity of the seasons and of the senses.

But who was Visvamata, Kalacakra's consort? As she raised her hands to take the black pebbles, might Ukyi Lhamo have been capable of becoming Visvamata? Had she been summoned by the *buddhadharma*? What exactly had Khanor Rinpoche imprinted on her heart and mind? The teacher appears only when the disciple is ready, as the saying goes.

But at the time, not only was Ukyi Lhamo not ready, she was not yet truly a believer. When she came to Tibet, she didn't have any real faith, she just wanted to affirm that more mysterious half of her blood, to see what there was to find on the road to religion. Not long after she had returned from France and moved to Lhasa, she saw in real life what she had once seen only in dreams: temples and monasteries everywhere, juniper and cedar smoke, snow peaks, butter lamps and, as ancient as all of these things, the Tibetan people. She knew her roots were in Tibet, and the search for those roots separated her from her former self and her friends. It excited her to feel, as if for the first time, the blood of half her heritage surging in her body, but this felt strange too, and her friends were confused by her newly awakened interest in Tibet. To some extent, she didn't belong to any place, she didn't belong to the Chinese interior, not to France nor Tibet, she was an exile, cast out by all three places, but she was also the blend of all three places. And this blend had many special characteristics, which made her different from everybody else. She knew, however, what was most important to her now: Tibet, only Tibet. For many years, nobody knew she was half Tibetan, even her best friends didn't know. For her whole life, she had always put down "Han Chinese" on forms that asked for her ethnicity. That is what was on all her IDs. Her student ID, her national ID card and her passport all said she was Han Chinese. She always took this as a given, but she knew, from when she was a little girl she knew, that she had something that made her different from everybody else. She was Shen Jiayuan. But she also had the name Ukyi Lhamo, and she never told anyone that she had this secret name, not in primary school, not in middle school, not even at university. Of course, if she was honest with herself, she would admit that she knew why she kept it a secret. When she was little, she didn't tell anybody because she was afraid of being different, and so she always carefully hid the secret about her heritage. But later on, she couldn't remember exactly when, the shame and fear she felt because of her secret name gradually disappeared, and not just that, her secret name suddenly became something that made her proud. But she still didn't tell anybody. After so many years, she had become used to never telling anybody, and she wasn't going to share her private point of pride with just anyone. She knew that sooner or later she would make a trip to Tibet, even though she hadn't been born there. She hadn't expected her mother to go first, but she did, she moved back to Tibet for good immediately after retirement. And now Ukyi Lhamo had come too. She thought of herself as returning home, but she found Tibet quite foreign to her, and because she didn't feel at home, she felt ashamed.

When she had imagined Tibet, while in the interior or Paris, she felt there was something in her that was Tibetan, it was hers by birth, it was her secret. But when she got to Tibet, she discovered that the Tibetan something in her, whatever it was, didn't grow stronger, it grew weaker. She and Tibet were far too different. But this was normal, there is always a gap between what we want and our reality. She tried hard to close the gap between herself and Tibet. She felt like a child too long away from home. From the bottom of her heart she loved the monasteries, the magnificent, calming butter lamps, the crimson *kasaya*, the magical festival days so markedly different from ordinary days. She loved the days of scripture reading, the ritual, the colour, the light. She participated in and appreciated her religious practice as if it were an aesthetic endeavour replete with complicated ceremony, even to the point of throwing herself into things by merely imitating what she saw others do. She found it all novel, she felt bathed in the crimson red of the robes and felt part of a mystical culture. But had she not encountered the young Khanor Rinpoche, would Tibet have come to capture her, body and soul? Abstract religion alone could not have changed her. She had believed a miracle was bound to happen sooner or later, but she hadn't expected it to happen so quickly! Ah, the young Khanor Rinpoche, the vastness in his eyes made her dizzy. His eyes overcame her, they threw her soul into a maelstrom, and something long latent within her burst to the surface. She had walked some distance from Nechung, she had come to a spot where she could see the blue Lhasa River down below but everything looked different to her now, and some strong desire pulled her back to the mandala.

She walked back to Nechung and into the centre of the mandala. She seemed possessed. She spoke to an old monk who was standing near Khanor Rinpoche. Boldly she said, Please tell Khanor Rinpoche that I would like to be introduced to him and want to study with him. No one had ever been so direct before, no one had ever asked to be taken as a disciple in such a fashion. The words didn't seem to come from her. Some other voice not her own was speaking for her. The elderly monk didn't understand Mandarin, but he recognised that there was something special about Ukyi Lhamo. He led her over to a young monk who was wearing wire-rimmed glasses, and to him she repeated her bold request, still in Mandarin because at the time she could barely speak Tibetan. She waited for an answer. She watched as the young monk in glasses went over to Khanor Rinpoche for instruction. He came back and told her that the Rinpoche said he and she knew each other already, he had known her for quite some time, and he welcomed her to his monastery for instruction.

—It was a miracle. I was so excited. You don't know how bold I was. I have never been so bold in my life.

—There was nothing miraculous about it. You're pretty, like the women on the *thangkas*.

—Really? Me, like the *thangkas*?

—Everybody likes beautiful things. Including the gods, including Living Buddhas. Beauty is the creation of the gods. Think about the White Tara or the wisdom consorts on the *thangkas* and wall paintings, is there a single one that isn't pretty? One who isn't beautiful?

—You make everything so base. That's not all there was to it.

—Of course not. If that's all there was to it, it would make him a lecher.

—You're nasty, Wang Mo. The gods are going to get you for that. Don't believe if you don't want to, but have a little respect.

—Just telling the truth.

—What truth? You're talking nonsense.

—As I've said before, you aren't just averagely pretty, you look like a woman in a *thangka*.

—Enough.

For Wang Mojie to say that Ukyi Lhamo looked like a woman on a thangka was to evaluate her with reference to her religion. Among all the men who had pursued her, there wasn't one who had ever considered her from the perspective of her religion, and her religion was important to her, and so she identified quite strongly with what Wang Mojie said. But when Wang Mojie made the remark about Khanor Rinpoche being a lecher, it dispelled any good feeling she had. Wang Mojie always did that. It was foolish of her not to expect him to ruin the mood.

But Wang Mojie wasn't always entirely conscious of how what he said or did impacted others, which Ukyi Lhamo knew. Ukyi Lhamo knew him to be straightforward, acerbic and opinionated, but it was precisely these characteristics of his that inspired her to want to open up to him. Each of us has something we can't share with others, and if we try to share it, we find we can only express part of it, and so we are always imagining somebody with whom we can talk, with whom we can share all our secrets without having to worry. Often this person is our fantasised lover or some made-up person we imagine lives in some far-off land just waiting for us, and we imagine that we could say anything to this person at all, dropping our guard entirely. Wang Mojie's objectivity about things made Ukyi Lhamo feel as if she could drop her guard. They went for long walks together or had tea or a drink, sometimes they talked all day and into the night, even all night and into the day. Ukyi Lhamo had a very unusual background, and once she began to talk about it, there was no going back. Wang Mojie would comment from time to time, very candidly, which just made her want to talk all the more. Sometimes they would forget the time and without being aware of it, they would walk beyond the Lhalu Wetlands and far down the bank of the Lhasa River, which they would then cross back and forth on a ferry raft of yak-hide. They were totally absorbed in the space-time of their conversation, the world around them was like an illusion. Wang Mojie was a patient, disinterested listener. Ukyi Lhamo could smell the animal on the prowl on all the men she knew. Wang Mojie was the only exception. Wang Mojie was pure, he made her relax completely. This surprised her, she couldn't understand it, it fascinated her. How could anybody be so objective, so disinterested? She couldn't believe it, and to her surprise this awakened in her a very strong physical desire.

12. Ceremony in Blue

Ah! Like so many visages of the moon reflected in water,
the myriad beings flow back and forth, trapped in the wheel of life and death.
In order that the souls of the myriad beings may remain in nature's void,
remain in life,
the bodhicitta *within me is born from the Four Immeasurables.*

Ukyi Lhamo could never forget the morning she went to see Khanor Rinpoche at his residence in a small monastery. After several days of rain, the sky over Lhasa had cleared and the world sparkled. It was nothing she hadn't seen before, but Ukyi Lhamo had never felt clearer herself, she felt as clear as the morning sky. She walked instead of taking the bus or riding her bike. She walked, her heart full of gladness, welcoming the rising sun after the rain, feeling for a moment that she was rising together with the sun, rising above the rivers and the shimmering Potala Palace lit with golden light. The sun was rising and everything seemed to be rising with it, Lhasa, the vault of heaven, and Ukyi Lhamo too, even the faithful prostrating themselves with each step seemed to be rising. She walked unhurriedly with a light heart. She watched the worshippers who lay prostrate in prayer after each step forwards and knew she was doing the right thing by walking, moving her feet over the earth. She felt connected to the earth as never before. She wanted to walk and didn't care how far.

She walked through Lhasa's western suburbs, by the Chagpori and the Potala Square, down Beijing Avenue and along Yuthok Road to Barkhor Street. She made three circuits of Barkhor Street around Jokhang Temple, and each time she came to the entrance of the Jokhang she stood with her hands raised in prayer, then lowered herself and touched her forehead to the ground. She was called to do it, it was natural, and she didn't feel timid any more.

She walked for about three and a half hours. Each time after that it took the same three and a half hours, seven for a round trip, but it didn't tire her, she felt boundless energy, the same energy felt by the worshippers who lay themselves down on the ground after every step. When the paved road ended, she had reached the hills and she saw, against a grove of willows, the red walls of the monastery.

Khanor Rinpoche was on the stairs at the entrance waiting for her, which surprised her because she hadn't told him what day she would visit. She asked him how he had known she would come that day. Khanor Rinpoche said he just knew, just as before they had ever met he knew they would. He said this with all seriousness, no trace of humour, but still Ukyi Lhamo felt puzzled. Because this wasn't a festival day, Khanor Rinpoche wasn't wearing his monk's hat, had no yellow fabric draped over his shoulder and was holding no gleaming ritual objects. No horns were sounding and no banners were flying, and because it was all so different from the magnificence and grandeur of the festival day at Nechung, at first Ukyi Lhamo almost didn't recognise Khanor Rinpoche, who looked ordinary, even a little boyish. He was wearing a *kasaya*, his right shoulder bare, his hair was short, and he looked like any young monk. If it hadn't been for the unchanging lake of his eyes, Ukyi Lhamo might have felt a little disappointed or perhaps she was disappointed. She was trying to recall in every detail the feeling she got from that gorgeous festival at Nechung, that brilliant rainbow of a spectacle, and nothing around her now felt as dreamlike as it had then. But when she looked more closely, she saw that Khanor Rinpoche's gaze was just as penetrating as before. His eyes were lowered at first, and when he raised them to her, it was as if she were gazing into a lake, and she was moved, just as she had been the first time. It was his eyes, like a deep lake, that made Ukyi Lhamo gradually forget about the festival day at Nechung and focus instead on the moment.

Khanor Rinpoche did not know any Mandarin, and at that point, Ukyi Lhamo spoke only a little Tibetan, so they communicated for the most part in silence with their eyes, just as the young Ma Dingge and Kangyur Rinpoche had done in Darjeeling. Khanor Rinpoche handed Ukyi Lhamo a copy of *The Annotated "On Buddhist Practice"* by Gyalse

Tokme Zangpo (also known as Gyalse Ngulchu Tokme). It was in Tibetan, so Ukyi Lhamo couldn't read a word. She looked at the book as a blind person might, feeling a little ridiculous. Should she give up? she wondered. Could there be any student of Buddhism as blind, deaf and dumb as she was? She had always planned to start studying Tibetan one day, but she needed the language now, so what was she to do? If she was going to learn about Buddhism, she had a very long road ahead of her, and she wondered if she had the perseverance. Not only did Ukyi Lhamo wonder about this, but Khanor Rinpoche did too. She was about to turn and leave, but Khanor Rinpoche didn't give her the chance. From a drawer in a small red table, he took out a pen and a string-bound notebook with a leather cover. He handed the notebook to Ukyi Lhamo and indicated she should open it. She did and found the pages blank. It was handmade, the paper not particularly white but very clean. Khanor Rinpoche said Ukyi Lhamo's name, pronouncing it somewhere between the Mandarin and Tibetan readings, then handed her the pen and indicated she should write her name. Ukyi Lhamo wrote her Tibetan name in its Mandarin transliteration in Chinese characters and read it to Khanor Rinpoche. He took the notebook and pen and below the Chinese characters wrote her name in Tibetan, དབུས་ཀྱི་ལྷ་མོ།.

—Ukyi Lhamo, he read.

Khanor Rinpoche made her repeat it, in proper Tibetan.

It hadn't occurred to Ukyi Lhamo that everything would start from her name.

She read her name in Tibetan until she mastered it. Khanor Rinpoche wrote Tibetan phrases in the notebook and taught Ukyi Lhamo to read them, pointing with his pen to help her follow along. She had learned English when she was small and studied French at university. She was exceptionally good at languages, and it didn't take long before she could read the words and phrases in the notebook accurately and fluently. She didn't know the meaning of what she was reading, nevertheless, some emotion she couldn't name filled her heart.

While Ukyi Lhamo was going over her lesson, Khanor Rinpoche walked away and came back with a monk who spoke Mandarin. It was the monk in the wire-rimmed glasses from the day at Nechung. His name was Nyima Tsering. He bowed to Ukyi Lhamo but didn't say much, as if to acknowledge that this was a classroom and not a place for conversation. He sat to one side, took the notebook, pushed his glasses up and under each line of Tibetan wrote the corresponding Chinese. As he wrote each Chinese word, Ukyi Lhamo's eyes brightened as if just released from a blindfold. Nyima Tsering glossed for Ukyi Lhamo the words "samsara", "anitya" and "karma" and the phrase "discover the *bodhicitta* within and follow the Buddhist path". He also translated the sentence "take refuge in the Three Jewels of the Buddha, the Dharma and the Sangha".

As Ukyi Lhamo read these words, tears fell from her eyes.

She looked at Khanor Rinpoche, longing to wrap her arms around him, she felt such a profound rush of emotion. But she could not do this, and her joy turned to anguish. Khanor Rinpoche lowered his gaze and spoke to her slowly.

—It is a rare and precious thing to be born as a human being, but this existence is *anitya*, impermanent, there is only reincarnation, the cycle of rebirth, so if you seek the path towards liberation from the six rebirth destinies, from *samsara*, it is to be found in the *buddhadharma*. When you begin to have faith in the *buddhadharma*, it is a rare and precious thing. As a follower of Sakyamuni, I will help you discover the path towards liberation.

He spoke quietly and calmly, and Nyima Tsering translated in the same tone.

Ukyi Lhamo's tears ceased falling to the ground, instead they flowed within her.

Something in her felt cleansed, she felt the truth of *sunyata*, and a great peace filled her heart.

Khanor Rinpoche picked up the notebook and wrote a few more lines of Tibetan, his writing careful and neat, leaving space between the lines. When he finished, he read it aloud, and it sounded beautiful, like poetry. Then he taught Ukyi Lhamo to say it, repeating after him syllable by syllable, the pen in his hand moving along and tracing the rising and falling of the pitch and emphasising the poetic rhyme.

It was a poem from a sutra that in Nyima Tsering's somewhat awkward translation read:

> Ah! Like so many visages of the moon reflected in water,
> the myriad beings flow back and forth, trapped in the wheel of life and death.
> In order that the souls of the myriad beings may remain in nature's void, remain in life,
> the *bodhicitta* within me is born from the Four Immeasurables.

Ukyi Lhamo found out only later that this referred to one of the

"Four Extraordinary Foundations", namely the cultivation of *bodhicitta*. In the practice of Buddhism, there are "Foundations" to undertake, including the Four Ordinary Foundations and the Four Extraordinary Foundations. The Tibetan Buddhist Triyana, the three vehicles (or teachings), are, in order, the Hinayana or Basic Vehicle, the Mahayana or Great Vehicle and the Vajrayana or Diamond Vehicle. Each leads to a higher level of enlightenment that is increasingly difficult to attain. Together they lead to the highest level of enlightenment, Buddhahood. Students of Buddhism must undertake and practise the Foundations before they can achieve any true success. The Four Ordinary Foundations are undertaken at all levels and in all sects of Buddhism, and the Four Extraordinary Foundations are the particular practice of the gate to enlightenment that is the Diamond Vehicle.

When the young Khanor Rinpoche began to transmit the *buddhadharma* to Ukyi Lhamo, he instructed her in the Four Ordinary Foundations and the Four Extraordinary Foundations, the Ngondro practices that are preliminary to tantric meditation. The Four Ordinary Foundations are deep reflections on: one, the freedoms and advantages of precious human rebirth; two, the truth of impermanence and change; three, the workings of *karma*; and four, the suffering of living beings within *samsara*. The Four Extraordinary Foundations are: the cultivation of *bodhicitta* or the Bodhi Mind; prostration to abolish pride; Vajrasattva meditation; and mandala offering. The Four Ordinary Foundations are the essence of Buddhism, while the Four Extraordinary Foundations belong to the poetic realm of the practice of perfection.

The small monastery where Khanor Rinpoche lived was astonishingly quiet and in a very beautiful spot. The natural beauty drew people outdoors and so the young, boyish even, Khanor Rinpoche did not always remain within the forbidding assembly hall when teaching. Sometimes he came outside and sat beneath a tree, just as Sakyamuni had. In summer, especially after rain, the normally arid air in Lhasa holds a little moisture and thin clouds drift through the sky, scraping one after another across the ridgetops of the mountains that surround the city or rolling up those mountains like a vision of swans or sheep. Sometimes a cloud forms over a grove of trees and drifts across the sky like a parasol, its shadow suddenly cool on the people below. The monastery where Khanor Rinpoche lived was surrounded by trees and there were some within the monastery compound. Under many of the trees were simple stone tables and benches, not polished stone but naturally rough. Often on a stone table would be a thermos and wooden bowls, sometimes the benches were wet from rain or dew but if so, there were red woven mats on which to sit.

Buddhism is closer to nature than any other religion. The Buddha taught that the entirety of the *buddhadharma* is in nature. For example, the cultivation of the Bodhi Mind is the result of a person's engagement with nature, such as with the moonlight. Sitting beneath a tree, Khanor Rinpoche seemed younger than he had at the scripture-reading festival at Nechung and younger than he did when teaching in the imposing setting of the assembly hall. He seemed less worldly, was more transparent, and he didn't keep his gaze lowered all the time. Ukyi Lhamo grew accustomed to the vastness in his eyes. Looking into his eyes was like looking into a lake that meets the sky at the horizon. And now when Ukyi Lhamo's eyes met his, her heart no longer beat so fast. Sometimes they exchanged a few words of casual conversation and talked about themselves. Ukyi Lhamo learned that Khanor Rinpoche had been born into a herdsman's family not far from Lhasa, and before he was five, he was identified as a reincarnated soul. Since then he had been at the monastery. It had been fourteen years, and he was not quite nineteen. Ukyi Lhamo knew by his appearance that he was young but never would have guessed that he was only eighteen. She had always assumed he was twenty-three or twenty-four, just a couple of years younger than her. He seemed so young compared to the many old monks at the monastery, who unlike Khanor Rinpoche seemed venerable.

—Are you really only eighteen?

Forgetting herself, Ukyi Lhamo spoke to him as to an equal, but to her surprise, Khanor Rinpoche was not bothered by the question.

—If you count my previous lives, I'm much older than that.

He said he was born already old, which touched Ukyi Lhamo, and she responded quickly.

—No, no, you're not old, but you don't seem eighteen, I thought you were my age, more or less.

—You are very young, Khanor Rinpoche said.

—Oh! Ukyi Lhamo exclaimed. She did not know what to say.

Khanor Rinpoche's voice didn't match his age, and, like his gaze, somehow didn't seem connected to his body. Indeed, Khanor Rinpoche seemed to exist in a time all his own, as if he inhabited several different eras at once. When he said Ukyi Lhamo was young, his voice was relaxed but it sounded like that of an older man and seemed to emanate from the vastness in his eyes.

Only now did Ukyi Lhamo realise why Khanor Rinpoche's gaze always made her think of light on a vast lake. It was because his eyes held all his past lives. Would you say of a lake that it was old? Not really and yet at the same time you would not say of a lake that it was young. This was the feeling that Ukyi Lhamo got from Khanor Rinpoche.

—Venerable Khanor Rinpoche, you are amazing! Ukyi Lhamo said with an involuntary sigh.

Ukyi Lhamo reminded herself to speak to the master with the proper deference. She wanted to do so. Khanor Rinpoche had already resumed writing in the notebook. The lesson continued. From then on, however, Khanor Rinpoche was different with her to a degree. They knew each other better now and were more informal with each other. Once, as they were sitting together under a tree reading a poem related to the Four Extraordinary Foundations, a bird flew over and with an audible plop, bird droppings fell on Ukyi Lhamo's head. She yelled out.

—Oh! What bad luck! Of all places, it has to land on my head!

Khanor Rinpoche responded immediately.

—Oh! What good luck! Of all places, it has landed on your head!

Khanor Rinpoche's expression was entirely serious.

—You mean it's a message? Ukyi Lhamo asked, puzzled.

Khanor Rinpoche looked up to where the bird had just flown.

—It's *adhisthana*. The bird has sent you a blessing.

—That's a blessing?

—Not just anyone has bird droppings land on their head. Some people wait for it their whole lives but never get it.

—Who?

—Many people. Those bird droppings are to remind you that you once flew here like that bird.

—I was a bird in my previous life? Ukyi Lhamo's eyes widened.

—To be reborn as a bird is quite good fortune, you know.

—Khanor Rinpoche, are you truly being serious?

—Yes, I am serious.

If it was a joke, it was profound. If it was not a joke, it was a moment of pure innocence. Ukyi Lhamo couldn't figure out which, but whether a profound joke or a moment of unaffected innocence, Ukyi Lhamo liked it, because either way it was out of the ordinary. A moment of perfect innocence might contain profundity. The *buddhadharma* is found in both profundity and innocence.

During this time, Ukyi Lhamo told Wang Mojie as they stood by the river, she made two trips to see Khanor Rinpoche each week. She always walked, reciting the Heart Sutra to herself. The language barrier between them was gone. Language had, in fact, become a bridge, but even when Ukyi Lhamo's Tibetan began to improve rapidly, she still insisted that Khanor Rinpoche write down in Tibetan everything he taught her and read it aloud for her to repeat as if at primary school. Ukyi Lhamo became used to this, it was a ritual she needed. She was able to persist in her study because of Khanor Rinpoche's profundity, his innocence and the mixture of the two that made it hard to separate the one from the other.

Over the course of approximately a year, Ukyi Lhamo studied the various paths to enlightenment in the Foundations, becoming fascinated by the blessings offered by each of several different rituals. As she saw it, the rituals of esoteric Tibetan Buddhism were the most aesthetic, complex and mysterious of all religious rituals, and the ritual implements, the vases, conch shells, mirrors, *vajra* sceptres, crystals, offering bowls, peacock feathers, ceremonial hats and bells, created a wonderful symbolic world. It is fair to say that Tibetan Buddhism is a religion of rituals, and the most common series of initiation rites is known as *abhiseka* (a Sanskrit term that means "anointment", "consecration", "empowerment" or "initiation"), which taken together comprise a surpassingly beautiful work of performance art. Khanor Rinpoche taught Ukyi Lhamo that the significance of *abhiseka* is that the teacher blesses the disciple, bestowing upon the disciple merit and virtue, which empowers the disciple to become a mature practitioner.

Khanor Rinpoche told Ukyi Lhamo that *abhiseka* can be tangible, such as with sacred water, the most common of the rituals. The blessing is done by offering water like sweet dew and is something that anyone who visits a monastery on a festival day may receive. *Abhiseka* can also be intangible, an oral transmission, an incantation, a revealing of a secret, or a teaching, all of which are *abhiseka* in the strict sense, performed not in public but privately by the master and the disciple. The ritual often begins with the rinsing of the mouth with sacred water, which is a symbolic cleansing of body and mind, then the master uses ritual implements to bless the disciple on the head, chest and palms. There are four types of *abhiseka*: vase empowerment; secret empowerment; the knowledge of wisdom empowerment; and the word empowerment. The most difficult is the knowledge of wisdom empowerment, also known as the consummate empowerment. It is difficult because, according to circumstances, it may take a variety of forms. Khanor Rinpoche told Ukyi Lhamo that the classic example is from the time when Sakyamuni was teaching the Dharma and is the story of the "Flower Sermon". Sakyamuni held up a flower and smiled but did not speak. Among all the disciples who were gathered before him, only Mahakasyapa understood, and he smiled, indicating that he understood

Sakyamuni and that his heart accepted what Sakyamuni's heart transmitted. When Sakyamuni held up the flower but did not speak, it meant that he possessed the marvellous mind of nirvana, and Mahakasyapa immediately understood the law of *sunya*, he understood that the ego and all phenomena were unreal. This was mind-to-mind transmission (or heart-to-heart, the meaning is the same), the most difficult of *abhiseka* practices, which is why it is also known as the consummate empowerment, and it is not available to just any ordinary disciple.

Ukyi Lhamo was fascinated by the *abhiseka* rites, and on her own she read a lot of books about them. But no matter how much she read, she would never know all that Khanor Rinpoche did. Over nearly a year, Khanor Rinpoche, sometimes in the assembly hall and sometimes outside under the trees, took Ukyi Lhamo through various initiation rites a dozen or so times, two of which left a profound, unforgettable impression on her. One was a remarkable rite that Ukyi Lhamo referred to as "Manjusri empowerment", and the other she thought of as "empowerment by tongue".

"Empowerment by tongue" is not "empowerment by kissing", but that is what Ukyi Lhamo thought it was at first, which excited her so much that she felt hot all over. She felt simultaneously as if she had a new insight into things but also completely confused. She felt a thirst, a yearning for a supreme spiritual uplifting, and she imagined Khanor Rinpoche taking her flying towards Shambhala. But she was mistaken. Khanor Rinpoche merely walked her over to a vase of flowers, which they admired for a moment. Then Khanor Rinpoche took a red aster and a white aster from the vase and brought them to his mouth. He closed his eyes, recited something and touched his tongue to each of the two flowers to bless them. Then he got Ukyi Lhamo to take the flowers into her mouth, chew and swallow the petals. This was empowerment by tongue. Within the symbolism of empowerment by tongue, the flowers represent the Red Bodhi and the White Bodhi respectively, which the disciple has no way of acquiring on her own. She must be given them by the Master. After swallowing the petals, Ukyi Lhamo felt uncommonly beautiful, as if she had floated into the wall paintings to join the ranks of the Tara depicted in them.

The latter sent her imagination soaring, while the former brought her into the realm of heart-to-heart transmission. The Manjusri empowerment was held in the hall for worship of Guru Rinpoche, Padmasambhava, which blazed with candlelight. What Ukyi Lhamo didn't know was that Khanor Rinpoche was preparing to leave for Bhutan and they would never see each other again. (Khanor Rinpoche departed in secret, and Ukyi Lhamo didn't find out he was gone until days later.) Manjusri empowerment was a knowledge of wisdom empowerment ritual, solemn and complex. Just as on that day at Nechung Monastery, Khanor Rinpoche was wearing a crimson *kasaya* with a yellow sash over one shoulder and a red ceremonial hat. Ukyi Lhamo, after her custom, was wearing a black Tibetan dress with a blouse with white sleeves, and in her hair she had a string of turquoise beads like Khampa girls wear, which she was to learn was inappropriate for the occasion. She had bought them the day before from a street vendor on Barkhor Street because she wanted to look more authentically Tibetan. With a smile, Khanor Rinpoche took the beads from her hair. He was disapproving but seemed to also take in with appreciation the sight of her long, perfectly clean black hair. Perhaps by the rules of the ritual, there can be nothing in one's hair, perhaps the beads would have been in the way somehow. Ukyi Lhamo didn't know and didn't ask.

During the Manjusri empowerment ceremony, named after the Bodhisattva of wisdom, Khanor Rinpoche used many different ritual implements, following a strict sequence. The first object used was a precious vase. Khanor Rinpoche sprinkled sacred water on Ukyi Lhamo's hair, and pearls of water rolled down her face like tears. Ukyi Lhamo caught the water on her tongue like sweet dew. Next was a blessing to the crown of her head with a *vajra* sceptre, then a conch shell blessing to her chest, a crystal blessing to her palms and a peacock feather blessing to the crown of her head. The blessings took a long time. In his left hand, Khanor Rinpoche had prayer beads, which he slowly placed into Ukyi Lhamo's hands. He extended his right hand and hooked his ring finger around the ring finger of Ukyi Lhamo's hand. They faced each other and turned slowly, hands together, step by step, a lotus, step by step, a levitation. Khanor Rinpoche's gaze flooded down, covering Ukyi Lhamo entirely, covering her entire world. Ukyi Lhamo felt she had entered a realm that was one vast expanse of clear, bright water. Khanor Rinpoche recited a sutra, line by line, and Ukyi Lhamo repeated each line after him, one voice high, one low, one light, one heavy. They stood close together, like dancers in the most wonderful of dances. There was understanding, commitment, heart-to-heart transmission, two heart-minds imprinted on each other.

Khanor Rinpoche was just eighteen. But much older than that too. Ukyi Lhamo's life was made in that moment, she would remain in that moment forever. They turned slowly, dancing, eyes locked together. But then, for just a second, Ukyi Lhamo's thoughts turned to her digital camcorder. She should get this eternal moment on film, she thought, even musing that if she did and then showed it in Paris, it would be a sensation. She could not have imagined that Khanor Rinpoche was soon to leave her. She didn't know why he left and never found out.

13. Tenpa Nyima

They were the unfamiliar eyes of an old man on the verge of death.
I was to be one of the last people he saw after a century of life.
It took a great effort for Tenpa Nyima to prise the old man's hands from their grasp on mine,
and in that moment the old man's eyes clouded over.

I rose early. The vultures that sleep on the cliffs rose earlier. Often, when the eastern sky had just turned fish-belly white, they had already finished their morning meal and were flying off into the sky on their sacred mission. They are the emissaries of the heavens. That day, even though I got up early, I arrived a bit too late. I searched the sky, but they were gone. I stood on the round platform built of rough stone. Grass grew thick around the platform in summer, but it was winter, and the grass was a desolate, warm, profoundly serene shade of brown. Looking at that expanse of warm brown gave me a quiet, dreamy feeling. I had been told that you can see the colour of the grass at night too. I heard that at night the colour was even more vivid, it was trance-inducing, they said. Looking at it under the warm yellow light of the moon makes you think you are dreaming, they said. I never visited the place at night, but the colour that morning was so rich that I could imagine what they meant.

It was morning. There was sunlight. The light changed gradually.

Each moment there was a small change, a slight shift, each moment a painting.

Look at a painting long enough and you will become part of it. That is what Cezanne came to believe when he was living in seclusion at Mont Sainte-Victoire. I stood looking at the platform for a long time, so did I become part of it?

I felt an inner tranquillity, I needed no one else, I didn't need Yu Youyan with her insipid seductiveness, and I didn't need Ukyi Lhamo with her fondness for long heart-to-heart talks. Thoughts of neither of them could interfere with the tranquillity I felt as I looked at the sacred ground where the sky burials are held. The sense of tranquillity was profound and made me feel solid, whole, as if I were one of the stones out of which the platform was built.

The low round platform was empty, and from it someone's soul had just been sent to the sky. The tools used by the *ragyaba* were there. Cutting tools. Strewn about. Worn from use, but their blades were still gleaming. There was a long-handled axe. A fingernail. Teeth. A red sweater was on the ground next to the platform, one sleeve bent up onto it. Bent up as if there was life there still, as if there was more to be said, as if reaching up to hold on to life. In the grass I saw two plaits of hair, they were tied with red string, neatly plaited, neatly laid in the grass.

There were withered flowers all around. Dried flowers. Withered but indomitable.

A young woman had just been there. She had slowly been taken up, rising with the morning, with the vultures.

But why then was the poor old man not taken?

During his last days, he had longed for his sky burial. The attendants, the *ragyaba*, dismembered the old man's body, and the emissaries from the heavens flew in, but they refused to descend. They circled but flew away. The old man's family called to them, the *ragyaba* called to them, and Tenpa Nyima yelled after them as if he had lost his mind, but they didn't come back. They flew far away, in refusal. This was extremely rare, so unheard of as to be the stuff of legend. It was something neither the living nor the dead could accept. The poor old man, the poor boy. Poor Tenpa Nyima. All of a sudden, he began to fly, his arms out, after the vultures. He ran into the hills, he ran over the top of a hill and disappeared, and he did not return.

It was always dark in Tenpa Nyima's house, and because the sunlight outside was so strong, every time I walked in, it took a long while before I could make out the layout of the room and see the silhouettes of the people and the furniture. It always felt damp at first, like cold damp air was coming from caves all around, but this was just an illusion owing to the dark. When my eyes finally adjusted, the first thing that slowly took shape before me was the old man lying on a *khaden* by the wall, his life's flame burning out. Every time I visited, he took me by the hand, he did not say anything but just looked at me. The last time I saw him, his face was distorted, his cheeks sunken, his mouth hanging half open. He lay on his back, and his face showed the effort it took for him to turn his eyes towards me. He could still move his eyes, but he could not move his head, that was the terrible state he was in. I had come looking for Tenpa Nyima's father. His father, only middle-aged but looking much older, came out from an even darker inner room. I told him why I had come, but he didn't seem to understand my poor Tibetan. I told Tenpa Nyima I needed someone who spoke Mandarin, so Tenpa Nyima translated this for his father, who nodded and then went out.

I was there because Tenpa Nyima had been acting up. He was missing school, not doing his work and sleeping during lessons, but worse than this, to my great surprise, he was constantly getting in fights. He bloodied Penpa Tsering's face and beat up Wangchuk, Lhakpa and Nyima Tsering (my student and Khanor Rinpoche's assistant had the same name). Tenpa Nyima was abusing his authority as class monitor and not setting a good example. Students, including many of the girls, complained about him. I called him in to talk several times, and every time he gritted his teeth and took the criticism. I thought he was just angry about having to obey, but what I didn't know was that he was hungry. He never got breakfast and sometimes did not have any lunch. He was fighting hunger when he made his promises to me to behave, but hunger always made him lose his head. It made him attack his classmates like a crazed animal. It never changed. I scolded him many times, but he never stopped, and I finally lost patience when he stole food from his classmates, disappointing me greatly. I stuck my finger in his face and yelled at him, called him worthless and said I regretted being stupid enough to make him class monitor, because now I had a class monitor who was a thief, a class monitor who stole from his classmates. I mocked him, saying he wasn't brave enough to try to take food out of somebody's hand, so he snuck around and stole when nobody was looking. I grabbed him by his collar and yelled, You should be ashamed of yourself, ashamed of yourself! But he glared right back at me, his hands curling into fists. I said, What? You want to take a swing at me? Go ahead! Go ahead! I had treated him well, and he had disappointed me deeply. His face was twitching like mad as he raised his fists, but then he lowered them. I whacked him on the chest. He started to flail out at me but stopped and hit himself on the chest instead.

He was sobbing, hitting himself and saying he couldn't take it any more, not any more. He said every day his dad yelled at him and hit him. He said his dad never let him eat enough. Usually he came to school without having any breakfast and there was nothing for him to eat at home during the lunch break. He said he was a good older brother and tried to keep his wild little brother in line, but still his dad hit him. He didn't want to go to school any more, he wanted to go back to his uncle's house in Nagchu and look after the sheep, but he couldn't bear to leave his grandfather. His grandfather was dying and needed him.

All of Tenpa Nyima's bad behaviour was because of his empty stomach, which I never suspected. I felt I had failed as a teacher, I had utterly failed to understand what was going on with him. But why had he never come to me to explain? I asked him why he had never told me. He yelled back at me, How could I tell you? I couldn't tell you! I didn't want to tell you! Tenpa Nyima was honest and straightforward. He stuck to me like my shadow, even like my bodyguard. We had spent countless weekends together, roaming around Lhasa, hiking, fording rivers, going to sacred places, offering incense in temples and sharing meals. He could eat a lot, and every time I took him for a meal, I told him to eat his fill. He could put away five steamed buns or three big bowls of rice, which I thought was eating his fill, but I found out it wasn't, because once I had invited a friend for lunch and cooked three *jin* of noodles, but my friend had to cancel, so I told Tenpa Nyima he had to help with the noodles. He ate them all, wiped his mouth and said, I am finally full.

During the Saga Dawa Festival, everybody visits sacred places or circumambulates sacred mountains. The festival lasts for seven days. Tenpa Nyima was the only student in my class who over the seven days made seven trips all around Drepung Monastery, prostrating himself with each step the whole time. He was covered head to foot in dirt because of the repeated prostrating, which also bloodied his forehead, palms and knees. He recited *om mani padme hum* thousands of times. Sangnyi went around twice and then gave up exhausted. Over the seven days, Sangnyi made more than a dozen bottles of yogurt for Tenpa Nyima, and for the last two days of the pilgrimage, Sangnyi's mother made knee pads for him and got Sangnyi to take them to him. Tenpa Nyima's piety and arduous pilgrimage made him famous.

Tenpa Nyima had come from his family's home in Nagchu to Lhasa when he was four. His parents sent him to a monastery, where his paternal grandfather looked after him. He stayed in the monastery until he was nine, when he moved to his parents' home on the grounds of the cement factory. His grandfather had worked his entire life in the monastery kitchen, gathering the firewood and doing the cooking. I once asked Tenpa Nyima if his grandfather was a monk or on the monastery staff. Tenpa Nyima answered that his grandfather was a monk, of course. But I don't think he could have been, otherwise he would have spent his retirement in the monastery rather than at home. This detail puzzled me, but I didn't pursue the matter with Tenpa Nyima, fearing it might bruise his pride.

Tenpa Nyima was sitting by his grandfather's side, speaking low into his ear, the two of them sharing a moment of closeness. I couldn't understand what he was saying. I watched as the old man extended a trembling hand, which Tenpa Nyima took and squeezed lightly. The old man looked very emotional. An odd sound came from his throat. I asked Tenpa Nyima what was wrong. Tenpa Nyima said that's just the way he is, he's old, and he cries a lot. I could see that, as he was crying. When the sound of his crying got louder, Tenpa Nyima took his grandfather's head in his arms, leaned close to his ear and spoke to him again. The old man seemed to say something back, but I couldn't hear what. Tenpa Nyima turned to me and said, Granddad says there is money in his bag and to make sure I don't go hungry. Granddad says after he dies, he wants me to carry him to Drepung for a sky burial. Then the two of them hugged, crying.

Tenpa Nyima's father came back, and Tenpa Nyima's teacher from primary school was with him, a man named Lodro. We knew each other. I described Tenpa Nyima's situation to Lodro. I said that I thought that because Tenpa Nyima had grown up with his grandfather, there was distance between him and his parents, so his parents didn't favour him, which wasn't good for the boy's development. I said Tenpa Nyima was a great lad with a great future. Lodro translated everything for Tenpa Nyima's father. I could tell he was also adding comments of his own. As we talked, Tenpa Nyima went and washed his face, then got the container of butter tea from the corner of the room and prepared some for us. It was ready quickly, and Tenpa Nyima poured a bowl each for Lodro and me, and for his father, then he took a bowl over to his grandfather, bending down and holding the bowl to his grandfather's lips. He fed the tea to his grandfather mouthful by mouthful, and tears again fell from the old man's eyes.

When I took my leave, I emphasised to Tenpa Nyima's father that he had to give the boy enough to eat and should not hit him over just anything. Then I went to Tenpa Nyima's grandfather, pressed my palms together and raised my hands to him. I told him not to worry about Tenpa Nyima. He reached his trembling hands out from under his quilt. I took them in mine and held them tightly. He opened his eyes wide and looked at me, as if to look deep into my soul. I couldn't tell from his eyes what he was thinking, but I knew they were the unfamiliar eyes of an old man on the verge of death. I was to be one of the last people he saw after nearly a century of life. I had to leave, but he had my hands and would not let go. It took a great effort for Tenpa Nyima to prise the old man's hands from their grasp on mine, and in that moment, as I remember, I seemed to see the old man's eyes cloud over.

He passed away two days later. There was no funeral, just silent prayers to send him on his way. The night before Tenpa Nyima's crisis, he came running over to the school to tell me that he was going to spend the night with his grandfather saying prayers for him to help his soul find peace. He said early the next morning he would carry his grandfather to the sky burial site. He said I could come to watch. He knew that I always wanted to observe the mysterious sky burial rite, but I said no. I knew strangers were not allowed to witness sky burial, in part out of fear that if strangers were there, the vultures would not descend.

I didn't know if I was a stranger to them or not.

I told Tenpa Nyima to see the old man off, and I said I would burn incense for him.

Tenpa Nyima was in deep sorrow but also relieved because his grandfather could finally go where he had longed to go. Tenpa Nyima said his grandfather had many times gone and lain on the sky burial platform at Drepung Monastery, praying that he soon could give himself to the sky. This amounted to promising yourself to the heavens in advance. I had never burned incense before, but on that calm night, smoke spiralled up in front of my window from incense I lit.

That night, I had the very clear sense that I could hear the murmur of a sutra being chanted somewhere, but I didn't know where. The sound fell on my window lattice just like the moonlight. It never occurred to me that the next morning heaven's emissaries would refuse the old man, approaching but then flying up and away.

14. Mother

Even during the Maoist years, Mother's will was indomitable,
nothing could overcome her. When she told jataka *stories*
about wise birds, the nine-coloured deer, the virtuous tortoise, and Prince Sattva
and the tiger,
she never explained the allegories or the Buddhist terms,
and so they just seemed like ordinary children's stories.

Even though Ukyi Lhamo's faith wasn't pure, it had been part of her psychological makeup since childhood. We are first brought to a faith merely as a custom to which we are introduced by our parents. Later, it may become true faith. But if we haven't formed the habits when we are young, if we don't have it in our blood, then our faith can never be natural. Why does religion seem so natural among Tibetans? Because their faith is, first and foremost, a way of life that is passed from generation to generation.

Ukyi Lhamo was her mother's youngest child. She had two older brothers and three older sisters. Her mother's name was also Ukyi Lhamo. Her mother had plans for her youngest daughter, which is why she gave her own name to the girl, as if completing a circle, a turn of the wheel of transmigration. This is a common custom in Tibet. Her mother was Tibetan but living in Beijing and raising six children during that age of conformity, she appeared to be exactly like any other young mother. She had a job and she took care of the household. She had long since put away her Tibetan clothing and even wore her hair in the same bowl cut that all women had in those days. Her children had Tibetan names, Ukyi Lhamo's siblings were Dawa, Nyima, Drolma, Yangzom and Jigme, but none of these names were ever used, and the family eventually forgot about them. The children had Chinese names, taking their father's surname. When they filled out forms, they always put down Han Chinese as their ethnicity, and the youngest, Ukyi Lhamo, was no exception. It was the 1970s and housing was tight. The family lived in a typical apartment building right on campus, there was nothing to make them different from any of the other families that lived there on top of one another. There was nothing that marked them as special, which was not permitted in any case.

The children knew nothing about Tibet, naturally, and didn't take much notice of the fact that their mother was Tibetan. Children don't want to be different in any way at all. They loved their mother, of course, that goes without saying. Indeed, they loved their mother much more than they did their strict father. Mostly this was because their mother could not control them and they never obeyed her. When she was looking after them, they ran wild. She was a Buddhist so they didn't respect her authority, they even found her religion ridiculous. For example, when she was anxious about something or something had upset her, she would put her palms together, close her eyes and recite something to herself, behaviour so unusual for the Maoist era, even towards the end of it, that it made them laugh out loud. For a time Ukyi Lhamo's mischievous older sisters liked to provoke her mother to prayer. For example, they might suddenly yell, Oh no! The building's on fire! Or, Shen Jiayuan (Ukyi Lhamo) fell out of the bed! Then Ukyi Lhamo's naughty siblings would wink at each other and say, Look, Mum's praying again! It worked every time, but Ukyi Lhamo (the mother) never spanked them, because hitting someone was unthinkable for her. She couldn't even speak harshly to anyone, let alone hit them. The most she would do was shake her head and sigh. Her bosses at the university criticised her more than once over her habit of praying, and she wrote countless self-criticisms about it. She was even taken into custody and investigated once. She managed to stop praying in public, but at home she did not stop.

If putting her hands together as she recited a sutra was merely a habit of Mrs Ukyi Lhamo's that her children laughed off, she did something else, usually in secret, which the children could not laugh about. She had a statue of a goddess that she kept hidden. It had many arms and looked exactly like the terrifying statue of the goddess Cundi kept behind the iron bars in the film *Serfs*. She was very secretive about the statue, and not all her children had seen it. For the children who had never seen it, it was all the more frightening to them in imagination when they talked about it. Some of them said Cundi's eyes were blue, some said white, but they agreed that her brows arched, her lips were red and she had an eye in the middle of her forehead.

The secret statue was kept locked away in a compartment inside a wardrobe. Mrs Ukyi Lhamo kept the key to the compartment on her at all times, even when she slept. A very, very few times, some of the children caught a glimpse of the scary, many-armed goddess. This happened when their mother thought no one else was home or after the children had gone to bed. Each time she opened the wardrobe, she did so quietly. She stood before it, hands together, then dropped to her knees and recited something. She usually did this on a day during an important festival, such as the Saga Dawa Festival, the Sho Dun Festival or Galden Namchot, the anniversary of Tsongkhapa's *parinirvana*. These were the times she prayed to the goddess in secret. But sometimes the children weren't asleep, and they would muster the courage to get up and look through the door crack, their scalps tingling with fright as they watched their mother. The many-armed goddess was terrifying. How could a person have so many arms? There were *khata* below the statue, which the children called "white scarves", and bowls of offering water. They watched as their mother carefully dusted the statue and poured more water into the bowl, then she got down on her knees and prayed quietly. It made them nervous to watch her. Ukyi Lhamo's brothers always said, It's the Buddha from *Serfs*!

They had all seen this famous film, more than once. And they had vivid memories of the long bronze horns, the gloomy temples, the many-armed Cundi, all the types of torture, the white walls of the palace, the terrifying palace steps that led up and up and up into the clouds with the horns blowing in the background, and they had a feeling that it somehow had something to do with them. They knew that the location in the film was supposed to be their mother's ancestral home. It was impossible for them to believe she came from there. They didn't want to admit that their mother came from such a terrifying place, but there was no denying that she had the statue from the film. They kept this an absolute secret, never mentioning to anybody that their mother was Tibetan or that their own blood was half Tibetan.

Ukyi Lhamo was still small and hadn't seen the film (she saw it many years later, of course), but she understood enough of what her siblings whispered about to know something was going on that felt strange and frightening to her. Nothing is imprinted more securely on a young mind than a secret that brings unease and terror, and her memory of her mother's statue became part of the very foundation of her psychological makeup. But she was still very young at the time and hadn't seen the film, so her fear was abstract, indistinct and nameless. If Ukyi Lhamo's sisters were terrified of the little compartment in the wardrobe, they thought it housed a devil, Ukyi Lhamo in contrast was as much curious about the compartment as she was frightened by it. Many times she dreamed of the blue-eyed, many-armed goddess her sisters had described to her, they liked to scare her by talking about the devil in the wardrobe, but oddly in her dreams, she wasn't afraid of it, because when she dreamed of it, she always dreamed next of a bird, and the bird changed into Cundi, who could fly. She rode on the back of this bird-like, many-armed goddess as if on the flying carpet from the Arabian Nights. Ukyi Lhamo was fascinated by her mother's secret compartment and its demon, and one time she stole her mother's key, an audaciously brave thing to do.

Ukyi Lhamo could never forget what happened that day. Her mother was taking a bath, her clothes draped on a chair. Ukyi Lhamo saw her mother's little key, and her mind went straight to the compartment in the wardrobe. Quietly, she went over to the clothes, unfastened the key from her mother's belt and went into the inner room. She had to pull hard to open the doors of the big wardrobe, then she dragged over a stool and hauled herself up on top of it. She was a resourceful child. The door to the compartment creaked as she opened it, and, oh my, she beheld the gleaming many-armed Cundi. She was not at all afraid and even dared stroke the little arms of the statue with her finger. She looked at the *khata*, prayer beads and bowls of offering water. The little bronze goddess was so pretty, its eyes looked to one side, and it seemed to be smiling. It had so many arms wheeling all around it. This was Mummy's secret. She had wanted to see it for a very long time, and now finally she could. But why were her brothers so afraid of it? She thought about the frightened looks on her siblings' faces and that made her afraid. The goddess didn't scare her but the look on their faces did. She boldly reached out and picked up the prayer beads, but she put them down right away as if they had burned her hand and almost fell off the stool because she heard her mother yell her name.

—Yuanyuan, Yuanyuan!

Yuanyuan was Ukyi Lhamo's Chinese pet name, she was only five at the time. Ukyi Lhamo calmly locked the compartment, put the stool away and walked out of the room. She was not at all afraid of her mother. Her mother never scared her.

—Yuanyuan, have you seen my key?

Her mother spoke Mandarin with a Tibetan accent.

—I've got it, Ukyi Lhamo admitted, but she put the hand with the key behind her back.

—Why did you take it? Give it to me, now!

—I won't. I want a key too.

—What do you want a key for?

—I want to see the goddess!

Her mother cried out in surprise and disapproval. She immediately put her hands together, closed her eyes and began to chant. It was many years before Ukyi Lhamo understood the meaning of the mantra *om mani padme hum*. Just like her siblings, Ukyi Lhamo always laughed when her mother chanted these words, but this time her laughter was hesitant, halting, because this time she could see her mother's eyes moving behind her closed eyelids. But then Ukyi Lhamo surrendered to laughter and happiness. Her mother opened her eyes and reached out and slapped Ukyi Lhamo lightly. Well, to call it a slap is an exaggeration. It was more like she brushed her daughter's face lightly with her hand, no force behind it. Ukyi Lhamo did not give the key to her mother. She ran around the room until her mother finally caught her. Ukyi Lhamo said, If you let me go, I will give you the key. But this was a lie. As soon as her mother let go, Ukyi Lhamo ran. Her mother was beside herself. Had it been any other object, she wouldn't have cared, but the key was no ordinary object. She was very upset but physical violence was inconceivable for her. She couldn't even bring herself to yell at her daughter. She was not capable of taking the key back by force. Not knowing what to do, she put her hands together in prayer again, her eyes tightly closed, the corners of her mouth and her eyelids moving rapidly. Ukyi Lhamo was so shocked she stood still. She saw tears fall from the corners of her mother's eyes. Ukyi Lhamo had been about to start laughing again, but her mother's tears scared her into seriousness. She had never seen her mother cry before. Ukyi Lhamo was scared, and quickly and quietly she put the key into her mother's hand, then she started crying herself. Her mother stopped crying and asked Ukyi Lhamo a question.

—Why are you crying?

At this, Ukyi Lhamo started to laugh again.

Ukyi Lhamo wasn't entirely sure, but she thought it was sometime after this event that her mother began to tell her the stories. Only later did she realise they were religious stories. Mother told the stories to her siblings too but not as many as she told Ukyi Lhamo and not as systematically. None of the children guessed they were religious stories because most were about animals, the deer of nine colours, the brave parrot, King Sibi and the falcon, Prince Sattva and the tiger, the good dragon, the lion and the woodpecker, many, many stories. Often, when her mother reached the end of a story, Ukyi Lhamo would ask, What does it mean? Her mother would then patiently explain, but Ukyi Lhamo would only partially comprehend. The stories, Ukyi Lhamo found out when she was grown, were *jataka* tales. When her mother told the stories to her children, she never explained the allegories or the Buddhist terms, so they seemed like ordinary children's stories.

Mother knew what she was doing. Even during the Maoist years, her religious belief remained indomitable, and nothing could overcome the belief she kept hidden in her heart. What she was doing was creating new versions of the *jataka* stories for the Maoist era. She carefully elided the religious messages but kept the core of each story, which made the stories more concise and livelier. Ukyi Lhamo kept trying to get the key. She wanted to see the many-armed goddess again. Her mother knew there was danger in this, but she also took it as a religious sign, there was something special about her youngest daughter, otherwise why would she have taken the key? It was obvious that among her six children, Ukyi Lhamo was her hope, and so the *jataka* tales were to be planted in her mind from a young age.

Many years later, her mother finally revealed who the stories were about, telling Ukyi Lhamo about Sakyamuni and the fact that every living being has had former lives. She said that the *jataka* tales were about the Buddha's former lives. The stories about the good dragon, the deer of nine colours, and the woodpecker and the lion were all stories from Sakyamuni's former lives. She said that before Sakyamuni became the Buddha he had been through countless reincarnations, sometimes as a person, sometimes as a god, sometimes as an animal, until finally, as a twenty-nine-year-old man, he came to enlightenment under the Bodhi tree. Her mother told Ukyi Lhamo this twenty years later when Ukyi Lhamo was preparing to leave for France to study. Her mother gave her a newly published Chinese edition of the *jataka* stories and told her to take it with her. The stories were a gift that Ukyi Lhamo's mother gave her youngest daughter when she was little. At the time Ukyi Lhamo left for France, her mother had decided to leave Beijing and go home to Tibet, but Ukyi Lhamo was unaware of this. She didn't find out, she told Wang Mojie, until her father called her in France to tell her that after almost forty years in Beijing, her mother had finally gone back to Tibet. Her father had accompanied her, but as soon as they landed, the altitude gave him heart trouble, and after a week in hospital, he returned to Beijing. Her mother didn't go back with him, and she never went back.

15. Secrets

Lungshar's handwriting was graceful and attractive.
He liked to use the occasional English word or phrase and
sometimes wrote entire letters in fluent English,
but his wife, Ukyi Lhamo, never wrote back, ever.
Not a word, right up until she disappeared.

My mother had other secrets. She never talked about her past. It was as if she had never had parents or siblings nor any relatives. She was like that big rock in our garden at home. It is so entirely covered in moss and lichen and overgrown with leafy plants that you would never guess that it is actually a meteorite. It came from the sky. Mother came from Tibet, which is like coming from the sky. No one knew that her father was none other than Lungsharwa Dorje Tsegyal, who is often referred to by the single aristocratic family name Lungshar. Do you know about Lungshar? I am sure you don't. You have never even heard of him, I bet. Nobody in the interior has heard of him. Even most Tibetans these days have never heard of him, but if you take a peek into those dusty old files in the archives, you are sure to come across the name of my maternal grandfather.

Lungsharwa Dorje Tsegyal, Lungshar, was one of the first Tibetans to meet Westerners. He and his young wife, my maternal grandmother, lived in England for four years. He presented gifts to the British Queen on behalf of the Thirteenth Dalai Lama, met with senior British diplomats and studied the British parliamentary system. His wife, Ukyi Lhamo – my grandmother, my mother and I all have the same name – was only seventeen when they went to England. She was so beautiful and spoke such perfect English that British aristocrats all swooned at her feet. She often appeared in *The Times*, there is a photograph of her with Queen Mary.

Nobody in my immediate family, including my father and siblings, knew that so many of our relatives played important roles in Tibetan history. None of us knew that so many Tibetan historical figures were connected to us in so many ways. We didn't know my uncle, my mother's brother, Lhalu Tsewang Dorje, known as Lhalu, had been the commander of the Tibetan army. He is still in good health and is a vice chairman of the Tibetan Committee of the Chinese People's Political Consultative Conference. We knew nothing about the family history, it was as if it hadn't happened or had nothing to do with us. I did not know that when Lungshar returned from Europe, he delivered a petition to the Thirteenth Dalai Lama that advised reform. You can look it up. In his petition he wrote,

> The snowy Tibetan plateau is vast, larger than Britain, France, Germany and Italy combined. It is rich in natural resources and precious gems, but we have no mines and lack electricity. We are cut off from the outside world. We are undeveloped. We are so weak that a British expeditionary force of fewer than two thousand soldiers, after a march over the Himalayas from India, was able to easily take Lhasa. How are we to progress if we do not change?

My grandfather advised the Thirteenth Dalai Lama to make a geological survey of Tibet, investigate corruption and tax evasion, replenish the treasury, increase soldiers' pay and provisions, and invest in armaments expansion. The Dalai Lama agreed with this advice, placed his trust in Lungshar and appointed him Tsipon, head of the revenue office responsible for grain levies, and not long after this, he made him the commander-in-chief of the Tibetan military. My grandfather had power in both the government and the military and was one of the leaders in the Thirteenth Dalai Lama's "New Government". My grandfather pushed hard for reform and relentlessly went after those who were avoiding taxes and fined them mercilessly. He applied new grain levies and, in general, undertook what people came to call the Lungshar Reform Movement.

But a storm can arise out of a clear sky, and my uncle told me that when the New Government was achieving great success, the Dalai Lama suddenly passed away and everything was thrown into upheaval. The conservative faction launched a vengeful attack on the Lungshar Reform Movement at exactly the same time that my grandfather, who had a lot of power, had decided there was an opportunity for him to realise his political ambitions. According to my uncle, my grandfather, who had been heavily influenced by the West, had become overconfident and so didn't conceal his aspirations. He contacted more than one hundred young aristocrats from Lhasa and with them established the Kyicho Kuntun – Society of Seekers After Happiness. They made the bold proposal that the *kalon*, the three ministers, should lose their appointments for life and instead be elected every four years. Candidates for election as *kalon* would first be elected from among the members of the National Assembly, meaning that the *kalon* would have to answer to that assembly. But before the Kyicho Kuntun could act on their plan, they were betrayed by one of their own.

One of the main members of the Kyicho Kuntun, a man named Kashopa Choegyal Nyima, went in secret to Chief Cabinet Minister Trimon Norbu Wangyal and revealed what the Kyicho Kuntun was planning. He also made the alarming but entirely false charge that Lungshar was planning to assassinate Trimon and take power. Trimon relayed this false assertion to the regent, the fifth Reting Rinpoche, Thupten Jamphel Yeshe Gyaltsen. When Grandfather was at Drepung Monastery for a festival and not on his guard, they arrested him and other members of the Kyicho Kuntun. Uncle says my grandfather was first held at Drepung and then moved to a basement prison in the Potala known as the Sharchenchok.

Trimon levelled fabricated and contradictory charges against my grandfather. He claimed Grandfather wanted to destroy Buddhism, assassinate the *kalon* and establish a parliamentary system of government, but he also said Lungshar and his faction planned to establish a communist government. Trimon even claimed that Lungshar was a demon in human form. He said that when they arrested Lungshar, they found black magic mantras hidden in his shoes. Lungshar, he said, had contempt for the *kashag*, the cabinet, and the proof was that Lungshar built his home on land higher than the Meditation Cave of the Dharma King in the Potala. All these charges were nonsense, and some were illogical. For example, how did it make sense to charge him with intending to set up a capitalist parliamentary system but also say he wanted to establish a communist government? Nevertheless, my uncle said, one clear morning in the fourth month of the agricultural calendar, on a day when all across Tibet people were celebrating the Saga Dawa Festival, the government sent messengers to Lungshar's home to order the family to stay inside, and they posted sentries to ensure they did. On that day, Lungshar was convicted of all the crimes he had been accused of. He was sentenced to have his eyes gouged out, after which he would remain in prison at the Potala. The verdict also stipulated that no one from Lungshar's family could ever enter politics again. They were banned from holding any government position whatsoever. And that's not all. His children were to be sent to Lungshar's ancestral home in Dromo. But before this verdict was made public, my grandmother learned of it from someone she knew inside the government, and she took her youngest daughter, my mother, to hide at the home of Yuthok Tashi Dondrup, whom she was later to marry.

Before the verdict was made public, the regent, the fifth Reting Rinpoche, distanced himself from it. He said, "I am a Living Buddha, I cannot sign this, sign it yourselves!" So Trimon handed down a "personal written instruction". My mother's second oldest brother, Chaba Rusu, had married into the aristocratic family of Shatra Paljor Dorje and so was not accused in the case, but because he submitted a vehement petition to the *kashag* arguing against the verdict, he was accused by Trimon of "disobeying his superiors" and sentenced to be whipped, after which he was made to put on clothes of white *pulu* wool and ride sitting backwards on a yak past the crowds of Lhasa, and then he was banished to Dromo.

My uncle Lhalu Tsewang Dorje, Lungshar's son, had been adopted into the aristocratic, powerful Lhalu family because they lacked a male heir. Lhalu at that time held a fourth-rank position in the government as *kandron* and was intelligent and capable. Therefore, he was regarded as the most dangerous of Lungshar's relatives, and he was sentenced to have his right arm cut off. The Khenpo at the Sera Monastery asked for mercy on his behalf, and the sentence was withdrawn, but he was still dismissed from his position in the government.

Uncle Lhalu was my maternal grandfather and grandmother's eldest son and had been born in England. His birth name was Lungsharwa Tsewang Dorje, but when he was young, he was given to the Lhalu family, one of the greatest aristocratic families in Tibet.

Both the Eighth and the Twelfth Dalai Lamas were from the Lhalu family, and the Lhalus maintained ties to all the Dalai Lamas from the Eighth to the Thirteenth. The Lhalu family name came from the name of its estate, "Lhalu Gatsal", which means "park where gods and Naga's children play". Lhalu Gatsal was large and stretched across the entire western limit of the city of Lhasa. Long ago there were huge trees there. It was sunny and warm and there were many natural ponds as bright as mirrors. It was absolutely gorgeous. The first to fall in love with the place was the Sixth Dalai Lama, Tsangyang Gyatso, who had a palace built on an island in the middle of a pond there. When construction was over, he often came in his monk's robes to Lhalu Gatsal to relax and enjoy himself. After Tsangyang Gyatso was deposed as Dalai Lama, he lived in the palace for a time and there wrote nostalgic songs and poems. The Lhalu family came to prominence after the death of the Seventh Dalai Lama. A regent directed a search that took years before finally, at a place called Lhari Gang near Shigatse, in the home of a farming family, they found the child reincarnation of the late Dalai Lama in the boy Jamphel Gyatso, and he became the Eighth Dalai Lama. As was the custom, his father, Sonam Dhargye, was given a title and land, he was made a duke, entitled to adorn himself with rubies and given the beautiful Lhalu Gatsal estate. And so, when Jamphel Gyatso became the Dalai Lama, his family took the name Lhalu, after their new estate.

Because the lives of the Ninth, Tenth and Eleventh Dalai Lamas were brief, after Trinley Gyatso was enthroned as the Twelfth Dalai Lama, the kashag *was faced with a problem. Finances had been exhausted by the bestowing of estates to the families of three Dalai Lamas in quick succession, making it impossible to provide anything similar to the family of the new Dalai Lama. The solution was found in the family of the descendants of the Eighth Dalai Lama. The family was rich but was without a male heir. So the* kashag *had the Twelfth Dalai Lama and his family adopted into the Lhalu family, raising the status of the Lhalus for a second time.*

When my uncle was adopted into the Lhalu family he was twelve. Lady Lhalu was already in her thirties but remained uncommonly beautiful. Her name was Yangdzom Tsering, and she was the youngest daughter of Shatra Paljor Dorje. She took

Buddhist vows at a young age but remained with her mother at the beautiful family estate by the Kyichu – the Lhasa River. The Shatra estate was just east of the estate of the family of the Thirteenth Dalai Lama. His elder brother, Duke Langdun, happened to meet Yangdzom Tsering, fell in love with her at first sight and soon married her.

But storms may rise out of clear skies, and in 1904 British troops invaded Tibet, easily overcame resistance and marched into Lhasa. The Thirteenth Dalai Lama fled to Mongolia. Duke Langdun accompanied him but died of an illness on the way. Yangdzom Tsering was left a widow and so was married to Lhalu Jigme Namgyel, a nephew of the Eighth Dalai Lama. In another unfortunate event, Lhalu Jigme Namgyel died suddenly when he was thirty-seven, leaving the unlucky Lady Lhalu a widow once again. She was left to maintain Lhalu Gatsal on her own. She had no children, had lost two husbands and was feeling hopeless. She wrote to the Thirteenth Dalai Lama saying that because the patriarch of the Lhalu family had died with no male heir, she requested that the Lhalu estate be turned over to Lhasa's three great monasteries and she be allowed to become a nun.

The Dalai Lama refused Lady Lhalu's request, commenting that the Lhalu estate was one of the most beautiful sites near the Potala Palace and that to break it up would be inauspicious. The Dalai Lama insisted that the Lhalu family must continue, and he directed that a male heir be found for it. A husband for Lady Lhalu was to be found in one of Lhasa's aristocratic families, and the major-domos convened to make this happen. They produced a list of names of young men, but when they presented it to the Dalai Lama, he rejected it and instead chose someone not on the list. He chose the eldest son of Lungshar, Lungsharwa Tsewang Dorje, which is evidence of how much the Dalai Lama valued Lungshar. But Tsewang Dorje was only twelve, therefore it was declared that he would be "first be the adopted son, later the husband". And that is how Lungsharwa Tsewang Dorje became the Lhalu family heir and why as Lhalu Tsewang Dorje he earned promotion to kandron.

He was given as the adopted son to the family matriarch, and his family name was changed to Lhalu. The affair of the Society of Seekers

After Happiness was massive, and as Lungshar's son, my uncle was no longer allowed to hold a government position. The matriarch, Lady Lhalu, knew that if they had no one in the *kashag* then even such a powerful clan as the Lhalu was not going to be able to hang on to its wealth. She had no choice but to humble herself and bribe high officials in the *kashag*. She managed to arrange the marriage of a distant relative of hers, a young woman who knew how to make herself desirable, to Trimon, who was then already nearly sixty. It worked. After some persuasive pillow talk from his beautiful new wife, Trimon consented to my uncle Lhalu's return to government. But the wily Trimon had a condition: before my uncle could return to the government, he had to prove he was not Lungshar's son. This was impossible, of course, but Trimon did not expect Lhalu to prove he was not Lungshar's son. His intent was to publicly humiliate Lungshar. Trimon obviously hated Lungshar, otherwise he would not have gone to such lengths to humiliate him. Surprisingly, Lady Lhalu agreed to Trimon's demand. At her persistent urging, my uncle made many trips to Yuthok's home, asking to see his mother. To meet Trimon's condition he needed his mother's help. But not once did he see her. It was always Yuthok who received him. Because he could not see his mother in person, he was left with no choice but to write her an urgent letter with a full account of the situation. He told his mother that for the sake of his future, he wished her to write a petition to the *kashag* stating that the father of her first-born son, Lhalu Tsewang Dorje, was not Lungshar but was some other man. My grandmother wrote the petition and sent it to her son. When my uncle got it, he went straight to Trimon. Trimon was satisfied, and my uncle was restored to his official post.

My uncle made frequent trips to see his father in prison, swearing to him that what he had done was not only for the sake of the Lhalu family but also to save him, Lungshar. My grandfather could never accept what his son had done, it was too great an insult to my grandmother, nevertheless, he was relieved that his son, my uncle, had been restored to his position in the government. My grandfather's circumstance was tragic, but his spirits never flagged. Like all revolutionaries, he was faithful to what he believed in, and even though he lived his days in darkness, he wrote poetry to keep himself encouraged. His poems were full of passionate idealism. Years later my uncle could still recite them from memory, for example...

Our grand undertaking has only just begun,
but I am thwarted, trapped in prison.
Butchers came in their numbers and
amid their curses, eyeballs fell to the ground.
But oh let them take my eyes,
for they cannot take my conviction.
Blinded, I live with darkness,
why then lock me away in a dark cell?
My prison may be dark,
but there is light in my heart.
Within me there is peace, piety and devotion.
Why then is the night so dark and deep?

So it was, Grandfather was in prison and his wife married Yuthok. Nevertheless, Grandfather remained a man of high ideals. He was very understanding of my grandmother, never saying a word that was critical of her. He never told her he missed her, he never asked that she come see him. The person he always spoke of was his youngest daughter, my mother. She was only three or four and hiding from danger at Yuthok's home with her mother. She had been only about a year old when Grandfather had been put in prison, so he couldn't have had any real impression of her, but again and again, he told my uncle that he missed Ukyi Lhamo. He was always talking about her. Of course, when he said he missed his daughter Ukyi Lhamo, he really meant he missed his wife. My uncle understood this, and whenever he was going to go see his father, he first went to Yuthok's home near Jokhang Temple to get my mother and bring her with him. My mother thought of Yuthok as her father, not Lungshar in his dark cell. Every time, the gloomy prison cell frightened her to tears, even though my grandfather would put on big glasses with dark lenses so that his empty eye sockets didn't scare her. He laughed and sang for her. He taught her nursery rhymes and told her stories from the *Sutra of One Hundred Parables*. And every time, my mother eventually stopped crying and cheered up. Whenever she left, my grandfather said the same thing, Say hello to your Mama for me. But you are too little, he said, you won't remember. Tell you what, take this letter to your Mama for me!

Grandfather had been blinded, but his writing was still neat and elegant. Sometimes he would include a beautifully written word or phrase in English and sometimes he would write the entire letter in English. But Ukyi Lhamo, my grandmother, my mother's mother, never wrote back, ever, not one word.

16. Tibetan Folksong

Her eyes had been smelted by the sunlight to the colour of amber.
The colour grew richer as her eyes brimmed with tears.
Karma Rishi was over, Sho Dun was over, the riverbank was empty.
We gathered scraps of wood and came home, arms full.

Sangnyi, I called, come down, come down, you'll fall. Come down, Sangnyi, come down, it's your turn.

Sangnyi climbed down from the Corkscrew Willow and almost fell, but Lhadron caught her. Corkscrew Willows are only two or three metres tall. They are pretty and spiral as they grow, hence the name. Sangnyi stood on one side of the tree, Lhadron on the other, their backs to the tree, facing two different watercourses, one the emerald Lhasa River, the other a tributary. Picture it. Two rivers. We were on an island, with water on both sides and a stone bridge to the bank. The island had a pretty name, Nyizhon Lingga. It was a natural playground for the children. My goal that day was to make all the children happy, and I had just about succeeded. As soon as they crossed the bridge they started to run around, they were very happy, racing about, setting up the blue-and-white tarpaulin, turning the island into our very own summer resort.

—Kalsang Dekyi, Kalsang Dekyi, I said, you lot can start. Sangnyi, get ready. After they've performed, it's your turn.

Kalsang Dekyi and her group ran out fast from behind the tarpaulin onto the grass. They were all dressed up, and they danced, flinging their colourful long sleeves. They looked like goddesses. It was a few days before the start of the Sho Dun Festival, and they were wearing their festival dresses. They sang as they danced. Gulls swooped from the river over the island, flying through the song, dropping diamonds of water on the girls. They sang and danced, water sprites among the trees, transmigrated birds. Lhadron, Chokyi and Sangnyi were all children from the village. But that day Lhadron was dressed every bit as nicely as the girls from the cement factory. In her long skirt, her ornamented braid coiled on top of her head and with her bracelets and silver and turquoise jewellery, she looked all grown up. Chokyi wasn't quite so done up, but she was dressed neatly and gracefully. Sangnyi was wearing what she always did, nothing particularly Tibetan about it. She had on her usual black trousers and trainers and the brown corduroy jacket she was already outgrowing. You could tell the jacket was freshly washed as it was worn white in a few places where it had been scrubbed too much.

All the children were eating snacks. Sangnyi had brought a small bottle of homemade yogurt and a bag of *tsampa* in brown sugar. I said, Sangnyi, give me a little *tsampa*, I've tried everything the others brought, now I want to try yours. Sangnyi stood there with her bag in her hand, not sure what to do. I took a little of her *tsampa* and ate it. Sangnyi, I said, your *tsampa* and brown sugar is really good. Sangnyi blushed. I said, Sangnyi, everybody else has done something. You're the only one who hasn't performed. I've heard you sing. You sing well. I told her that once when I was walking back from the monastery, I heard her singing. She had a load of firewood on her back and was taking the path back to the village from the mountain. She was singing as she walked. As soon as she saw me, she stopped singing and hurried towards home. Sangnyi didn't answer me. She blushed and wouldn't look at me. I could see the bashfulness on her face but there was something else there too. I sang to her softly, The mountain stream, it flows to the east, My valley home, it lies to the south. Then I said to her, That's what you were singing that day. After a while, Sangnyi stood up, turned towards the river, looked into the distance, and sang.

The mountain stream, it flows to the east
My home, it lies to the south
Please, oh please, take the turn
And bring me to my door

The mountain stream, it flows to the east
My home, it lies to the south

The sun is going down
The sheep still graze beyond the mountain

Sangnyi sang only fragments of songs, never the whole thing, and her school attendance was rather "fragmentary" too. There was always some problem at home. Once, I realised that Sangnyi hadn't missed just a day or two, she hadn't come to school for almost a week, so I knew something was wrong. I also felt guilty and irresponsible because a week had gone by before I noticed her absence. I asked Lhadron, Where's Sangnyi? She shook her head. I asked Chokyi. She shook her head too. I decided to go and look for her. I told Tenpa Nyima, Lhadron and Chokyi to come with me, and we walked out of the campus gate. We took the path up through Danba towards the monastery. Sangnyi's house was at the highest part of the village at the edge of the monastery grounds. The wind off the mountain reached Sangnyi's house before it hit the rest of the village, and so when it started to blow, it was the prayer flags on her house that waved first. I remembered the irregular shape of her family's courtyard and the little winding brook by their front gate. I remembered that after the little barefoot boy came back to the house, he got spanked by Sangnyi and then by his mother. When I heard about this, I gave Sangnyi fifty yuan to buy shoes for her brother. She took it but later made me take it back.

It was midday and the sun was beating straight down, glaring off the walls, shining on the water. The sun was so severe I didn't dare glance at it. But my students did, they were used to the sun, and they weren't afraid of it. Their eyes were smelted by the sun to the colour of amber, even when they were still very young, like Sangnyi's little brother.

—Sangnyi! Isn't that Sangnyi? Chokyi said and pointed into the distance.

Up ahead I could see two small figures coming around a bend, their backs bent under loads of firewood. Lhadron said the one on the left was Sangnyi. Chokyi and Tenpa Nyima agreed. I couldn't tell which one was Sangnyi because all I could see of them was their feet moving under the big burlap sacks of firewood. Lhadron and Chokyi yelled Sangnyi's name together. The burlap sacks stopped and turned heavily and slowly until we could see the two girls, their sweat glistening in the sunlight. They stopped for only a moment and didn't seem to see us, then they turned back around and continued on their way. I asked Chokyi if it was Sangnyi or not, Chokyi said yes, and Lhadron and Tenpa Nyima said yes too, so we all started to yell together. Sangnyi stopped again. Her companion continued walking rather hesitantly and kept turning to look back. Sangnyi stopped but didn't turn around, so I still only saw her legs and the sack on her back. It was a vision from a dream, a burlap sack walking along a mountain path.

—Sangnyi, where have you been? Why haven't you come to school?

Sangnyi lowered her head, saying nothing. The big sack on her back blocked the sun but even in the shade her face looked hot, her hair steamed with sweat, as if she had just washed it.

—Put the wood down, I said.

Sangnyi moved a few steps and leaned her load against a wall. With the weight on the wall, she was able to bring her hands forwards and untie the rope around her chest. She slowly squatted down and carefully settled the sack of firewood on the ground. It was going to be very hard for her to get such a load on her back again. It was so heavy that she had to bind it to herself until she got home. If she stopped to rest on the way, it would be with the wood still on her. I had no idea how far she had walked already or where she had found the wood. Chokyi told me Sangnyi picked up the wood from a sawmill run by the military near the river and that she did the same. I turned and looked down beyond the road, beyond the wetlands and the barracks, and I could just make out the white glare from the Lhasa River.

—Did you miss school to collect that firewood?

Sangnyi wiped away some sweat, giving no sign she had heard me, and her look said she did not want to answer. In the sunlight, Sangnyi's eyes were the colour of amber. I had noticed that Tenpa Nyima's eyes were the same colour. I didn't know what the colour of their eyes said about their feelings for the Tibetan sun. I said to Tenpa Nyima, On Sunday we'll go to the sawmill together. OK, Tenpa Nyima said earnestly. He knew I meant that we would do it to help Sangnyi.

—Sangnyi, you come to school tomorrow.

She ignored me and didn't look at me. I decided I had better go to see her dad. I had heard he worked in Lhasa. I asked Sangnyi, When is your dad coming home, when is his day off? Sangnyi looked at me blankly, as if she couldn't understand what I was saying.

—I want to have a talk with your dad.

Sangnyi said nothing. It was still as if she couldn't hear me. Sangnyi never spoke much but this time was different. It was always hard to get through her silence but this was different. Then her lip started to tremble and her eyes filled with tears. Her eyes had been smelted by the sunlight to the colour of amber, and the colour grew richer as they brimmed with tears. I realised that I had forgotten a warning never to mention Sangnyi's father if I could help it. I found out later that

Sangnyi didn't know who her biological father was. Her father had stayed in the village for three days and then left. Nine months later, Sangnyi was born. Her stepfather stayed around a little longer but left for the city after two years. He had a stall on Barkhor Street selling miscellaneous stuff, ritual implements for worship, prayer wheels, tinned goods, army caps and so on. Sangnyi didn't cry easily, she kept her feelings to herself. I changed the subject and asked Sangnyi where her mum was. Sangnyi wiped her eyes and pointed ahead. The tears changed something in Sangnyi, made her drop her silent armour, softened her and made her obedient.

I told Tenpa Nyima to carry the firewood, but Sangnyi grabbed it and held on. Tenpa Nyima kept fighting for it but couldn't get it from her, she was stubborn to her bones. She hoisted the sack onto her back and let Tenpa Nyima help her tie the thick rope, like he was tying her up. Obviously, Sangnyi and her companion had helped each other the same way.

We walked to the threshing ground. I had my reasons for expecting Sangnyi's mother to be a particular sort of woman, but I was surprised. She was nothing at all like her daughter. She was wearing a thick black robe, and she looked tough. Her headscarf framed a face with a light complexion, sharp, strong bones and large eyes surrounded by wrinkles. She had been pretty when young but the anger that came later had warped her. She was working, a wooden threshing rake in her hands, and she looked at me with hostility. I told her why I had come. She answered sharply, saying that one of the children had hit Sangnyi and called her dirty and smelly, so when she told her to go to school, Sangnyi refused. She went right to the point, her jaw tight, and it was clear that it wasn't her idea for Sangnyi to stay away from school but Sangnyi's own. My students had been bullying Sangnyi.

—Is this true? Sangnyi, tell me, who was it?

Sangnyi said nothing. Her stony look told me she did not want to say.

—Do *you* know? I asked Lhadron and Chokyi, but the anger on my face scared them and they said nothing. Tenpa Nyima told me that it was mostly Wangchuk, also Penpa Tsering. They mocked Sangnyi all the time, called her smelly, and hit her too, he said. Penpa Tsering, that little bastard! I poked Tenpa Nyima in the chest.

—You're the class monitor, why didn't you tell me?

—I, I beat up Penpa Tsering, Tenpa Nyima said.

And Wangchuk! I stewed over his name. I had been to his house, and of all the homes I had seen, it had the fanciest prayer room, the nicest furniture and the biggest colour TV, and his dad gave me beer to drink, not just barley wine.

—If this is what it's about, Sangnyi, tomorrow you come to school, I said.

Sangnyi shook her head but looked at her mother.

—Don't look at me. Tomorrow take your brother back to Lhasa, get him settled, then leave him there.

As her mother spoke, Sangnyi teared up again. Apparently, her missing school was also because of her little brother. She had to look after the little brother who had floated his shoe down the stream like a boat.

—Sangnyi, how about this? Don't go to Lhasa tomorrow, instead find some time to come over to the school. We'll talk about getting you back to school, OK?

That was what she wanted to hear, so she wiped her eyes and nodded. I wanted to talk to her about her little brother, I wanted to help in any way I could. I told her to make sure she came to school the next day. But she didn't turn up. I knew it wasn't going to be easy to help Sangnyi, it was likely to be very difficult in fact. I didn't know what to do. I had to stop myself from punching Penpa Tsering. One morning a week later when I was thinking about going to see Sangnyi's mother again, I looked up to see Sangnyi standing in front of me in the classroom. She took her seat. I knew nothing need be said. I asked her, How is your little brother? She turned red and didn't answer, but I knew the storm had blown over. The next time I visited Wangchuk's house, his father offered me beer again, but I asked for barley wine.

That Sunday I took Tenpa Nyima and Sangnyi to the sawmill. Tenpa Nyima brought some rather poor barley wine, Sangnyi brought yogurt, and we had the wine and the yogurt by the river. Karma Rishi was over, the Sho Dun Festival and the Ongkor Festival were over, and there was nobody else there on the riverbank. We collected woodchips, sticks and bark and came home, arms full. Sangnyi sang,

The mountain stream, it flows to the east
My home, it lies to the south
Please, oh please, take the turn
And bring me to my door

The mountain stream, it flows to the east
My home, it lies to the south
The sun is going down

The sheep still graze beyond the mountain

During my years in Tibet, I collected more folksongs than I could count, but I had never heard the song quoted by Wang Mojie. Tibetan folksongs are soul-stirring, always surprising in their melody and lyrics. I wrote an essay, "Tibetan Folksong", with my thoughts about the genre. Wang Mojie read it and said nothing at first, but eventually he said it was one of the few things he had ever read that captured the real Tibet. I don't mention this to brag but to establish that Wang Mojie is one of the very few people who understand my writing. It is because I have Wang Mojie as a reader, and other readers like him, that I take my writing so seriously. Wang Mojie hasn't done much writing himself, but I find him to be among the most insightful readers of literature of our generation. I suggested to him once that he should write something in the manner of what Barthes and Derrida wrote, not your typical literary criticism but a sort of philosophical essay. In our lifetime, philosophy to a degree has become a form of literature, and literature has become a type of philosophy. Wang Mojie said I overestimated what he was capable of or more correctly, I overestimated what our generation was capable of producing. True, I very likely overestimated our generation; my passion for literature sometimes gets me a little puffed up, and while Wang Mojie's level-headedness deflated me, I admired it.

I have included my "Tibetan Folksong" essay below for any interested reader.

I like to listen to the silence of the open spaces in Tibet. There is something to be heard in that silence.

There is beautiful music in the rivers that wind across the land. A river with a skein of birds can sing like a harp. There is music in the pastureland and music in the villages. There is music in the air. It is carried on the wind. There is song trembling in the air. You hear someone singing from far away, and the sound echoes so that you can't tell where it comes from, and you stand alone in all that empty space, the singing all around you.

If you are open to it, the very stones will sing to you. The stones sing the songs of long ago. They sing of the Stone Age.

They sing of calloused hands. When I look at my hands, I can feel how distant that past is. The folksongs come from that same distant past.

This feeling is especially strong when you hear someone singing at twilight or in the quiet of the night.

When you are walking through those wide-open spaces, if you just listen, you will hear the singing. I spent days walking over grassy slopes and along lakes. There were bright points of light in the snow on the mountains like innumerable suns. I felt as desolate as the emptiness all around me. I walked and walked. I stopped in villages where only stones grew. I might stay for one or two days, I could have stayed for years, anything was possible. Even when I was feeling completely lost and alone, I never felt lonely because I was out in the natural world, and I could feel myself expanding outwards into nature. I walked through wilderness, I walked along river after river, I passed through village after village. Stones lay across the landscape. There were villages built of stone. There were windows of stone. Sometimes I would stay in a village for days. During the day, I felt I was sleepwalking, and at night I never slept deeply. I was always alert to something, but not because I felt in any danger, it was just a half-waking state of consciousness that became my habit. Once I heard folksong that didn't seem to be drifting over from a distant hillside, the song seemed to suddenly fill the window of the house I was staying in, and it was as if the window had become a portal to somewhere else, and in that instant, in that ksana*, my world was turned upside down, and I felt a spiritual connection to the Tibetan sky.*

Here are the lyrics to one of the songs as I wrote them down in my notebook. Ukyi Lhamo translated them for me.

Let's talk about me
My love is a mountain
that can't be moved or shaken

Let's talk about you
Your love is mountain snow
that melts in the sun

Let's talk about me
My love is an emerald on the river bottom

that can't be washed away

Let's talk about you
Your love is a fish in the river
that is gone on the current

Let's talk about me...

I love the dialogue in this, the way the singer addresses his beloved. I love that even though the singer is a spurned lover and is sad, the song has its humour.

Tibetan folksong is the product of hard lives and a lot of suffering, but the songs are never heavy or depressing. They are uplifting, you just have to get into the mood they create. The songs are about universal concerns — birth, death, love, heartbreak, happiness, grief — all the emotions we experience in life, the eternal cycle of life, but the songs still sound personal and individual. It is like the singer is singing to the wildflowers. The songs speak of the resilience of the Tibetan people. Amid suffering and grief, the glad sound of the cries of the newborn still ring out in the air on bracingly cold mornings. Tibetan folksong turns the memory of suffering into lyric beauty. When a young woman becomes a mother, her songs no longer lament, her songs no longer are full of tears. She becomes a goddess, and her songs become lullabies. Her songs are mother's milk. Her songs are spring water. Her songs are moonlight. You can hear the sound of the heavens in Tibetan folksong.

At any moment on any night, any patch of sky over any village hidden in any mountain valley is likely to start to tremble with song, and sometimes a comet will trace snow-white across the sky at the same time. Even mountainside monasteries interrupt the quiet of the sky with song, and this song comes from dark temple halls where the sunlight barely reaches. Monasteries are unworldly places, but that can't stop the red-robed boy monks from singing. They are too full of life. Whenever they have the chance, or when they just can't help themselves, they break out in song.

A young monk stood on the topmost terrace with the vast white monastery compound spreading along the contour of the mountain below him. A huge, dense, disordered white jumble. Like a massive relief sculpture carved on the mountain itself.

Like glacial till deposited in the Cretaceous Period. There were innumerable small, dark windows in the monastery, a honeycomb of them. Up on the terrace, the boy could reach out and take a handful of cloud or pluck a star. And when the transcendent sound of his young voice broke through the silence of the night sky, it was natural and beautiful.

It was Galden Namchot, the day that honours Tsongkhapa.

Butter lamps burned in all the stone windows of the village. The points of lamplight on earth blended into the points of starlight in the sky. Galden Namchot celebrates the birth, parinirvana *and Buddhahood of Tsongkhapa. The butter lamps symbolise the vanquishing of spiritual darkness. The butter lamps and stars are Tsongkhapa's eyes. On the night of Galden Namchot, everyone seemed to be waiting for something. It was astonishingly quiet. Something felt imminent.*

Before dawn, I walked out of the village and up through the darkness and saw the lamps in the monastery windows blazing on the mountainside. The night went from black to blacker. The enormous shadow of the mountain was blacker than the night sky. The light of thousands of butter lamps broke through that darkness. The lights from the monastery lamps formed a fantastical geometric shape above me. It was ethereal, mysterious. It could have been the spirit of Tsongkhapa made manifest. It was beautiful. They burn juniper and cedar as an offering to the gods, and the long trails of juniper and cedar smoke rose softly into the empty sky above the monastery. Streamers of smoke, soaring slowly, and I imagined the trails of smoke were arms about to lift the entire monastery into the sky.

I felt my way forwards, the darkness rose up from my feet like water. It was about to submerge me, and I started to panic. I tripped and fell on the stone steps, but my hand felt something warm and soft. It was one of the many stray dogs that live in the monastery. It didn't seem surprised. It got up and leaned against me, like a brother. This startled me. It moved me. The warmth of it almost brought a tear to my eye.

In the now pale morning light, I could see the shadows of people flickering here and there on the terrace higher up in the monastery. They were like the shadows made on a wall by hands, now there, now gone. I thought I could see faces peering down, and although I couldn't make out any features, they seemed to be smiling. I had the sense that they were up there in nirvana, while I remained down in the mortal world in samsara. *Me and the dog, that was the world, but suddenly it didn't seem real, their world up there in nirvana seemed real, and I was excluded from it, I was not capable of enlightenment. This was a difficult thing to accept. The morning dew made everything damp, so now I was damp and dejected, but I was tough like stone, I decided, and the damp wasn't going to kill me, I didn't have to worry about that. I decided to have a smoke, but when I lit the cigarette, the dog, my brother, jumped up and vanished. The flame had spooked it. It wasn't my brother. It was sad to think there was no brotherhood in the world. Is there no brotherhood in the world?*

I was starting to think it was all a dream, a nightmare, and I was feeling a little afraid, and so I'm grateful to the young monk who started to sing. His voice broke the morning like a shout, dispelling the darkness and freeing me from the nightmare. I smoked cigarette after cigarette as I watched the boy and listened to him sing. My cigarette smoke rose up with the juniper and cedar smoke. My brother the dog hadn't liked it when I smoked, but I didn't need its company any more. I was back in the real world, my world, and reconciled to it, afraid no longer. It was just a man sitting below a monastery smoking a cigarette and a boy up in the monastery singing.

The young monk was out on a shift as a nightwatchman. I felt like a nightwatchman myself.

Up on the terrace, the young monk walked back and forth. When the wind blew out a butter lamp, he relit it. The flames from the lamps danced against his robe, and the light shone on his bald head and his girlish face. He was only fourteen or fifteen. The sky was getting light, and the slight fear I had felt in the dark was gone. As I watched the boy, I was thinking about children's stories. I was thinking about The Little Match Girl. *The boy looked composed, calm and focused. It surprised me that one so young could be so responsible in carrying out his job, and in fact, he couldn't. I watched as he started to play. He skipped and hopped across the terrace and suddenly started to sing. His voice was good, a boy's voice still, not a man's. At first, he was singing under his breath, but then as if he couldn't help it, he sang louder and louder. He had his eyes on the lamps and a burning torch in one hand. He skipped about, touching his torch to lamps that didn't need it because they were still burn-*

ing. He was dancing. His song had only five syllables. It was like a chant. He drew out the last word with something like a sigh. It sounded to me like this,

Yi-ya
Yi-yo – yo

It was beautiful and full of emotion and meaning. In the dawn light, the long, soft sigh made me relax completely, as if I were floating on air, rising slowly, flying through the sky. I wasn't sure where my soul was soaring to, but as the long last syllable faded away, I returned to Earth. There was a brief pause, and then his song started again. His voice caught the morning sun and rose up to the dawn sky. The world was flooded with light. The sky was now in full light, and the boy was like a paper cut silhouetted against the sky. The butter lamps were still burning.

I turned and left. I felt I had received some sort of enlightenment after my escape from the night. "Some sort of enlightenment", that's what I was thinking as I walked back down and reached the edge of the village. The morning was extremely still, and kitchen smoke curled up into the air. I thought I should go, go into the mountains and make a pilgrimage to Kailash. I wanted to pay my respects to the mountains and to the pastures. I wanted to find the origins of the young monk's song. I would not be daunted by distance or loneliness.

---

17. Avalokitesvara

My then eleven-year-old mother could hear nothing
because she was sitting on her round yellow khaden, *reciting* om mani padme hum.
From afternoon to twilight, she never moved from that spot.
When the butter lamps in the beautifully decorated Buddha niche brightened,
my eleven-year-old mother was illuminated with golden light...
like the thousand-armed Avalokitesvara.

More than once I asked my uncle Lhalu why Grandmother never wrote back to Grandfather and why she never went to see him. If she was afraid somebody might read her letters, she could have written in English. Isn't that what Grandfather did? Had she fallen in love with Yuthok Tashi Dondrup? If not, why did she marry him while Grandfather was in prison? Had Yuthok taken advantage of Grandfather's misfortune or had Grandmother forgotten her former love and shut herself away to lose herself in a new love? My uncle never answered. In Tibet it is acceptable for women to divorce and remarry, fate may bounce them from man to man, but my grandmother was unlikely to have been swayed by custom. She had been influenced by Western culture and didn't unthinkingly submit to tradition. She wasn't one to accept setbacks without a struggle. Who knows what she was thinking, so no wonder my uncle couldn't answer my questions, if he even cared about what I was asking. What he liked to talk about from that time was how he got his father out of prison. He said it was the most important thing he did in his life.

By the time my uncle Lhalu was promoted from *kandron* to *kadrung* (a secretary-aide to the *kalon*), Grandfather had been in prison for seven years. After his promotion, Uncle had more influence and was determined to rescue his father. He used his status to lobby important government officials and wrote a petition to the regent, the fifth Reting Rinpoche, that made a strong argument from the facts. He demonstrated that Trimon Norbu Wangyal's charges against his father were false. He described the poor conditions in the prison and said that because Lungshar did not have long to live, he hoped the regent would allow him to go home. The regent was sympathetic and approved Lungshar's release. This was happy news, but anyone who loved Lungshar and saw him could not be happy. My grandfather was a noble, dignified man, handsome and suave. He had been the most forward-thinking member of the *kashag* and had such uncommon ability that the Thirteenth Dalai Lama had seen Tibet's future in him. Lungshar's reputation was such that when the Lhalu family needed a male heir, they turned to his son. After seven years in prison, my grandfather was in such bad condition it hurt to look at him. He was thin and weak, his eyes, once so full of life, were now two dark, scarred holes. According to my uncle, when they came to remove his eyes, to bolster their courage for carrying out this awful, bloody deed, they drank a lot of barley wine. They drugged my grandfather with *langchen nyonpa*. They put yak's knucklebones on his temples. The bones were bound to his head with a leather strap that was tightened until his eyeballs bulged. It didn't work the way it was supposed to, his eyes didn't come all the way out, and so they used a knife. They cut out his left eye and held it up to his right eye, then they cut out the right eye. They poured boiling oil into his eyes to seal the wounds.

Lungsharwa Dorje Tsegyal came home, but the family mansion had fallen into disrepair, cobwebs were everywhere. In its heyday, the home had been elegant and modern, with guests always coming and going, but now it was dark and cold. Grandfather, however, couldn't see what the house looked like now.

Grandfather's sole wish was that my grandmother would return to him. But she didn't come to see him after his release, in fact, he never saw her again. Still, Grandfather missed her as strongly as ever, and he seemed lost without her. He would often go out on the balcony in the sunlight and "look" into the distance, he would do this for hours. He had lost the fervour of his youth, he was old and his spirits were low. At one point, according to my uncle, Grandfather got up the courage to write a long letter to my grandmother, spending months on it, pages and pages, and then he wrote to Yuthok. By then, Grandmother had been with Yuthok for almost a decade and they had a son. She didn't write back, of course, but Yuthok did. His letter made Grandfather happy because Yuthok promised to allow Grandmother to return to him. Grandfather thought Yuthok's promise was as good as an answer from her. But things didn't turn out as he expected. Grandmother did come back to the Lungsharwa mansion, bringing her nine-year-old daughter (my mother) with her, but she only came to the door and didn't set foot inside. One morning she brought her daughter to the door of the mansion and left her there. Then she walked away, disappearing into what for Lhasa was a rare misty morning. She was gone just like that, and no one in the family ever saw her again. Uncle later learned she had become a nun at the Tsamkhung Nunnery down an alley not far from Barkhor Street. She refused to see visitors, including family, and she wouldn't even consent to see her young daughter, my mother.

After she moved into Lungshar's home, my nine-year-old mother, as if following her mother's example, refused to speak. She had lived with the Yuthok family for eight years and everything in her new home was unfamiliar. They told her that she was now in her real home, but it didn't feel that way to her. She had two different fathers: Yuthok, with whom she had spent her whole life, and Lungshar, a father to her in name only. One father she knew from eight years of life with him, the other had been in prison the whole time. One father loved her as dearly as he loved her mother, one father was a man in dark glasses who told her tales from the *Sutra of One Hundred Parables*. She had lived with this contrast of heaven and hell her entire life. When her older brother, my uncle, came to collect her to take her to visit the prison, her mother, who never visited the prison herself, insisted that she go. She cried and argued back, saying she didn't want to go and that she would go only if her mother came too. But her crying and yelling were of no use, and she always had to follow her brother from the heaven of Yuthok's home to the hell of Sharchenchok Prison. From heaven to hell, this created a rupture in my mother's psyche from a young age, and when my grandmother left her with Lungshar, it was like being left in hell, especially when she saw those dark holes where his eyes should have been. Fortunately, the light of the Buddha illuminates everything. Fortunately, the eyes of the Buddha look down on all the world with compassion, and fortunately, Mother could see this light from the moment she was born.

The eyes of the Buddha gaze down on the world and all the myriad beings with mercy, and they looked with mercy on my mother and her father.

My mother could not bring much happiness to my grandfather, she could not replace my grandmother. After Grandmother disappeared, Grandfather fell into depression. He broke down completely and only recovered somewhat when word came that Grandmother had gone to Tsamkhung Nunnery. But then he grew more and more forlorn. He did not understand why she would refuse to come home or why she had gone to the nunnery. Had he known that things would turn out as they had, he would not have written to Yuthok. Not only had she not come back to him, but she had also turned her back on her entire family. Grandfather loved Grandmother and had never wanted to see her suffer, so he was grateful to Yuthok for looking after her. He just wanted his wife back, he didn't care about anything else, but now he had been deeply injured twice and was full of regret.

After Grandmother's disappearance and taking of her vows, my grandfather felt hopeless. He was too depressed to eat, and his health took a rapid turn for the worse. He was blind but still had butter lamps lit for him. During his final days, he would allow no one to sit with him except my mother, little Ukyi Lhamo. She was only nine, but Uncle says she was such a solemn child she seemed much older. Her voice sounded older than her years too, she had a husky voice, just like her mother did. I inherited this too, there is an unbroken chain of transmigration linking the three generations of Ukyi Lhamos.

Once, my uncle said, after Grandfather had been declining for a long time, he suddenly said something in English to my mother, who was eleven by then, and she answered him in simple English. Grandfather knew right away that she had learned her English from her mother. After that, he started to give my mother English lessons, which made him so happy and energised that for a time he seemed almost back to his old self. But this happiness did not last long, and one day my grandfather suddenly fell back into dark despair. He stopped teaching English to my mother and lay in bed all day saying nothing. Sometimes, for reasons we do not understand, the light in a life can just go out.

Grandfather did not speak. It was as if he had gone to sleep, never to wake. Mother did not speak either. Often the two of them were together all day, as silent as the dust dancing in the beams of sunlight. But even during those silent days, sometimes the frowning corners of his mouth (his eyes gone, he expressed himself with his mouth) would turn up in a small smile at some happy fantasy. From his fantasy, he would call out "Ukyi Lhamo", my mother's name, his wife's name, his wife's mother's name, her grandmother's name, the names of my maternal ancestors, generation after generation of Ukyi Lhamos, there has always been a Ukyi Lhamo. Ukyi Lhamo was many people: wife, daughter, grandmother and ancestor. And she was one eternal person, this was the thought that brought a small smile to Grandfather's face.

During Lungshar's last few days, his youngest daughter, my then eleven-year-old mother, spent each day by her father's side reciting the mantra of Avalokitesvara, preparing him for the next life. The sound of her reciting *om mani padme hum* lingered in Grandfather's ears, bringing him some peace. Her voice did not sound familiar to him, it was even like the voice of a stranger, but precisely for this reason, it seemed to him he was hearing a blessing bestowed upon him by the universe, as if a goddess was speaking to him from heaven. With a young girl's voice speaking the mantra to him, Grandfather was content.

Uncle remembers clearly that Grandfather died on the afternoon of 4 February 1944. That afternoon he woke up after being unconscious for days, he called his children to his side, held their hands and said he felt poorly and wanted to eat a *renchen rilbu*, a precious pill, to prepare for the road to the next life. He wanted the ritual text placed over his face, a piece of dark blue paper with a sutra written on it in gold. My uncle Lhalu had obtained both it and the pill at the Draklha Luguk Monastery below the Chagpori. Uncle says that Grandfather squeezed each of his children's hands in turn and then made them leave the room, but asked my eleven-year-old mother to remain with him. Mother was not afraid because she had spent many of Grandfather's last days alone with him. She followed his instructions and did everything correctly. She gave him the precious pill and removed his dark glasses. She paused and calmly studied the dark holes of his eyes, then she slowly put the blue paper with the sutra in gold over his face. Grandfather's last words were to ask if she was afraid, but she could not hear him, she was in some other space-time. Like the Bodhisattva of Compassion, she was sitting on the round yellow *khaden* she used for meditation and was chanting *om mani padme hum*. The sound of her young voice, as if from heaven, rose above her father and filled the room, filled the universe. From the afternoon into the evening, my mother, still only a child, sat by her father and repeated the mantra over and over. Finally, the butter lamps in the room abruptly grew brighter and then the largest of the lamps went out. At this, my uncles came back into the room together. They saw my mother sitting motionless, illuminated by the lamplight, looking like a little thousand-armed Avalokitesvara, the Bodhisattva of Compassion. Grandfather was gone, but she kept on reciting the mantra.

Grandfather was gone, and for a long time my mother's soul seemed to have departed with him, and she rarely spoke to anyone. Every day, Uncle said, when she wasn't sleeping or eating, she was sitting on her round yellow *khaden*, facing the Buddha in its pretty niche, reciting the mantra. Later, when Uncle took my mother with him to Lhalu Gatsal (dislocation, again), she still kept the *khaden* with her.

It was unusual for a dying soul to be seen off by a child, and it was very unusual for a dying father to be seen off by his daughter, but this is what my mother did, and it stayed with her for the rest of her life. At the Lhalu family estate, Uncle looked after my mother. To cheer her up he often took her to Tsamkhung Nunnery, and even though they never managed to get my grandmother to come out and see them, just spending time there made my mother happy.

You can't say that Lady Lhalu mistreated my mother, indeed she treated her so well you would think she had adopted my mother as her own. But to tell the truth, she didn't like my mother because she spent all day every day sitting on her *khaden*, never saying a word, ignoring everybody. Lady Lhalu suggested to my uncle that he send his sister away to be a nun since she sat in front of the Buddha all day anyway. Uncle said he liked the idea but kept putting it off. He didn't want to let her go. He had status as the male heir to the Lhalu name, but he was still relatively young and his position wasn't secure, especially after everything that had happened with his father, which marked him out as an outsider. He had never led the family, and even after he was promoted to *kadrung*, all the power in the family remained in Lady Lhalu's hands. Her suggestion for my mother was not acted upon, but this wasn't, of course, regarded as anything important. Not long after, however, the clan major-domo brought out the petition that had been presented to the Dalai Lama describing the family's need to find a male heir: they needed a husband for the widowed Lady Lhalu. He went back through the details, reminding everyone that when my uncle had come to the Lhalu family he had been taken in as a son because of his young age, but the plan had always been for him to marry Lady Lhalu. The major-domo said my uncle was now of age and should marry Lady Lhalu. She stayed out of it but sent word that she accepted the plan.

My uncle had no say in the matter. Five months after my mother moved into the Lhalu home, Lady Lhalu, who was fifty-six, and my uncle were married. Mother and son became wife and husband. They lived as such for seven years, after which she found him a proper bride, a young woman from the Thonpa family, Thonpa Sonam Dekyi, who was seventeen. Thonpa Sonam Dekyi was pretty, vivacious, cultured and interested in religion, so as soon as she met my mother, who was so reserved and eccentric, it was as if she had discovered some rare flower, and they became fast friends immediately. My mother was fifteen, so they were close in age and became like sisters. Similar to Lady Lhalu, as a girl Thonpa Sonam Dekyi had shaved her head like a nun and undergone rigorous education at Neuchungri Nunnery, which was famous as a sort of private school for the daughters of the aristocracy. Thonpa Sonam Dekyi was astonished to discover that despite my mother's entirely secular upbringing, she had a powerful, innate spirituality.

Thonpa Sonam Dekyi was impressed by my mother's character and bearing. My mother had spent her time living in seclusion at Lhalu Gatsal, except for trips with her brother to Tsamkhung Nunnery to try to see their mother. She stayed in her sun-filled room, reading sutras and praying to the Buddha. She had a large, sunny room on the first floor of the compound's watchtower that opened onto a big terrace with flowers and a small, foreign-style fountain (a servant took care of the flowers and the fountain, and Mother rarely went out on the terrace). The room was ornate, and circular banners with scriptures hung from the carved ceiling. The room looked like a scripture hall. It was filled with statues of Sakyamuni, Padmasambhava and the thousand-armed Avalokitesvara, copper bowls of offering water, butter lamps, *khata*, *thangka*, prayer flags and offerings of barley. And the round *khaden* that was always with my mother and on which she had sat when she saw her father off on his way.

Mother didn't need to go to a monastery because after my uncle married Lady Lhalu and had authority over the household, he brought in lamas from Drepung and Sera Monasteries to teach her. The lessons were about the Dharma, scriptures and mantras but also included more general cultural topics. For a time, Uncle employed an English teacher for her so she could continue her education in the language that she had started with her mother. At first, she worked diligently, but one day she just stopped, didn't give a reason and just wouldn't study any more. There was nothing Uncle could do with her. It had been seven years since Lungshar's death, but to Uncle it seemed that my mother had never been able to move on from that day or get over seeing grandfather off. Time seemed to have stopped for her. Uncle said Grandfather's shadow stayed over my mother, part of his soul was with her. This, of course, was some consolation to my uncle, it made him happy to be able to see his father in his sister. It was as if his father's life hadn't been extinguished but was still there with them, reincarnated in the body of his sister. But Uncle was worried too that his sister was lonely. No matter how devoted to Buddhism she was, she was still young and needed friends, she needed a life: even Shri Devi liked to play. Luckily, the arrival of Thonpa Sonam Dekyi eased my mother's loneliness, and she began to smile and laugh sometimes.

Thonpa Sonam Dekyi's cheerfulness had an influence on my mother, and for a time, Uncle said, when the two of them were together it was as if his sister had been awakened from a deep sleep. Together, their laughter made the sunny days that much brighter. He didn't need to ask anything of Thonpa Sonam Dekyi. Whenever she was free, Thonpa Sonam Dekyi liked to spend time with my mother. Mother's room became their shared scripture hall, and her terrace, unused for so long, became a place the two of them went often, because Thonpa Sonam Dekyi said she liked it. In spring, the ice and snow melted from the Lhalu Gatsal grounds, streams flowed, migratory birds arrived in flocks that blotted out the sky, and in the waters of the Lhalu Wetlands were the reflections of the blue sky, the white clouds and the two young women who walked together in nature, among the birds. Thonpa Sonam Dekyi loved the large Lhalu estate, especially all the white birds, so much so that often she couldn't stop herself from chasing after the birds as they flew. Mother watched this, almost impassively, it seemed natural to her. Thonpa Sonam Dekyi, she thought, was like a bird. Mother was a lot happier than she had been. Sometimes Thonpa Sonam Dekyi would be chasing after a bird and she would stop, turn and stare at my mother, as if she had suddenly realised something. She would yell, Hey, Ukyi Lhamo, how did you train yourself to be as content as a bird? Hey, I know what you were in your previous existence. A bird! Amazing!

Their usual topic of conversation was Dharma study, their shared language was that of sutras, doctrine and ritual. Together they studied *In Praise of White Tara, The Wish-Fulfilling Wheel*, which was their most common topic of discussion. They also discussed *jataka* tales and told them to each other. In winter they went out on the terrace in the sun to tell the stories they never tired of: the deer of nine colours, the woodcutter and the bear, the brave parrot, King Sibi and the falcon, the good dragon, the lion and the woodpecker. All of the stories were, on the surface, about animals, so they had fun telling them and acting them out. It was their main source of amusement during their free time. My mother didn't usually speak that well, but when she told the stories she was articulate, clear and precise, not a word out of place. Thonpa Sonam Dekyi wasn't as good and wasn't aware that there were 509 such stories, but my mother knew, and she could tell you every single one of them, which Thonpa Sonam Dekyi admired. But this happy time lasted only for a few years, until Thonpa Sonam Dekyi had children and became the lady of the house with responsibilities in the mundane world. Their interests and routines inevitably diverged, never again did they discuss the Dharma or perform rituals together. Mother returned to her life of seclusion, sitting alone with her statue of the Buddha.

The big change came in 1956, the year my mother turned twenty-three, when the Tibet government sent a group of young people to visit Beijing. My uncle was in the group. When he came back, he talked enthusiastically about everything he had seen and shared the news that the Central Academy for Nationalities was accepting its first class of students from Tibet and was recruiting throughout the region. Uncle jokingly asked his sister, How about it? Everyone assumed he was teasing her and didn't mean to suggest that she apply. He had been fretting over a match for her because at twenty-three she was old to be unmarried. This was Uncle's biggest worry, and it had to be addressed, but every time he brought it up, she said if they didn't want her at home any more, she would go to Gari Nunnery and become a nun.

Maybe Uncle wasn't entirely joking, maybe he had some thought that a change of scenery and exposure to more of the world would do her good, but certainly, he could not have expected that as soon as he mentioned the idea of her going to Beijing, Mother would immediately say she wanted to go. Uncle regretted bringing it up and tried to scare her off by telling her stories about how terrible life in Beijing was, but it was no use. Mother remained composed and resolute, just like when she sat in meditation.

No one knew what my mother was thinking. There are worlds upon worlds and the *buddhadharma* is vast. Perhaps her Buddhist mind gave no thought to the affairs of the world. Perhaps distance meant nothing to her, perhaps home meant nothing to her, perhaps everything was another turn of the wheel of the cycle of rebirth, like Gautama Buddha living hundreds of different lives. If so, then Tibet, Lhasa, the Lhalu estate and Beijing were all the same, weren't they? Perhaps this was a call to yet another life? But this was all meaningless speculation, my mother did not say what she was thinking, so nobody knew.

On the last day of March, the day before she was to leave, everyone in the family was busy helping my mother pack, the servants dizzy with work. Uncle said my mother seemed no different that day from any other, and in the morning, she recited the *In Praise of White Tara, The Wish-Fulfilling Wheel* mantra. She was about to make a long trip to a place she had never been, but it didn't seem to mean anything to her. She sat on her *khaden*, facing a statue of Usnisavijaya and went through her ritual as she had done every morning for years: she filled an offering bowl with water, presented a *khata* and recited...

> I and *sunya*, all the sentient beings, from now on take refuge in all the great masters, take refuge in Sambodhi and all the Revered Buddhas of the World, take refuge in the true Dharma (repeated seven hundred times), pay homage and take refuge in the three treasures of the masters, in the Buddha, Dharma and Sangha, make vows unceasingly, bless me, bless all sentient beings, bless all sentient beings (repeated five hundred times), to attain the Buddhahood of Enlightenment and save all sentient beings from *samsara* and the sea of suffering of the three existences, I practise the ritual of *In Praise of White Tara, The Wish-Fulfilling Wheel* (repeated seven hundred times).

It typically takes three sessions, morning, noon and evening, to recite all of *In Praise of White Tara, The Wish-Fulfilling Wheel*, requiring more than two hours altogether, but that afternoon she was going to go to Tsamkhung Nunnery and Yuthok's home to say goodbye, so she sat from morning until noon and recited the entire mantra without a break.

Uncle says that immediately after lunch, my mother pressed him to leave for the nunnery. Mother never left the house alone and had never travelled far, but she was about to travel two and a half thousand kilometres from Tibet, and Uncle couldn't believe how calm she was. For reasons he didn't understand, he was always a bit afraid of his sister, so he did exactly as she asked, he didn't dare not. Grandmother was no longer at Tsamkhung Nunnery. Quite a while before, she had moved to a different nunnery to stop her daughter from coming to look for her, but Mother kept her connection to Tsamkhung, visiting it every so often. In the Lhasa afternoon, the sun was high overhead, its light flooding the Barkhor Circuit. The light seemed to add to the energy of the place, there were street vendors, one next to the other, and crowds of people busily going to and fro. Uncle led Mother through the sunlight and the crowd of sunlit people and into the quiet of the nunnery.

Tsamkhung Nunnery is down an alley and secluded, unlike Jokhang Temple, which sits in the middle of the Barkhor Circuit. Tsamkhung is not a place full of people and clouds of incense smoke. All year round, it sits quietly under its small patch of sky, keeping to itself, as is fitting for a nunnery. The site was the location of a cave where a seventh-century Tibetan king meditated and prayed for the Lhasa River not to flood. A disciple of Tsongkhapa erected buildings over the cave, brought in a dozen nuns and established a nunnery. The number of nuns increased and a two-storey scripture hall, meditation rooms and a dormitory were added. The walls of the courtyard enclosed by the buildings are all decorated with wall paintings. A striking custom at Tsamkhung Nunnery is that for centuries, when the east glows red in the morning, two young nuns climb high above the courtyard and blow into snow-white conch shells as the sun slowly rises over Lhasa.

My mother never got to see her mother, of course, but years had passed and she had come to accept this. To her, the nunnery was her mother, its tranquil, lonely light made her think of her mother. That day, as she did on every visit, my mother first went to the scripture hall on the first floor and knelt and kowtowed to the statue of Tsongkhapa in his yellow hat. Tsongkhapa's hands were in the Dharmacakra mudra, symbolising the turning of the wheel of Dharma, lotus flowers on his palms and his four female disciples at his sides.

The nun my mother was best acquainted with was Tenzin Sangmo, and Tenzin Sangmo was the person at the nunnery who best understood my mother. When she was a child, on every visit to the nunnery my mother sought out Tenzin Sangmo, pointed at a wall painting and asked, Is that Tara? Did she come from tears? Tenzin Sangmo always answered, Yes, child, all the Taras you see were created from tears. The tears and the Taras made an indelible impression on my mother, and no matter how many times Tenzin Sangmo told her the story of Tara's origin, my mother asked again on every visit, and every time Tenzin Sangmo pointed at the wall painting and told the story again. She said, Avalokitesvara, in his mercy, saved myriad creatures from torment but once, after Avalokitesvara had already saved many lives from the sea of suffering, he looked and saw the number of sufferers had not diminished, and so he wept tears of compassion. His tears became the White Tara, Green Tara and Black Tara, they are all manifestations of the Bodhisattva Avalokitesvara, and they went right to work delivering people from danger and fear. On her visit before she left for Beijing, my mother did not, of course, ask Tenzin Sangmo to tell her the story, she simply stood by the wall paintings for a long while.

She went up on the highest terrace above the courtyard where every morning nuns blew on the conch shells. Uncle said my mother rarely went to the top floor, and if she did, he didn't, because the space was cramped, but this time Uncle climbed up with her and stayed by her side because he was thinking about the journey she was about to take and their uncertain future, which made him uneasy. There was a series of wall paintings that depicted Sakyamuni with a crazed woman at his feet, her hair in disarray. In the paintings, the woman was variously biting into the skull of a child, holding a child, wailing in a frenzy, rushing about wildly, holding her head in her hands and kneeling in front of Sakyamuni. Uncle said my mother looked at them for a long time. It was the first time he had seen these shocking paintings, and he asked his sister how he could have missed them. He asked her what they meant. My mother shook her head and said nothing. He was going to ask Tenzin Sangmo, who was standing behind them, but my mother stopped him. She handed something wrapped in ceremonial yellow cloth to Tenzin Sangmo and asked her to deliver it to her mother. Tenzin Sangmo sighed and shook her head, but she took the bundle. Uncle didn't know what was in it, and he didn't dare ask, as he knew she wouldn't tell him.

They left Tsamkhung Nunnery, walked away from bustling Barkhor Street and soon reached the huge front door of the Yuthok mansion. Uncle hadn't realised that my mother planned to go there. When they had passed it on the way to Tsamkhung Nunnery my mother hadn't said anything, and Uncle thought Mother had long since forgotten about Yuthok, but he was wrong. She had planned it, and when they neared the house, she stopped. She didn't say anything, she just stopped and wouldn't take another step. Uncle thought she was having second thoughts, so he walked up and knocked. Mother would not let him come in with her to see Yuthok, and as Uncle was there only for his sister, not to pay his respects to Yuthok, he was happy not to go in. He crossed the street and waited in a teahouse famous for its sweet tea.

My mother was in the house only briefly before she came out, seemingly unaffected, and Uncle assumed she had said a quick goodbye to her adopted father. The teahouse where uncle waited stuck in his mind because in the short time he was sitting there he had a premonition that when he said goodbye to his sister before she left the next day it was likely to be the last time they would see each other. He was thinking that he was the one who had put the idea of going to Beijing in her head. Still, at the time, Uncle never would have guessed that after she left, she would be gone for almost forty years, during which she never wrote. Years later Uncle said he had nothing but the memories of sitting in the teahouse waiting for his sister, of the Yuthok Manor House, now gone, Tenzin Sangmo's face and her stories of Tara and the tears, and of Tsamkhung Nunnery before its destruction. He said that his memories felt unmoored because the teahouse was gone, Yuthok was gone, and the original nunnery had been destroyed. It was hard to make sense of it all, he said, everything seemed to have disappeared so quickly.

Tsamkhung Nunnery was destroyed in 1968, and although it was later rebuilt, as with anything rebuilt or remade, the copy is not the same as the original. Younger people who don't know their history can't tell the difference, and that includes my friend Ukyi Lhamo, but when people of the older generation return to places they have been to when young, the difference to them is enormous, they can't find their memories, they can see only destruction. This was true of my friend Ukyi Lhamo's mother and uncle, and it is true of many people who still remember. In 1995, when my friend Ukyi Lhamo came to Tibet for the first time and visited Tsamkhung, she didn't understand that her mother and uncle could not find their memories at the rebuilt nunnery. After the nunnery was rebuilt, her mother and uncle visited it only once because the rebuilt Tsamkhung had no history. The original nunnery had a history of hundreds of years. The new Tsamkhung seemed no older than the young Ukyi Lhamo, just back from France, or even younger.

But my friend Ukyi Lhamo wasn't aware of any of this. When she learned from her mother and uncle that her grandmother had become a nun at Tsamkhung, she became very excited and asked them to show her the room where her grandmother had lived. Neither of them told her that the place had been destroyed and then rebuilt, not her mother, not her white-haired uncle. She wanted to visit, and so they said nothing and came with her. She even made them climb with her up to the terrace where they blew conch shells every morning. All around the terrace were brightly coloured wall paintings, but Ukyi Lhamo could not find the paintings of the frenzied woman at the feet of Sakyamuni. Finally, her Uncle Lhalu leaned close to her ear and whispered (he didn't want anyone to overhear him) that the nunnery wasn't the original place but a reconstruction.

Ukyi Lhamo's 1995 visit was, however, a success because in something of a miracle she met Tenzin Sangmo. She was over ninety, old enough to seem as if she was from another planet. She was wrapped in a crimson robe and walked with a cane.

Her eyes were sunk in their sockets but opened wide when she saw Lhalu. Lhalu's eyes opened wide too. They stared at each other for a long time. Each had assumed the other was long since dead, neither could quite believe their eyes.

—May I ask how old you are? my friend Ukyi Lhamo said in a loud voice. How long have you lived here?

Tenzin Sangmo didn't answer, she stared straight ahead.

—I am looking for Madame Ukyi Lhamo. Do you know where she is?

Still no answer, still no expression on Tenzin Sangmo's face. Uncle Lhalu spoke next.

—Do you recognise me, Sister Tenzin Sangmo? I'm Lhalu Tsewang Dorje.

A light came to Tenzin Sangmo's eyes, she clearly recognised Lhalu, but she didn't answer him. She slowly turned towards Ukyi Lhamo's mother and looked at her intently. Her lips trembled and she spoke.

—Are you, are you Ukyi Lhamo? Tenzin Sangmo asked. She could speak, she remembered.

—I saw your mother, but I couldn't get the bundle to her, it's been lost, Tenzin Sangmo said.

She still remembered the bundle wrapped in yellow cloth that Mrs Ukyi Lhamo had given her. Mrs Ukyi Lhamo remained calm but her daughter, my friend Ukyi Lhamo, cried out, What? You saw her? You saw my grandmother? When? Where?

—I can't remember... We did labour together... Swept the streets... I wanted to give her the bundle but it disappeared.

Tenzin Sangmo's eyes were on the mother, Mrs Ukyi Lhamo, not the daughter.

—Please think, please think. I'm her granddaughter!

At this, Tenzin Sangmo finally turned her eyes to the younger Ukyi Lhamo and stared at her. Ukyi Lhamo quickly removed her hat and straightened her long hair, as if this would prove who she was.

—Are you Ukyi Lhamo? Tenzin Sangmo asked.

—Yes, I mean, no, I'm Madame Ukyi Lhamo's granddaughter, Ukyi Lhamo.

Tenzin Sangmo's gaze drifted away, then she slowly closed her eyes.

—Sister! Sister!

My friend Ukyi Lhamo called out to the venerable old nun,

but the nun kept her eyes closed and slowly brought her hands together. She sat down and became utterly still, detaching herself from everything in this world. Ukyi Lhamo had never seen anything like it before. What Ukyi Lhamo didn't know was that this was the reaching of nirvana, an extinction, the blowing out of a flame, a happy death. Only a year later, after Ukyi Lhamo had come back from France for good and had decided to settle in Lhasa, did she learn that at that moment Tenzin Sangmo achieved parinirvana. *Ukyi Lhamo was convinced that she had been the last image to register in the venerable old nun's mind.*

---

18. A Long Talk

The emptiness in your eyes might appear at any time, at any place,
as if you feel yourself alone, it can come at any time, like your depression.
Even when you danced with abandon on that night under Venus,
I could see the lonely emptiness in your eyes.

I want to go back to Neuchungri Nunnery, said Ukyi Lhamo. Oh yeah, also Gari Nunnery. Grandmother could be at one of those two places. All the other nunneries are small, I've been to them but didn't find her. Neuchungri and Gari are big, you can't see everything in one trip. Do you know that Neuchungri has the most beautiful scripture hall of any nunnery in Tibet, the whitest dagoba and the prettiest dormitory for the nuns? It's a little yellow structure. Neuchungri used to be the place the young women from the Tibetan aristocracy or wealthy merchant families came to study or take vows, so it's possible that Grandmother ended up there when she wanted to hide from everybody. The special thing about Gari Nunnery is that everyone there practises yoga for longevity, and many of the nuns are even older than Tenzin Sangmo was. They are like so many ancient trees, so old they are genderless. For all we know, Madame Ukyi Lhamo could be living there in a little yellow room. When can you go to Neuchungri with me? And Gari? Who knows, we might find Madame Ukyi Lhamo.

—Which is it, Madame Ukyi Lhamo or Grandmother? asked Wang Mojie.

—I don't feel close to her when I call her Grandmother, I actually feel very close to her when I call her Madame Ukyi Lhamo. She's historically important, but she's my grandmother. It's weird, Tibet gives me all sorts of strange feelings, it's completely different from the interior.

—Of course, I'd like to see Neuchungri but aren't you interested in the wrong grandparent? Your family's history is not well known, most of Tibet's history is not well known. There were Tibetan revolutionaries, that was news to me, and your grandfather was one of them. I would think that he should be the focus of your attention, but you seem to be interested in only the mysterious Madame Ukyi Lhamo, who no one in your family has seen for fifty years.

—There is nothing mysterious about her to me. She was alive during the Cultural Revolution, Tenzin Sangmo saw her!

—The Cultural Revolution ended twenty years ago, Ms Lungsharwa.

—I'm not interested in "revolution", I'm sick of hearing the word. Name me a revolutionary movement that didn't cause suffering and disaster. Isn't even the French Revolution criticised now? My grandfather was influenced by the West, I respect him for the idealist he was, but I like my grandmother more, she was amazing. My grandfather suffered, he was willing to die for his beliefs, his sort of willpower is incredible, but the way I see it, his decisions forced my grandmother to make decisions of her own that were even more difficult. Women the world over have always been treated as nothing but companions to male heroes, they are expected to be faithful to their men, but my grandmother would not go along with that. For the sake of her children and herself, she accepted a marriage to Yuthok. She was an ordinary person, she wouldn't be the wife of some hero, she wouldn't be a chaste martyr. Even when he asked her to say that my Uncle Lhalu was the child of her affair with another man, she signed her name to it in black and white for the whole world to see. She was a great person.

—She deserves sympathy, but that doesn't make her great. That's a confused value judgment.

—Don't talk to me about value judgments, all the standards that women are measured against are bullshit! Stop lecturing me, Wang Mo, I'm not confused in the least. Why should a woman be expected to remain faithful when her husband gets himself into trouble? By what right can we place that expectation on those poor women? As everybody expects that of women, you sincerely think that's what my grandmother should have done, don't you? Listen, Wang Mo, what makes my grandmother a great person is that she was willing to take action and live with the consequences.

—You're worked up about it only because you aren't sure about it, right? You're not so confident you're correct.

—Spare me, Wang Mo, what makes you think you're so special?

—Who said I'm special? I'm a shallow sort of bloke.

—You make me so angry! Are you suggesting I'm shallow?

—Yes, confused too, I'd say.

—You really don't understand how complicated everything is. Who do you think you are?

Ukyi Lhamo was red with rage, but Wang Mojie ignored this and kept talking.

—Of course, I can understand your superficiality and your confusion. True enough, our traditional moral standards have always held that when the husband is in extremis, the wife must be steadfastly faithful to him, the examples are too numerous to mention. It's the foundation of our system of moral standards for women, and it explains our obsession with building monuments to chaste widows. It's fine to discuss the possessiveness and legalistic thinking behind the notion that a woman might be "unfaithful", being "unfaithful" is after all simply a natural impulse. But that is no reason to take things to the other extreme and denounce fidelity and say being unfaithful is admirable and makes a person great. That's where your thinking is muddled.

Ukyi Lhamo realised she was no match for Wang Mojie in an argument, and she eased off when she replied.

—It wasn't easy for her. She never wrote a word to Grandfather, never once went to see him, you think that was easy for her? I understand her very well, I think it was painful for her but she was resolute, it wasn't easy for her at all. I think that maybe it was Yuthok who hurt her more than anybody. He shouldn't have married my grandmother. But he was certainly magnanimous with my grandfather. When Grandfather got out of prison and asked that his wife come back to him, Yuthok agreed, if you can believe that. Grandmother was educated, in the Western way, so how could they send her back and forth like some piece of property? Did Yuthok take her wishes into account? I think it's all too sad.

No matter how worked up Ukyi Lhamo became, Wang Mojie stayed perfectly calm.

—It's fine to sigh over how difficult she had it, but your grandfather recognised this, and I fail to see that he ever blamed her for anything. Quite the contrary, he wanted her back, unconditionally, with no fault ascribed to your grandmother. He still loved her after she married somebody else, which is not something most men would be capable of. It seems to me that for Tibetans, relations between the sexes are in part a social contract and in part the way of nature, or instinct, plus there is a religious aspect to it, an outlet for spirituality. A culture with no outlet for spirituality is a dangerous one, lacking a capacity for forgiveness, a culture capable of evil that can lead us straight to darkness. On the other hand, when we have a made-up moral code hanging over our heads like a sword, we end up going down the same road to ruin. Tibet seems to have neither of these problems, which is something you should think about. Of all the people involved in the Lungshar Incident, I think that it's your mother who is the most atypical. There's a lot about her character for us to consider, she's the real riddle in this chapter of history. You know her better than anybody, but she's still a stranger to you.

—I used to think I understood my mother, but then I suddenly found I didn't. It's like she changed into somebody different when she came back to Tibet.

—She is hard to understand, right?

—Forty years, she never told us anything, she never said a word about any of it.

—She loved you, what more do you want?

—Yes, I know, she is the kindest woman on Earth, completely selfless as a mother, but she is also the most steel-hearted of mothers, you can't get into her heart. I study Buddhism, read scriptures, recite mantras, all because I want to understand her world, I want to understand how she thinks. But Buddhism is so deep, Buddhism is about letting go of the self. Buddhism tells me not to be attached to the things of this life, but with that mindset, I'm starting to feel that my mother is more and more like a stranger, more and more unknowable, more and more unreal.

—The same thing would happen with you and your grandmother, if you were to find her, I mean. What could she tell you? What would you say to her? Besides, she is even more committed to her religion. Religion is a path that leads one to oneself, not to other people. If you keep looking for insight into someone else, you won't gain insight into yourself.

—I know, that's true, but I don't know what to do, I'm all muddled up.

—You've got some muddled-up contradiction in your very blood, you're a mix of everything, you carry with you every sort of influence.

But then again, that is what makes you unique, there are things about you that nobody else has. Your mysterious charm comes not just from your looks, it owes more to your confused identity, which can be taken as a positive. But even if you take it as a negative, it means that looking at you, I see not just you but also, just barely, the whole lineage: you, your mother, your grandmother, three generations of Ukyi Lhamos, connected by history, connected by blood. Your grandmother left your grandfather, your mother to all intents and purposes left your father, and you, who have you left? Or who will you leave? I saw how broken-hearted that maths professor-poet fellow was, you couldn't get more broken-hearted. But you and him, that's different, the times are different, your lives have been different. All the same, there is still something in all these stories about the different Ukyi Lhamos to make a man wary, they are all connected by something that no man has control over. In any case, of the three of you, your mother is the most interesting to me. I don't think your grandmother is that special, she's quite ordinary, as are you, of course, that goes without saying.

—Who do you think you are, Wang Mo? I can't stand that tone of yours.

—You asked for my opinion, so don't complain about my tone.

—Can you please stop being so pompous? Please?

—You deserve it. You don't take things seriously enough.

—You drive me mad.

—Let me finish what I was saying.

Wang Mojie took a sip of tea, cold now. He didn't touch alcohol, he drank only tea. But Ukyi Lhamo was drinking a lot lately.

—There is some dimension to your mother that is different from other people, something spiritual. She had two fathers, lost them one after the other, and her mother left her too. She was abandoned and had to move again and again. She was still little when she stopped talking much, what she had to live through was much more than a child of her age could endure, but she simply bore all of it in silence. You said yourself, her repeating *om mani padme hum* sounded to your grandfather's ears like the voice of someone he did not know, like a child speaking to him from heaven, in other words, like an angel's voice. She was only eleven when she sat with her father to see him on the way to his next life, and after that, she was never far from that round yellow *khaden* of hers, her life wasn't her own any more. And if all of that isn't enough to make her special, then consider the miracle that for almost forty years in Beijing she kept her secrets locked away. She raised six children and gave them all her love, she never caused any of you any pain, and then suddenly she left, she left because she had finished something that her mother had not finished. That to me is what makes your mother special, she never placed herself above the world. She has her faith in the Buddha, but she knew what her responsibilities in life were and she fulfilled them, and one of those responsibilities was finishing what her mother had not. When she went to Tsamkhung before leaving for Beijing and stood there for a long time in front of the paintings of that mad woman, she was thinking about her mother, there was a heart-to-heart connection between her and her mother. I think she was trying to feel what her mother had felt, trying to feel her suffering, feel what her life had been like. Likewise, she never forgot Lungshar dying, and I think that changed her utterly. I think your grandfather presented her with what amounted to a prophecy. Really, your mother is an amazing person, that spiritual quality of hers was there even in her secular life and finally, she left in pursuit of an entirely spiritual life.

—Wang Mojie, that is insightful, really, very insightful, how can you know my mother so well?

—That's all from what you or your uncle said. I don't understand your mother that well, everything I said is just a footnote to what you said, a kind of free association. Maybe the woman I've described is not your mother but just a discursive space constructed from what I know of your mother, a woman entirely of my imagination.

—Why do you say that?

—If we are to understand a thing, we cannot stereotype it, all things should endlessly open themselves to all sorts of possibilities.

—But what you said was exactly right. Really, that's what my mother is like.

—Even so, what I've said probably doesn't capture even a fraction of who she is.

—But even that fraction nobody else has ever talked about with me.

—Just a matter of a difference in expertise and interest.

—What do you mean "interest"? You are so strange.

Ukyi Lhamo took a sip of her red wine, swirling the glass out of habit, then put the glass down on the red tea table. Wang Mojie studied her as she went through these motions, then unhurriedly went on with what he had to say.

—Interest in you, of course, but... just an interest. Before you told me anything about the history of your family, Yu Youyan gave me the gist, but I think she got some things wrong. She said you were Lhalu's granddaughter, but to be honest some things about you make me see why one might think that. I never imagined it was all so complicated, so tragic, so profound. Other than that, what matters to me, as I've said, is that since I've started to learn about Tibetan history, which I knew nothing about, I've realised the depth of my ignorance, and from this I've drawn the following conclusion. If you don't know Tibetan history, then when you come to Tibet, no matter how much you feel that your experience is unique, no matter how deep into yourself you get, no matter how pleased with yourself and your life here you are, anything you might have to say about Tibet is going to be superficial. I used to refuse to engage with the world or think about the past or plan for the future. I thought my inner life was rich enough on its own, but as soon as I learned the history of your family, Tibet became real to me. Tibet became more than just landscape and lamas, and I realised that my self-satisfied rejection of everything must have made me seem quite ridiculous.

—What's ridiculous is that you think you are so profound. You are such a narcissist.

—I'm very self-critical.

—That's just part of your narcissism.

—Really? Why didn't I realise that?

—You are so exhausting. Right, are you coming with me or not?

—To where?

—Neuchungri Nunnery, of course, and Gari Nunnery.

—You haven't given up trying to find Madame Ukyi Lhamo?

—I can't, I've been searching for her for two years now.

—If you gave up, you wouldn't know what to do with yourself, would you?

—I don't know what to do with myself as it is.

—I can tell. So what do you want to do with your life?

—I don't know.

She lit a cigarette. She blew out a long puff of smoke towards Wang Mojie, it caught in his throat and he coughed, he waved the smoke away with his hand. Ukyi Lhamo laughed, she was a little drunk, a little flirty, a little forward, but Wang Mojie ignored it. It wasn't that he didn't understand, he truly wasn't interested.

—Think about your mother, maybe you'll be able to figure out who you are, and maybe you'll gradually find something of your own. Of course, most people live dull, boring lives and in comparison with most people, you might decide you're quite happy with yourself. Do you want to hear my opinion of you? All right, I'll tell you. As I've said, your confused identity is a positive, it's what makes you so enchanting. You have a degree in French literature, you study Buddhism, immersing yourself in the mysterious rituals of esoteric practice, and at the same time, you have endless affairs, go to bars and parties, you're always surrounded by people. And you decided to come and teach at a school in a remote spot outside of Lhasa, becoming the centre of attention out here. This was a peaceful place but you've upset that peace. You don't let anything go, you want to hold on to everything, you even want to dredge up forgotten history, the epic and tragic long history of your people. You answer to many masters. All this makes you complicated and colourful. So far, you seem to be handling all this pretty well. Everybody wants to know who you are behind your mysterious persona, but I'm guessing that you know that you don't have an answer unless it's confusion and emptiness.

—Go on, don't stop, Ukyi Lhamo said, blowing another long puff of smoke into Wang Mojie's face.

—I've noticed that the emptiness in your eyes might appear at any time and any place, just like your depression. Even on that beautiful night during Karma Rishi when you danced with abandon with that man, I could see the emptiness in your eyes. That's normal, it's true of all of us, anyone can suddenly realise they don't really know who they are, but what makes you different is there is something about the emptiness inside you that has this quality of looking down on the rest of us from a height with indifference and sadness. It has something of the "emptiness" they talk about in Buddhism. That's enough to make you attractive to men but not enough to drive them crazy. At the same time, you are a Beijing girl, unconventional, outgoing, carefree. You are open and make friends easily. And that proves you didn't make a rational choice to hollow out your heart and detach yourself from life, it's just part of your emotional make-up. You aren't a rational person, you can't control your emotions, but you don't want to, and that is what gives men the opportunity to let themselves go with you. You don't care, you don't care at all, because you know nobody can capture your heart. Your heart is far away where nobody can reach it, but when that enormous emptiness threatens to overcome you, you will give yourself to any man who will have you. But you are capable of staying out in the snow half the night, you can even make the snow melt... There is something in you that was passed down from your mother and your grandmother, you share some fate, but the connection between you and them has been broken. There's no solid line from you to them, it's a dotted line, or to put it another way there's been some change from them to you. You'll never be your mother. Or your grandmother, despite your obsession with her. What will you make of yourself? Heaven only knows.

—Are you some sort of shaman? How can you know me so well? What do you think I can make of myself?

Wang Mojie finished his tea and pushed his cup across to Ukyi Lhamo before replying.

—I've been drinking cold tea, and now even that's gone. Serves me right for being pompous. May I have some hot water, please? You should look after me.

—I'll pour some wine for you if you want. If you want tea, get it yourself. Want some wine?

Wang Mojie gave her a look, picked up the thermos and poured some hot water onto the tea leaves in his cup.

—If I were a shaman, I would know what you will make of yourself, but I'm not and I don't.

—Have you noticed that I'm starting to admire you?

—I noticed that a long time ago.

—You are a shameless braggart. What should I do with my life? Ukyi Lhamo asked, holding her glass in both hands.

—I already said, think more about your mother and less about the Madame Ukyi Lhamo of your imagination, think less about your grandmother.

—My mother has a spiritual quality to her, I don't.

—I'm surprised you're so clear-headed about that, Wang Mojie said and smiled.

—I'm doing my best to find the Buddha, I'm happiest when I feel near to the Buddha. But I know that maybe what would be best for me would be to give myself entirely to some man, but I know the right man doesn't exist and never will exist. And he's not you, Ukyi Lhamo said, as she stared at Wong Mojie, took a sip of wine and lit one of her long, slender cigarettes.

—Don't drag me into it, Wang Mojie said. I've told you what I think of you.

—What do you think? Tell me, tell me! Ukyi Lhamo was a little drunk.

—I'm interested in you but just in an everyday sense, you make an interesting study.

—You're such a saint, a scholar.

—No, you're wrong there, but I have very particular needs, complicated needs, didn't Yu Youyan tell you?

—I haven't seen her in a long time, she just vanished.

—She didn't tell you?

—What happened with the two of you?

—She came here.

—Oh? How come I didn't know?

—I took good care of her.

—You have no shame.

—I'm trying to improve.

—How?

—That's my business, you never mind.

—Tell me, what are you doing to improve? Is there something you should be praised for? Tell me, tell me, go on.

Ukyi Lhamo was drunk now, she didn't seem to care at all about Yu Youyan.

—OK, we've talked too much, Wang Mojie said. He stood up and asked, When are we going to Neuchungri Nunnery?

—Neuchungri Nunnery? Oh, right, the nunnery. Tomorrow, we'll go tomorrow.

—Also, when are we going to go see Ma Dingge again?

—Go by yourself, he's always mentioning you.

—OK, sweet dreams. See you tomorrow... Wow, look at the time, it's already tomorrow, the sun's about to come up.

—Then we're going today, we can leave in the afternoon, this morning we'll sleep.

—OK, good night.

—Good morning, sir, said Ukyi Lhamo, correcting Wang Mojie.

—Good morning.

19. Cakrasamvara

She taught him how to make the Vajrahumkara posture, she rose above him,
wrapped one leg around his waist, then both legs.
The degree of difficulty was high, the feeling was extraordinary.
But suddenly he couldn't contain himself, he let go,
she saw his face convulse as he lost control and shuddered.

It was the winter morning after their long night of conversation. The glasses and ashtray were still on the table.

Wang Mojie had left. There were many such nights that they talked. This time he stayed longer than he ever had. They did not say good-night, they said good morning. You could already hear the yaks grunting from the village in the distance. Ukyi Lhamo wasn't sleepy. She stared at the door after she shut it and lit a cigarette. She took a few drags from the cigarette, then put it out. She had had too many, she didn't want another. Typically it's the man who smokes and the woman who inhales the second-hand smoke, but with them it was the reverse. She envied him for not smoking. She had had wine, she drank the whole bottle herself, he didn't touch a drop. He was a puritan. They talked all night, then suddenly he was gone. It was if she hadn't seen him go. All she saw was the door closing. He had walked out into the clear, empty light of dawn without looking back.

That wasn't just pompous, that was cruel.

But she needed the cruelty. It made her heart ache. Cruelty was the only thing that could make her feel something. But soon she felt empty again, as empty as the silent rising light of the pale dawn. There was no snow, but if there had been, she could have gone to the empty playground, into the deep snow to sit there motionless like Ma Dingge. But there was no snow, just the daybreak, and it was as meaningless as the snow. She didn't like the dawn, she was used to the night. In the night, no matter how deep in the night, she could close her eyes and become part of it. But she couldn't get used to the way dawn pierced the night. She was afraid of the dawn. It was terrifying. She asked herself if he might come back. Maybe he forgot something and will come back for it, she thought.

Many times after he left, she would sit in a daze, thinking he would suddenly walk back in. She would wonder if he had left something behind. Then she would feel something she couldn't name, some feeling would float up. Two nights before, she had dreamed that Wang Mojie was kneeling in front of her, begging her to let him stay, but she steadfastly refused. It made her happy, she felt quite excited when she woke. The strange thing was, when he was with her, she didn't have any clear idea of what she wanted, but as soon as he left, something powerful welled up in her. She just couldn't get used to the way after their long talks he suddenly was gone, leaving the room feeling deserted. He left so casually, which made her feel hurt somehow. Why didn't he hesitate even a little?

This time, with the sky already light, the feeling was particularly strong.

She hated him. He always did this to her after he was gone.

The windows were glazed with light. The sky was brightening fast, its pale blue slowly turning white.

She felt afraid. She suddenly saw her face reflected in the window, looking like the face on a wax figure.

She stood still. She lit a cigarette. She put it out. A wax figure.

She looked at the wax figure and picked up the telephone.

According to theories of the mirror stage, the place of the self may be taken by the other we see in a mirror. We unconsciously identify with this other in the mirror, taking it to be our true self, which it is not. The theory holds that this is a common psychological stage. It can be short-lived or sometimes long-lasting. The theory is very difficult to explain, to do so is beyond my competence. I am, however, confident that when Ukyi Lhamo saw her face in the window and thought that it looked as if it were made of wax, the feeling didn't last long. At any rate, when she described to me what she had seen in the window glass, and I looked at her, she didn't look to me as if she were made of wax, not at all.

The dawn and the vision of that face of wax shook her deeply.

She made a call. Not to Wang Mojie. He didn't have a telephone.

She wouldn't have called him even if he did.

The call was brief, she said just a sentence or two then hung up.

She wanted to get away, she wanted to leave right away.

There was no way for her to sleep now, the sun was up. She washed her face and brushed her teeth, then stood in front of the mirror for a long time. She looked lost and exhausted, like a still from some film. She packed a few things, she wanted to get out of there, it didn't matter where to, the farther away the better. She needed the jolting of a car, she needed a long trip, she needed her mountain climber and she needed to sleep. She couldn't stand it any more, so she dialled his number again. He didn't answer, he was already on the way. She was furious with Wang Mojie, she was almost ready to murder him. She pictured him dead, stabbed to death, sprawled out like a dead body on a film poster. If he died, she wouldn't care.

Her mountain climber – the man who taught climbing at Tibet University – arrived. He had been quick. He looked at her with puzzlement. Calmly and with all the emotion of a talking wax figure, she said nothing was wrong with her except for insomnia and that she would sleep in the car. Her tall mountain climber asked her where she wanted to go. She said Dromo. Dromo was five hundred kilometres away, but the man said nothing, he just stepped on the accelerator, and they drove away from the quiet school grounds. She sat in the spacious back seat of the SUV, her eyes half shut, saying nothing. She looked out at the morning, at the Lhasa suburbs, at the rosy glow of dawn across the sky, at the vault of heaven, at the Tibetan sky. The SUV raced along, the speed soothing her icy, terrified heart. The daybreak had scared her. Wang Mojie, looking himself like a man of wax, had scared her. Wang Mojie was like some inhuman spectre. She told her mountaineer to drive faster, she needed the speed, the space, the distance, she needed to get away and she needed silence.

She loved her mountaineer, she loved that he never had much to say. She loved his silence, his speed, she loved this good man. She slowly closed her eyes, leaned against the seat, then lay down, and as she did, the car gradually slowed, as if to help her sleep. She started to drift off. Snippets of her many night-time conversations with Wang Mojie ran through her mind to the jolting of the car: talk of her childhood, her mother, Tibet, Grandfather, Uncle Lhalu, Grandmother, Mother, Yuthok, monasteries, the Lhalu estate, Neuchungri Nunnery, a face of wax, a film still, a passing over into the next world, *In Praise of White Tara, The Wish-Fulfilling Wheel*... so much talk had passed between them, she couldn't stop it from running through her head... her head felt like it was about to explode.

—Stop the car! Ukyi Lhamo yelled out.

The car pulled over to the side of the road. The mountaineer jumped down from the driver's seat and opened the back door. The wind was strong, the smell of the river on it, and it lifted the long hair fallen across Ukyi Lhamo's face. Her eyes were closed and she sighed deeply. He didn't say anything, he sat down next to her, took her by her shoulders and looked into her face, then straightened her hair. She opened her eyes, shut them again, then put her arms around him, her lips searching urgently on his face. She kissed him all over his face, then she found his lips. She kissed him hard, she grabbed at him with her hands, pulling him to her with a frenzied strength.

—Wait, wait, he said coolly.

He pulled away from her, got out, then climbed back into the driver's seat, turned the key and slowly drove off the road down to the stony bank of the Lhasa River, right to the water's edge. They were near the confluence of the Lhasa and the Yarlung Tsangpo where the riverbank was broad. He turned the engine off and got into the back with Ukyi Lhamo. The seat was big and soft, a good place to make love. Nothing needed to be said. They held each other, kissed and took off their clothes. He had turned the heat up in the car. As they made love, the wax faces she had been seeing vanished and the clamour of voices in her head stopped. The tension left her as she filled her senses with him, and she came close to losing consciousness. She felt a powerful fulfilment, he always made her feel that way, he understood her, he made her feel new. Again and again, he touched her deep within. All the dawns, all the pieces of dreams, all the fragments of language in her head were driven out by him, it was good for her body and her soul too... She loved him, she loved him, and she felt the orgasm coming, slowly flowing through her body like a tide, like the fire-red sun rising over the Lhasa and Yarlung Tsangpo rivers. All those dawns after Wang Mojie left her were driven away, and with abandon, she turned over for him, so he could reach even farther inside, penetrate her deeper, take her to heaven. This position she liked best, it was the best way to do it, and now he felt completely different to her. She usually didn't cry out or moan during sex. Even when they had once made love in a field, her on top of him as the sun set behind her, she hadn't cried out. This time he was too much, he understood her so well, even though they hadn't said a word. He was fierce, focused, she braced her hands against the window, her bare arse catching the morning sun rising over the Lhasa and Yarlung Tsangpo rivers. She turned her head and looked at him, in that instant she felt him deep in her heart and, exorcising all that had been haunting her, she cried out with the sound of a wild crane. The shorebirds on the shoals were startled into flight, but he didn't stop, his breath stayed even, and he said nothing. She surrendered, she was freed, utterly. Then she fell into a deep sleep. No consciousness, only mountains.

The boundless mountain peaks reached into the sky, the sky was crowded with them. The car clung to the side of the mountain and slowly climbed, the wide Yarlung Tsangpo dropping away to just a thread. To get to Yamdrok Lake you cross the Gambala Pass. The peak of the 5,800-metre Gambala Mountain is always snow-covered, always out of reach. Like all the other vehicles on the mountain, their Toyota Land Cruiser crawled up the road like a beetle. The road over the Gambala Pass is known as one of the most perilous in Tibet, and every year, cars and trucks fall from the mountain to the Yarlung Tsangpo, looking like tumbling beetles as they go, so they say, rolling over and over all the way to the river. On one side of the road is vertical rock, sharp and straight as if cut with a knife, on the other a deep gorge with the swiftly flowing river at its bottom. There are hairpin turns one after another, one mistake and you can drive straight off the cliff and fall thousands of metres. Yamdrok is the second most holy of Tibet's four holy lakes, and Ukyi Lhamo had set her mind on going there. She wanted her mountaineer and his Land Cruiser on the mountain, and he was more than man enough for it. He and Wang Mojie were two entirely different species of men. Wang Mojie couldn't be mentioned in the same breath as her mountaineer.

Few men would have dared drive over the Gambala Pass after sex, any postcoital weakness in your legs could cost you your life. You might not be able to brake hard enough, and one moment's carelessness and you could miss a turn and drive straight off the road to your death. They say that a moment's debauch did lead to one couple falling to the Yarlung Tsangpo, so drivers know to stay out of the mountains right after sex and definitely avoid the Gambala Pass. Ukyi Lhamo didn't know about this taboo and wouldn't have cared. The mountaineer did, but he didn't say anything about it. Ukyi Lhamo's mountaineer was thirty-eight, he was not famous as a mountain climber, so he supported himself by teaching climbing. You can't be famous if you haven't reached the summit of Chomolungma, or Everest as Westerners call it, and he hadn't, but many excellent climbers don't. He had climbed 12 seven thousand-metre mountains and three higher than eight thousand metres. He had tried Chomolungma once but failed. He stopped just thirty metres from the top when his entire team was driven down by a snowstorm. He came close to conquering Chomolungma, but he had never reached such heights again, so he didn't brag about his climbing.

He was a simple man, dedicated to his teaching, a good dancer, and he had the physique of a younger man. What made him a good dancer, they said, was his grace and ability to keep a beat, he was musical. In fact, in Lhasa he was more famous as a dancer than he was as a climbing instructor or athlete. Women said that next to him they felt like a cloud by a mountain peak. He had never married, he lived alone, but he was charming and so never lacked for female companionship. He could easily have been a playboy, but he kept his sex drive in check. This was because of his climbing, he loved mountains more than he loved women, so he exercised restraint when it came to sleeping with women.

Ukyi Lhamo was different, of course, and equal to any mountain. If they hadn't met at the university, they would have met somewhere else. If the poet hadn't introduced them, which he did at least in part to show off Ukyi Lhamo, they would have met at some social function. Lhasa is not a big city, their social circles overlapped, so they were destined to meet. After they did, when they saw each other at a dance party, there was a charge in the air between them. He was sure of himself, she was haughty. They danced and it felt wonderful to them, and after that, he sometimes invited her out to dance. They practised a Latin dance, but she wasn't very good at it, so he taught her. They practised at Lhasa's only private dance club, the dance was strenuous, like aerobic exercise.

He was a man with mountains on his mind and such a man is a man of lofty thoughts, as climbing is not just a challenging physical activity, it is also an intellectual exercise. When you climb, you face dangerous situations and circumstances that present themselves suddenly, so mountain climbers have to be sensitive to everything around them. In many ways he and Ukyi Lhamo were completely different, he was clear about that, as clear as he was about how far he could safely make it up any given mountain. He had climbed many mountains where he could not reach the summit, but still he was satisfied. The summit is the goal, but you don't necessarily need to reach the goal, and feeling the despair of having your goal in sight but beyond reach is also a way to be fully alive. He knew he couldn't possess Ukyi Lhamo entirely and didn't want to, so he kept himself under control, content with demonstrating to her that he was a man of quality, measured and appropriate in everything. They didn't get together often, they avoided any romantic entanglement and kept a check on their physical passions. After their infrequent love-making, they waited a long time before the next time, and in between they acted as if they were just friends. He loved her, for sure. Tibet's sacred mountains have sacred lakes as companions, and of course, he wanted the remarkable Ukyi Lhamo to be the lake to his mountain, but he knew that this would be to lose her. The truth was that if she had wanted to possess him completely, he would have left her, and he knew she felt the same way. When two equally remarkable people get together, neither can keep the other for long. Sometimes they didn't see each other for a month or two at a time, but they knew they would never forget each other.

He knew she could sometimes take things to an extreme, women are emotional creatures, and this is even true of exceptional women. But he had never seen her act this wildly, they had always exercised some discretion, been private, but they had just done it by the side of the road, which surprised him. He hadn't hesitated and hadn't asked her any questions. He liked to express himself not with words but with actions, he took everything in his stride. Her call had come with no warning, and she wanted to make such a long trip. His calm reaction showed how experienced he was in dealing with avalanches, rockslides and climbing accidents. Dealing with a woman's emotions is like dealing with any of that, it is a chance for a man to show his strength to the woman he loves. When she called, she woke him from sleep, and he had no idea what was going on, so he simply said he would be there in ten minutes. Ten minutes was impossible, it took him longer than that, but only a couple of minutes longer. When he arrived at her house, he saw her standing there in a trance, her face like wax, and though he wasn't in the least prepared for it, they got right on the road. He didn't need an explanation, he wanted to give her what she wanted, make her feel safe and let her find a match for her mood in the speed and jolting of his car. She seemed to fall asleep as soon as she got in the car, and he thought she was sleeping as peacefully as the dawn river in the distance. It surprised him when she suddenly yelled for him to stop. She looked directly at him, her eyes confused and fevered. He knew this was desire and knew what to do. So he did something dangerous, something he shouldn't have done. But he had done it right, he stopped himself from ejaculating. That took a mountain climber's self-control.

For four hours straight, his car clung to the Gambala Pass road without the slightest mishap, and he took each turn as gently as possible for the sake of his passenger asleep in the back. Had he ejaculated, he wouldn't have been able to make it. This was part of the composure and self-control he learned in the mountains. Mountain climbers need self-control more than most people. Just like Ukyi Lhamo, he had a Han Chinese father and a Tibetan mother. He was born in Tibet (his father was an officer in the 18th Army Corps), raised in Chengdu and then came back to Tibet as an adult. He never claimed to be Tibetan but didn't think of himself as Han either. He belonged to no ethnic group, which was the source of his solitude.

After another hour, the car reached the top of the pass and rolled to a stop by Yamdrok Lake. The lake was frozen, a plane of undisturbed ice and snow. Ukyi Lhamo had woken up once on the way, but it was misty and she couldn't see anything. A trace of her conversation with Wang Mojie lingered in her mind but just a trace, as indistinct as everything out there in the mist. She fell back asleep, deeply asleep, and when she woke up she felt refreshed, all the anxiety she had carried since that moment at dawn was gone. She remembered nothing, not even making love, it was all gone, leaving nothing but the mountains all around her and the snow on the lake. She didn't know how she got there. She was alone in the car, she got out and ran towards the lake. She took a handful of the pure snow and washed her face with it, it was so cold it burned, it was invigorating. Her mountaineer came up from behind her and handed her a snow-white towel.

—Is this a new towel?

—Yes, there's a pile of them in the car, he said.

—Thank you, she said, hugging him.

—Did you have a good sleep?

—It was great, she said, turning to look at the landscape, now fully back to herself.

—It's bitter out, don't catch cold. Let's get back in the car.

They continued down the road along the ridge above the lake, you might say they were driving along the ridge of the Himalayas. Yamdrok Lake is long and narrow, lying in the peaceful embrace of the Himalayas, surrounded by dazzling tall peaks. The sunlight off the lake stings the eyes, and the otherworldly twin snow peaks of Gambala

Mountain stand side by side, thrusting up into the sky. The blue sky seems to flow down from the peaks, a Yamdrok Lake in the sky. The peaks sometimes stand out starkly and sometimes are shrouded in clouds, within the clouds snowstorms howl, one look at them makes you feel cold to the bone. How could you possibly climb those mountains? Ukyi Lhamo thought about her man climbing a mountain in a snowstorm, which she found impressive in the extreme, but this simply proved her ignorance, no one climbed during a snowstorm. He was concentrating on driving and didn't say much, but he did say that once they got past Nangartse they would be able to see the famous Nojin Kangsang, which he had climbed many years before. Ukyi Lhamo was curious to know how many years. He thought for a while, not answering right away, then said it had been nine years, he had been twenty-nine. Twenty-nine, he repeated. Everyone is nostalgic for their youth, even someone who still seemed as young as he did. Nojin Kangsang, its summit just above seven thousand metres, is one of Tibet's four tallest mountains. He told Ukyi Lhamo that there are two climbing seasons, April to May and September to October, which made her realise her mistake in imagining him climbing in a snowstorm. He said Nojin Kangsang was a world of ice and snow, its peaks and valleys giving birth to dozens of glaciers, and there can be avalanches on the mountain. He said two friends of his lay buried on the mountain.

—Are they still there?

—Yes. For nine years now.

—Aren't they turned to ice by now?

—Of course.

—Really? Can you still see their bodies?

—No.

—How come?

—It'd be good if you could, though. Something for the tourists, right?

He could be very subtly sarcastic. Ukyi Lhamo usually caught most of his sarcasm, but this was the thing that kept a distance between them. Despite herself, her thoughts turned to Wang Mojie, and she wondered what it was that kept a distance between them. Wang Mojie was never subtle, he was always straightforward. Wang Mojie was completely different from her mountaineer, so how come she couldn't free herself from that miserable bastard? The beautiful peaks rising into the heavens faded from her vision, and in her head the sound of Wang Mojie's voice faded, along with the image of his face.

—You should sleep some more, her mountaineer said.

—I always get sleepy in cars, she said and, embarrassed, she opened her eyes wide.

—Want to move to the back to sleep? he asked, slowing down.

—No, let's listen to some music.

He put on *Eagles of the Snow Peaks*, which he liked to have on when he drove. It is good, very Tibetan, but hear it too much and it becomes just background to whatever you are thinking about and doesn't move you any more. Music in a car is like that, you can't listen with your full attention. Music in the background can make you start to think about the past, and travel can make you turn things over in your mind again and again, more so than usual, so when you are travelling you are always both where you are and somewhere else. At all times, human beings are such indeterminate things. The conversations she heard in her head started again, now unstoppable, more and more voices, the words coming faster: Mother, Grandmother, Uncle Lhalu, *In Praise of White Tara, The Wish-Fulfilling Wheel.*

She longed to be understood, she longed for things to be made clear to her. There had been so many long talks on so many days and so many nights, talks that took her journeying back through the mists of the past. The difference in their genders seemed not to matter, and she often forgot Wang Mojie was a man. But oddly, slowly over time Wang Mojie had become part of her thoughts, and she could not get him out of her head. He was right, she needed to think seriously about her mother. Why had she never thought seriously about her? All the things that Wang Mojie had said about her mother during their long talk played back in her head. Her mind raced… Wang Mojie's voice kept talking and talking in her head. It didn't stop until she looked out and saw they had reached Nangartse, finally giving her something else to think about.

The town of Nangartse sits at a high elevation and, looking down on a lake, seems even higher than it is. The sun was bright on the snow peaks all around and stung their eyes. The prayer flags fluttered in the wind. Nangartse is a small town with a single crossroads, the road is four metres wide at most. Two- and three-storey wood and stone buildings run for maybe two hundred metres along both sides of the road. On one side are half a dozen restaurants run by people from Sichuan, one next to the other, as if they need to huddle together to avoid being blown away by the strong mountain winds. The restaurants are small, with just a few tables in each, all of them furnished in more or less the same way and none of them terribly clean. Ukyi Lhamo looked out at Nangartse and was not impressed. Seeing she was awake, her mountaineer spoke to her.

—You slept another hour. Did you sleep well?

—I slept all right. It's like sleeping on a plane, you're just out.

—I was driving slowly.

—I shouldn't sleep any more. I've slept too much already, she said, stretching.

—Let's get something to eat, then we can go to Samding Monastery. No sleeping there, even if you want to.

—Wow, Samding! How much farther?

—Not too far now, we're close.

—Excellent!

He knew Nangartse and had been there countless times on climbing expeditions. He was almost a regular at the best restaurant, the best because it was the cleanest. He knew the couple who ran it. It was on the ground floor, rooms for rent were on the first floor, and from the first-floor balcony you had a view of the mountains rising behind the building. The blue-green mountains looked crystal clean, there wasn't a tree on them, no vegetation, just colourful prayer flags flapping in the wind high up on the peak. They looked at their room, and Ukyi Lhamo's mountaineer asked that it be cleaned. The innkeepers had changed the sheets and quilt and cleaned the floor and the bathroom, but he had them change the bedding and clean the room again. It was the best room available but still a bit shabby. Yet the view was wonderful, and after it had been cleaned, they were satisfied and went downstairs to eat. He asked her what she wanted, and she said she didn't care. She was used to letting him take care of everything, which he did well. When he asked her if she wanted wine or beer, she hesitated before saying she did. He said she might get sleepy again if she had something to drink, which might make the trip up to Samding uncomfortable for her, so she gave up the idea of a drink. Samding Monastery is about fifty kilometres from Nangartse. He had told her it wasn't far, but distance is relative. It is usually pointless to ask your driver how far away a place is because near and far mean different things to the driver and his passengers. Fifty kilometres on a mountain road would take them more than an hour. It is a good thing Ukyi Lhamo didn't drink, as it would have put her back to sleep. Her mountaineer knew what he was doing. He was experienced behind the wheel, experienced in life and in affairs of the heart.

The road to Samding Monastery leads out along a peninsula that juts into Yamdrok Lake. The peninsula is a hill and Samding Monastery, with its crimson walls, is on top. Because the monastery sits alone under clouds above a lake, and because few tourists visit it, Samding Monastery seems like a secret. Another thing that lends Samding Monastery an air of mystery is that its abbess is the twelfth incarnation of the Samding Dorje Phagmo. The first Samding Dorje Phagmo was a fifteenth-century princess named Chokyi Dronma, who was identified as the *tulku* of the tantric deity Vajravarahi, known as Dorje Phagmo in Tibetan. Dorje Phagmo is the consort of Cakrasamvara, as well as the *dakini* of practitioners of Atiyoga or Utmost Yoga, so Samding Monastery has many images and statues of Dorje Phagmo (Vajravarahi) entwined with Cakrasamvara in the *yab-yum* posture. Because the historical Dorje Phagmo, along with her monks and nuns, long practised the esoteric methods of Vajravarahi, many incarnations of Dorje Phagmo could shape shift and use the same power on others. In researching Samding, Ukyi Lhamo learned that early in the eighteenth century, when a Dzungar army invaded Tibet from Mongolia, their chieftain came to Samding and demanded that Dorje Phagmo demonstrate her shapeshifting ability. She refused, so the Dzungar army attacked the monastery. When they rode in, they found that Dorje Phagmo had transformed her 160 monks into 160 roaring beasts. Dorje Phagmo's powers overawed the Dzungars. Not only did they not destroy the monastery but they became great patrons of it.

After they had been on the road for almost two hours, Ukyi Lhamo could see the monastery in the distance at the top of the hill, its various levels rising like a staircase. She looked at the lake, the snow peaks, the clouds, the blue sky, and wondered if perhaps when her grandmother disappeared during the Cultural Revolution she had come to Samding for refuge and maybe was still there. This was a realm of the *dakini*. Grandmother belonged to no man, not to Lungshar nor Yuthok, she didn't belong to her children or grandchildren, and maybe her grandmother had always belonged to Samding and so her journey should have ended there. Ukyi Lhamo had long wished to come to Samding, so perhaps her passion that dawn had not come only from the physical desire of a moment.

20. Vajravarahi

She was so close to him that the badge on her hat brought back for him the terror of that day.
Amid the sound of death, they fled the Square. Death. Humiliation.
She slapped him. It was the right thing to do.
She stepped on his lower back, exerting almost all her weight. Slowly he began to levitate, his field of vision dimmed, then everything went black.

Ukyi Lhamo had assumed Samding was a nunnery, but she discovered this was not so. Everyone affiliated with Samding, with the exception of the twelfth incarnation of Dorje Phagmo and her attendants, was a crimson-robed monk, and Dorje Phagmo and her retinue weren't even at the monastery, they were in Lhasa. Ukyi Lhamo didn't see a single nun. She lingered at the monastery for more than two hours, feeling calmed down, calmer even than she had felt after she and her mountaineer had made love in the car, calm now in a deeper way.

She interrupted a monk's chanting to ask him if there was now or ever had been an elderly nun in Dorje Phagmo's retinue, but the answer was no. She asked where the older nuns lived, but the monk did not know. There were no tourists at Samding and only a very few local worshippers, so there was an otherworldly quiet on the top of the hill. Ukyi Lhamo was used to coming up with nothing, she had done so many times, and each time she told herself that it was all right because a failure to find her grandmother on one day only meant she would find her on another day. Her search was the expression of faith, she accepted the suspense of not knowing, she knew she was looking for something that might not exist, and this suited her psychological make-up. Her thoughts were on her grandmother only fleetingly. She prostrated before the statue of Sakyamuni in the main hall and then knelt in prayer for a long time, now she too belonged to emptiness, belonged to nothingness, but just at this moment when she surrendered herself to the Buddha and felt aware of the nothingness of existence, she slowly felt something rushing in to fill the void. To those who have an innate aptitude for enlightenment, or a particular psychological make-up, a monastery is the soul's mandala, the soul's surrogate, the soul's *triloka*. Ukyi Lhamo was no longer aware of her surroundings or her body, her soul had taken on three dimensions, one for each of the monastery's three levels.

Samding is not large but its layout is complex, fortress-like, circles within squares, each part linked to the rest by winding corridors, stone steps and steep staircases. Wang Mojie would feel lost at Samding, thinking he had walked into a maze, but Ukyi Lhamo seemed to have an inborn familiarity with the labyrinth, just as she knew well the tangled confusion of her thoughts. She went into every one of the halls, making an offering in each of a few yuan, no more than five or ten yuan at a time, which was the habit of someone who often visited monasteries. She found the Stupa Hall where the first to the eleventh incarnations of Dorje Phagmo are venerated. It was filled with shadows cast by butter lamps, and she suddenly felt some delicate spirit overcome her. Nowhere else in Tibet was there a stupa hall with the bodily remains of eleven incarnations of a Living Buddha, and Ukyi Lhamo was so moved she left almost every yuan she still had as an offering. At no other monastery had she experienced such an impulse. She liked Samding, even the incense there smelled different to her, and she told herself she should have come to Samding long before. Those eleven women were her previous selves, her sisters, her mother, grandmother. Generations of women, depicted in the paintings in various postures, some young, as young as she was. Whether from happiness or some other emotion, she was moved to tears that she could not stop from falling. She was alone in the Stupa Hall except for two young lamas in their red robes (actually, to call them lamas is incorrect, "lama" means guru or "superior one" and is a title reserved for monks who have attained a high level of enlightenment, and the young men were ordinary monks). When the young monks saw Ukyi Lhamo make her offering and start to cry, they led her to a door at the back of the Stupa Hall that led to an ancient room for tantric practice. Did they take her for an incarnation of a *dakini*? They opened the rusted lock on the door and invited her to go in.

The door opened onto a splendid scene of butter lamps like stars in a morning sky, *thangka*, wall paintings and bronze statues of deities in the *yab-yum* embrace of tantric practice. She had seen such figures before but not so exquisite and not in so many positions. It was like a dream to her, a vision. Cakrasamvara and Dorje Phagmo, with eight arms, twelve arms, twenty-four arms, in yellow, in green, in white, the two deities in sexual embrace, standing and sitting, facing each other, in union, soaring together... a glorious combining of souls and bodies, both spiritual and secular. A depiction of love, blissful love, love that connects one to the gods, eternal love, love that can lead to Buddhahood.

Her mountaineer had some of the qualities of Cakrasamvara, pity he wasn't beside her. He was waiting in the car, he never came into monasteries with her. She stayed there for quite some time, reluctant to leave, her heart like a lotus in bloom.

When she walked out, there was an aura around her (or so it felt to her), but her mountaineer, sad to say, didn't seem to notice. Apparently, he had none of the qualities of Cakrasamvara after all, that had been just her fantasy. He hadn't slept, he had passed the time sitting in the car listening to music. He wasn't a Buddhist, he was not interested in religion. Religious life, monasteries, Cundi, *dakini* and all that didn't exist for him. For him, the world was mountains. They both were in pursuit of some sort of ultimate fulfilment, but their ideas of what this meant could not have been more different. He poured some tea from a thermos into a paper cup for her, it smelled good, and it was hot. He and the tea both met her standards.

—Learn anything?

She knew he was asking about her grandmother, and she didn't know how to respond. She said, I'll need to come back.

—Any news of your grandmother? He made the question specific.

—No, she said, shaking her head. After a pause, she said, Women never have homes, but women are home here, this is their home.

—Is that so? I'm sorry, I don't understand Buddhism.

—No need for you to, she said, looking at him.

—How is this monastery different from the others? You look like you've learned something. He was not unobservant.

—The remains of eleven women are in there, all covered in gold leaf, they go back almost a thousand years, some died when they were very young, younger than I am.

—The gold leaf makes them last forever, he said. He took a sip of tea, then said, Tibet has other ways of doing that.

—What other ways?

He took her cup and carefully refilled it from the thermos.

—Well, for example, there's mountaineering, he said with authority.

—Mountaineering?

—Yes, mountaineering. There are many mountain climbers whose bodies are going to last forever.

—Are you talking about the men who were on that climb with you? What a thing to say.

—They are part of the mountain now.

It was getting dark, he turned the headlights on. They sat and drank their tea, making no move to leave. The SUV was new, it had all the latest bells and whistles. They sat, surrounded by high mountains. The SUV was like some futuristic monster, light from its eyes beaming out into the night and vanishing in the distance. The monastery sat in darkness at the top of its hill, its lights weak but eternal, shining like faint stars at morning.

—So, are you going to end up lasting forever the way your friends did? Ukyi Lhamo asked.

—Just don't know when, he said.

—Do you want that day to come?

—I wouldn't say that, but we all go someday, one way or another.

—Your way is too cold. Faith makes you warm.

—I should be a Buddhist mountaineer?

—What's wrong with that?

—Climbing is about overcoming something. Is Buddhism about overcoming something?

—And you say you don't understand Buddhism. You have potential, really, she said, feeling a sort of hope.

—If I didn't climb, I could be a very, very devout Buddhist.

—All those mountains you've climbed are sacred, people worship them.

—That's *kora*, that's circumambulation, not mountain climbing.

—Anybody can be a Buddhist, you can be a Buddhist and climb, climbers are just people.

—Marry me, stay with me forever, the two of us, one of us climbing mountains and one of us worshipping the Buddha. He caressed her hair and kissed her.

—I think you can say that love is the Buddha, the Buddha is love. Can you accept that?

—Now that I haven't heard before. I suppose I need to go inside the monastery and have a look around, to see if I can find the love.

—You lack understanding, it wouldn't be visible to you.

—And you only recently gained your own understanding, no?

—I was seeking it for a very long time, that's what matters, not that I've only just found it.

—How long would it take me?

—I don't know.

—You're determined to change me, aren't you?

She kissed him, he kissed her back, a long kiss.

—You better stick to climbing mountains, she said.

—Exactly right. The truth cannot be expressed in words, so sayeth the Buddha, Ukyi Lhamo's mountaineer said.

They embraced and kissed but stopped short of making love in the car again.

That evening, Ukyi Lhamo drank a lot until her face was flushed and her eyes were glassy. They were at a roadside inn, out on the Tibetan Plateau on a winter evening. She put her arms around his neck, her legs around his waist, straddling him, lotus position, feeling every inch of him. At first, she didn't moan. Four arms. Eight arms. Twelve arms. Twenty-four arms. One thousand arms, one thousand eyes. She taught him how to make the Vajrahumkara posture, she rose above him, wrapped one leg around his waist, and then both legs. The degree of difficulty was high, and the feeling was extraordinary. But just when she moaned, long and loud, her eyes full of ecstasy, he suddenly couldn't contain himself, he let go, lost control and came. She saw his face convulse as his body shuddered.

He stilled, became motionless as a clay statue, and the next instant he was asleep, his head on her naked breast. She took the condom off him and went into the bathroom to wash. She looked at the person in the mirror, she studied her face. She studied her eyes and looked at her damp hair. She looked lost and exhausted, a still from some film. She was at five thousand metres above sea level in a little town on the Tibetan Plateau. In her mind's eye, she saw the dawn shadow of Wang Mojie. She wondered if tomorrow she should continue on the trip. Tomorrow would take them even farther, and then it would be too late to turn back. She stayed up late and woke up late the next day. Her mountaineer was reading a month-old copy of *The Tibet News*. She had read it the night before, he seemed to be very interested in it. She asked the time, and he said ten. She gasped.

—Ten? Why didn't you wake me up?

—Why would I do that? This is a nice place, it's nice and sunny outside, and nice and toasty in here.

From the window she looked out at the sunny day, at the snow peaks, the light bounced off the peaks and shone in on her, it was very bright.

—Been up long? she asked, smoothing her hair back, her body moving as if in yoga.

—I've been out twice already. I got petrol and bought some bottled water and snacks. There's a market with all kinds of stuff, it's like a mini Barkhor Street, want to have a look?

—No.

He put the newspaper down, stood up, went to the bed and stood looking down at her.

—It was quite novel to see you lying there asleep, in sunlight, under mountains, really super fantastic. Hungry? There's coffee and bread here. Downstairs in the restaurant, there's noodles and congee that's been waiting for you all morning.

She felt a sharp stab of desire that was hard to resist. Her mountaineer bent down and kissed her forehead. He moved to kiss her lips, but she turned away. She jumped out of the bed and took off her nightdress, she was never modest with him. He kissed her again, told her she was beautiful and started to caress her, but desire had left her. She was thinking not about him but about a feeling, she couldn't quite say what it was, that seemed to be growing inside her, sparked by the sunlight and the unfamiliar surroundings. Later she would realise it had something to do with Wang Mojie. Was that why she had turned away from his kisses? Was this all because of Wang Mojie? She found the thought ridiculous. She got dressed. Then she gave her mountaineer a long, hard kiss. It was near noon when they got back on the road and left Nangartse. He drove like someone in touch with the mountains all around them.

The eternal mountains, the snow, an eagle.

That afternoon under the same sun in the same sky in the same moment, Ukyi Lhamo watched an eagle while Yu Youyan watched the eagle-like Wang Mojie. He was standing in a shadow in a wrinkled black cotton jacket. He looked to her like an eagle with wings spread. Actually, because of the black jacket, printed with odd circular patterns, he looked more like a bat than an eagle. Of course, if we want to be picky, we really have no reason to connect the two "moments". The eagle that Ukyi Lhamo watched was soaring upwards, up to a silvery snow-covered peak, but Wang Mojie, more a bat than an eagle, looked caught, like an actor in a cage on stage. Yu Youyan was sitting, legs crossed, in the high-backed chair where Wang Mojie often sat to read. She was wearing her uniform, she looked stern, her white gloves were clean and bright.

She looked imposing in her tie and sharply creased trousers, the badge on her hat and the buttons on her jacket glinted in the afternoon sunlight. She was dressed exactly as she dressed for work, and she had her workface on. She had learned something since their first time doing this (the first time she had looked pointlessly angry, amateurish, she had just vented her anger in a frenzy, not following any of the rules of the game). But this time she was cold, haughty, distant and sexy. She looked professional, intimidatingly so. She gave Wang Mojie a look, nothing needed to be said between them.

That was how the game began, her look was an order that Wang Mojie understood. He got up, closed the curtains and turned the electric space heater all the way up. January is the coldest month of the year in Lhasa, and so he also turned on the hot plate that he cooked on. Then he spread a sheet, the same one they used the previous time, on the floor, one end of it under Yu Youyan's raised glossy boot.

He took off his jacket, sweater and trousers. When he was down to his sleeveless T-shirt and a woman's lace-waist thong, he paused. Calmly and confidently, as she had done the first time, Yu Youyan slapped him hard in the face and directed him to take off the rest of his clothes.

She spoke softly, which made a nice contrast with the crisp sound of the slap she had delivered with dispassionate professionalism. She was much better at it now, she had improved fast, the progress she had made in just three days was impressive. Clearly someone had given her some tips (only later did Wang Mojie learn that it was the maths professor-poet who had clued her in on what she needed to know). She had also seen some videos, which she had access to at work (in Lhasa, just as everywhere else in the country, there is a crackdown on prostitution and pornography every year, and every year police confiscate many pornographic videos).

When Wang Mojie hesitated before taking off his T-shirt, she slapped him again, which was part of the game. His face turned one way with the first slap, the other way with the second, he took it with docility, also part of the game, they both understood without speaking that the slightest disobedience was to be punished.

Naked, Wang Mojie shivered, not because of the cold and not because he was frightened, quite the contrary, he shivered because he was excited. In the instant of each sharp slap to his face, Wang Mojie felt stirred and stimulated and started to remember the many times before. Yu Youyan was strong, her strength came from anger, and she had been taught what to do. She was much more forceful with him than his wife had ever been, so it was more real and exciting to him.

It never felt exactly right with his wife because she always held back, never fully got into the role, so he had to rely on fantasy for some of what he needed. Wang Mojie knelt at Yu Youyan's feet and kissed her boot. He kissed the shaft, then inch by inch moved down to the upper, the toe, the heel. He was worshipful, completely into it. Yu Youyan, of course, could not be satisfied with this, and she gave him an order in a loud, firm voice, as if on stage.

—Lick it! Don't kiss it, lick it! You know what lick means? Use your tongue and lick.

She raised her boot and looked down at Wang Mojie. This was a new demand, he had always kissed the boots rather than lick them, kissing made it into a sort of romantic ritual. Licking was starker, more raw, more direct, sexier, it was shameless, it dispensed with the very last bit of Wang Mojie's concern with the aesthetics of it all. Tasting with his tongue was different from feeling with his lips. When the tip of his tongue touched the tip of her boot, the taste of boot polish in his mouth made him feel complete debasement.

—Faster! Stop messing about, she ordered, disdainfully.

He sped up, his tongue turning black.

—Say, "I'm a dog". Say it. Are you a dog? She took off her belt and held it up as a whip.

He did not speak. The belt came down on his buttocks hard, she held nothing back, a welt bloomed on Wang Mojie's buttocks, more welts bloomed in profusion as she whipped him again and again, waves of pain spread through his entire body.

—I am, yes, I am, Wang Mojie said under his breath.

—Louder. Say it and use the word "dog".

She whipped him again, twice. That was savage, Wang Mojie thought. He didn't say anything, he began to grow angry, and in the moment it was hard to separate what was role-playing and what was real. She kept hitting him with the belt, it wasn't a game any more, it was real pent-up hatred. But weren't real humiliation and pain what he wanted? What was sufficient humiliation? What sort of humiliation from what sort of violence? How debased could a man be? How far had he debased himself before? How was he to endure this debasement and humiliation? He needed the violence and humiliation in order to find release.

—Yes, I am, I am.

—Say you are a dog!

—I am, I am a dog.

He wanted to cry but there were no tears.

—Whose dog?

—Yours.

Whack, whack, *she whipped him again.*

—Whose?

—Yours! Yours, I'm your dog.

—Bark. I want to hear you bark.

—I'm your dog.

Whack, whack, *she whipped him twice. Wang Mojie barked, very loudly.*

—Who said to be so loud? Quieter.

Whack, whack. *Wang Mojie gave a softer bark, like a pug. He was self-conscious before the first bark, but now he didn't care, he would bark any way she wanted him to.*

—Come here, let's put this collar on you. Good boy, are you a good boy?

He barked softly. She put a dog collar around his neck, tightly, then had him get on the bed on all fours and crawl back and forth. She showed him some mercy by not making him crawl up and down on the hard stone floor, which would have skinned his knees. But the bed wasn't that soft and his knees soon hurt, making him shift the weight to his hands. Yu Youyan soon acted on her recent new idea and told him to crawl under the chair in which he often sat to read and take notes.

— OK, in you go, there's your kennel, in you go, in you go.

This innovation of Yu Youyan's wasn't bad, it was amusing, it met Wang Mojie's long-standing interest in ridiculing himself, so he was happy to crawl under. He had many times asked his wife to play the kennel game with him, but she never gave him the satisfaction, she wouldn't play along. She was willing to whip him and stand on him in her high heels, but she would not call him a dog. If he barked wildly at her, she just called him a pig. There wasn't much room under the chair and nothing to lie on, so it was more uncomfortable than an actual dog crate. The first time this was as far as they got before Yu Youyan walked out. As she left, she turned to him and said, You stay there, don't come out, I'm going grocery shopping, be a good boy and wait for Momma to come home, when Momma comes back, you get a treat. She waved to him, even blew him a kiss from the door. He thought she was pretending to leave, still role-playing, so he stayed under the chair for a good long while after she walked out, it took a long time before he realised she wasn't coming back.

This time, however, it was clear the game wasn't stopping here. When Yu Youyan arrived, Wang Mojie had noticed the nice black leather briefcase she had. She had put it on his desk. Now, from under the chair, he heard what sounded like a combination lock turning, then clicking as it opened. A moment later he saw that he had been right, it was a briefcase with a combination lock, the sort for safeguarding important legal documents. If she had taken from the briefcase and read out loud to him a court verdict, an investigatory finding, someone's testimony or an accusation against him, anything of that sort, it would not have surprised him, it would have been a new game, and of course he would not confess to the charges easily. Eventually he would, of course. After the torture (the torture would be impossible to endure), he would submit and confess to everything, he would name his accomplices or take it all on himself. If a written statement of remorse was required, he would sign obediently. He longed for her to put him on trial, he longed for the mental and physical pain. He had many secret fantasies he wanted to tell someone, he wanted the chance to testify. At the click of the briefcase opening, all these crazy thoughts ran through his head, but then he heard the clack and rattle of something metal. There were no legal papers, they weren't needed. From her briefcase, Yu Youyan took gleaming, honest-to-goodness handcuffs and shackles, merciless things. All his theatrical fantasies vanished at the sight of the shiny stainless steel. The handcuffs and shackles waved near his eyes, and he could see his thin face reflected in the metal. They weren't props or toys, they were the real deal they used in jail. Yu Youyan's job was an advantage, and the same had been true of his wife.

Yu Youyan wasn't as practised at using the handcuffs and shackles as his wife had been. She wasn't clumsy, not at all, just not as practiced, but that was just because of circumstances, as his wife had the chance to get more skilled. Because she wasn't that adept, Wang Mojie's knees suffered some more, and he got an abrasion on an ankle, from which blood seeped. He wasn't stark naked any more. Besides the dog collar, he wore handcuffs and shackles. With difficulty, he crawled up and down a few times. Giving Wang Mojie an arrogant, scornful glance (she looked very like an actress in one of the videos she had studied), Yu Youyan said, Get up. He got up. She was a much better actor than his wife, no doubt because she was a show-off by nature. He stood up, unsure of what she would do next. He couldn't predict, they hadn't planned this, which was the only way to make it all new and exciting.

It surprised him greatly when she took out white nylon rope and began to tie him up as she reprimanded him. Unlike the handcuffs and shackles, the rope was amateurish, it should have been hemp or climbing rope or canvas strapping. Nylon rope is never used. She didn't know how to bind him either. Aesthetics matter in bondage, a person should be tied up in a way that is pleasing to the eye. It should be brutal but beautiful. Yu Youyan was cruel enough, she tied him tightly enough for the rope to cut into his skin, but it looked coarse, no order to it. Her choice of nylon rope and the way she tied him proved that despite her ostentation she was rough and unsophisticated. She quite clearly had never learned any handicraft, and Wang Mojie doubted she could even sew or do needlepoint or any of that sort of thing. It was hard to believe she was a university graduate. Any way you look at it, there is a difference between coarse cruelty and elegant cruelty, like the difference between the locust swarm of the Japanese monsters in contrast to the neat and tidy German brutes in World War II. In no way could his wife ever be capable of the roughness and savagery that was part of Yu Youyan's nature. His wife came from a prominent family of police officers. All established families (even a family of police) pass down their own civilising traditions. But, goodness, what traditions do we have left? Do we have any left? Wang Mojie asked himself these questions as he watched Yu Youyan, who he decided lacked culture. He missed his wife. He owed his wife an apology.

—Lie down. Face down. Hear me? Lie down. You're asking for a whipping!

Whack. *The belt came down on him again.*

The pain from the belt added to the pain from the rope. He was bound head to toe, lying face down, defenceless. He suddenly felt really at peril, they were about to cross a boundary. It was too late for any sort of self-protection, they had not set a safe word, and so Yu Youyan had the power to do with him whatever she wished to, without constraint. He realised that with Yu Youyan, what started as play could turn real, and the roughness and savagery in her nature had no limit. What if he couldn't withstand it? This was a real test but also very arousing, he felt real fear.

He always wanted to experience true fear, he wanted to study it. Only by knowing real fear, only by crossing a boundary, could he be freed from fear. His wife never gave him satisfaction in this regard.

He couldn't see Yu Youyan's face or her hands, only her boots as she slowly lifted and lowered them. She stepped slowly over his head and for a second he had an up-close look at the sole and heel of a boot and he could smell the glue. The pattern on the sole was as complicated as a map of the Fengtai transport hub in Beijing. He had hidden there for days. The pattern on her boot reminded him of this, and it brought back to him the fear he had felt, it reminded him of Fengtai in Beijing and this made him afraid.

He tried to slow his breathing, he tried to calm his fear, he tried telling himself he was a hero, but when he felt her boot lower onto his skinny, frail back, he cried out loudly.

She was standing on him, or it felt that way to him, but in truth she had put only one foot on him. His fear exaggerated the pain.

—Wang Mo! She shouted his name, and only then did he realise that she had put only one foot on him because as she shouted, she lifted her foot and poked him in the buttocks with her toe. She wasn't standing on him yet, which made him feel a lot less heroic.

—Wang Mo, you should see yourself now. You think you are so tough. If you're tough, don't yell.

He had to yell because as she spoke, she put her other foot on him, she stepped on his defenceless lower back, he yelled in pain, his breath moving the sheet in front of his face.

—Wang Mo, you think this is a game? I don't play games. This violence is real, it's real, real! Look at that thin waist, like a dog's. How could I have had a crush on you, that was ludicrous of me, ludicrous, ludicrous!

As she spoke, she stomped down on him with enough force that her hat fell off. Her short hair fell across her eyes as she bent down to pick up the hat. Wang Mojie saw this out of the corner of his eye and found it exciting. It was a good thing Yu Youyan wasn't as tall as Ukyi Lhamo, a good thing part of her big bust was just padding, otherwise she might have broken his back while he was distracted by her hair. She put her hat on and straightened it, she even took out a compact mirror and checked it. The pain made Wang Mojie sweat profusely, but the momentary vision of the hatless Yu Youyan was simply wonderful, and that made Wang Mojie feel there was nothing he could not bear, he felt pleasure. Had it not been for the pain, the sight of the hatless Yu Youyan would have done nothing for Wang Mojie, rather like the sight of a flower as we walk through a ruin is more touching than a flower we see in a walk in a garden. He had been through the ruin, he saw her short hair, he was satisfied. He even longed for her boots, he longed for her powerful boots and her beautiful short hair.

But she was panting for breath now, panting for breath as she stomped on Wang Mojie.

—Rubbish. You know you're rubbish, right?

—Yes, I am, Wang Mojie said happily, his face to the floor.

—Listen to me, no high heels today, high heels would stab straight through your back!

—Uh, uh, the boots are good too.

—Crap. I wore stiletto heels last time, I wish I'd worn them today, that's what the women in the videos wear, I should have worn them, then you'd be covered in blood. Rubbish, I'm letting you off easy, understand?

—Thank you, thank you, thank you for the kindness.

—Kindness? I'll show you kindness. She stomped on him again, he shrieked.

—I thought you were better than those other men, I thought you were different from them, I thought you had culture, I thought you were deep, I thought there was something special about you, but I never guessed that what's special about you is that you're a pervert! You tricked me, you tricked me, you tricked me. You're a rotten person. Tell me, are you a rotten person? Are you?

—Yes, I am, I am, yes, I'm the worst person.

—You want me to stomp you to death, don't you?

—Yes... I like you.

—Don't make me sick. I should stomp you to death!

But now she was no longer standing on his lower back, her feet were on his buttocks, which were pulled apart by the way he was bound. She was supposed to stand on his buttocks, not his back, she stood on his back only because she hated him. Still, it wasn't too late in the game for her to stand on his buttocks, in fact it was a perfect time. Unlike the pain in his back, the pain in his buttocks was also a kind of pleasure, plus when she stood on his buttocks the pressure was transferred to his crotch. He felt the stirring in his penis, felt it engorge, grow hard. His erection against the hard stone floor hurt, so he raised himself up a bit. There was danger here in that if Yu Youyan exerted her full weight on him now, it might break his prick! This was a horrid thought, he had to turn himself over, get himself on his back, but he was tied up and it was difficult to move. He took a breath, arched his back – this was the crucial moment – and with a yell he flipped over, like a beetle.

She was startled when he flipped over and what startled her was his big fire-red sausage of an erection that was covered in scars. Instinctively she stepped back, and as she did her eyes grew wide, her expression seemed to say it hadn't occurred to her that he could still get it up, especially with all the rope tied around him. When she was tying him up, she hadn't touched that limp dead thing, and had paid no attention to it, remaining as indifferent as a doctor. She had seen many men, and she wasn't embarrassed. Now she turned away at the sight of it but immediately turned back around. Her face was a little flushed, not with embarrassment but with arousal. Had she been embarrassed, she wouldn't have kept looking at it so boldly.

Now it was time for some S&M with his penis, she had to know that. The theatrical, cold, haughty expression returned to her face. She knew, she must have known, what she had to do now. She moved the hard toe of a boot near it, as if she were about to stamp on it, but she didn't. She touched it a few times with the toe of her boot and she started to shake, her face went red and suddenly she withdrew her foot and turned away, covering her face with her hands. She was no pervert, she was normal, her anger was normal, it came from frustration because what she wanted was sex, not any of this. She shook, not knowing what to do, by the rules of the game this was when she was supposed to be most cruelly dominant with him, but she couldn't do it. She was fine doing anything else to him but not this. If it was flaccid, she would step on it no problem but red and erect like that, it left her at a loss. She pushed it with her boot toe again, it stiffly bounced back, and at this she suddenly cried out and threw herself down on top of Wang Mojie. She squeezed his neck in her hands.

—Wang Mo, I hate you, I hate you, I want to strangle you, I want to strangle you.

Wang Mojie hadn't been prepared for this and was helpless to do anything about it anyway. Yu Youyan was out of control, out of her mind, and while this lasted only briefly it was long enough for her to have really strangled him. He was on the verge of passing out. Wang Mojie knew that the highest level in the game was losing consciousness, and it wasn't everybody who dared take it that far, but Yu Youyan was unaware of this fact, she was utterly unfamiliar with the concept. Wang Mojie started to black out and just before he did, he couldn't repress a despairing sigh. He didn't want to die this way, no matter how empty his life was.

His last hazy thought before he passed out was a prayer. He prayed, Don't let this be real, this isn't happening, it isn't happening... He slowly began to levitate, his field of vision dimmed, then everything went black. As he fell into the blackness, his prayer stopped, but then he began to perceive the light again, he saw what looked like a river of white in the distance, and above the river he saw himself, he called himself back.

Next, he saw a uniform hat, close up, its badge, the national seal, right up in his face, filling his field of vision. He felt as if he were back on the Square, looking up from the ground, seeing everything at a tilt, seeing the torches and national emblems on the Great Hall of the People and the National Museum. He saw Yu Youyan's mouth open as she yelled at him, but what he heard was all the yelling on the Square. She was too close to him, her hat filling his field of vision and bringing back the terror of that day. Amid the sound of death, they fled the Square, death, humiliation, a trip through hell, worse than death. Yu Youyan was slapping him, which was the right thing to do. She tried to make him come to, she had to make him come to, her face was almost touching his. As she slapped him, her face slowly came into focus for him, her nose, her eyes, her tears, he knew he had been pulled back from the Square, and he understood what she wanted.

—I want you to rape me, he said.

—No, Yu Youyan yelled.

She kissed him, nuzzled him, bit his lip.

—I want you to rape me, he said, his voice steady.

—No! No!

—Rape me, you'll feel better.

—No!

She stood up, losing her composure. She threw herself on the bed and rolled back and forth, her body convulsing.

—Come on, rape me. I'm ready for you.

Yu Youyan lay still. After a good long moment, she got up from the bed and looked around the room. She found what she needed. She cleaned herself up, checked herself in the mirror and straightened her hair, always keeping her back to Wang Mojie. When she finally turned and looked at Wang Mojie, who was still bound and lying on the floor, she was quite calm. She wasn't wearing her hat. Now Wang Mojie could stare at her uniform and short hair rather than catch only fleeting glimpses. She reached down and unlocked the handcuffs and shackles and began to untie the rope, which was wound around him crazily, the knots snarled, she worked at them but couldn't undo them, which made her lose her cool again.

—Don't worry about the rope, I can get it off myself, we can use it next time.

Ignoring him, she put the handcuffs and shackles back in the briefcase. She stood up and gave a long, relieved sigh. She had opened the door and stepped out through it when Wang Mojie said, Officer, your hat, don't forget your hat. She came back in and picked up her hat without looking at Wang Mojie.

—Practise on the rope for next time.

—Next time I will kill you, she said, standing in the doorway and looking down at Wang Mojie.

—You couldn't kill me, he said.

—Then you will have to kill me, she said, then turned and left.

—Hey, he shouted after her, close the door. Close the door. I can't get up.

There was no answer, but luckily it was the winter break and the school was deserted, and it was twilight. No one was around. As he worked on untying himself, the sky grew dark. When he had freed himself of the rope, he closed the door and then heated water, filled a bath with the hot water and soaked in it to relax his muscles and get his blood flowing. He looked down at the purple marks all over his body left by the tight rope. They were ugly. The pain and the pleasure, the two things didn't separate for him, would stay with him all that night. He stayed awake for a long time, thinking about his body. He hadn't expected to still be caught up in all this after he moved to Tibet. He didn't drift off to sleep until it was almost morning, and he woke up soon after.

He always got up early.

---

21. The Order of Things

It was morning. The mornings were always like paintings.
Each moment there was a small change and each was a painting.
Look at a painting long enough and you will become part of it.
I stood at the centre of the round platform, my arms held up to the sky.
I didn't know if I was welcoming those emissaries or directing them,
but I had no influence on them whatsoever, none descended.

As I have said many times, I am an early riser. And as I have said, the vultures got up even earlier, they rose before the sun, bringing the darkness of the predawn with them. They circled and soared. They were in their world, I was in mine, they were in their space, I was in mine. They were silent, always silent, a silence that lasted from birth to death. They filled the empty sky with the shadows of the night, so when they flew off it was hard to say if they flew towards the sun or the moon, but perhaps to the soul of the departed it made no difference.

It was morning. The mornings were always like paintings, each moment there was a small change and each was a painting.

Look at a painting long enough and you will become part of it.

I stood at the centre of the round platform, my arms held up to the sky in a V.

I went there often, so I often write about it.

True, I didn't know if I was welcoming those emissaries or directing them. But either way, it didn't have the slightest influence on them. None descended, they don't take orders from the earth, they answer only to the sky. Then again, if my arms were held up in welcome, maybe it wasn't just for them, not just for the vultures, maybe I was reaching out to a life that has gone or to a time that has been forgotten.

I walked through the village and saw three different sorts of time. Three different sorts of time in one space.

An old man, a child, a tree. The tree was at the edge of the village, a child stood in a hollow in the tree, the old man sat in the sun. Each in their own time. But what about the woman in black who was drawing water and glanced over at the tree, the child and the man? Her glance took in the old man, the child and the tree, and the instant of her glance was its own time, yet another type of time. A fourth sort of time?

Her glance did not take me in. She and her glance were within my field of vision.

And in what time – what disordered time – did I exist? Who was watching me in what broader field of vision? Who was watching the woman, the old man, the child and the tree? And who was watching the watcher in an even broader field of vision?

I stood on the round platform for a long time, it was low and empty, and grass grew high all around it. It was desolate. An abstract symbol of something. I didn't know what the gesture with my arms signified, nor what the platform signified.

And I don't know what Wang Mojie's grey checked scarf was supposed to signify. It was knotted once under his chin loosely and hung down in front of his chest. It was like an object in a still life painting, it was a relic of something, it represented an ideology, it stood for the afterlife, it symbolised reincarnation. It looked like a noose, it was a symbol of his soul, it looked like a nerve plexus, like stalks of hay, like wildfire fed by the spring wind. It was a memento of something, to be kept forever, it triggered memories that brought endless tears and boundless sweetness. He wanted the scarf as soon as he saw it at a stall on Barkhor Street, like it was made for him, the scarf was him. You couldn't really say what its style was, it didn't look Chinese but neither did it look Tibetan, maybe it was a mix of both. Maybe he just liked the way it looked. He thought of it as his personal trademark. He never noticed that he and the poet shared the habit of always wearing a scarf.

That day no soul was being sent on its way into the sky, but the tools used by the *ragyaba* were still there, always there. Cutting tools. Worn from use. Strewn about. The blades gleaming. A long-handled axe. A stone trough, its hollow shaped to hold a head. A fingernail. Teeth. A red sweater was on the ground next to the platform, one bent sleeve on the platform, as if reaching up for something, as if there was more to be said.

When I returned to the platform on a different but similar morning, everything looked just the same at first. But then I saw that the plait of hair that had been in the grass was gone. Who had taken it? Had they done so out of love?

I was missing Tenpa Nyima and Sangnyi. They had both vanished from my class. The students said Sangnyi had gone to her dad's, who had a stall on Barkhor Street. I looked at the sky. I felt completely lost.

A footpath in winter. A grove of trees, a mill house, the mill house was easier to see in the winter.

I walked through a field of barley that no one was going to harvest, crossed a road and walked into a second unharvested field of barley. I was once again walking down the footpath between the stream and the sluice. The water wheel was splashing but it was not grinding barley. The huge wheel was used for that only occasionally. Dolma was up and already at work, but Penpa Tsering was still in bed. My home visits were always a big deal to the students' families. I was used to the way Dolma would often put her hands together and say a prayer under her breath. It was just the Tibetan custom. Ukyi Lhamo's mother had preserved it while living in Beijing for decades. I went into their prayer room that overlooked the water and waited for Penpa Tsering to get up. He didn't get out of bed until Dolma had made butter tea.

I asked the sleepy-eyed Penpa Tsering about his homework. He rubbed his eyes and said he had finished it. I told him to go and get it, but he dawdled until it was clear he hadn't done it. It was all too familiar. I didn't say much, just gave him the usual lecture, I said what teachers say. I said, Make sure to do your homework every day and hand it in on time. When I left, Dolma presented me with a bag of eggs. I took them, gave them to Penpa Tsering and told Dolma that I still had a lot of homes to visit and couldn't take the eggs right then but would come back for them. Dolma put her palms together and bowed to me, up and down, over and over.

I left the mill house and walked back along the river. The water in winter was shallow and clear, everywhere running over rocks. The river ran near the cement factory dormitory building, and people were out washing clothes in it, I suppose they weren't bothered by the cold. I visited about a dozen families in the factory dormitory, it took most of the day. I had lunch at Wangchuk's apartment. His father got out both beer and barley wine, I accepted just a drop of the barley wine. Wangchuk had done a good job with his homework, he had been neat and thorough. He had a future, no doubt about it. The good life always goes to these sorts of people, every child's fate is determined by the family he happens to be born into. Most of my other students came from families that lived much more simply, more naturally. Most of the students were more like Penpa Tsering, who would either claim he did his homework but would be unable to produce it or, blushing, would show me the meagre line or two that he had written or simply say he hadn't done it. Wangchuk was the exception. I praised him. His father, the cement factory boss, told me I should go to the hot spring at Dezong for a break and enjoy the waters. Dezong was about one hundred and fifty kilometres from Lhasa, the factory ran a workers' sanatorium there, and they had a van that made the trip. I thanked him for the suggestion.

There was no news of Tenpa Nyima. None of the students knew where he was. I expected one of them to tell me some incredible story about what had happened to him, but they just shook their heads with a look of mystery and repeated the story of Tenpa Nyima running up the mountain the morning of his grandfather's failed sky burial and not coming back. They said they didn't know more than that. Typically, my students loved telling me wild stories about people in the village, but nobody had any crazy story about Tenpa Nyima. Was that because he had been touched by bad luck? Because his grandfather wasn't taken up into the sky? Was it because Tenpa Nyima was there that his grandfather wasn't taken? Or had his grandfather taken Tenpa Nyima with him? Who had been taken and where and by whom? What happened to his grandfather was sad, it was rare, unimaginable, and maybe that is what everyone was frightened of. It was what everyone dreaded deep down.

It was nearing twilight, and I was wondering if it was a mistake to have come to Tenpa Nyima's house. The last couple of times I had been turned away at the door, but I was already there, and after hesitating a moment, I knocked. The house was quiet, a foreboding silence that I can't quite describe. I should leave, I thought.

I walked back along the river, the sky was getting dark, and I could see the lights of the mill house in the distance. They were the only lights in the area, and they looked warm and welcoming. I wondered if Penpa Tsering was doing his homework. I had lectured him about his homework that morning, so surely he would be doing some of it. He usually obeyed my specific instructions to him, so I told myself that the more often I visited him at home to remind him about his homework, the more of it he would do. Then again, I didn't want Dolma always giving me eggs, but maybe if I came by more often, then it wouldn't seem special, and she wouldn't feel the need to give me any.

I felt comfortable in the mill house, it felt welcoming. I didn't feel like an intruder, as I had at Tenpa Nyima's house when I stood there by the door. I made up my mind to come to the mill house more often. I went right inside. I looked directly at Dolma's cataracts. She was covered in barley flour, it was on her white hair, her robe, her colourful *pangkhep* apron, on her rough hands and her weathered face. It all seemed very traditional, ancient. The flour was even on the lightbulbs that shone against the dim light of dusk. Penpa Tsering wasn't home, he was no doubt messing around outside, maybe playing *carrom* on the street or loafing in a teahouse. He would come home when he got hungry, all the village boys were like that. A lot of the girls too. The girls hung out in groups of two or three outside teahouses. They never went in, always stayed outside, as the old custom that teahouses were strictly for men was still strong. They would snack, giggle, playfully push and shove one another. If there were no boys in the teahouse, there would be no girls outside it and vice versa. That is what spring was like in Tibet, that was the routine, it never changed, it was timeless like the seasons, like the sunlight. And it was fine, why would anyone want to do all that homework, I sometimes wondered.

As if from habit, however, I checked Penpa Tsering's homework. I sighed, thinking that teachers are shackled to homework. But if we didn't assign homework, could we still be called teachers? In any profession, some things are so deeply ingrained by habit that you just do them without thinking, and they even make you feel secure. Dolma had very poor eyesight, but she opened her son's assignment notebook at the page with his latest work and handed it to me. She looked happy. Penpa Tsering had done a fraction of his work, less than a page, it was a joke, but I praised him to his mother anyway. I asked her if her son had other assignment notebooks for his other lessons. She grew flustered. She said she didn't know, she said she didn't know about maths, history, physics, politics or the rest. I let it go. She seemed unsettled as I left, and her happy look was gone. I had robbed her of her happiness. It may have been just the bliss of ignorance, but if I hadn't mentioned the rest of her son's homework, she would have stayed happy. I sighed.

Where had Tenpa Nyima gone? How could he just disappear? There were things about Tibetan culture that were eternally impenetrable to me, mysteries to me, taboo for me, things beyond my experience that belonged to tradition and could not be put into words. I thought about asking Wangchuk's father to talk to Tenpa Nyima's parents for me. I thought his parents had to know where their son was, but I decided that would be a bit too pushy, me asserting my power. I didn't want to do that, I don't like it when people assert power. I went back to the school. I walked past Ukyi Lhamo's house, my eyes unconsciously turning to her door, which was still locked. It had been locked for days. She often just suddenly disappeared. She was a hard person to figure out. But once I was back in my house with my books in their rows on my shelf, I felt happy.

I washed up, turned on the lamp and lay down on the bed to read. I always keep a lot of books by my bedside to pick up and read whenever I want. I'm not the sort of person who reads one book at a time cover to cover, I read several books at once, and I don't necessarily finish them all, and sometimes it takes me years to get all the way through a book, like for example Foucault's *The Order of Things*. I liked it, I had been reading it for a long time. It is known as a deep, difficult book that is full of insight. Foucault is unusual among the leading French structuralists and post-structuralists, unusual compared with Lévi-Strauss, Louis Althusser, Lacan and Barthes, for example, because with each of these four, it is clear what the defining characteristic of his thought is, but with Foucault it isn't clear. It is difficult to judge Foucault by any of the conventional criteria because each of his books takes a different approach. *The History of Sexuality*, *Archaeology of Knowledge*, *Discipline and Punish*, the titles alone tell you they aren't conventional works. But the real reason it isn't easy to categorise Foucault's work is not just that it encompasses the study of the discourses of madness, prisons, authority, sexuality and violence, but because he arrives at his insights using the tools of structural linguistics. In Foucault's opinion, language doesn't just disseminate knowledge, it produces knowledge. He held that the evolution of intellectual history is, in essence, the repositioning of the relationship between words and things. Foucault's most important contribution is to argue as follows: in order to lay bare the deep structure of intellectual history, we must rid ourselves of our traditional methods of doing history, which are based on the principle of continuity and, just as archaeologists dig up relics of human history from the ground, we must unearth the structures of intellectual history, which lie hidden in their many layers. We must study the ways knowledge is encoded. We must find the fissures deep within knowledge. This is the method of intellectual archaeology, and it is what separates Foucault from traditional intellectual historians.

That said, I do not think *The Order of Things* is as abstruse as some make out. I think the reason people find it difficult to understand has a lot to do with the way it's been translated. Maybe it is true that Foucault's manner of expression is complicated, but it's entirely within the power of a translator to take Foucault's French and make it fit the conventions of other languages so that he reads smoothly and clearly in translation. But that's not what they do, so the translations are awkward. An example I have at hand is the following:

> This book first arose out of a passage in Borges, out of the laughter that shattered, as I read the passage, all the familiar landmarks of my thought – *our* thought, the thought that bears the stamp of our age and our geography – breaking up all the ordered surfaces and all the planes with which we are accustomed to tame the wild profusion of existing things, and continuing long afterwards to disturb and threaten with collapse our age-old distinction between the Same and the Other.

Michel Foucault, The Order of Things: An Archaeology of the Human Sciences, *translated by Alan Sheridan (New York: Vintage Books, 1994), p. xv.*

Maybe Foucault's use of "geography" is a little abstruse, but the rest of his meaning is not difficult to understand. If we consider the word carefully, even what he means by "geography" isn't that difficult to grasp.

Moreover, Foucault's concept of "epistemes" is no more abstruse than Derrida's "différance", and actually it is the latter concept that is truly abstruse because it argues that meaning is *always "differential" and postponed in language. Guo Yancheng of Nankai University published an article titled "Buddhist Philosophy and Derrida's Deconstruction" (*Mt Wutai Researches, *2007, no. 2, pages 8 to 11), in which Guo wrote, "Derrida's 'différance' is obviously derived from Zeno's arrow paradox, one of the ancient Greek's four paradoxes of motion. In the arrow paradox, Zeno asserts that a flying arrow at each instant is at rest in a specific place, and if at every instant the arrow is at rest in a specific place, then at no moment is the arrow in motion. The concept of 'différance' holds that only when the present instant is regarded as lying on the 'trace' of the continuity from past to future, in other words, only when the present instant is not regarded as a self-sufficient structure, only then can the idea of motion be understood. By this reasoning, Derrida concludes that 'presence' must be considered from the perspective of time as 'différance'."*

What Guo means is that although the "instant" may be an extremely short period of time, Derrida still regards it as a product of the continuity of past and future, rather than as a self-sufficient structure... Guo writes, "In fact, the Buddhist classics present a clear, systematic explanation of the structure of space-time. Works such as Specifics of the Sutras and Vinayas, A Forest of Pearls from the Dharma Garden *and* An Illustrated Guide to the Dharma Realm *undertake an intensive investigation of the question of space and time. This is particularly true of the discussion of the* kalpa *in the latter work, which considers the measurement of time from a macroscopic perspective; a* kalpa, *the Buddhist 'aeon', is an extraordinarily long period of time. The Buddhist scriptures also express the impermanence of all things through the microscopic perspective of the notion of the* ksana, *which is an instant, a split second, the twinkling of an eye. In the* Taisho Tripitaka *it is written that, 'The shortest measure of time is called a* ksana; *the time of a snap of the fingers contains 320 trillion* smrti, *one* smrti, *the time of a thought, equals ninety* ksana, *one* ksana *contains 900 instances of formation and annihilation.' It is thus clear that Buddhism holds that the world is in a constant state of change, arising, abiding, changing and ceasing, a cycle of birth, life, sickness and death. This process will never end, and time will never stop at any particular instant. Moreover, a* kalpa *is infinitely long, and a* ksana *is infinitely divisible. Derrida's abstruse concepts of 'différance', 'trace' and 'presence' are similar to the Buddhist notions of 'form' and 'emptiness'.* The Prajna Paramita Heart Sutra *says, 'Form is no different from emptiness, emptiness is no different from form, form is emptiness, and emptiness is form...' In other words, 'form and emptiness' and 'existence and non-existence' are not absolute opposites but are interrelated and interpenetrating concepts. The world is the unification of existence and non-existence in a single instant. Time and time again Derrida explicated his notion of 'différance', arguing that there was only 'différance' and never any 'origin'. But Derrida also said that 'différance' is the origin of differences, the production of differences, the play of differences, the difference of differences... It is evident that Derrida negated neither the 'existence' of 'différance' nor the 'non-existence' of 'différance', which happens to coincide with the Buddhist idea of 'Non-complete Emptiness'. But Derrida did not consciously theorise or think through in any systematic way the relationship between 'existence' and 'non-existence', and his notion of 'différance' does not approach the depth of Buddhism's systematic explication of 'existence' and 'non-existence'." That is what Guo wrote about Derrida and Buddhism. I frequently fell asleep thinking about these abstruse concepts, often forgetting to turn off the light.*

Wang Mojie was always quoting from authorities, always analysing, but the reader can skim through this sort of thing, or just skip it completely with nothing lost, but please do note Wang Mojie's last sentence:

I frequently fell asleep thinking about these abstruse concepts, often forgetting to turn off the light.

---

22. The Poet

Yes, the poet died. All right, all right, concerning the death of the poet, there were a variety of theories, some said suicide, some said murder, some said drunk-drowning, some said he challenged the goddess of the Lhasa River...

I don't deny it, my reading habits are like my sexual habits, that is, I tend to take things to extremes. Is there a connection between the two? I think so, but I have never been able to figure out exactly what it is. Do they reinforce each other? Or do they keep each other in check? Or both? If reading is a kind of masochism, is masochism rather like some sort of reading? Are they hard to separate? Whether I like it or not, I don't think they can be separated easily. I have to accept my habits as they are. My reading habits and my sexual habits are entangled, and that makes me who I am. My acceptance of my masochism, which is like a kind of reading, is not without its intellectual basis. Foucault had a taste for S&M, and he once wrote that those who believe that physical pleasure must always come from the sexual organs are mistaken. He held that the erotic theatre of S&M could turn any part of the body into an organ of pleasure. This, he maintained, allowed us to imagine unlimited new forms of physical pleasure. He argued that the pursuit of physical pleasure through erotic theatre must be free of ideological control. He wrote that the idea that those who are dominant in S&M must harbour some unconscious desire to commit violence is outdated and obsolete.

I agree, in the main, with the former argument but not with the latter argument. I agree that "erotic theatre" can allow us to "imagine unlimited new forms of physical pleasure". I don't, however, accept Foucault's denial that when we are violent during S&M, we are expressing an unconscious tendency towards violence. Also, Foucault's argument is an implicit dismissal of the much more complicated psychology of the submissive partner in S&M. I think Foucault reached his conclusion far too hastily, at least when it comes to Eastern cultures. When Western philosophers discuss "human nature" in the abstract, it never seems to occur to them to consider how "human nature" is understood in the East. In the same way, when philosophers in ancient China wrote about "the world" or, as they put it, "all under Heaven", they were thinking of no place other than China. The arrogance is the same, East and West, and so is the naivety.

No matter how Wang Mojie tried to rationalise, intellectualise or theorise who he was, a competing discourse in a different space defined him quite differently. In that discourse, he was depraved, bizarre and risible. His enjoyment of "erotic theatre" inevitably became the subject of gossip that everyone found fascinating and couldn't wait to spread. This was, of course, not a surprise. Wang Mojie never tried to keep it a secret, and in fact, the word didn't get around as fast as he thought it would. He didn't mind. No one who had done the amount of lonely soul-searching that he had done would care what others thought. He was an individual, but he was also a type, and so he made himself the subject of his own philosophical investigation. He was indifferent to everything else. He did eventually admit, however, that he never imagined that everything would turn out to be such an unbearable mess. What bothered him was that it became a farce, to the point that people got together to share details of what went on in Wang Mojie's "erotic theatre". And what surprised him most was that Yu Youyan played the leading role in this farce and she spread the news. The tales she told made no mention of anything that would have reflected poorly on her, of course. She didn't mention that she got a thrill from inflicting pain on Wang Mojie, that it turned her on, or that she had writhed on the bed. Wang Mojie thought it was foolish of Yu Youyan to think that telling these stories, even her edited versions, could possibly be good for her. He didn't understand how she could be that stupid. She would have been so much better off had she limited herself to telling just one friend, Ukyi Lhamo, for example, or the poet – the mathematician-poet – someone like that. Wang Mojie could understand that it would have been difficult for her to keep it all to herself, but why in the world did she choose the occasion of the poet's "birthday" party to tell everybody? Wang Mojie found out what happened only after the fact.

Yu Youyan wasn't entirely at fault because from the start of things until their conclusion she was manipulated by the poet, who was a very cynical man. When Wang Mojie had left her feeling frustrated, she complained to the poet that Wang Mojie had "unusual" tastes. The poet was keeping to himself at the time because he was feeling the sting of being rejected by Ukyi Lhamo, who had left him for her mountaineer, but he perked up when Yu Youyan gave him the news about Wang Mojie. He was more worldly-wise than Yu Youyan, and he had even seen some Japanese S&M pornography. He did a little research, and he and Yu Youyan spent many evenings watching videos they got from her contacts in the judiciary. They observed, studied and learned. He was the instigator, he did all the planning, and Yu Youyan was under his control. The poet told all this to Wang Mojie before he died.

Yes, the poet died. All right, all right, OK, I'll tell you about the poet. There were all sorts of theories as to how he died, some said suicide, some said murder, some said drunk-drowning, some said he challenged the goddess of the Lhasa River. I think the last theory is probably closest to what actually happened because more than once the poet told me he planned to challenge that icy blue river and swim from the north bank to the south bank. As you of course know, the Lhasa River is called the "Goddess of Death" because no one has ever successfully swum across it. I am told that every few years some possessed soul gets a great notion and tries it, but without exception they are taken by the blue river forever. In any event, concerning the death of the poet, there was no consensus as to how it happened, all was confusion. In the end, even the police couldn't come to a conclusion, and they put down the cause of death as simply the vague "death by drowning". And oh yes, where they found him is interesting, because it wasn't where he died, just where he ended up, and it was obvious that he died while trying to swim across. Even more interesting is that his body was found on the south bank, which means that yes, he was dead but still, no matter what you say, he made it across the river. No one can claim that the current carried his dead body all the way from bank to bank, that would be impossible, and to claim so would be unfair to the poet's indomitable spirit. If we wish to eulogise him, then we may say without fear of contradiction that the poet was the only person to ever successfully cross the river. Or to retreat slightly and be more accurate, we may proclaim that his was the first corpse to cross the Lhasa River successfully. No corpse had ever made it from one bank to the other, but by the grace of God, the poet's corpse had.

The poet's death caused some bother for me and for Ukyi Lhamo. I didn't mind at all. Looking at it the way a surveyor might, we may observe that his corpse ended up on a shoal on the south bank of the Lhasa River at a spot that, as it happens, was directly across from my stone house. When the police came to talk to me, I said they should also talk to my neighbour Ukyi Lhamo, because there was only one house between hers and mine, so if my house was directly opposite the spot where they found the poet, then her house was too. If I was a suspect, then she was too. I told the police there was something else they should know. I said Ukyi Lhamo had been the poet's lover shortly before he ended his life in despair. I stressed "despair" so they wouldn't miss it. When the police came to talk to her, Ukyi Lhamo lost her temper and swore at them (they were Tibetan, and she wasn't afraid of them). She got rid of them, then she started a big argument with me. She pointed her finger at me and swore at me. She was furious.

—What are you, bored? You have nothing better to do?

—Did the police come to talk to you?

—Why did you bring up my name with them? she asked, furious. And why did you say that we were involved? What did you mean by that?

—I'm glad we are getting this out in the open, but listen, I said nothing about the two of us being involved.

—So how did the police find out about us?

—Find out what about us? I asked.

—Don't play dumb.

—The police have ways to get any information they want, I said.

—You're awful. And why make up something about a love triangle?

—Did I need to make it up? It was plain what was going on.

—He is dead. Have you no sympathy at all?

—I think that by giving people a reason to keep talking about him, I am showing him a little sympathy.

—You're just as bad as he was. You're the same.

—Well, there's at least some difference between us, you should know that, I said.

—Yeah, there is. You are worse than he was! she yelled.

—In some ways that's probably true, I said breezily.

—At least he was normal, she said gravely.

—You think his death was normal? I asked sarcastically.

—Yes! she shouted, then she turned and walked off.

I believe that one must always be fair, so I had insisted to the police that because both Ukyi Lhamo and I lived across from the spot where the poet's body was found, then if one of us was going to be a suspect, we both had to be. The police agreed, which satisfied me, and I didn't care about anything else in the whole boring affair. I am, of course, partially joking about this. I was interrogated by the police not only because the poet's body was found on the riverbank opposite my house. There were two other reasons. First, the poet had come to see me before he drowned, and second, on his body they found a book by Walter Benjamin. It was a small paperback edition of Charles Baudelaire: A Lyric Poet in the Era of High Capitalism, *which was very popular with poets and scholars at that time. My name was in the book, and below it I had written the date and place I had bought it. This was my habit, but I discovered it was a bad habit. If it was the book that had killed him, I wasn't going to be able to shirk responsibility, but luckily for me the police didn't give the book much thought. A book as a murder weapon is an idea that could occur only to an eccentric who is both a librarian and a novelist, someone such as Jorge Luis Borges for example. Not only did he write fiction, he was the director of his country's National Public Library. But he went blind, leaving him unable to read any of the books in his library, and after that he liked to pass the time thinking about all kinds of wild stuff to do with murder. I have already mentioned that Borges attracted Foucault's own eccentric interest.*

But I digress. I was talking about the fact that the book itself did not interest the police, but because it was my book, I became a suspect, and I was subjected to an investigation that tried to make something out of nothing. So, of course, when the police made the connection between where the poet had been found and the location of my house, I had to drag Ukyi Lhamo into it. The whole thing was ridiculous already, so I would make it even more so. For example, it could have been a crime of passion. She and I were neighbours and there might have been a relationship between us, you could not rule that out. At any event, the crime of passion theory was dismissed after a lot of hullabaloo, but that didn't change a basic fact: while the poet's body had been found on the bank opposite our houses, that was only where he had ended up, it wasn't where he had drowned, so it had nothing to do with Ukyi Lhamo and me. And so, in the end, just as I expected, the case fizzled out. I even got my book back, Walter Benjamin's Charles Baudelaire: A Lyric Poet in the Era of High Capitalism *(Joint Publishing Company Co: first edition, 1 June 1989; thirty-ninth printing, 1 June 1994. That is right, it's quite the coincidence, both editions came out on International Children's Day, but that doesn't mean anything, it doesn't mean that a poet is the child of all humanity. Of course, there is a date a few days after 1 June that is important too, a date with a more complicated significance, and so perhaps that the book came out in early June 1989 was some sort of prophecy).*

I didn't say much to the poet, and I can honestly state that when he left my place that day, it never occurred to me that he would die. His death shocked me. He stayed about two hours, and start to finish he talked and I listened. He was very worked up and very confessional, but I couldn't really follow what he was saying. Nothing suggested to me that he didn't have long to live, and I didn't pay much attention when he picked up the thin blue Benjamin book on his way out. I do remember what he said. He said, Wang Mojie, in the future I will stand for you, assuming you are still alive. I have no idea what he meant. Later on, I spent some time thinking about the book, but I could never figure out just how Benjamin had killed him, the poet for our times. I also wanted to take another look at my Borges, but I couldn't find it, which was strange. In sum, I had no idea that when the poet took the Benjamin and left that he was going off to challenge the Lhasa River, the "Goddess of Death". By the way, some of his poetry wasn't bad at all. For example, there is, "let water flow into water / let the one become the one", lines like that.

As I've said, when he came to see me, he was worked up and confessional, almost crazed. He was smoking, and every time he lit a cigarette, he inhaled almost a third of it in one drag, he was that worked up. I never suspected that it was the thought of death that made him so excited. He told me he had been doing everything he could to destroy my reputation, and when he had found out about me and S&M it made him so happy he couldn't contain himself. He said that he went around telling everybody about me, trying to make me sound as depraved as possible – he talked about how I liked to lick boots, how I played at being a dog, barked like a dog and crawled into my "kennel". He made it sound as if he had seen it all himself. I had done all that, and so I listened to him with dispassion. He told me that he had organised a "birthday" party for himself – it wasn't his birthday, which he never celebrated anyway – so that he could gather everyone to hear Yu Youyan's "announcement". I can imagine the scene: they must have been drinking, talking, joking, telling dirty jokes, everybody letting themselves go, with Yu Youyan the butt of most of the dirty jokes. I had been to a few of their parties, and I had discovered that Yu Youyan liked it when men made dirty jokes about her. She blushed but she stood up to it, she even came right back at them with the same sort of talk, which of course just thrilled the men who were joking with her. This wasn't all just teasing and play, a lot of people desire sexual talk, it's just like physical desire, and sexual talk can bring the same satisfaction. At the poet's party, I of course became the focus of discussion. But as my case was far from typical, it didn't give them quite enough to talk about, because Yu Youyan and I never actually had sex. We took what we did seriously. They could laugh about her ordering me to act like a dog, but how were they going to laugh about her tying me up, whipping me and putting her heels on my prick? All that would have sounded incredible to them but it wouldn't titillate them. I had a hard time imagining the scene of Yu Youyan telling them about me, and the impression the poet's manic account gave me turned out to be quite wrong. Yu Youyan hadn't stood up and given a long, detailed account of me, which the poet claimed she had, that was his exaggeration. I learned later that the poet had orchestrated the whole thing. He made her talk and then interrogated her relentlessly, and others asked her questions too. I can imagine him bullying her into talking, which was no doubt why the two of them finally fell out.

The poet didn't know everything. For example, he didn't say anything about the way my erection stood up from my bound body. That is something he never mentioned, which is how I know that Yu Youyan kept some things to herself. There were things she would have found difficult to speak about openly. I am sure that everybody who heard the story asked her about the sex. After they had heard about all the bondage and S&M, which they no doubt took as just so much preamble, I am sure they wanted to know about the sex. But we didn't have sex, not even of the S&M sort, such as pussy torture, and so to them everything we did was just bizarre foreplay. The poet didn't say anything about this to me, which I'm guessing meant that his interest actually wasn't prurient, all he really cared about was destroying me, and he succeeded to some degree.

Right after Ukyi Lhamo returned from Dromo, to her annoyance she had to attend the poet's "birthday" party. She was in a good mood after her trip, which had been rewarding, as she believed she had found her grandmother living in a monastery deep in the woods in Dromo. She couldn't be absolutely sure, her mother and her uncle had to confirm it. She would have to convince those stubborn old folks to make the trip to Dromo, her mother would be especially difficult to persuade. Other than her mother and uncle, the person she was most eager to tell about her discovery was Wang Mojie. In part because he was her most important confidant outside her family, in part because she and her mountaineer had split up. She had left him and his SUV in Shigatse and hitchhiked alone to Dromo. Getting back to Lhasa from there took her three days on a dirty, slow long-distance bus. At night she slept next to snoring people on smelly, lice-ridden communal beds in roadside inns. But whenever she thought of Wang Mojie, she felt happy and, though she barely admitted it to herself, a little bit excited. It made her happy to think about sharing her discovery with Wang Mojie, in part, of course, because it would put him in his place. He had always made it clear that he thought her search for her grandmother was a fool's errand, and now she could tell him that there was nothing foolish about it. She had found her grandmother, which meant she had found herself and her connection to history. So what happened at the poet's "birthday" party was like a kick in the gut, her happiness, and her excitement, vanished in an instant.

She should have seen it coming. Wang Mojie had intimated there was something between him and Yu Youyan, and the person who called Ukyi Lhamo to invite her to the party mentioned Wang Mojie's "scandal", so she knew something was up. But when the person who called to invite her used the words "perversion" and "masochist", she was entirely ignorant of this sort of thing and the words had no real meaning to her. She didn't care if Wang Mojie and Yu Youyan were sleeping together, she cared about souls, not bodies. On the way to the party, she was thinking about asking Wang Mojie to visit Dromo, about renting a car and asking him to come with her when she took her mother and uncle to Dromo to confirm that she had found her grandmother. But at the poet's party, when Yu Youyan told them, with great disdain and enthusiasm, all about Wang Mojie, with the poet egging her on and getting her to share all the details and act it out, Ukyi Lhamo was left in shocked disbelief. She had been revelling in the joy of finding her grandmother and the pleasure of imagining the scene when she told Wang Mojie, but the good feeling was gone now.

Wang Mojie knew nothing about any of this, he didn't know that Ukyi Lhamo had gone to Dromo, he didn't know their entire social circle was in an uproar because of the gossip about him and he didn't know about the party. He had assumed that sooner or later gossip about him would reach Ukyi Lhamo's ears. Actually, he was looking forward to it. That night after their long talk – it was near dawn – when Ukyi Lhamo said that she didn't know what was going on with him and Yu Youyan, he had been a little surprised. And because he and Ukyi Lhamo had agreed to go to Neuchungri Nunnery together, he had been a little surprised when he woke up and went back to her place only to find she was gone. Her door was locked, she had left without a word. But she always came and went like the wind, so Wang Mojie didn't think much about it at the time.

Then one evening days later, the lights in Ukyi Lhamo's house came on and Wang Mojie knew she had come back. He was about to go over and knock on her door as usual but didn't. Wang Mojie decided that since she was back after having been away for a long time, she should come to say hello to him. He waited all evening but she didn't appear. He thought it was probably too late, and she would come over the next day. She was back, that was all that mattered. But the next morning her door was locked again. Wang Mojie began to feel something was wrong, but he had known this day had long been coming, and the good times were over between them. This was not surprising, and he didn't feel as if he had lost anything.

On many nights and many days and during many walks, they had had many long talks. Spending time together had become their habit, and all habits need to be changed. He felt lonely, for sure, but loneliness can become a habit too, and if he could overcome the feeling of being ungrounded, if he could stare harder into the emptiness of existence, he would be able to more fully understand who he was.

And so Wang Mojie went back to the round platform where sky burials were held and stood at its centre for a long time, now looking down, now looking up.

He walked through the winter fields, his sloping shadow on the levee.

It was winter. Everything was laid bare. Wang Mojie seemed to perceive the trees in their essence, the sunlight reflected from branches, trunks, bark, from even the last dead leaves, and the trees were bright, as bright as water in the sunlight. And he visited his students. He went to the cement factory, dropped in on a student, had a cup of butter tea and a talk with a parent, then visited a second student and had a second cup of tea and a talk with a second parent, they were all alike to him.

One day he had just walked out of his door when, as if he were dreaming or hallucinating, he saw Ukyi Lhamo walking towards him. They stopped and looked at each other, neither spoke. They both made sure they weren't dreaming, many thoughts ran through their heads. She spoke first, very stiffly despite her effort to sound casual. She asked Wang Mojie if he was heading out, which was just a way to say hello. It was two or three in the afternoon, the students were on a long holiday, and the school was empty. Wang Mojie said he was going out for a stroll. They fell silent again until Wang Mojie, also trying to be casual, asked Ukyi Lhamo how things were going. He expected the usual "Good" or "Not bad" in answer but she looked right at him and said things were going badly.

—When you get back, come and find me, I need to talk to you, she said.

They walked off in separate directions. She was wearing a beige fur jacket and high brown boots, her long hair fell to her shoulders, and there was nothing particularly Tibetan about her appearance. She looked as if she had stepped out of a French film, a Jean-Luc Godard film to be specific. This is what Wang Mojie was thinking as he walked out of the school gate and down to the road. He didn't know where to go. Had he not run into Ukyi Lhamo, he probably would have crossed the road and walked through the field and along the stream to the woods, a route he took by habit, but encountering Ukyi Lhamo left him feeling confused, and he walked down the road aimlessly. It was cold, the tarmac was shiny in the afternoon sun, and trucks roared past now and again. He had almost reached the edge of the cement factory grounds when he stopped, turned and headed back, hurrying along the road until he was back at the school.

He went straight to Ukyi Lhamo's door and knocked. Her house always smelled of cigarette smoke, Wang Mojie didn't like it, but he had learned to put up with it during their long conversations. Today, however, her house smelled of tea and incense, the aromas were vivid in the dry, cold air. It was the smell of hospitality. The aromas of tea and incense created a mood of anticipation. The tea smelled fresh and warming, and the incense gestured towards the spiritual. He sat down and inhaled deeply, the room was warm with memories. Ukyi Lhamo's fur jacket was hanging up, her boots placed below it, making it look as if Ukyi Lhamo's double was standing there. She was wearing wool trousers, wide at the thighs and tapering to the ankles, the colours and pattern like a *pangkhep* apron, and with the trousers she had paired a grey woollen shirt with a high collar. She no longer looked like she had stepped out of a Godard film, but she didn't look Tibetan either, her look was hybrid. Wang Mojie didn't ask Ukyi Lhamo what it was she wanted to talk to him about, he just started to chat as if all was normal. Ukyi Lhamo talked about her trip, she talked about her mountaineer and his SUV, there was emotion in her voice when she was talking about him, but we needn't dwell on that. They were both uncomfortable but managed to relax somewhat.

—Sounds like you went off on a sort of honeymoon, Wang Mojie said, with well-intentioned humour.

—We went a long, long way. We went way out there, but it was always nice and warm in the car, she said, not denying what Wang Mojie had said.

—Is that what you needed to talk to me about? You wanted to tell me you two had a good time?

—I found my grandmother, she said as calmly as she could.

This was beyond anything Wang Mojie had ever imagined, and he couldn't believe how calm she was.

—Really? he asked, amazed.

—That's what I wanted to tell you.

—I never expected you would find her. You really should be congratulated.

After receiving a positive response from Wang Mojie, Ukyi Lhamo stopped pretending to be calm and turned serious.

—Tenzin Sangmo saw my grandmother during the Cultural Revolution, so I decided that if my grandmother didn't stay in Lhasa, she probably went back to Dromo, where her people are from. There are two roads from Lhasa to Dromo, one goes past Yamdrok Lake and through Gyangtse, the other past Yamdrok Lake and through Shigatse. I've travelled both roads, and I've been to all the nunneries along the way, but I didn't find her, not a trace. I went to Dromo by myself. Dromo is near the border, it's where my grandfather's family is from. I always wanted to visit it, and I thought Dromo had to be the place.

—Wait a minute, you just said you went to Dromo by yourself?

—Yeah, she said, pausing a second before continuing. Both my maternal grandparents were born in Dromo, both of them were born into the Lungsharwa clan, they were cousins. I didn't find that out until after I got back and my uncle told me. He said the Lungsharwa family were descendants of three great Nyingma Rinpoches. He said Nyingma monks are allowed to marry and have children, and the Lungsharwa family lived in Dromo and also Pakri. Both my maternal grandparents were gifted children, the family hired many famous teachers for them. They studied English and Sanskrit, and Tibetan medicine. They learned how to treat illnesses, wrote poetry, and were musical, they could dance and could play several instruments. My grandfather was twenty-one and my grandmother was only sixteen when they came to Lhasa so he could take the test to get a government job. He stood out among all the sons of aristocratic families, and his career took off.

Time seemed to flow backwards for Wang Mojie, weeks into the past, back to those days and nights of conversation. But he noticed that the trip had changed Ukyi Lhamo, now she was more serious, and she sounded like she was giving a lecture to a tour in a memorial hall or museum. Perhaps there should be a memorial hall for Lungshar, he had earned it, Wang Mojie thought, but why had Ukyi Lhamo gone to Dromo by herself? What happened to her mountaineer? They left in his car, and she hadn't minded when he called it their honeymoon. He was waiting for her to explain, but she hadn't, was she avoiding the subject?

—Are you listening to me? she asked, noticing his distracted look.

—Yes, Wang Mojie said. Your maternal grandparents were a talented couple with important places in Tibet's early modern history and their end was tragic.

—You seem to be able to have your mind on two things at once.

—So do you. You're telling me some things, but there are things you are thinking but not saying.

—You're right, she said, looking at Wang Mojie and speaking slowly. I broke up with him. In Shigatse.

Wang Mojie stared at her, she stared back at him before continuing.

—He came back to Lhasa, I went on to Dromo by myself. As to why we broke up, don't ask. I spent three days in Dromo but didn't find a trace of the Lungsharwa family, not a thing. But Dromo was pretty. The houses are made of wood, everybody keeps fresh flowers on their windowsills.

—Dromo is close to India, right?

—Yes, Sikkim is on the other side of the border. From Dromo you can see Sikkim's capital, Gangtok.

—How did you manage to find Madame Ukyi Lhamo? Wang Mojie asked. He had no further interest in her mountaineer.

—I found her in a Nyingma nunnery. I knew it was her as soon as I saw her. I started crying and hugged her. The tears just came as soon as I saw her. She hugged me back, she knew who I was.

—Maybe you are her when she was younger, one turn of the wheel of *samsara*, Wang Mojie said. He could see no reason not to believe her, she certainly believed it, and her belief seemed to possess her entirely. When he looked at her, it was as if he could see her grandmother's image superimposed on her.

—It's just a shame she's so old. She can't really speak, you can't understand what she's saying.

—So how do you know it's her?

—I just know. I knew as soon as I saw her. She understood everything I said. I talked about my grandfather, my mother, Yuthok and Tenzin Sangmo, and I could see in her eyes that she understood. She kept touching my hair. Her hands are skin and bone, and very dry. I was sobbing.

—What do people call her in the nunnery? Do they call her Madame Ukyi Lhamo?

—They call her Ukyi Lhamo, just like my name!

—Wow, it really is a miracle. It was worth all you went through.

—But my mother doesn't believe it. She barely reacted when I told her, and no matter what I say she doesn't believe it.

—Is it that she doesn't believe you or that she has put her former life behind her? Does your uncle believe you?

—He said he believes me, but he didn't seem too excited, it was like he was humouring me. I don't understand it.

—Their reaction is odd, Wang Mojie said. Maybe there is something to this that you don't know about. Did you take a picture of her? That would be proof.

—I left my camera in his car in Shigatse, and he drove off with it.

—I have faith in your intuition. That said, it does sound rather incredible.

—This is what I needed to talk to you about.

—How can I be of any help? I'm not like your mountain climbing friend, I don't have a car, and I can't drive anyway. Of course, if it had been me, no way would I have left you to go on to Dromo by yourself.

—Enough, what do you know about that?

—What do you mean?

—Nothing, she said. She composed herself, lit a cigarette, and continued, If you believe me, then help me convince my mother. I have to make her believe me, otherwise I'll never get her to go to Dromo.

—Your mother doesn't know me at all.

—She knows about you, Ukyi Lhamo said, blowing a puff of smoke for emphasis.

—She knows about me? Wang Mojie asked loudly.

—Don't be so pleased with yourself, I can't stand it when you get so pleased with yourself. I just need you to back me up when I talk to her.

—But I wasn't in Dromo with you, how can I back you up?

—You know the family history.

—That matters?

—Will you help me or not? If not, fine.

—I would be delighted to have the pleasure of meeting your mother. When will this be?

—It's almost the start of Losar, are you staying here?

—Where am I going to go?

—I'll let you know when I have a specific date, Ukyi Lhamo said. She stood up, as if to bring the conversation to a close.

—I'll wait to hear from you, Wang Mojie said, reading her body language and standing up too. Almost forgot, if possible I'd like to meet your uncle too. Does he know about me too?

—Everyone in the world knows about you. I must get going. You may leave now.

—You're not staying at the school any more?

—No.

—Why?

—No real reason. Sorry, if you don't mind...

She opened the door and almost pushed him out. She had not mentioned the business with Yu Youyan, but it was obviously on her mind. She didn't leave immediately, and it wasn't until an hour later that Wang Mojie heard her lock her door.

23. Imprinted on the Heart, The Heart's Imprint

Silence can be a form of communication,
it can even allow for a richer form of communication than speech.
Silent communication, communication without language, is always taking place.
Sakyamuni wordlessly held up a flower and Mahakasyapa understood.
This was heart-to-heart and mind-to-mind communication,
each heart-mind imprinted on the other.

Ukyi Lhamo's mother was the most serene of women, but her serenity was not that of a monastery or Barkhor Street early in the morning. It is hard to describe, but it reminded you of pure, still water in sunlight. It was Losar, so she was dressed in her best, a long dark-coloured Tibetan robe that covered her feet. You could see only the motion of her feet under the robe as she moved along silently. She was dressed splendidly, but her hair wasn't plaited, coiled on her head and adorned with jewellery in the Tibetan fashion. She still wore her hair in a bob, with black hair grips on the sides, a style fashionable in the Chinese interior in the 1970s, which told you that she had lived in that part of the country back then. There wasn't any particular reason she hadn't changed her hairstyle, she was just used to it. In terms of hair, Mrs Ukyi Lhamo looked more like somebody from the interior than her fashion-conscious daughter, who liked to wear colourful strings in her long hair. But overall, Mrs Ukyi Lhamo looked like a typical transcendent Tibetan woman.

She was in her sixties, not that old, with white hair, and you could tell she had been beautiful as a younger woman. She had worked in a university library reference room for almost forty years and had an air about her that came from having spent so much time among books. This is different from the quality you get from spending time with sutras in a monastery, but the dark prayer beads she wore changed the librarian quality about her into something more noble and ethereal.

She didn't talk much but was crystal clear in everything she did say. Her voice sounded like a harp compared with the drum of her brother Lhalu's voice. He was almost nineteen years her senior and had a head of white hair, a deep, sonorous voice and laughed readily. He looked and sounded so cheerful that you would never have guessed he had spent fifteen years in a Reform Through Labour camp. He said prison life had made him physically tough. He did all kinds of work in the camp, so there was nothing he couldn't do, he said. He was always very entertaining when he got drunk on barley wine and bragged about his fitness to his children, grandchildren and guests. He was a member of the standing committee of the Chinese People's Political Consultative Conference of the Autonomous Region and in line to be made deputy chairman of this body, the higher-ups had advised him. It was amusing to hear him talk about this because he was pleased with himself and self-deprecating at the same time. It was hard to tell how he really felt, and maybe he didn't know himself. He was upbeat and witty. He enjoyed his drink, which he always took from a wooden bowl inlaid with silver. When he was younger, he always maintained the reserved poise proper to an aristocrat and so when he drank, he never used to let himself go the way the working classes do, but all those years in the Reform Through Labour camp changed him, and now he spoke loudly and drank with gusto.

The Lhalu family was flourishing once again. They had a big home with winding corridors and high eaves around a central courtyard just off Barkhor Street. It couldn't compare to their Lhalu Gatsal estate, but in contemporary Lhasa, it was a mansion, a relic of the aristocratic past. They had it because Lhalu Tsewang Dorje's case had been cleared up in a manner that was quite favourable to him. He didn't have the entire three-storey mansion to himself, other families lived there too, but like Lhalu they were all people of importance. The building had an antique charm, it was distinctly Tibetan. The blue-and-white curtains on the windows were kept clean the whole year round. The windows were hand-carved with Buddhist symbols, so you knew that inside you would find tapestries, *thangka*, carved beams and painted pillars. Unlike the village where Wang Mojie lived, at the Lhalu mansion you got a sense of both the prosperity of the past and the politics of the present. Of course, it was all just shadows. It might seem as if something from the past had survived up to the present, but it had not. False appearances, however, have their persuasive power and can contribute to the writing of false history.

Lhalu Tsewang Dorje had four sons and many grandchildren. The Lhalu extended family was now larger than it had been in the past. Lungshar was dead, but his son had brought fresh blood and energy to the family, which was especially evident in the flourishing younger generation. Lhalu's grandchildren had given up Tibetan dress for Western attire, some favoured elegant brand name jackets, others the latest fashion in winter coats. Some wore their hair long, some smoked pipes, and others sang in bands that performed in clubs. Lungshar had been among the first modernisers in Tibet, and the spirit of modernity was only stronger among the current young generation of the Lhalu family. They were so thoroughly modern it was difficult for the older people to understand them. They had not, however, forgotten the old etiquette. When they drank to their elders, the granddaughters, who looked like fashion models, raised their wine bowls above their heads and sang the traditional song of salute. Still, if it weren't for the fact that they sang in the Tibetan language, you would swear they were university students from Beijing or Shanghai. And you would not be wrong, as one of them was at Fudan.

Next to Lhalu's grandchildren, Wang Mojie, who was in his early thirties, and the twenty-seven-year-old Ukyi Lhamo didn't seem so young any more. There was another generation coming of age, and while it was hard to say what defined them, they were the new driving force in the family. Ukyi Lhamo was half Han, but she seemed more traditionally Tibetan than the Lhalu grandchildren. She had on a lilac-coloured Tibetan dress with long sleeves, a colourful kerchief and many ornaments in her long hair, and two multi-coloured hair strings fell over her chest. She looked like a wealthy young lady from the old days. Ukyi Lhamo walked among the several different generations as if walking through history, all of them together comprising a sort of museum, as if she were there to oversee the meeting of past and present.

Ukyi Lhamo took a glass of barley wine offered to her by one of the grandchildren, and they sang *Shambala My Home*. Then she and all the young Lhalus and their guests of a similar age linked hands in a line and danced around the long red tables and among the veranda pillars, singing and drinking as they went. Ukyi Lhamo was very happy, and the wine seemed not to affect her. She stood out from the crowd. She drank a toast to her always serene mother, then hugged and kissed her. Her mother accepted this placidly, she was used to her daughter's ways. Mother and daughter were very different, and it was easy to see that the daughter had Han blood when she was next to her mother, but it was also clear she had inherited something special from her mother. When Ukyi Lhamo drank a toast to her Uncle Lhalu, once an aristocrat, she looked at him with affection but also with a teasing twinkle in her eye. On Lhalu's face was an expression of detached amusement earned from long experience and a difficult life. The look that passed between them was almost like that of lovers from different generations. Lhalu drained his bowl of wine and looked at Ukyi Lhamo. She poured him another bowl. He looked surprised, but he did as she asked and drank it and then a third bowl, after which Ukyi Lhamo gave him her hand so they could dance. They had danced together once already, and now she pulled him to his feet, hugged him, and they danced again. Not a Tibetan dance and not any of the familiar ballroom dances but a dance popular in the 1940s that involved a lot of swaying and shaking of the shoulders, something truly old-fashioned. Afterwards, she told Wang Mojie what it was like to dance with Lhalu. She said her uncle was the only one she could dance that particular dance with. She had tried it with her mountaineer, but the feeling just wasn't right. Lhalu Tsewang Dorje was a personable, elegant old man, and his grandchildren could not get enough of him. His granddaughters surrounded him and tried to get him to dance with them, but he shook his head, laughed and said he only danced with Ukyi Lhamo. He told Ukyi Lhamo to dance with the girls.

Other cultures had influenced Lhalu's grandchildren, but they were still Tibetan. They had trendy hairstyles and were wearing fashionable leather jackets, fur coats, jeans and boots, but they were unmistakably people of the plateau, it was in their faces. One look at Wang Mojie made the difference clear. Wang Mojie hadn't suffered the vicissitudes of life the way the Lhalu elders had, and he lacked the vitality that the younger Lhalus possessed. His features were lopsided, and while this might have given him some character, he had spent so much of his life bent over books that his face, not handsome to begin with, had become lifeless, the blank cover of a reference book, a book five hundred years old, or a thousand, who knew. His face was strikingly different from all the happy faces around him, and those other faces were like Lacan's mirror for him, because when he looked into them, he was made keenly aware that his own face was a mask that lacked subjectivity. But no one knew he felt this way. Even Ukyi Lhamo had only a superficial understanding of him, although she had managed to get beyond some things about him that were off-putting and now was somewhat enamoured with Wang Mojie's instrumentalist approach to life. Instrumentalism is a type of deformed power, which is exactly what Foucault warned against. In other words, knowledge is power. It is human nature to want power, and we are always pursuing one sort of power or another.

That night everyone looked into Wang Mojie's face with respect. They gave him the seat of honour next to Ukyi Lhamo's mother, a significant gesture. Ukyi Lhamo had brought boyfriends home before, but they were never seated next to her mother, they were treated as ordinary guests. Wang Mojie, of course, had a mission, his job was to get the mother to do what the daughter wanted. Ukyi Lhamo told Wang Mojie that her mother wasn't an easy person to talk to. She said that no matter how festive the occasion or how large the crowd, her mother just sat and counted her prayer beads, speaking only when ceremony required it. Which was exactly how she was behaving. Wang Mojie toasted her, she didn't drink, but she poured more wine for him, rare for her, and as she did, she thanked Wang Mojie for coming. Her Mandarin was crisp and clear, a cool breeze. Wang Mojie wished her good fortune in Tibetan and Mandarin, but that was the extent of their conversation. They sat together peacefully and watched the new year come in.

For a long time, Wang Mojie didn't speak to Mrs Ukyi Lhamo, he stayed even more still than she was. He had been feeling out of place at the party, but now he and Mrs Ukyi Lhamo had created their own space, a space for attaining wisdom from beholding the unreality of the ego and all phenomena or a space for grasping Derrida's notion of "non-presence". (Wang Mojie believed the Buddhist notion of the unreality of the ego and all phenomena and Derrida's notion of "non-presence" were two different ways of talking about the same truth, his comparative research into these two ideas was ongoing.) Wang Mojie and Mrs Ukyi Lhamo were strangers but were surprisingly similar, like fellow travellers, like mother and son. By convention Wang Mojie should have tried to engage Mrs Ukyi Lhamo in conversation, it was the proper thing to do. But he didn't. At first, he couldn't think of anything to say, and then he chose not to speak. He knew silence wasn't polite because it might make a person uncomfortable, but she didn't look uncomfortable in the least. Her silence was more powerful than his own, so powerful that it calmed him. Silence can be a form of communication, it can even allow for a richer form of communication than speech.

Silent communication, communication without language, is always taking place. A few times Ukyi Lhamo came over and got them talking, but as soon as she left them alone, their conversation stopped, like a wind dropping away.

Ukyi Lhamo asked Wang Mojie to dance. She said she didn't understand how he could just sit there, she wasn't displeased, just puzzled. As they danced, Wang Mojie explained to Ukyi Lhamo that he had been enjoying an unusual form of silence, he had been in silent communication with her mother, and their silent conversation went deeper than any ordinary talk. He could sense what was in her heart, and she clearly could sense what was in his. Each time Ukyi Lhamo came over to get them talking, she just got in the way of the silent conversation they were having.

—Put simply, I am communicating with your mother heart-to-heart, or mind-to-mind, which mean the same thing, right? Wang Mojie asked, leaning close to Ukyi Lhamo's ear. I'm not sure I grasp it entirely, but I remember the story about Mahakasyapa you told me. I forget where it happened, but Sakyamuni wordlessly held up a flower and Mahakasyapa understood. Neither of them spoke. This was heart-to-heart communication, each heart imprinted on the other, two people sharing the same heart-mind. I don't know what I have come to understand, but I do know that what's in your mother's heart is extraordinary. If you don't have something similar within you, or don't at least pretend to have it, you're never going to be able to really communicate with her. Sitting next to your mother I feel a kind of quiet strength, a strength that stops me from engaging her in small talk, and I'm trying to express to her with my own silence what understanding I do have. Don't you think that is better than talking?

What Wang Mojie said was reasonable to Ukyi Lhamo, it moved her, she hugged him and didn't seem to want to let go. They moved close to each other, turning slowly but not in time with the music. After a long moment, Ukyi Lhamo spoke in a whisper.

—I can't figure you out, I don't understand you. I don't understand how somebody as smart as you can go for that bizarre stuff. Never mind, I didn't mean to bring it up. I know it's your private business, but I just don't get it. You are a pure-hearted person, you can communicate with the Buddha directly, which is something I've always wanted to do but have never been able to. You can do it even though you don't believe in Buddhism, which I just don't understand. But how can you do that sort of thing? I'm sorry, I didn't intend to talk about that. No, you don't have to explain, and I don't mean to criticise. I don't have any right to criticise you. But Wang Mojie, I can't be without you, I'm in love with you.

—I think I do need to explain, as soon as I have a chance. I'm stuck in my ways, and it will be hard to save me. Don't overestimate me, I just have a feeling for the metaphysical. And at the moment I can feel your mother watching us.

They turned their heads and met the old lady's gaze. She didn't look away, she kept looking at them calmly. They looked at one another for a moment. Wang Mojie was the first to look away. He asked Ukyi Lhamo, Could you tell what your mother was saying to us? Ukyi Lhamo, calm now, answered immediately.

—I think she was giving us her blessing.

—The Buddha said, "The truth cannot be expressed in words... " You should attend to the rest of your guests, you're the host, Wang Mojie said.

—I have a hard time controlling myself sometimes, don't take it seriously.

—I don't know what you are saying.

—I'm not saying anything.

Wang Mojie sat back down. He nodded at Mrs Ukyi Lhamo, he felt he was back in a special place. After a time, the connection between them was reestablished, they were removed from the space around them, and the words Wang Mojie was speaking in his heart-mind grew more distinct.

My father disappeared when I was three years old. It was 1968. A group of students took him away, he never came back. He had been labelled a Rightist in 1957, one of the younger people to be condemned as such, he was only nineteen. In 1968 he was a technician in a factory, a chemist, and the people from the factory told my mother that the students who took him away weren't from any of the local high schools, no one knew where they were from. But when they caught my father, they acted like they had found some treasure. They had been looking for class enemies, and I suppose they reasoned that if my father had already been a Rightist back in 1957, then a decade later he must have been even more reactionary. My mother looked for him everywhere. She went to a local school, but the Red Guards there were convinced she was lying. They thought she was hiding him, and they demanded she turn my father over to them. They locked her up for three days and beat her up badly, they almost killed her. That's how my father vanished, and I've never seen him since. I lived in fear my whole childhood. I had a stepfather later, I called him father, but I knew he wasn't my real father. My father was in heaven, I always believed he was somewhere in heaven. I once looked through the dossiers of people who had been locked up and subjected to struggle sessions, but I didn't find any record of my father, and his name wasn't on any list of people who had been killed. But I did find some leads for other people who were looking for their own "disappeared". Their tears of gratitude moved me, and we became friends, like family. But eventually, I stopped looking for news of my father and gradually forgot about him.

Wang Mojie drank his tea, he didn't look at Mrs Ukyi Lhamo, his eyes were on his teacup. But he knew she was listening. He paused.

—Did you go to my university and search records there? she asked. She wasn't looking at him either. Her eyes were straight ahead.

—The Central Academy for Nationalities? No, I only went to high schools.

—They might have been university students, she said. Clearly, she was thinking about what Wang Mojie was telling her, she took it seriously.

—That never occurred to me. Maybe they were students from my father's university, that's where they made him a Rightist. But there is no point in pursuing it any more, I want to leave him in peace. I like to think he is in heaven and happy.

—*Moksa*. Liberation. *Moksa* for you is *moksa* for him. We seek liberation not just for ourselves but also for others, for our past lives and our future lives. My daughter claims she found my mother. But she has made the same claim before. Three times she has asked Lhalu and me to come with her, and all three times it was not my mother. Different things are predestined for different people. If it is not predestined, there is no awakening. I should tell her that one of them is my mother, that would liberate her and some others as well. I am still attached to things, I am still far from *moksa*.

—Maybe this time she has found her. It's the ancestral home of the Lungsharwas.

—There is no ancestral home, the Lungsharwas do not exist, not for me.

—I understand, but many things exist despite our refusal to acknowledge they exist, and believing something exists doesn't mean it does.

—Well said. But haven't I heard my daughter say that you have no faith, you don't believe in Buddhism?

—Correct, I don't.

—Why not?

—As I see it, faith is primarily just a matter of habit, something we are taught when young, the seed is planted in us as children. But I don't have that seed, I never did.

—You are able to enlighten others. That requires something like faith.

—It might seem to, but it isn't the same as faith. I should tell you, I am not a person who observes boundaries, and I'm a very cold person.

She filled his bowl with wine, surprising him, and he quickly took the bowl in his hands.

—My daughter likes you. She told me.

—I know.

—May the Buddha bless you.

They fell silent, as one.

The space adjacent to them grew more and more raucous, all the guests singing and dancing, having reached the most euphoric stage of intoxication. Ukyi Lhamo seemed oblivious to everything, she danced alone, a silver inlay wooden bowl in one hand. She was feeling good, she was happy, her long braid with the colourful hair ties and her lilac-coloured floral Tibetan dress twirled as she twirled with the bowl in hand. She held her drink better than many of the men. She saw Wang Mojie and her mother in conversation off in a world of their own. She had never seen her mother like this before, and it made her very happy. She was revelling, drunk, dancing, and her joy was infectious. When Wang Mojie and her mother fell silent, as if to reward Wang Mojie, Ukyi Lhamo got her cousin Dege to invite him to dance. They glided into the ranks of the dancers. Dege was in her first year at Tibet University, and she was wearing a pretty Tibetan outfit. Tibetan girls are great dancers, they can learn any new dance right away. Dege was very close to Wang Mojie, around him like a cloud, but she was just being hospitable, and as soon as the song ended, they separated. Wang Mojie went back to Mrs Ukyi Lhamo, but he had only just sat down when she said she had been sitting too long and needed to rest. Palms together in salute, she welcomed Wang Mojie to visit her anytime.

When she saw her mother about to leave, Ukyi Lhamo ran over to escort her out of the room, and Lhalu did as well. Lhalu laughed happily as he accompanied his niece Ukyi Lhamo taking his sister Ukyi Lhamo back to her room to rest. (Wang Mojie only learned later that she had retired not to rest but because it was time for her to recite a sutra.) Watching Lhalu and his sister you could imagine how well he must have looked after her when they were young, and all these years later he was still looking after her. Despite all the changes he had been through, he never changed towards her. The two of them together had an unbroken link to the past. Wang Mojie wasn't easily moved, but as he watched Lhalu walk away and thought about how he had taken such good care of his sister for his whole life and into his old age, he got a little choked up. When Ukyi Lhamo and her uncle came back, Wang Mojie said he had to be going. When Lhalu heard that Wang Mojie was leaving, he grabbed hold of Wang Mojie.

—Hey, you can't leave, if you leave, she won't know what to do! You're going to take her heart with you when you go, Lhalu said in Tibetan. Wang Mojie only partially understood, so Ukyi Lhamo translated. Wang Mojie wished the old man a happy Losar in Tibetan, and then he spoke to Ukyi Lhamo.

—Your mother left, and that space she and I were in has vanished. I'm not so good at parties, and it's late.

Ukyi Lhamo said she would walk him out and told Wang Mojie to wait for a moment while she got a coat. They went downstairs and out through the main door. The lights along Barkhor Street were bright, and prayer flags fluttered, but there was nobody on the street.

—What are you going to do at home all by yourself? Ukyi Lhamo asked.

—Nothing, read I suppose, go to sleep.

—For Losar? On New Year's Eve? How boring.

At a junction, a taxi stopped and the driver, who had a Sichuan accent, called to them to get in.

—What did you and my mother talk about?

—Not much, but I think maybe she believes you now.

—Really? Ukyi Lhamo said, as she straightened Wang Mojie's collar.

—Come on, get in, the taxi driver said.

—I'm going, Wang Mojie said. You should get back, you're needed in there.

Ukyi Lhamo looked at Wang Mojie as if waiting for him to do something, but nothing happened. She turned and left. Wang Mojie got in the taxi. He told the driver to wait for a moment, and he watched Ukyi Lhamo walk away without looking back. There on ancient Barkhor Street, her beige fur jacket and long hair blowing in the breeze looked unreal. When she reached the entrance of the alley to the Lhalu mansion, she instinctively turned, looked back and waved at the taxi. Wang Mojie didn't move. And only now did he begin to feel ashamed of himself. He was playing back in his mind, like a scene from a film, the moment that had just passed, when he had done nothing but wait for her to turn and walk away. Slow motion. A long take. His voice-over.

No, no voice-over, what could he possibly say in a voice-over? He had performed brilliantly, start to finish, as if in a black-and-white New Wave film, exquisitely composed, austere. He hadn't been acting out his life as much as he was living a performance, and it was difficult to tell what was real and what was an act. Who was he anyway? Was he who he thought he was? Or someone else? Or both and neither? He couldn't control his reality, reality was a trap. Every word he had said about his father was the truth, but at the same time, it was all a story, as if he had been making it up, changing reality into fiction. He couldn't stop. Even when it came to this goodbye, he was trying to turn it into a truthful fantasy in the style of Godard.

When he got home, a different sort of film started that began with close-ups of a bookshelf, nylon rope, books. He undressed slowly, throwing each article of clothing onto his bed until he was wearing nothing but a black lace-waist thong. He owned about a dozen pairs. Their shape was meaningful, they were a simple form of bondage, and for him, they stood for professional women in the metonymic sense. He stood in front of the bookshelf, on which the nylon rope was coiled just so and placed carefully among the books for maximum visual impact, but it would have looked even more appealing were it a hemp rope or canvas strapping, as it should have been. He thought about replacing the nylon rope. There were stalls on Barkhor Street that sold all sorts of military gear, ration packs, boots, climbing rope, canvas strapping, everything. But then again, nylon hurt more, the pain coming close to what he experienced under the rough treatment from Yu Youyan. He picked up the rope. A close-up of his hand picking up the rope. He uncoiled it. Let it hang to the ground. Measured it with his eye. The scene was lit from above, the rope cast a shadow. His hand was slender. The rope was slender. A two-shot of the hand and rope like the two-shot of the books and rope, with little difference between them, two objects in a still shot. This was his own hand. White, thin, warmer than the rope but not that much warmer. He began to tie himself up, wrapping the rope around and around, and soon he had encased himself in a beautiful web of rope, like barbed wire. If he had the chance, he should teach her how to do it, he thought. There was beauty in everything, even in pain. He got in the bed, pulled the quilt up, turned out the light and entered the darkness. He fell asleep wrapped in rope, on New Year's Eve.

24. Vajra

The realm of the unconscious is yet another ideological construct.
Therefore the so-called "individual" is non-existent.
Our ideas of "human nature" and of the "self" are illusions, fabrications.

Wang Mojie lived his life as if everything was a metaphor. One might think that the rope that bound him confined him, but to him the rope stood for liberation, and one might think the books on his shelf offered liberation, but to him they represented imprisonment. One afternoon during a holiday, Wang Mojie could no longer remember exactly when it was, he sat reading, the sun shining on his open book. He read this from Fredric Jameson:

> In the past, we always believed that we could control our own language, language was a tool and man was at the centre of language. But this is actually not the case. The fact is that when we speak, we think we are controlling language but in truth we are being controlled by language. Man does not speak language. Man is spoken by language.
> (Fredric Jameson, *Postmodernism and Cultural Theory*, Peking University Press, 1997, page 32, lines 2 to 9.)

As Wang Mojie would later realise, it was as he read these lines that Yu Youyan walked into Ukyi Lhamo's house. He had heard the knock on her door, but at the time he had not known it was Yu Youyan knocking.

Foucault held a view very similar to the idea that "man is spoken by language". Foucault believed that subjectivity was created by language. Without language, Man could exist as a biological animal but would have no subjectivity – and no capacity for intellectual activity – but the subjectivity created by language was often not fully human and was not our own, it was a product of ideology. Althusser went so far as to argue that,

> The realm of the unconscious is yet another ideological construct. Working from the outside in, ideology creates 'human nature' and the 'self'. Because of the workings of ideology, the subject is deprived of all freedom, and before the birth of an individual, ideology and Ideological State Apparatuses will have interpellated that individual as a subject. Therefore the so-called 'individual' is non-existent. Our ideas of 'human nature' and of the 'self' are illusions, are fabrications.
> (Louis Althusser, *Philosophy and Politics*, China Social Sciences Press, 1996.)

As Wang Mojie turned to page 89 and read about the "fabrication of the self" on lines 25 to 26, he was unaware that Yu Youyan and Ukyi Lhamo were next door "fabricating" him, they were discussing him. According to Foucault and Althusser, all language functions to "fabricate". Yu Youyan had come to see Wang Mojie, but passing Ukyi Lhamo's house she decided first to say hello to her, and Ukyi Lhamo happened to be in. Earlier that afternoon Ukyi Lhamo and Wang Mojie had eaten lunch together and talked about going to Dromo together. After the Losar party, her mother had agreed to make the trip once the weather got warmer. At lunch, Wang Mojie and Ukyi Lhamo talked about the trip, it wasn't like a date, but Ukyi Lhamo was still a little taken aback when Yu Youyan showed up. She had been avoiding Yu Youyan, she tried not to think about her and had almost forgotten her, and so when Yu Youyan appeared at her door, it was like waking from a dream. They discussed Wang Mojie or we could say they "fabricated" a Wang Mojie.

Is "I" a fabrication of the self? It seemed to Wang Mojie that what Althusser said about the "self" had a lot in common with Ma Dingge's assertion that "I" does not exist. Two very different types of philosophical inquiry had reached the same conclusion. Wang Mojie recalled Ma

Dingge saying that when we are blind to the real conditions of our existence, we become blind to ourselves and blind to others. "I" is nothing but a flow of consciousness, which can be divided into past consciousness, present consciousness and future consciousness. "I" is nothing but innumerable moments, but "I" cannot be the totality of these moments taken all together because such a totality does not exist at any particular moment. It seemed to Wang Mojie that Derrida's concepts of "différance" and "trace" were also ways of thinking about this indeterminate river of time and consciousness... As Wang Mojie was thinking about all this, he heard Yu Youyan's knock on his door. There was a break in his consciousness. He opened the door and was not surprised in the least to see Yu Youyan.

—Was that you knocking on the door over there? Wang Mojie asked.

—What if it was? Am I not allowed? Yu Youyan put her black briefcase on the table, deliberately pushing the Jameson book aside, and Jameson almost fell off the table.

Wang Mojie picked up Jameson and closed him but didn't put him back down.

—You stayed away a long time, Wang Mojie said.

—Miss me? she asked. Her uniform was pressed, the badge on her cap was imposing and her lipstick was bright red.

—Yes, yes, Wang Mojie said emphatically.

—Aren't you worried she'll hear us? Aren't you worried she'll hear you shriek?

—It is a worry. I don't want to bother anybody. But I have this...

Wang Mojie put Jameson down and took a small radio from the bookcase. He turned it on, tuned to a station playing music and slowly turned the volume up, almost all the way. Symphonic music rose and fell.

—My new radio. That's Rimsky-Korsakov, *Scheherazade*.

—What a racket! Can you turn it off for now?

—With music playing, she won't hear anything, Wang Mojie said. He turned the music down.

—She said she'd be over in a moment. We were just talking about you. She's with me in trying to get you sorted out.

—Well, OK. She's more than welcome, but then we don't need the music. He turned the radio off and put it away.

—Is it really all right if she comes over?

—Let her. You two want to do it together? A threesome? All right, are we going to wait for her?

—You're feeling impatient?

—That's right, I am. I've been waiting for the two of you for a long time.

Whack. *A slap landed on Wang Mojie's face, out of nowhere. Wang Mojie, stunned, thought to himself, That was so good, so arousing, she's getting better and better at it.*

—Kneel down, clothes off! Yu Youyan yelled and slapped him again.

Yu Youyan knew what she was doing, her slap was crisp, her lipstick was redder than red, bright and very attractive, Wang Mojie thought as he stared at her lips. Then Ukyi Lhamo walked in. Wang Mojie had already stripped down to his underwear. As if in greeting to Ukyi Lhamo, Yu Youyan gave Wang Mojie another resounding slap to the face. Ukyi Lhamo was wearing her long beige fur coat and high boots and had on sunglasses with red frames. She looked fashionable and coolly detached. Wang Mojie hesitated for a moment and then, looking at Ukyi Lhamo, started to slowly take off his underwear.

—Keep that on! Who told you to take off your underwear? Did I tell you to take it off? Yu Youyan yelled, punctuating each sentence with one crack of her leather belt on Wang Mojie's body. Wang Mojie pulled his black thong back on.

—Ukyi Lhamo, get a load of him in his women's panties, a thong at that, and lace-waist too, it's disgusting!

Ukyi Lhamo stood stock still, her arms crossed tightly over her chest, hugging herself. She didn't react, and whatever was in her eyes was hidden by her sunglasses. Doing this with an observer present was a new test for Wang Mojie and something he had never thought about. The other thing that had Wang Mojie's heart beating fast was the fact that this time Yu Youyan wasn't wearing her work boots, she was wearing slender stiletto high heels. They were pretty and looked dangerous. Wang Mojie thought about how wonderful it would be to have those heels on his body but then again might it be almost lethal if she stepped on his back in those? Wang Mojie was now oblivious to Ukyi Lhamo's presence, his attention was entirely on Yu Youyan in her uniform and red lipstick. She was sitting in the high-backed chair where a moment ago Wang Mojie had been reading Jameson and Althusser. She had one leg over the other,

her toe pointing at Wang Mojie. Wang Mojie kissed her shoes, starting at the toe, inch by inch to the heel, then he took the heel in his mouth. He was greedy for it, saliva ran from his mouth.

—That's enough. Now bark like a dog. Tell me, are you a dog?

She whipped him, berated him. Without hesitation Wang Mojie started to bark, and he sounded exactly like a Pekingese, it was cute. He turned in circles, catching glimpses of Ukyi Lhamo's boots. He barked at her and crawled towards her, but before he could reach the boots, they started walking as Ukyi Lhamo turned around, opened the door and suddenly was gone. A draft of cold air came in when she opened the door, and it sobered Wang Mojie somewhat. At least she had been good enough to close the door on her way out, and she had even banged it a few times to make sure it latched. Wang Mojie barked at the closed door, almost petulantly.

—Enough! Back in your spot. Who said you could bark at her, you're so nasty.

Yu Youyan kicked Wang Mojie in the buttocks, then opened the door and went out. He could hear her knocking and knocking on Ukyi Lhamo's door, but Ukyi Lhamo didn't answer. Yu Youyan came back. Wang Mojie started barking at her again. Yu Youyan stood blankly for a moment, she took off her uniform hat and stared at Wang Mojie.

—That's enough, stop barking, get up, Yu Youyan said listlessly. She took off her uniform jacket, and Wang Mojie slowly got to his feet. He was naked, he moved close to her, the look on his face now very different, and he spoke with a candour as naked as his body.

—What were you and Ukyi Lhamo talking about just before you came over?

—Nothing, I just told her about our previous few times. She wanted to see. She really hates you too. Why aren't you getting dressed?

He grabbed her hands, pulled her up from the chair and said softly, You're not going to do this any more with me, are you? She lowered her head but did not answer. He pulled her to him and said, I understand, nobody wants to do this with me, I'm sorry. Wang Mojie stroked Yu Youyan's short, straight hair. She had obviously recently washed it, it smelled of shampoo. She slowly put her arms around him, but she did not put her head on his shoulder, she stood still and stiffly accepted Wang Mojie's caresses. He said, Thank you, it's finished. Yu Youyan suddenly pulled herself free of Wang Mojie and slapped him across the face.

—You think you get to decide when it's finished? I hate you, Wang Mojie, I hate you, I hate you. I won't wear this uniform next time, but I will still beat you, beat you, beat you! she said and slapped him three more times.

He put her hat back on her head, but she took it off and threw it to the floor angrily. She lashed out at Wang Mojie like a wife attacking her husband. Wang Mojie found this absurd and felt a rush of disgust, but in thanks for how brilliantly she had done their previous few times, he reached out and hugged her. She did her best to fight him off, but he managed to get his lips to hers. She kept resisting at first but when she felt his tongue in her mouth she relented, and they shared a long kiss. But that is as far as Wang Mojie went. They slowly moved apart, it had been a moment's dream.

—You still don't love me, do you? Yu Youyan asked, looking right at Wang Mojie.

—Don't ask that question, Wang Mojie said flatly.

—Do you love her?

—Same sort of question.

—Wang Mojie, you really deserve a beating, you do! She lifted her hand to hit him, but he grabbed it and held it before she could.

—I told you, it's finished, he said.

—No! No! No!

Wang Mojie closed his eyes, feeling complete despair. Yu Youyan slapped him several times, he made only a half-hearted attempt to duck the blows. He was upset but it was his own fault, it wasn't Yu Youyan's fault. Everything has its cost, and this absurdity was the price he had to pay. It would have felt different if she had been wearing her uniform jacket and hat, but she wasn't. Yu Youyan was in the right, she was innocent, and he did deserve a beating, just a regular beating. Yu Youyan stopped, put her arms around him and stood still. He caressed her clean, pretty hair. They hugged for a long time but didn't kiss. They were like two people made of wood. She suddenly pulled away from Wang Mojie, put on her uniform jacket like putting on armour, and she put her hat on too.

—Kneel down, she said calmly as she opened her black briefcase.

He knelt and it resumed. Handcuffs. Shackles. Bondage. Stomping. Moaning. Howling. Shrieking.

But Wang Mojie's desire to be raped went unfulfilled.

This time when Yu Youyan saw his purplish erection sticking out from amid the bondage, she remained composed. She had her choice of torturing his penis with the heels and toes of her shoes or using candles, and she chose the latter, which she used with detached, surgical precision (in S&M, birthday cake candles can be used to drip hot wax on the abdomen, pubic hair and even testicles). Wang Mojie did not have to ask anything of her, it all happened as an unspoken part of the game. He watched her closely. His eyes burned with desire and helpless supplication. Yu Youyan didn't notice, she concentrated on lighting the ring of candles she had set up around his penis, each candle held in place by a small clothes peg, the wax dripped steadily, and the little tingles of pain felt splendid. This was something even Wang Mojie had never thought of. Desire surged through his body, and he perceived a completely new kind of a very powerful strange beauty. He almost asked Yu Youyan where she had learned this or if she had thought it up herself. He longed to be raped, longed for it, he looked at Yu Youyan, his eyes hungry.

—Happy birthday, Yu Youyan said, in an emotionless tone.

—Thank you, I love you, Wang Mojie said.

—Getting off on it? Yu Youyan asked, bending over to kiss him.

—It's wonderful, ingenious, you're the best!

—But I won't rape you, I'll never do that.

—I could tell, that's all right, it's reasonable.

—Shit. What's reasonable about any of this? Look at yourself. Listen to me, this is the very last time, you're never going to see me again, I don't want to see you ever again.

—Thank you, I won't forget you.

—I'd rather you forget me. I want you to forget me. I studied forensic medicine, I know how to push suffocation to the limit, I want you to suffer that one more time. And if you die, well, that's your tough luck, sorry.

The unpredictable Yu Youyan choked Wang Mojie hard. His eyes bulged, his body jerked, knocking the candles over and scattering them, you could hear the hiss when the flames touched his skin. He was incapable of resisting, he grew weaker and weaker, everything grew dimmer and dimmer, more and more dreamlike…

When he came to, the room was pitch black. He couldn't see a thing and he wondered if he was in hell. But he was awake and alive. He could feel the burns on his body, and in his mind he pictured the beautiful birthday candles.

25. I Knew it was not a Simple Emotion

I knew it was not a simple emotion.
The new year had brought not joy
but rather a pervasive tranquillity.
I was suspended in time, as if in the middle of a lake,
in Yamdrok Yumtso, or Namtso or Drangkhok Tso.
The water didn't flow away, on the contrary, more water flowed in.
So much time rushed in,
so many rivers, so many birds, I felt tranquil, replete.

I knew it was not a fleeting emotion, the new year had brought not song but rather a pervasive tranquillity. It was the start of a new term. There was no Tenpa Nyima and no Sangnyi, but all the rest of the children were there in front of me like so many fresh apples, how could I not love them? I promised I would take them to the ravine, and on a calm sunny day I did. We walked out of Danba past the back wall of Sangnyi's house – I kept looking back – and into the quiet, empty ravine that runs down one side of Mount Gephel. Clouds and mist blow over the mountain's peak, its surface is rocky and bare, nothing but weather-worn boulders, no vegetation to speak of, but the ravine is the exception. The ravine is sheltered from the wind and from the extreme changes of temperature from day to night. A stream runs through it, it gets plenty of sunlight and is full of plant life. It seemed always to be green there.

Once, on a sunny winter day after a snowfall, I walked alone in the ravine by the cold, clear stream. I studied the places where the ice had built up. Many of the nearby streams froze over every winter, but the stream in the ravine did not. It was still running under the patchy ice, with open water along much of its length. Where the stream was in shadow all day, it froze into ice shelves, ice caverns and icefalls. Where there was sunlight, the water ran bright and noisy. The grass on the sandy banks was still green, like it was spring. When spring came to the ravine it did so suddenly, lasted only briefly and was surreally beautiful, with wildflowers everywhere. Flowers even grew in the still, dark, damp mouths of caves and crevices on the sides of the ravine. The flowers had red blossoms and delicate leaves, and the sun reached them only for a very short time each day. Some grew and even bloomed where there was never any sun. They stayed in bloom for a long time, standing there as if on watch, and when you touched them, water oozed from their roots, like tears. Little sandy rivulets flowed from the caves and crevices down to the stream. Grass grew on the silvery, sandy banks. It was like someone's well-tended lawn but much lusher. The ravine was a refuge, a paradise, the reward for all that spinning of prayer wheels, a place where you could be one with nature and with your spirituality. I loved the ravine. I called it the Valley of Inner Wisdom.

I had always wanted to bring my students to the ravine for a geology and botany lesson. I knew a little about stuff like sedimentary rock, basalt, granite, shale, gneiss and so on. It seemed to me that the rocks spoke the oldest language on the planet. If I didn't know the rocks and their types and their origins, how could I get to know the mountain, how was I going to talk to the mountain? We have to know the language and history of the rocks if we want to get to the bottom of anything. Plants tell us things every day too. Elms are taciturn, like grumpy old men, but wild roses and gardenias with their sweet-smelling flowers make a ruckus, and the baby's-breath and rock jasmine never stop chattering all day long, they like to gossip about their fragrant neighbours. The language of plants is the richest of the Earth's languages. Pick any of the flowers that are common in the mountains, and it is very possible you won't know what it is called. If you are feeling lonely, coming across a flower you can't name makes you feel ignorant and useless. There was a common wildflower I studied for a long time without knowing its name. I finally learned that it was called Kalsang, which means "happiness". The legend goes that a monk from India saved the Tibetan people from an epidemic by getting them to eat it as medicine. The only word of Tibetan he knew was the flower's name,

Kalsang, and so they called him Kalsang Rinpoche, the Living Buddha Kalsang. I love the name and the story behind it, and after I learned what it was called, every time I saw it, it was like seeing an old friend. When I saw Kalsang flowers I squatted down and talked to them and didn't feel lonely any more.

And so it felt to me that the time didn't pass. I was suspended in time, as if in the middle of a lake, in Yamdrok Yumtso, or Namtso or Drangkhok Tso. The water didn't flow away, on the contrary, a lot of time flowed in. So much time rushed in, so many rivers, so many birds, my life was tranquil, replete. All those children, all now adults. We were in the ravine, my young students surrounding me. I was still young myself. They asked me endless questions, as if I was their prophet and knew everything. I said that actually human beings don't know much about the world, and we will never know everything there is to know about the rocks and flowers. We are just a part of everything, a very small part.

We sang as we had our lunch. My students danced on the grass and sang. We hadn't come as well prepared as we were that day at Nyizhon Lingga. This time we didn't have a tarpaulin and the students weren't as dressed up, but that didn't stop them from singing and dancing. Every time we had a field trip they would spontaneously sing and dance, I couldn't have stopped them if I had wanted to, which I didn't of course. I couldn't stop them from bringing barley wine on our outings either. Every time I have barley wine I think of them, and I remember our picnics. I see myself among them, but I also remember that even when I was with them, I was apart from them too. I see myself holding up a leaf and explaining to them how to recognise different plants by the shapes of their leaves. I see myself standing up to yell at a boy climbing up a rock face at the side of the ravine. Come down, I yell. Then I see myself at Nyizhon Lingga yelling, Sangnyi, come down, come down, you'll fall.

Come down, Sangnyi, come down, it's your turn. Sangnyi climbs down from the Corkscrew Willow, she almost falls, but Lhadron and Chokyi catch her. Sangnyi stands on one side of the tree, Lhadron the other, their backs to the tree, facing two different watercourses. Kalsang Dekyi and her group dash out from behind the tarpaulin onto the grass. They are all dressed up, they dance, flinging their colourful long sleeves, they look like goddesses. It is a few days before the start of the Sho Dun Festival, and they are wearing their festival dresses. Gulls swoop from the river over the island, flying through the song, dropping diamonds of water on the girls. They sing and dance, water sprites among trees, transmigrated birds. Only Sangnyi is wearing what she always does. She has on her usual black trousers and trainers and the brown corduroy jacket she is already outgrowing. You can tell the jacket is freshly washed, as in a few places it is white where it has been scrubbed too much. All the children are eating snacks, Sangnyi included. Sangnyi has brought a small bottle of homemade yogurt and a bag of *tsampa* in brown sugar. She only has these treats because the festival is near. I say, Sangnyi, give me a little *tsampa*, I've tried everything the others brought, now I want to try yours. Sangnyi is not sure what to do. She is not happy at the thought of giving me any, but she lets me take a little. Sangnyi, your *tsampa* and brown sugar is really good. Sangnyi, everybody else has done something. You're the only one who hasn't performed. I've heard you sing. You sing well. Even I can sing it. I sang, The mountain stream, it flows to the east, My valley home, it lies to the south, Please oh please take the turn, And bring me to my door. I sang softly. It was just a fragment of a song, I heard her sing it on the mountain. As soon as she saw me, she stopped singing, but I had already heard part of the song.

Down in the ravine, we heard someone whistle from a distance. The students were curious and stood up, and so did I. We looked up the mountain, and at the same time my mind went back to the image of Sangnyi, running on the slope above the village, just her shadow, and no sound of her singing. I had been distracted by the whistle, but I was still obsessing over Sangnyi's disappearance. Sangnyi, I was thinking, where are you? She had stopped coming to school not long after Tenpa Nyima disappeared, I was told she refused to come to school no matter who spoke to her or what they said. It seemed to me that she stayed away because Tenpa Nyima wasn't there, and she needed his protection. I could only protect her from the things I could perceive, I couldn't help her with the things I didn't understand. I couldn't get inside her head to find out what was bothering her. Both Sangnyi and Tenpa Nyima were just gone. Some said she had gone into the mountains, some said she had gone to the grasslands, but everybody concluded her disappearance was somehow connected to Tenpa Nyima. I didn't know what had happened. I went to her house, and her mother told me Sangnyi was at her father's place in Lhasa. I rushed to his stall on Barkhor Street but he was very unfriendly, he said he hadn't seen any Sangnyi and didn't know who this Sangnyi girl was. I waited there by his stall all day but Sangnyi didn't show up. Over the next few days, I went back many times until I started to think that maybe the man was telling the truth about not knowing Sangnyi. That just made things more confusing. There was no clue as to where Tenpa Nyima was, and now Sangnyi's whereabouts were a mystery too. Any information I got just made it clear that there was a lot I didn't know. It was like being in a fog that got thicker and thicker. But one day I suddenly calmed down about it all. Everything is as it is, I thought. I decided I didn't need to know any more than I already did, I didn't even need to know any more about the lives of the students I was closest to. I decided I didn't even need to know that much about myself, all I had to do was keep myself on an even keel.

All this was going through my mind while I was looking up the mountain trying to figure out where the whistle had come from. It seemed to have come from a pile of rock above the ravine, and I was thinking, OK, maybe rocks can whistle. On that particular mountain it was pointless to try to separate the possible from the impossible, so I was ready to accept anything, even rocks that whistle. Then to my surprise the rocks started to move, which shocked me out of my reverie. I was startled to see the rocks assume human form. I saw a face with sparkling black eyes and shining white teeth. Then I saw five or six dust-covered faces. The pile of rocks was a group of boys. The students said the boys were yak herders, and they spent most of the year in the mountains. I had guessed this already. I had seen yaks moving slowly across the slopes, but I had never seen the boys who tend to them. Looking up from below the mountain, you almost never saw the yak herders, they blended into the background, like rocks on the mountainside. Those boys had never attended a single day of school, but I didn't think they should be brought down from the mountains and made to attend. I thought that what they needed was a classroom, not an entire school, just one room built up on the mountain, out of thatch or stone, just something to keep out the weather. Children who live in nature should be educated out in nature. I daydreamed about standing on the mountainside by a stream, sunbirds all around, delivering a lecture. Those boys might listen to me lecture and talk about history with a lot more attention than the children down the mountain or in town ever did.

I was no saint, but I had washed myself of the world.

It was spring. The sun was strong. The sky was clear and empty. It snowed in the spring sometimes, but it melted away in a day or two. The last patches of snow were on the riverbank. The snow concentrated the sunlight, setting itself on fire, setting the sunlight on fire. I could see the burning snow from the ferry landing and then from the ferry as we crossed. But when I got closer, the flames turned into water vapour, into mist that rose into the air and evaporated. When I set out on a walk, I always eventually found myself walking to the ferry landing by the Lhasa River. There were only a few people who took the ferry each day, and sometimes I was the only passenger the old ferry master saw all day. Many times, I wasn't intending to cross the river, I was just walking by the river in the sun, but the old man always smiled at me and gestured for me to get on the ferry.

It was spring and the Lhasa River was blue, clear and running fast. As soon as the ferry, a leather bull boat, was pushed out on the water, it turned parallel to the shore. The old man poled the boat, crossed with the current and expertly delivered me to the opposite bank. There was no purpose to this trip, which I had made many times. I walked about, stopped and looked at the mountains, I was lonely, like a fatherless child, like a child who never knew his father. I often gazed at the mountains and the ravines and gullies that climbed their slopes and thought there must be secrets hidden there, but those secrets were never revealed to me. The sunlight was like fire, and the blue water rushed over the white stones by the bank. In the summer they are well under water, in the winter they are exposed by the bank. Each stone caught and reflected the light, it looked like a scattering of suns along the banks of the river. The river was bluer than blue, icy blue, implacably blue.

Against the icy blue of the river the bright stones dazzled the eye, and the way the birds swooped down over the water was dazzling too. It made me want to go into the water, into that deep, glassy blue and never come out, never come back to the world. I think I had come to a better understanding of the mathematician-poet. I realised he wasn't crazy, he had just been dealing with some difficulties and temptations, I don't know whether it was all in his mind or real, but it was fatal. But I could do nothing about that, and so I walked in the sun, I was born for the sunshine, I was like a mountain, a traveller.

I walked over the scree at the foot of a slope and started up a ravine, craning my neck to look up at the mountain that rose above me. Snow covered the peak all year. I asked myself, Did this mountain arise out of nothing? Did I come from nothingness? Did the mountain come to the river's edge or did the river flow to the mountain? Mountains are always moving, they are travellers on the Earth. The mountain was weary but was about to be on its way again. And wasn't the same true of the river?

I walked up a ravine, I walked in the wind.

I saw withered grass and stacks of yak dung. I saw a village at twilight, prayer flags flying from roofs. If it weren't for the motion of the prayer flags, it wouldn't have been easy to see the village there under the setting sun, it was camouflaged like a lizard on a desert floor. The prayer flags meant people lived there, and they meant deities lived there too. Life is very hard there. I didn't have time to climb a different slope up a different ravine. I might have found another village if I did, but I would never be able to understand it. And besides, the old ferry master was waiting for me. He could have gone back to the other side to see if any others wanted to cross, but he was determined to wait for me. He charged one yuan for the round trip, half that for one way. He wore an old felt cap, the wrinkles on his face and his smile made me think of how the sun could etch one like a knife. The sun etches everything in the mountain, and it had etched his face. One yuan. The ferry was his livelihood. He didn't like to make the trip for nothing and so he waited for me, as we had agreed. As I walked up, he gave me a silly smile, like a rock cracking into a smile, and my heart was filled with sunshine.

There was not a lot of difference between spring and winter, but in the spring the mountain tops were often cloud-covered, and tendrils of cloud rose up from the mountains into the sky, higher and higher. Sometimes the clouds grew thick and suddenly turned into snow that fell back down on the mountain tops. I loved the snow, I was always hoping to see snow clouds rising up from the peaks. When it snowed, I always took my students outside, and I would have done so even if they didn't ask to go out, but they asked every single time, of course, especially when it snowed in the afternoon.

26. A Poet Like the Snow

A poet like the snow. A melancholic black trench coat. A red scarf,
coarse hair, a faint, sad smile through the snow. It reminds you of Bei Dao.
This photograph taken in a snowfall is etched on the poet's tombstone.
Because it's enlarged, his smile is all the more moving,
as if he lives forever on the tombstone out in the snow and wind.

When the mathematician-poet showed up at Ukyi Lhamo's on that snowy day in April, there were signs that his death was imminent, but neither Wang Mojie nor Ukyi Lhamo recognised the signs. That evening, as the snow was flying, he showed up uninvited because he had heard the latest about Wang Mojie, whom he liked to call "the philosopher". He had heard that not only had "the philosopher" crawled around naked, barking like a dog at Yu Youyan, but Ukyi Lhamo had been there too, and he had barked at her as well. This was a new development, shocking news, and very exciting to the poet. He got so worked up he started trembling. He tried to get Ukyi Lhamo to talk about Wang Mojie, he would have been happy with even a few words from her, but she steadfastly refused to engage. Once she had ended their relationship, shortly after the night by the river during Karma Rishi, he had left her alone, and so she didn't think badly of him, but she couldn't understand why he was now pestering her like a crazy person, nor why the business with Wang Mojie excited him so.

The poet had first entered Ukyi Lhamo's emotional life not long after she had come to Tibet, just after the mysterious disappearance of Khanor Rinpoche, and when she thought back on her time with the poet, she had no regrets. She never had regrets after an affair. After Khanor Rinpoche left, she was devastated, and the poet's wildness was exactly what she needed. She was even more wild in bed with him than she was with other lovers, because it felt different with him, because she was releasing pent-up desire. All her lovers were special in some way, her lovers had to stand out from the crowd, and the poet met her standards. He seemed to be an exceptional man with a certain aura. He was a professor in the maths department at Tibet University, and he wrote poetry. He always wore a red scarf. He taught algebra, he taught topology, and he wrote poetry. It was a rare combination, plus he studied Buddhism and had friends who were lamas. Ukyi Lhamo had been introduced to Ma Dingge by the poet, and that made him all the more fascinating. He seemed to know something about everything. He talked with ease and confidence about his love for Tibet, his belief in Tibet and why he had come to Tibet. He said he came to Tibet in the winter of 1989 and had never once been back to the interior. He swore that unless this or that happened, he would never return. You would never have guessed he was a maths professor, he seemed more like a nineteenth-century Russian Eastern Orthodox intellectual. He was always talking about the Decembrists, he looked a bit like a Decembrist himself. He had a big, unkempt beard, he was tall, thin and rather stooped, and with his red scarf his looks alone made a big impression on people, to say nothing of his ideas. He liked to criticise everything about the Chinese interior, which is why he made a point of vowing never to go back, and he built for himself a homeland out of the trinity of mathematics, poetry and religion, which he called his mandala. He hadn't published a single poem in almost a decade because he believed that if the argument that "it is barbaric to write poetry after Auschwitz" still had relevance, then for him to publish poetry during those years would certainly be barbaric.

Ukyi Lhamo quickly discovered that the poet was a liar. He liked to boast that he had never been back to the interior, but in conversation with Ukyi Lhamo he mentioned the time he went to Du Fu's thatched cottage in Sichuan to do whatever one does there, and he talked about going to the Triangle on the campus of Peking University for something, some memorial or other. But this didn't really matter, everybody exaggerates. What bothered Ukyi Lhamo about the poet was not that he lied about never going back to the interior but his tendency to try to exert absolute control over other people. He wasn't any less authoritarian than the people he claimed to oppose. As soon as he and Ukyi Lhamo went to bed together, he started to treat her as his personal property and forbade her to have any contact with other men. He poked his nose into all her business, and he didn't let her go to any party or social function without him. His behaviour, of course, was the expression of instinctual possessiveness. He seemed to think that Ukyi Lhamo had been sent by the heavens to save him, and it terrified him to think some other man might take her from him. He was madly in love with her, to the point of absurdity, and for her he wrote hundreds and hundreds of lines of "ladder-step verse", maybe as many as Vladimir Mayakovski himself wrote.

Ukyi Lhamo had no room in her extraordinary life for the poet's foolishness. She had not expected his "aura" would turn out to be so bogus. She also found out that his interest in Buddhism was specious. This was proved by his tendency to be verbally abusive, which often shocked her, as there was nothing remotely Buddhist about it. For example, he had called out Wang Mojie for living only a "pseudo-bucolic" life, an inflammatory accusation that hit Wang Mojie where it hurt. He said Wang Mojie was more like the neighbourhood cop than a rural sage, and he wasn't about to let a poser like him besmirch the memory of Tao Yuanming. Back in the interior, the poet's foe had been a huge, powerful, impersonal system, against which he could do nothing, any resistance was only for show. Now he had a flesh and blood enemy, and that enemy was Wang Mojie, who seemed to him weak and silly, and therefore he could feel safe and righteous when he vented his anger at him. The poet was convinced that his cause was just and right was on his side, so he believed Wang Mojie's "pseudo-bucolic" lifestyle had to be attacked head-on. The night they all got drunk had set the poet free. Like a soldier going into battle, he laid waste to the "pseudo-bucolic" garden, he stomped on the big padlock, then picked it up and threw it as far as he could. There was nothing spiritual about him, in his heart was only hatred, righteous, crazed, extreme, inexplicable hatred. If anyone had been able to dig into him just a little, they would have found he was a shallow person with no organised ideas about anything.

The poet's out-of-control, ridiculous behaviour was so very different from the way Wang Mojie conducted himself that Ukyi Lhamo started to see Wang Mojie in a new light. Wang Mojie had been wronged, but he seemed to rise above it, and there was something spiritual in that. She got over the poet, she transcended the poet, and she began to see the climbing instructor openly, the man Wang Mojie usually called "your mountaineer" when he talked to her. Her mountaineer was guileless and untamed, and the combination was the perfect purgative for the poet's hypocrisy. She was done with talk of culture, poetry, the battle for justice and so on. The kind of passion she felt when she was with her mountaineer was as pure as snow on a mountain top. It was true that she saw Wang Mojie with fresh eyes now, but she merely had realised how interesting a person he was, no more than that. She picked her men by their looks; Wang Mojie was not handsome, and so she discounted him without really being conscious of it. Both the poet and her mountaineer fitted the conventional ideal masculine type. The former had soulful, sad eyes and the latter had a chiselled physique and was taciturn. Wang Mojie was no match for either of these men, his body wasn't so great, of course, but more importantly the first thing that Ukyi Lhamo had noticed about Wang Mojie was that his face looked somehow lopsided. It was hard to say exactly what it was, but there was something wrong with his face. She even felt sorry for him for being so ugly, but in any case she could never get involved with someone who looked like Wang Mojie. This was her first impression of him. Her impression of him changed after the incident over his garden when he had stayed so calm that he reminded her of Ma Dingge – was it really possible he reminded her of Ma Dingge? – but what never changed was her condescending sympathy for him for being ugly.

Wang Mojie was, of course, an exceptional man. If Ukyi Lhamo was honest with herself, she would have to admit that it was the brazen way that Yu Youyan had gone after Wang Mojie that had made her start to feel somewhat differently about him. Yu Youyan was completely wrong for Wang Mojie, she thought. In truth, she was feeling jealous, but she convinced herself that she just didn't like seeing them together because it wasn't good for either of them. In the first place, Yu Youyan was running the risk of getting used again, and in the second place, Ukyi Lhamo hated to see the deep-thinking, philosophical Wang Mojie fall for seduction like any other man would. Yu Youyan was not pretty, but she knew how to attract men. She played around, or at least she often got played around with. Ukyi Lhamo's sympathy for Yu Youyan was genuine and long-standing. Her concern for Wang Mojie was equally sincere, even if she did seem to have an ulterior motive. Whether her motive was pure or not, she never imagined that her well-intentioned word of caution to Wang Mojie about getting involved with You Youyan would be thrown right back in her face by him, bluntly and unsparingly. This was the first time she realised how truly formidable Wang Mojie was, and in that very same moment somehow Wang Mojie's features seemed to rearrange themselves before her eyes, and he didn't seem that ugly any more. Everything he said to her was spot on. She didn't have any right to feel sorry for Yu Youyan. She thought she was better than other people and feeling sorry for Yu Youyan was just a way to make her feel superior.

What had she got out of her love life? Had she ever got what she really wanted? And if not, what was the point of all her casual affairs? What was the point of her affair with her mountaineer? Why was she satisfied to be nothing more than the object of so many men's attention? If the same men went after her and Yu Youyan, what made her think she was any different from Yu Youyan? This question had never occurred to her before. Wang Mojie's sharp words cut straight to her troubled heart. She no longer felt so self-satisfied and superior. She was full of confusion and lack of conviction, and in fact, the nameless feeling of being at a loss came precisely from this confusion and lack of conviction, but nobody could tell she felt this way. All she ever heard was flattery, but Wang Mojie saw right through her.

Of course, when Wang Mojie and Yu Youyan first got involved, Ukyi Lhamo didn't have a thought that something might happen between her and Wang Mojie. Her reaction to Wang Mojie getting involved with Yu Youyan was to introduce him to Ma Dingge, although at the time she wasn't entirely sure why. Ukyi Lhamo knew only that whatever that special something was that Wang Mojie had, she needed it, she was sure of it, and nobody else had it. She longed for the sort of heart-to-heart conversation possible only with someone with a man's intellect, and Wang Mojie could provide her with that. Even his cold, cutting candour was satisfying. She wasn't afraid of it, she had enough self-confidence, which freed her to be candid and unguarded with him. She told him all her secrets, including her infatuation with Khanor Rinpoche and her adoration for Ma Dingge. When she introduced Wang Mojie to Ma Dingge, was she making a gift to Wang Mojie of what she held most dear? Or was she trying to demonstrate her spirituality to Wang Mojie? Or was she subconsciously hoping that Wang Mojie would be influenced for the better by Ma Dingge? Her many motivations were difficult for her to articulate, they were unclear, but she made the introduction, and that was what was important.

In her love life and in her faith Ukyi Lhamo walked a single path that she kept secret to herself. She wasn't sure where this path was taking her but she stuck to it, even sometimes without meaning to. Wang Mojie had no religious faith whatsoever, he was quick to admit it, but when he and Ma Dingge, a great man of faith, met, they immediately established a deep rapport. This surprised Ukyi Lhamo and even made her envious, and she had never before envied anybody anything. Wang Mojie and Ma Dingge interacted as equals. Wang Mojie was not obsequious, and as the connection between them grew stronger and their talks went deeper, Ukyi Lhamo often ended up just listening to the two of them. After a few of these meetings, the things about Wang Mojie's appearance that had always seemed wrong to her stopped bothering her, they even started to fascinate her. She wondered if his out-of-kilter face was the necessary corollary to his balanced intellect. She started to like that face.

For Ukyi Lhamo, the months when she and Wang Mojie often visited Ma Dingge were a time of complex emotions and secret happiness. Many times she, Wang Mojie and Ma Dingge would stand on the terrace high up in the monastery at twilight, quietly watching the river and the setting sun. Slowly they would be illuminated by the beautiful light of sunset that fell on the river, the light seeming to shine through their bodies. In the moment the sun suddenly disappeared behind the mountains beyond the river, the light on their bodies blinked off, the world was still, and their minds were open and clear.

Once, as they stood there, Wang Mojie and Ma Dingge talked about consciousness, interiority and the self, and Wang Mojie insisted that we can't stop our thoughts. He said that even in a moment of utter tranquillity, our thoughts do not stop, and though we might be unaware of it, our subconscious mental activity can actually grow more lively. Ma Dingge said something interesting in response. He said that when you first try to stop your thoughts, it is difficult, your thoughts spill out like a waterfall over a cliff, and you think you are having more thoughts than usual, but you aren't really. He said that as we make spiritual progress, our thoughts become like the river down below, sometimes the flow is fast, sometimes it is slow, but it is never again a waterfall. And then the mind becomes quiet, like still water. From time to time, like ripples on water raised by a breeze, thoughts might pass through our minds, but these thoughts remain on the mind's surface, they reach no depth. Ukyi Lhamo couldn't get a word in, but when Wang Mojie spoke of an "existential crisis", she realised he had put a name to what she had been feeling for so long. She also found that what Ma Dingge said cleared up many things for her. It was like clouds had parted and the sun had come out. She pictured the three of them as in a painting. They were soaring over the rivers of thought, led by Ma Dingge, each of them flying at his or her own level, Ma Dingge in the centre, Wang Mojie on his left, Ukyi Lhamo on his right, the three of them ascending in light from the flames of butter lamps and the setting sun.

She pictured this many times and dreamed about it many times. She described it to Wang Mojie, but he wasn't impressed by the tableau. Wang Mojie did not believe that contemplation could extinguish thoughts, he believed the opposite, that it made us more fully aware of our thoughts. He said that what we feel and think during contemplation are at the essence of what it means to be alive, and on this point, he and Ma Dingge disagreed. Wang Mojie was interested in the lucid flow of thought that exists during contemplation. He tried to catch those thoughts, he tried to catch each thought at its inception, and he found doing so to be one of the greatest pleasures of his life. The conversations between Wang Mojie and Ma Dingge were conversations between two different approaches to life, this was something that Ukyi Lhamo had never imagined might happen. Wang Mojie and Ma Dingge were different, but because of this, they became friends. This shocked Ukyi Lhamo, and as a result, she opened up her past to Wang Mojie, she told him her mother's story, and she told him the long history of her family, none of which she had ever even hinted at before. She sighed and said that while she was the product of that history, she had never had a grasp on it, and she didn't know how to deal with it now that her family's history was suddenly confronting her. Now that she was living with that history, what should she do with her life? She was different now but not completely so. There was a lot of evidence that her grandmother was still alive, she had looked for her everywhere, but no one had helped her. All that history she had learned seemed unconnected to her current reality. But she believed there had to be a connection. She felt that having a history had given her life new meaning, she just couldn't say what the meaning was. She was like a millionaire who wasn't sure exactly where her money was. Now history was open to her. She just didn't know how to connect it to her reality.

She had so much she wanted to share. She longed for somebody to join her on her journey into history and religion; she didn't think she could love a man who didn't know history and didn't have religion. She couldn't give herself completely to a man like that. During those unforgettable days, those days and nights, she told Wang Mojie more than she had ever told anybody. She told him all about her past and all about her life now. What she said was a confession, an offering, a promise. Did he not understand that? He was part of her now, she had fallen in love with him, she was sure of it, and he should have known this from all the hints in what she said to him and how she looked at him. She wasn't acting on emotion, she had thought it through. She made the decision to love him, it was a conscious decision, not a surrendering to emotion.

She told him that she didn't think she could find herself until she found someone she could give herself to, but she said such a person didn't exist and Wang Mojie wasn't him, which was actually a hint to Wang Mojie that he might be the one. She wasn't being emotional, she had thought it all through, she had a plan, and she felt she couldn't be direct with Wang Mojie because he was always ironic with her. When he had told her that he was interested in her but only in an everyday sense because she made an interesting study, he wasn't telling the truth. But on that morning after they had talked all night, when she was ready to give herself to him, once again he just walked out, seemingly indifferent to her. It was too much, she couldn't take it any longer.

On that wretched morning, she had looked at him with a naked need that begged him to stay. He saw the look, he understood what she wanted, but he didn't waiver, he was not moved, his eyes were cold and, as he always did, he turned and walked straight out without a glance back. She hated him. He had hurt her, and so she decided she had been right to find him ugly. His nose was lopsided. She told herself that he didn't deserve her love. How could she possibly love him? He was ugly! She decided to get far away from him, forget him. He had made fun of her for trying to find her grandmother, and so she would, she would do so right away, now, it no longer had anything to do with Wang Mojie. She still was in love with her mountaineer, and she called him. Wang Mojie had humiliated her, and she almost wanted to murder him for it.

She felt a bleak, broken sexual need, she needed her mountaineer, she was lucky to have her mountaineer. She wanted him to drive everything from her mind, make her forget everything... she got what she needed... it brought her peace... she loved him... when she woke up, she was in the snowy mountains, it was like another dream... everything with Wang Mojie was all behind her now, as if it had never happened.

As her mind went back to Wang Mojie, the music in the car and the picturesque snowy landscape outside the windows faded from her attention. Her fear, anger and hatred were gone, she felt at peace now. Travel is a temporary escape, it gets us away from our routines, but it is when we are on the road that we are most likely to think about what has happened to us in the past. Now that she was away from Wang Mojie, she began to feel love for him, she began to miss him, and the farther away she got from him the more she missed him, the more she knew she forgave him, and the more she felt at fault. Love is a journey, don't they say that? It is true. Her decision that she and Wang Mojie would be together had been made out of arrogance. She seemed to think he ought to feel grateful to her for deigning to love him. But who was Wang Mojie really? He certainly was no ordinary man. He had an impressive inner strength. And he could hold his own in any argument, even with Ma Dingge.

While on the road with her mountaineer, Ukyi Lhamo fell in love with Wang Mojie. Up in the Himalayas, as far from Wang Mojie as she could be, she fell completely in love with him. And because she had, she didn't want to make love to her mountaineer any more, and she started to turn him away each night when they stopped at a new town. Finally they talked, and she explained everything to him.

She went on to Dromo alone.

She couldn't believe that Wang Mojie and Yu Youyan would do such shocking things, it was beyond imagination. If Wang Mojie loved Yu Youyan and not her, she could accept it. But she didn't give up on him, she gave him an opportunity, she told him that her relationship with her mountaineer was over. And Wang Mojie had given her reason for hope when he had been so wonderful about talking to her mother. That had surprised her, it touched her, she admired him for it, and so she stopped caring about Wang Mojie and Yu Youyan. But she was disappointed to find that Wang Mojie persisted in his behaviour. He hadn't changed at all.

She had seen his disgusting behaviour with her own eyes. He had barked at her, he had actually barked at her. He didn't even seem human. At all. He had chased her, barking at her heels, she couldn't stand it, so she turned and left. She pulled the door shut behind her and had to try several times before she could get it to latch. As she struggled with the door, she was surprised to find that suddenly she didn't hate him any longer and started to feel sorry for him.

A few days later, Ukyi Lhamo got a call from the poet. He said he didn't want to bother her, he just wanted to talk about Wang Mojie with her because he heard she had seen him in the act, so he had to talk to her. On the phone, his voice was hoarse with excitement. During the whole affair, the poet acted like a madman, he had hold of Wang Mojie and wasn't going to let him go. He didn't try to hide the fact that he was so elated and so excited that he couldn't sleep, which was obvious from his bloodshot eyes. He was so animated and exuberant when he recounted to others what he knew, that while he may have succeeded in making Wang Mojie sound dreadful, he also revealed how crazy he had become.

He walked to Ukyi Lhamo's house through the snow, which covered his black leather trench coat and red scarf. She was sitting by the window reading the copy of The Diamond Sutra *that Ma Dingge had given her. She was feeling distracted and struggling with it. She read, "Dispositions of mind, or modes of thought, whether relating to the past, the present or the future, are alike unreal and illusory." This was an insight intended to help us recognise the truths of impermanence and non-self and help liberate us from the cycle of rebirth, but she couldn't concentrate, and her mind kept wandering off into daydreams. She was surprised when the poet appeared at her door. She couldn't believe he had come to see her. It made her heart sink, it felt like somebody was playing a joke on her. If he had been content just to sit in silence or chat about the weather or make small talk about how she had redecorated since he was last there, then maybe it would feel like old times. But as soon as he came in the door, he began to talk excitedly (in retrospect, this was a portent of his impending demise).*

—You didn't want me to come, but I came. We have to talk, we must talk, I have a lot I need to say, and when we are done talking tonight, that's it, we'll be done with each other for good. I haven't said a thing to anybody about you and that climbing instructor, what's going on between you two is completely normal, that man is all right, but Wang Mojie, that's a whole different thing!

There was alcohol on his breath, he had had a lot to drink.

—I'll be quick, and you don't have to get me tea or anything, I'll say my piece and then I'll go, but you have to listen to me say all I have to say. It's so great, it's too great, they say you saw Wang Mojie's disgusting behaviour with your own eyes, he even barked at you, he barked at you, woof woof woof, woof woof, *that's so amazing, I can't believe it, it's too perfect!*

There was nothing she could say. She poured him some tea in the hope it would sober him up. He took the tea but put it aside.

—I'm really happy, I'm so happy, and why hide it? Why would I hide it? We hide too much. What happened, happened, why not bring it all out in the open? Who am I to hide anything, why would anybody want to hide anything? We should all stop

pretending to be who we are not. Why do we pretend? Given what the world is like these days, why do we keep pretending? We're all suffocating from it, it isn't worth it, it's not worth it. OK, let's get back to business, let me ask you a question, how are you feeling? Gone to pieces? Hopeless? You can admit it, we all feel hopeless. But you are doing better than Wang Mojie. The bloke's a basket case, you saw it with your own eyes, right?

He took a sip of tea, it burned his tongue, he sucked in a quick breath of air but was otherwise unfazed.

—But that doesn't matter, what matters is that he is such a phoney, worse than anybody, he even had me fooled, and I'm usually a very good judge of people. Actually, my initial impression of him was spot on. The first time I saw him "picking chrysanthemums by the eastern fence", all "carefree, gazing at the Southern Mountains" like he is Tao Yuanming, it pissed me off. What is up with that act? Who is he trying to impress? He is trying to impress you! Of course, as soon as he opens his mouth, he gives himself away. I've heard the way he lectures you, the fellow thinks he is the neighbourhood cop, and to think that he studied philosophy! He gives it a bad name. I'll show everybody how phoney a philosopher he is. And what was up with that lock? How ridiculous was that? Didn't that piss you off? OK, I know that he doesn't give a shit about us, also maybe I did go too far but still, I was surprised when he didn't react, he treated it like it was a natural disaster, that surprised me, it really surprised me. His garden was wrecked, by me, and he just bloody sits there meditating on it, like he is supposed to be Gandhi. I came over here and watched him, he seemed foolish to me at first, but the longer he sat there the more he did seem like some sort of monk or priest. Then when he cleaned it all up and started to rebuild it, that really dumbfounded me, I started to think he really did have something of Gandhi in him. He's stronger than me, he's stronger than all of us. He lives his trauma, no that's not right, he is surviving his trauma. The man is a cut above the rest. He makes me feel inadequate, I can't compare with him, I've just made myself look bad. You left me, I knew you would sooner or later, I deserved it. No one is ever going to completely tame you. I'm satisfied just to have had you. I know that the mountain climbing chap is better than me in some ways, he is more natural, for example, he's got all that energy, he's into mountains, he was able to take you away from

me. But that's what I thought before that night during Karma Rishi, because that night I found out that Wang Mojie might be even more impressive than your climber.

—I'll tell you what I think of him, I respect the way he accepts everything with equanimity even more than I respect the way he keeps to himself. Yu Youyan was quicker on the uptake than the rest of us, she grabbed him straight away, and it wasn't a game to her, other people thought it was, but I could tell it wasn't. She may not be the best person, but she's very intuitive. But she's one of those people who overestimates herself, she overreaches all the time, no chance that Wang Mojie was going to be interested in her. He has got his eyes on you, and I think that maybe in him you have found the man who can control you. You're a beautiful person but you don't know who you are. If you don't know who you are, how is anybody else going to know who you are? That's just depressing. But I think Wang Mojie has a chance, I'm just worried that if he falls in love with you, he's going to make the same mistakes I made, and I really want to see somebody tame you. I want to explain you to Wang Mojie. Isn't that noble of me? Aren't I the best? You actually don't know me at all.

—Don't always look down on me. When I want to be noble, I'm more noble than anybody. I'll sacrifice myself. I'll pay the price. My past proves it. All these years I've been fighting the good fight in my own way. Do you know anybody else who has always refused to go back to the interior? You don't care about any of that, which is fine, even if I'm really suffering.

He had finished his tea, but she didn't refill his glass.

—Of all the people I have something in common with, Wang Mojie's got the greatest inner reserves of strength. I reached out to him, I thought we could be friends, even though I know he doesn't need a friend like me. I've always been wishing him the best, I feel that with him around, I don't matter, I don't even care if I live or die, or what my life's like. I feel he can live for me. God, how candid I am, how noble. I even wrote a poem for him: "Oh, Mojie, / let water flow into water, / let the one become the one." I think Wang Mojie is the "one", and "one" stands for reason, transcendence, strength. But, ha ha, ha ha, ha ha! It's so great, God likes a joke. One day Yu Youyan suddenly shows up looking for me. She says she's just come from Wang Mojie's and she's shaking. She

says Wang Mojie kissed her boots, he kissed her uniform buttons, he got her to whip him with her belt, he made her torture him and interrogate him! Before she finished what she had to say, I understood. I could've slapped myself for being so stupid. I must've been crazy not to believe myself from the beginning. I was right about him from the beginning. I knew there was something creepy about him, something phoney, something perverted. I didn't know what it was exactly, and whatever it was I let it go. I even started to idealise him when I was feeling so down. And then, ha ha, it's just too perfect, he finally showed us who he really is. The devil took off his disguise. He's a mess. Life's ripped him to shreds and so he protects himself by being so sanctimonious and aloof. He's not better than me, he's much worse. I may be a weak man but I'm a man, deep down he is a dog, ha ha, a dog, a dog, like in some cartoon...

To make him stop the deranged talk, Ukyi Lhamo threw her cigarette lighter down. This was her third effort to get him to shut up, the first two times she had failed.

—Are you done yet? Are you done? Are you ever going to stop?

—No! No! No! he yelled back at her. You let me finish, you can't be tamed by anybody, Wang Mojie is a phoney, everything about him is fake, ha ha, you let me finish and then I'll leave.

—I don't think you're ever going to stop talking, she said. Listen to me, I'm still attracted to him.

—What? What? You love him? Are you saying you still love him?

—I'm not the only one it seems. Yu Youyan still loves him, a lot of people love him, but nobody loves you, no one cares even one iota about you. You can leave now.

Ukyi Lhamo's words were unsparing and they upset him.

—What? What? What?

—He's real, he's brave, I hadn't realised it but everything you've said has made me see it. He has his fetish but that's not all of him, he's more than that. You are nothing more than what I'm seeing now. He deserves sympathy from the women in his life. Do you? Do you know what happens when a woman feels sympathy for a man she respects? She loves him more!

Ukyi Lhamo was surprised at what she had said. It hadn't been planned, it just came out because she wanted to hurt the poet, but when she said it, she felt a rush of emotion, she felt hopeful.

—You both love him? Yu Youyan too?

—Yes, the two of us are going to save him! she said, once again surprising herself.

—You two? Together?

—Yes, she said resolutely, even though she didn't know exactly what she meant when she said she would save Wang Mojie.

There was a knock at the door. It was Wang Mojie himself, and his arrival surprised Ukyi Lhamo as much as the poet's had. Given that she had been trying to get rid of the poet and given what Wang Mojie said about Ma Dingge (he said Ma Dingge was sitting out in meditation in the snow), it was easy for her to decide to leave with Wang Mojie right then.

—Wang Mojie and I are leaving, she said to the poet.

That was an invitation to him to go. She draped a white wool shawl over her shoulders and waited for his reaction, but he didn't react. She felt like giving her arm to Wang Mojie just to make the poet give up, she was feeling suddenly bold, but she and Wang Mojie had not talked since he had barked at her.

When she got back, the poet was bent over the table writing her a note, and he had put on his coat and scarf. When he saw her come in, he picked up the note and smiled happily.

—Back already. Did you see Ma Dingge?

She couldn't hide her disappointment to find him still there.

—Why are you still here? she asked loudly. She let the door stand open, and snow blew in.

—What he said about Ma Dingge was nonsense, I knew it as soon as he said it. Ma Dingge wasn't out there. Haven't you figured out what sort of person he is yet? When I came here today, his door was wide open, in all this snow, his door was open, and he was just sitting there staring into space, and I'll bet you he was thinking about Yu Youyan. He came to see you only because there's no Yu Youyan today. I know I'm right. I know his type all too well. He likes the snow, he likes to go outside and freeze, ha ha, he likes the feeling, he should strip naked and get down in the snow!

—Get out, now, get out! she said, her hand on the door.

—Just one more thing. That climber fellow is good for you. At least he has his mountains, Wang Mojie has nothing.

—Get out, get out!

He stared at her, his gaze was different from Wang Mojie's gaze but the two of them shared something too, they were two different people but also the same person, that was Wang Mojie's type of logic, she thought, and it was fitting to turn it back on him.

—Wang Mojie and I will meet again. I wish you the best, he said with sincerity.

Ukyi Lhamo had no idea what he was talking about. She watched him leave, expecting him to stop at Wang Mojie's house, but he didn't (Wang Mojie wasn't back yet anyway). The poet disappeared into the snow somewhere beyond the school gate.

The two of them ought to have a talk, Ukyi Lhamo thought to herself. In some ways there is no difference in their characters.

The poet came to visit Ukyi Lhamo the night Wang Mojie asked her to come with him to see Ma Dingge meditating on the rock in the snow. The poet was still there when she came back, and immediately after he left, she called her mountaineer. The phone rang, and he answered. She said, I want to come back to town, but it's snowing too hard, come get me. He said he wasn't at home and it would be a while before he could come for her. She could hear music in the background.

—Forget it, then, never mind, I'll walk, she said, hanging up before he could say anything.

She started to pack, then stopped and sat staring into space for a while before finishing her packing. She heard his SUV and saw its headlights. He had come in a hurry, which touched her, made her feel a little dizzy. She looked at the snow falling fast and hard in the bright beams of the headlights shining on the campus wall. Brighter than Wang Mojie's stupid little torch, she thought. She yelled out to her mountaineer to tell him to wait just a minute while she got her things. She hadn't been in touch with him since she got back from Dromo, and he hadn't called to find out if she got back safely. This was typical of them, no different from when they were seeing each other. It was always impromptu when they got together, he would call her or come to see her out of the blue, or she would do the same, usually it was her surprising him. This was their old habit. She grabbed her handbag and got in, he turned the car around on the snow-covered ground in front of Wang Mojie's garden, like so many times before, but Ukyi Lhamo felt a little different this time, she felt stronger. They drove east towards Lhasa and soon the city's misty lights emerged from the snow.

Ukyi Lhamo caught a glimpse of the poet walking down the road in the snow all by himself, but she didn't say anything to her mountaineer until they had driven past him. When she told him, he pulled over and started to turn around, but she told him to keep on driving.

—But come on, the snow is heavy, there isn't a single taxi out, her mountaineer said.

—Don't worry about him, he likes the snow.

They sat there for a moment before he slowly drove on. They arrived at Jokhang Temple Square, the street up to it lined with bars and bright lights that gleamed off the snow. They were only a few minutes from Ukyi Lhamo's family home just off Barkhor Street when she told him to stop the car.

—Are you free for a bit longer? I'll buy you a drink, she said. They went into a bar she frequented. She knew the owner, who greeted her warmly. She got herself a small bottle of red wine. Her mountaineer had beer. As usual, the owner gave her free snacks and a discount on the drinks.

—I wanted to take you out for a drink, that's why I didn't let you pick him up. He was walking back from my house, Ukyi Lhamo said.

—Is he all right?

—Not really. He did have some nice things to say about you.

—Oh yeah? he said and took a sip of beer.

—A lot has happened lately. Have you heard?

—I heard about some of it, he said, being honest.

—I've been so stupid.

—Don't say that.

—OK, enough of that, let's change the subject. Let's talk about you. What have you been up to?

—The usual, working out, climbing. Spring is here, so I'm getting ready for a climb. I'm going to a peak in the middle stretch of the Himalayas.

—What mountain?

—Makalu. It's not very famous. Heard of it?

—No. Is it big?

—Fifth highest in the world.

—Oh. Fifth highest? How tall?

—8,463 metres.

—Over eight thousand metres? Has anybody ever climbed it?

—No. It's a virgin peak.

—Watch out, virgins are formidable, she said and laughed.

—We're not climbing the main peak this year. We'll go up one of the two subsidiary peaks.

—Subsidiary peaks?

—Peaks that are part of the same mountain but not as high as the main or highest peak. Makalu has two major subsidiary peaks, Chomo Lonzo, 7,804 metres, and Kangchungtse, which is also called Makalu II and is 7,678 metres. We have a three-year plan. This year we'll climb Makalu II, next year we'll climb Chomo Lonzo, and the year after that we'll do our best to get to the main peak.

—Is it dangerous?

—Of course, all mountains are dangerous.

—Why don't you just start with the main peak and get it over with?

—That's not what it's about. If you just want to get it over with, you shouldn't be climbing.

—Climbing Makalu sounds the same as climbing Chomolungma.

—I'll never climb Chomolungma again.

—Why not?

—I know my limit. Some things just aren't meant for me.

—You are very rational about it.

—Of course I am. At the end of the day, mountain climbing is about making rational decisions, it's not about being daring, and it's not about "getting it over with".

—I get it. It's about the journey, not the destination, Ukyi Lhamo said with a chuckle.

—More or less, yes. I'm not very good at explaining it.

—I apologise for Shigatse.

—I understand your nature. I respect strong women.

—Am I strong?

—I don't know, you seem strong to me.

—I'm not. A lot of the time I'm pretty fragile.

—So? Mountains are fragile too. Look at the clouds on the mountains, clouds are mountains in their fragile state, and just as beautiful.

—Everything with you is mountains.

—Mountains are what I know. And I know them well.

—You know mountains and so you know a lot of other things too.

—That's right.

—I feel better after talking to you.

—Cheers.

—Cheers.

Music was playing softly in the background, the snow was piling up on the square outside, clean glasses hung over the bar, like an upside-down glass harp. They finished their drinks and sat listening to the music. It was a weekday, early spring, and only a few other people were in the bar, and they looked as if they were always there, part of the decor along with the screens and prayer wheels that gave the place a Tibetan feel.

—Hate to say it, but I have to teach in the morning, Ukyi Lhamo said. First period, I hate having a lesson that early.

—I'll come and get you in the morning. I'll drive you to school.

—You won't need to come and get me, because I'm not going to my mother's place, I'm coming to your place. Makes it easy for you to give me that lift.

—You haven't been to my place for a long time.

—We won't make love, OK? Agreed?

—Of course. It's a given.

—What's a given?

—That we won't make love. In Shigatse, remember? You made that the rule.

—And you remembered? And you don't mind?

—Of course I mind, but there are things more important than sex, so it's fine if we don't.

Ukyi Lhamo was overcome by an emotion she would not have been able to express. She was with a man, but there was to be no love-making. She trusted him, he deserved her trust. If he had really wanted to make love, she wouldn't have refused, but it would have been the last time he would see her, and she would no longer hold him in her heart. It wasn't for Wang Mojie's sake that she didn't want to make love, it was just that for some reason she was feeling an aversion to sex. She wanted love without sex, she would be happy to lie on the bed with him, and she wouldn't mind if they kissed and cuddled, that she could accept, but she did not want sex. She couldn't bear the thought of being penetrated, she didn't want anyone in her body, it was as if she had a secret to protect that lay not within her heart but in her body. She had never felt this way before, it was an odd feeling but very strong. They walked back out into the snow, and it was beautiful in the city light. She knew she could trust him. By the front gate of Tibet University, they saw the poet again walking alone in the snow in his leather trench coat and red scarf. He was slightly obscured by the misty snow. He was a poet like the snow.

He was a poet like the snow. That's what my friends in Tibet always said when they talked about the poet after he was gone. It wasn't just Ukyi Lhamo but all of us who did our best to forget about his odd behaviour in the period before his death. We chose to remember him having a swim in the "Goddess of Death", we chose to remember his endearing, admirable, indomitable spirit, we chose to remember him as the hero of the Lhasa River. We chose to remember him looking so melancholy in the black leather trench coat and red woollen scarf he always wore, his head of coarse hair, a hint of a sad smile through the snow (in appearance, he reminded you of Bei Dao).

We had the photograph of him in the snow enlarged and etched onto his tombstone. Because the photograph was enlarged, he seemed to live on among the lonely graves, his smile all the more touching, like on the tomb of a departed national leader. We planted a few small trees by his grave. I don't know if they will live, I think if we look after them, they will, but it is hard to say. It's difficult for plants to survive in that high, dry climate, and even if we went to water them a lot, they still might not make it. But we planted them anyway, to make ourselves (and the poet) feel better: No tree is certain to survive / but a tree that does not survive is still a tree / there are many such trees in the world.

Everyone came to the funeral with the sole exception of Wang Mojie, who more than anybody should have been there. Wang Mojie had his unreasonable streak. There was nothing keeping him from the funeral, he just refused to participate, he even questioned us for going, or maybe he was mocking us. That is the one thing about Wang Mojie I can't stand. There is something inhuman in him, in his bones, and it makes him a lot less likeable than the poet was. He said all that we did for the funeral was meaningless. I agree, it was meaningless, but we were right to do it. Wang Mojie has something in his character that makes him almost a Nazi, almost like Martin Heidegger, and when a person with such a tendency gets involved with the structures of power it is very dangerous, but luckily Wang Mojie never came close to holding any sort of power.

27. Notes on Zero

The symbol for zero was first invented by the Sumerians.
It was passed on to the Greeks, who found it ridiculous and rejected it.
"Conceived of as having no name, it is the Originator of heaven and Earth;
"Conceived of as having a name, it is the Mother of all things"...
"Nothingness" in the Dao De Jing *is closely related to "zero",*
it is at the foundation of Eastern philosophy.

Wang Mojie had been pondering the concept of zero for a long time. He kept a notebook with his thoughts on the subject. Over time, these thoughts became more ordered and clear, and he put a title on the cover of the notebook that he grew to like more and more: "On 'Zero': The Starting Point for Mathematics, Buddhist Learning and Philosophy". As Wang Mojie understood it, zero was most important not as a number but as a metaphysical concept, and so philosophers should have as much to say about zero as mathematicians did.

In his notebook Wang Mojie wrote down something from "Zero and Metaphysics: Thoughts about Being and Nothingness from Mathematics, Buddhism, Daoism to Phenomenology", by Ni Liangkang and Cheng Zhengzhi: "What would it be like if there was no zero in this world? Not so terrible, it seems. There is no record of zero in the ancient history of China... The ancient Chinese would say *wushi* (five tens) or *liubai* (six hundreds) to denote fifty or six hundred, the same as the Greeks used 'murias' to denote ten thousand, and the Romans used

X to signify ten... zero came to the West around the tenth century CE, and had not existed there before then... Although the Greeks had been the first to bring forward the notion of mathematics, their mathematicians, even those as great as Archimedes, able to think of numbers as large as 10^{63}, still had not invented a symbol for zero. Moreover, in their geometry, which was extremely well known to Socrates, Plato and Pythagoras, there was neither zero nor the need for zero."

Frontiers of Philosophy in China, *October 2007, Vol. 2, No. 4 (October 2007), pages 547 to 556.*

Wang Mojie copied down this abstract musing on a topic far from the concerns of daily life. He was working on putting into writing his ideas about the difference between the Indian word for and notion of "zero" and the Chinese word for and notion of "nothing", when Ukyi Lhamo walked in. Wang Mojie asked her to wait as he finished what he was writing. Ukyi Lhamo sighed. She watched as Wang Mojie, seemingly oblivious to her, continued to write in his notebook. It gave her an odd feeling to see him at his desk at work while she could picture him crawling around on the floor barking at Yu Youyan. How could this be the same person?

She had come over because she had to. She had to talk to him about Ma Dingge's father because he was soon to leave France for Beijing, where he would stay only briefly before flying to Lhasa. He had been in contact with Ukyi Lhamo, who was making all the arrangements in Lhasa for him. He couldn't stay at the monastery. A hotel would be best but that would not be convenient because even the nearest one, the Tibet Hotel, was a good distance from Drepung. He could get a car from the hotel to the monastery, but it would be difficult to get back to the hotel from there. Ukyi Lhamo was worried about what he was going to eat, where he could rest, what medicine he would need and who was going to be by his side each day. She agreed with Ma Dingge that his father was too old to handle the altitude, and she had opposed the trip from the start. Wang Mojie, however, wanted him to come. All he cared about was his chance to meet Jean-Philippe Robert, and he didn't give a thought to how the altitude would affect him. If Robert had been coming to Tibet for religious reasons or as a father who missed his son, Ukyi Lhamo would have been happy to host him, but not only was he not coming for either of these reasons, he was coming as a challenger.

He claimed his purpose in making the trip was to engage his son in conversation, but the truth was he needed material so he could finish a book he was writing that was a critique of Buddhism. Ukyi Lhamo was confident that Ma Dingge would get the better of any argument with his father, but she still didn't like the whole idea. She had thought about solving the problem of Robert's accommodation by letting him stay in her house, and she would go back to Lhasa every night. But when she looked at her shrine with a figure of the Buddha and bowls of offering water and her *mani* stones, she couldn't bear the thought of letting somebody who rejected Buddhist beliefs sleep there. It would be better for him to stay at Wang Mojie's, it would be perfect in fact. The two of them were both sceptics, they could keep each other company. The thought made her laugh, at which Wang Mojie finally put his pen down and looked up. She couldn't resist having some fun at his expense.

—What are you writing? Your philosophical magnum opus? she asked, stressing the last two words.

—Nothing so grand, he said as he stretched, but maybe close, an opus at least. I've been working on this all day, so let me ask you a question. Do you know when the symbol for zero first appeared? Do you know when the Chinese first started to use it?

—I don't know, she said quickly, uninterested.

—Well, I'll tell you. Want to hear it?

—No.

—The symbol for zero was first invented by the Sumerians. It was passed on to the Greeks, who found it ridiculous and rejected it, and then it made its way to India, and only then was it resurrected. Do you know why? Because ancient India was Buddhist, and the Buddhists had the idea of *sunyata*, emptiness, which is the idea that all things are empty of intrinsic existence or nature. I learned this from an article called "Zero and Metaphysics".

Not caring if Ukyi Lhamo was interested or not, Wang Mojie went on, as if lecturing to a class.

—In Greek philosophy, in Western philosophy in general, there is little discussion or understanding of what in Chinese we call *kong*, which is our translation of the Sanskrit *sunya*, empty, and *sunyata*, emptiness, and little discussion or understanding of what we call *wu*, nothing or nothingness. Westerners misunderstand Eastern philosophies of "emptiness" and "nothingness" and mistakenly conflate them with nihilism, and so they have little to say about them. And that is why the Greeks ridiculed the idea of zero, but the ancient Indians embraced it.

Wang Mojie picked up *A Comparative Analysis of Greek and Indian*

Thought, flipped through it, put it down and picked up a copy of the *Dao De Jing*. He continued to speak.

—The Chinese didn't invent zero, but the idea of zero appears very early on in Chinese history. It's in the *Dao De Jing*. Look, right here in the first section we find these sentences: "Conceived of as having no name, it is the Originator of heaven and Earth; Conceived of as having a name, it is the Mother of all things." Are you listening? If you don't listen carefully, you're not going to follow me, are you?

—I didn't listen to a word you said.

—That's a shame.

—I have no idea what you are talking about, she said, her head held high.

Wang Mojie closed his notebook and put away the books that were lying open on the table. He tilted the desk lamp up a little and the room grew brighter.

—We've been talking in the dark, Wang Mojie said as he straightened up. OK, tell me, what's up?

—You seem to be truly an intellectual, she said, not ready to let things go.

—What do you mean? Wang Mojie looked at her, his mind seemingly still on zero.

—Now I know that there is something you have faith in. You have faith in zero.

—Zero is the origin of everything, it's at the heart of Eastern ontology, and so you can say I have faith in zero, in that sense you're correct, but not really. Philosophy and religion are two completely different things. The crisis of our time is that we know a lot, but we have no faith in anything. I won't discuss why this is, everybody knows the reason. My question is, how do we live, even for one more day, if there is nothing we can have faith in? There are many different sorts of faith, and I don't think that just thoughtlessly converting to Christianity or Buddhism is going to solve anybody's crisis of faith. Religion is just an expedient, a crutch. But then again, a lot of people do need a crutch.

—You're the one with a crutch, Ukyi Lhamo said, turning red with anger.

—I know people who have converted to Buddhism, which is to say I know people who have picked up a crutch, and crutch is the right word, and generally speaking they're happy because being among like-minded people gives them a sense of belonging. To me they're just a big group of people all walking along leaning on the same type of crutch. They parade along, looking like they have left all their troubles behind, but that has come at the cost of their agency.

—Do you have agency? I thought everything was zero.

—Maybe I don't have real agency, but I still don't need a crutch.

—Right, you don't need a crutch because you bark like a dog.

—I bark, I play at being canine, that's right, and in life I am dog-like, I put my tail between my legs, I cower, I beg, but I'm not turning to God to save me, I take responsibility for myself. I know how debased I feel inside, and I know that I may have to live with that feeling my whole life.

—And you would rather feel debased than use a crutch? I hate that word "crutch".

—Come on, you think that converting to Buddhism after all we've been through isn't just an escape?

—What do you mean "we"? You're the only one debasing yourself.

—OK, OK, good for you, good for you for being able to be so unaware of the way you duck reality.

—I know what you're trying to say. You think you're so great, you think you're the victim, you have to bear it all, what a saint you are.

—Well, now that you say so, maybe I am. Not much difference between my life and being a saint.

—I've never met anyone as shameless as you.

—OK then, what did you come to see me about?

Wang Mojie wanted to change the subject. Ukyi Lhamo didn't answer at first, she was still thinking about what they had just been debating. After a moment, she told Wang Mojie that Ma Dingge's father was about to leave France for China.

—What are you going to do to help? she asked.

—If you don't want the bother, leave it all to me.

—Leave it all to you? Okay, he'll stay with you! Ukyi Lhamo didn't mean to laugh, but she did, loudly, she couldn't help it.

—What's so funny? What are you laughing at?

—Nothing, nothing, Ukyi Lhamo said and put her hand over her mouth.

—You want him to stay with me? You'd do that to me?

—Well, where else is he going to stay?

—I want to know what's making you so happy.

—Who's happy? Ukyi Lhamo started to laugh again.

—Ukyi Lhamo, I thought you were always pretty fair about things, but now I've discovered that you can be bad.

—You're the only one who gets to be bad? I have to be good all the time?

—You find the thought of Robert and me sharing a room funny?

—Me? Think that? How could I find the thought of two sceptics sharing a room funny? You can be sceptical of each other.

—It wouldn't be convenient for either one of us.

—No, it wouldn't, Ukyi Lhamo said, laughing so hard now she could hardly speak. She asked, But what else can we do?

Ukyi Lhamo hadn't felt so happy in a very long time. People are like that, they have a moment of joy, sparked by the smallest of things, and it releases all the tension and worry they have been carrying around, and they feel suddenly and truly happy. Ukyi Lhamo was trying to hold on to the feeling.

—It'll be inconvenient, but just deal with it. He'll be sceptical about you, but he might just like you, and he might end up staying longer than he plans. If so, you be sure to take good care of him, she said with a laugh.

—Ukyi Lhamo! This is Ma Dingge's father we are talking about. Ma Dingge is your guru, not mine!

—Ma Dingge likes you more than me now.

—Can't you clear out of your home for a while? You can go to your mum's house in Lhasa. Can't you just go back and forth?

—I don't want that old man sleeping in my bed, she said definitively.

—I thought you were taking care of his housing.

—No, you are, she said with a smile.

—You're saying that not only is he going to stay with me, but I also have to cook for him, I have to make his coffee, get him milk, make him toast, and I have to buy another bed? And right, I have to buy all the stuff I'll need, something to make coffee with, a microwave, bedding, crockery and cutlery, toiletries... my goodness, I have to take care of all of that? And you do nothing?

—Yup, precisely.

—Fine, I'll do it, but you have to split the cost of all that with me, Wang Mojie said loudly.

—OK, sure, no problem.

—I'm going to tell Ma Dingge that you are doing nothing to help.

—He won't believe you, Ukyi Lhamo said and blew out a puff of cigarette smoke.

—Bad luck for me, then. First time anybody's got the better of me.

—You were planning on getting the better of me in this?

—Of course. What is it with you today? Why are you in such a happy mood?

—You should go and buy a bed, she said. She smiled, she was happy. She noticed a stiff, silly look on Wang Mojie's face.

—You have to arrange his lift from the airport. Get your mountain-climbing friend to pick him up, Wang Mojie said.

—He's not in town. Looks like you'll need to take care of that too.

—What? I have to? I have to find someone who can pick him up? Who do I know that has a car? Where did your mountain man go? Why did he take off just when we need him? Let me say it again, Ukyi Lhamo, Ma Dingge is your guru, not mine.

Wang Mojie was genuinely angry. He said, I'm taking care of everything else, it's asking too much to make me pick him up too!

—This is the first time I've seen you lose your temper. It makes you seem more normal, she said.

—I'm not angry, why would I be angry? Don't talk to me about your mountaineer. That's no connection to me. He's your business.

—He's off to Makalu, she said and lit another cigarette.

—Makalu? Never heard of it, some stupid mountain? No one has ever heard of it.

—8,463 metres.

—How high?

—8,463 metres, fifth highest mountain in the world.

—Really? Wang Mojie said, drawing a deep breath. And I thought the only thing he was good at was dancing.

—He left yesterday. He might be at base camp already.

—Fine, I'll find a car, Wang Mojie said, slamming his fist into his palm. His mood lifted as it occurred to him that Wangchuk's father, the cement factory boss, had access to a van.

—He introduced me to a friend of his who has a car we can borrow, Ukyi Lhamo said and blew out a long puff of smoke.

—Really? Your mountaineer is the best, Ukyi Lhamo, you should count your blessings.

—I don't need you to tell me that.

—However, Wang Mojie said, knocking on the table with a knuckle, we have to reconsider Mr Robert's accommodation, we really do, not for my sake, for his sake, he's old. But that's not the real problem. The real problem is we are both men, and Westerners have this thing about two men sharing a room. If he was an old woman, then I could sleep with him in the same room no problem.

—Don't be stupid. This is nothing to be flippant about, Ukyi Lhamo said.

—Who's being flippant? I'm serious.

—He can stay in your house, and you can stay somewhere else.

—Where? Like I'm supposed to stay with a student's family?

—Stay at mine.

—Sorry? What?

—You clear out of your house and let him have it.

—And where will you be? You mean you and I are going to share your house?

—Would you have a problem with that? Ukyi Lhamo asked, putting out her cigarette and not looking up.

—Is there something wrong with your head? That would not be good for you. Even if we behave ourselves and nothing happens, imagine the gossip. Have you been plotting this? Don't be stupid. Think. That mountaineer of yours is a catch. You know of any other man around here who is both a skilled climber and an excellent dancer? He's not your average fellow. He is completely different from me and from our friend the mathematician-poet, and what's more he seems to be pretty spiritual too, in some ways. Don't be a fool. Besides, you have your mountaineer, I've got Yu Youyan, and you and I can stay friends who can be completely open with each other. What could be better than that?

—Easy for you to say. Listen, I don't care about gossip. What does it matter what people say? Robert can't stay in my house, and I'm not going to go to my mother's. If you don't want to move in with me, then you can get Robert to move in with you.

—You'd really let me move in with you?

—Why wouldn't I? What are you going to do? You tell me, what could you do?

—Deal. Shake on it. I have to hand it to you. You've got me figured out.

Wang Mojie extended his hand, but Ukyi Lhamo did not take it. She gave him a piece of paper. It was a shopping list with all the things they needed to buy before Robert arrived, divided into three categories. There was a lot for just the bedding: pillows, pillowcases and a blanket, a quilt, a quilt cover and so on. Also crockery and cutlery, glasses, oxygen canisters, toiletries, medicine, utensils, napkins, a reclining chair... Ukyi Lhamo had thought of everything.

—Don't you have to teach tomorrow afternoon? We should go into town to buy what we need, Ukyi Lhamo said, but Wang Mojie didn't hear her.

—You don't have a bed for me on this list, he said, looking at the list. If I move in with you, I'm going to need a place to sleep. We need to buy one of those folding camp beds.

—Add it to the list. What else do we need?

—We need, I think we could use a...

—What? Say it.

—I think maybe we should hang up some sort of a curtain between us. Otherwise, I won't be able to get to sleep.

—Write it down.

The next day they went to the large department store in Lhasa that had opened just a few weeks before. It was the city's first modern superstore, and once inside it you might as well have been in any city in the Chinese interior. It was easy to forget that you were on the roof of the world in the heavenly city of Lhasa. Just like in similar stores in the interior and the world over, the customers were overwhelmingly younger people, couples, newlyweds, and young parents pushing buggies up and down the aisles. The superstore was a sign that Lhasa was not going to be the exception in the face of the homogenising force of globalisation.

Wang Mojie and Ukyi Lhamo walked, now side by side, now in single file, up and down the aisles through each of the store's departments filling up their shopping trolley. Ukyi Lhamo chose the best of almost everything. Wang Mojie didn't say anything at first, but eventually he began to protest. He didn't see why they needed to buy French wine. He told Ukyi Lhamo that Robert should try one of the dry reds from Great Wall or a Chateau Changyu. Changyu wines won gold medals a hundred years ago at the Panama-Pacific International Exposition in San Francisco. They were as good as French wines. They should give Robert a little taste of China. Same with yogurt. They should get Tibetan yogurt, he said, made with yak's milk, local and cheap, and Robert would have nothing to complain about. Wang Mojie started to scrutinise every purchase. He checked the price, place of manufacture and quality guarantee on every item. His marriage had lasted less than a year, but except for his bizarre sexual habits, he had been a model husband. He looked after the finances, he did the shopping, the cooking, the laundry and the cleaning. His wife's job kept her busy, she had no time to shop, not even for bras and panties or tampons. Wang Mojie bought those things for her.

Wang Mojie's ex-wife was not what you would call beautiful, she had single fold eyelids, she was thin and elegant, but there was nothing especially striking about her that would make her stand out in a group of girls. In uniform next to her male colleagues, however, she was a rose among thorns. Born into a family of several generations of Beijing police officers, she had internalised the culture of the metropolitan police force: she liked order and worried about everything. The culture of China's police is different from that of its military. China's modern police force came into existence when the modern Chinese city did, it is a product of the modern city and is inextricably tied to it. This is not true of China's military, which is why soldiers look so out of place in the city. Girls brought up in military families are arrogant, but girls brought up in the families of police are subdued, professional, calm and collected, and just like their parents they believe in public service. The children of police often become police, most daughters of police marry sons of police, many of whom are outstanding young men. Often these matches are made among classmates in the police academy.

Wang Mojie's ex-wife never imagined she would end up with a university lecturer or an intellectual (the two seemed to be mutually exclusive categories), but one day while she was out on the beat, a stranger came up to her and said a few years back he had once given her a bottle of fizzy drink, and he wanted to know if she remembered him. She didn't remember at all. The police nearby, her colleagues, were suspicious of the stranger, and they came over and crowded around. The stranger said at the time she was a police cadet and he was a college student. He had handed her a bottle of Arctic Ocean, the fizzy drink they all loved, the orange soda, which you couldn't get any more. He said in 1989 Arctic Ocean fizzy drink sales topped 100 million yuan, 13 million in profit, the most successful year in its history. At this point, her colleagues decided the stranger wasn't a threat and walked away. The stranger went on talking about the drink. He said Arctic Ocean went into a joint venture with Pepsi, discontinued the fizzy drink and started selling bottled water under the Arctic Ocean name. He had researched it, he said. He missed that drink. He asked if she was sure she didn't remember him.

He said, "Nobody could believe it when you police cadets

came out too, it was so encouraging to us. You know, I'm wrong, I didn't give you just a bottle, it was a case. There were a whole lot of you cadets but just a few of you were girls. I opened the bottles for you girls myself, with my teeth, bottle after bottle. You said to watch out that I didn't break a tooth! The drink was just my way of showing some respect for you folks, I was so surprised you cadets were joining in, in uniform no less. I remember you, it was you, I know it was you, it was you for sure. What happened to those other girls who were with you?"

She remembered somebody handing her a fizzy drink but during those days somebody was always handing it out. She didn't remember the face of the student who had given it to her, and she didn't remember which university he was from. She didn't remember Wang Mojie. Not at all. She stood, walkie-talkie in hand, shaking her head. He asked for her address, phone number and pager number so he could get in touch. She wasn't sure about him and hesitated. He gave her his card (his university and title were on it) and a bit reluctantly she gave him her pager number. Then she asked him to move along, she was working. She was serious, she was tired of his talk, and her walkie-talkie kept crackling with chatter.

They were in a busy part of downtown Beijing by a three-storey Western-style building with police cars parked on either side of it. Wang Mojie walked away but stopped at the next junction and stood watching her. Everything he had said to her was the truth, it had all happened just as he said it did, whether she remembered him or not. After that, he kept paging her and calling and leaving messages. He kept asking her out, said he hoped to see her again, and by pager text message he sent her his memories of the spring of 1989. He thought back to that time and that place. He started to remember details about her, which he described to her and complimented her for. In his messages she read a profile of the person she had been when still a cadet, it brought her past back vividly.

We all think we know who we were in our past, but we can't be sure we're right. We would all like to know what we were like, and if somebody who knew us in the past describes our past self to us, it all comes rushing back. It is like looking in a mirror and seeing that past self. We always have a desire to see ourselves, we desire a mirror, other people are our mirror, language is our mirror, a photograph can't show us to ourselves the way another person's description of us can. She had been so young in 1989, she had photographs from that year, but they didn't seem quite real to her. What he wrote to her, on the other hand, made the past seem very real. He wrote that he remembered beads of sweat at the ends of her hair, that she hiccupped after taking a drink of Arctic Ocean, and she covered her mouth and laughed. He remembered she told him to stop opening the bottles with his teeth because he was going to break a tooth, but he said that for her and the other girls he would happily take that risk. He was relentless with his texts and messages, but he tried to be entertaining, and he stayed absolutely respectful of her. Touched, she said she would meet him, but when they did get together, she said it was to be only the one time, no repeats, because she had a boyfriend already. He said that was OK with him, he was happy to meet just the once, after which he promised to leave her alone. This put her completely at ease and so they had a great conversation. They quickly forgot that the first time was supposed to be the last, and they got together again and again and yet again. She wore her uniform the first two times, but on their third date she showed up in very nice understated casual wear, which left Wang Mojie deeply disappointed. He didn't say anything about this until they were seriously involved, and then he asked that she always wear her uniform when they went out. He asked that she wear her dress uniform to the wedding, at which he recited the poem "Militia Women" by Mao Zedong. After they were married, he took responsibility for all the housework, all the shopping and all the cooking.

It had been a long time since Wang Mojie had been in a department store, but he still knew his way around, he had not forgotten how to shop for good deals on quality products, and he understood the semiotics of marketing. Every brand name was a signifier of something, a lifestyle, an attitude, an aspiration, which we were assumed to desire. He believed philosophers should study the marketplace. There were similar stores around the world, an empire of signs, and with globalisation this sort of consumerism had changed countless lives and altered countless cultures, homogenising human societies. If his divorce hadn't changed his life, Wang Mojie might have undertaken a philosophical inquiry into the culture of the superstore.

Ukyi Lhamo was surprised by how experienced a shopper Wang Mojie was. He wasn't just a pedant, after all, he was a better shopper than most women, which impressed her, and so she let him make a lot of their decisions. Wang Mojie's knowledge was practical as well as theoretical, he knew the specifics about the quality and the proper retail price of a lot of things they were buying, and he explained it all to her in detail. At first, Ukyi Lhamo was astonished by Wang Mojie's ability to find bargains, but she began to grow tired of having to listen to him lecture her about every single product, as if he worked there, and she began to get peevish with him.

—Can we just shop, please, without the commentary?

Wang Mojie did not realise that a model husband can get on your nerves.

On two different days they spent a few hours shopping and bought everything they needed, by which time, Robert was already in Beijing and due to arrive in Lhasa the next day. Wang Mojie went through the receipts and paid Ukyi Lhamo for his half of what they spent. Ukyi Lhamo had not planned on asking Wang Mojie to pay for anything because as he said, Ma Dingge was her teacher, not his, but it didn't occur to Wang Mojie not to pay for half.

—What are you doing? You really want to split the cost? Ukyi Lhamo asked.

—Of course. Want to check my maths?

She glanced at Wang Mojie's figures and said, You owe me a lot more than that. Do the maths again.

—What do you mean? I checked it. It's right, to the penny.

—Robert is living in your place and when he leaves, all that stuff is going to stay with you, so you should pay more than half.

—Nonsense. I don't want stuff he's used.

—You need it.

—OK, the microwave I'll take, maybe the crockery, but the rest I don't want. You take it.

—His mattress, quilt, pillowcase, that all goes to you.

—As soon as he is gone, I'm throwing all that stuff out, he said loudly.

Wang Mojie's house was transformed, the windows now had net curtains and fabric curtains and there was a square rug on the floor. The rug caused a big argument. Wang Mojie thought it was extravagant, they didn't need it, but Ukyi Lhamo was adamant. He finally relented but insisted they spend as little on it as they could, which is what they argued about. They compromised and bought one priced right in the middle. The rug made the house seem nicer and gave it a Tibetan touch. The books on the shelves were the only things left to remind you that it was still Wang Mojie's house. They also added a red tea table in the Tibetan style and two *khaden*. The *khaden* were Ukyi Lhamo's idea. She said the two philosophers had to have something to sit on while they talked. She couldn't have one sitting on the sole chair in the room and one on the bed while they conversed. All was in good order. Ukyi Lhamo turned on the floor lamp.

—Now it looks like a proper home, it's finally fit for human habitation, she said teasingly, but Wang Mojie pretended not to get her meaning.

—Are you hinting that you think I should pay an even larger share?

—You have a rug now. You won't need to put a sheet down on the floor any more. The rug is much classier.

—I don't want the rug, you're taking it after he leaves, Wang Mojie said emphatically.

—I'm just thinking of what's best for you, she said.

—I shouldn't sleep on the new mattress tonight, right? Wang Mojie asked, changing the subject.

—You could sleep on the camp bed.

—That's right... the camp bed. It's at your house.

—Go and get it.

—But I'm moving in with you tomorrow. What difference does a day make?

—Of course there's a difference. Go and get the bed.

—But tonight could be an experiment. We can give it a try. If it's no good, we'll know that we have to make other arrangements.

—Give what a try? What are you suggesting?

—Nothing. I'm a little nervous.

—You're itching for the belt, I bet. If you can't sleep, I can whip you.

—Really? Well, now I can relax.

—Go and get the camp bed!

Wang Mojie did as he was told, and then they talked about the upcoming trip to Gonggar Airport to meet Robert and ran into another point of contention. Wang Mojie thought that Robert should stay in a nice hotel in Lhasa for a few nights before he came to the school so he would have a chance to adjust to the altitude in comfort. He also said that the 1 May Labour Day holiday was coming up and that would give them a few days when they would be free to take Robert up to Ma Dingge at the monastery. It just wasn't convenient for Robert to come straight to the school.

—He can afford a hotel, he's not in a rush to get back to France, so it would be good for him to stay in a hotel a few days. Think about it, why be in a hurry to get him here? I'll be moving in with you sooner or later, don't be impatient, Wang Mojie said.

—Who's impatient? Ukyi Lhamo said and blushed.

—I was kidding, sorry, I shouldn't make silly jokes. Just think about the logic of having Robert go to a hotel first, please.

—I hate you, really, I hate you.

—I said I was kidding. It was a stupid joke and I apologise for it, all right? Let's get back to Robert. In my opinion, listen, he should stay in a hotel for a few days and rest, we'll make sure nobody bothers him, we'll go and check on him every day but just a quick visit. We can go together the first day, then take turns. After a week he'll be adjusted to the altitude, and everything will be easier. If he comes straight here, he's still going to have to rest for a few days before doing anything anyway. He can't go right to Drepung to debate with his son on his first day here, right? There is still time to book him a hotel room.

—I'm going back to Lhasa. Do whatever you want, you don't need my input, Ukyi Lhamo said and then walked out. Wang Mojie walked out after her.

—If you're OK with it, we can book a room right now, he said to her back.

—Go ahead. Will you please leave me alone?

—You have to call them. I don't have a phone.

—You can ride your bike and book in person. There's still plenty of light.

Ukyi Lhamo went into her house and closed the door. Wang Mojie was puzzled by her sudden anger, but he felt relieved because putting Robert up in a hotel for a few days bought him a little more time, and if she was going back to Lhasa because she had decided to stay at her mother's place while Robert was there (had she changed her mind?) then things were playing out the way he had hoped they would. When he said he was a little nervous, he had pretended to be joking but it wasn't a joke. Ukyi Lhamo said nothing was going to happen between them, but the knowledge that nothing turns out as planned or expected made Wang Mojie nervous. It was a physical tenseness, an edginess in his body, not a mental state. Mentally he felt fine, he was happy, extremely happy, but his body protested, and he often let his body rule his life. But he kept his mind on the upcoming conversation between Ma Dingge and his father, which was the most important thing to him at that moment.

Wang Mojie got on his bike and in thirty minutes arrived at the Tibet Hotel. He then went to the Everest Hotel. He thought long and hard about the choice. Both were first-class hotels, the Tibet Hotel had more local flavour, its design echoed the architectural style of Tibetan palaces and monasteries, but it was only three storeys high and so its rooms didn't offer the sort of views that the Everest did. The Everest was twelve storeys and its architecture reflected the shape of the mountain it was named after. From rooms in the Everest there were good views of the Potala and also the Jokhang and Barkhor Street and, in the distance, the clear blue water of the Lhasa River and the snow peaks beyond. Was it going to be a little local flavour for Robert or a spectacular view of the whole city? Wang Mojie finally settled on the Everest, because to him Robert was first and foremost a tourist, come for the sites, and only then was he an interlocutor in a conversation about spirituality. Wang Mojie assumed he had the measure of the old man, and while Robert might not be interested in any discussion of Tibet as a state of mind, Tibet's transcendent quality and its beautiful scenery were enough to impress anyone, even those who live the life of the mind, and so might that not temper his scepticism? Wang Mojie hoped that Robert's attitude would moderate somewhat, even though he had not even the slightest doubt that Ma Dingge could hold his own in debate with his father.

Wang Mojie did the paperwork for the reservation and was about to leave when across the lobby on the far side of a huge rug, which was embroidered with an image of Chomolungma, he saw Yu Youyan, whom he had not seen in weeks. She was in a small group of people, all of them in the full-dress uniform of officers of the judiciary. He had taken an unthinking glance over at them and was startled to see Yu Youyan. She stared at him coldly, as she had seen him first. Wang Mojie stood still, she looked away, turning her attention back to her colleagues. Yu Youyan was pretending not to have seen him, but she had, no mistake, she had given him a searing look. Wang Mojie pretended not to have seen Yu Youyan either, and he walked towards the big revolving front door, but the image of Yu Youyan was still in his mind's eye. He was thrilled to have seen her in her neatly pressed, pretty dress uniform. He assumed she was there as part of the entourage for some VIP. He hadn't seen her in her dress uniform before, just her work uniform. The dress uniform was lovely, especially because she wasn't wearing work shoes with it but those stiletto heels he knew so well, which changed her posture completely. Man, is she sexy, Wang Mojie thought to himself with regret. The men with her looked imposing in their uniforms, but they seemed faceless and anonymous. Still, they made a nice background for Yu Youyan, who looked all the more slim and graceful among them.

When Wang Mojie reached the revolving door, he suddenly turned around and marched across the lobby towards Yu Youyan. As he was about to reach her, she stepped forwards to stop him from coming any closer, as if confronting a beggar accosting her on the street. Wang Mojie held out his hand but she did not take it.

—What do you want? I'm working.

—I saw you over here. I can't keep pretending I didn't.

—I'm busy, she said, looking exasperated.

—Somebody important here from Beijing?

—None of your business. Go away.

—If you don't shake my hand, your colleagues are going to assume we're lovers and you're cross with me for something.

—We were never lovers. Go away!

—That dress uniform is very nice. I like the shoes. You look very pretty.

—That's enough. Please just leave, please.

—Don't you want to know why I'm here?

She sighed. Her colleagues were watching them and so she had to hold her temper.

—Why are you here? she asked grudgingly.

Wang Mojie told Yu Youyan he was there to book a room for a French philosopher who was arriving the next day, an important Western public intellectual. He made no mention of Ukyi Lhamo, this was half unconsciously. Yu Youyan did not listen to what he said, she didn't react to Wang Mojie's boasts about Robert's importance. She had an important assignment, welcoming the VIP was far more important than anything else. Finally she could bear it no longer and interrupted Wang Mojie. She grabbed his hand, shook it, gave him a formal, awkward-looking smile, said, Goodbye, then turned and strode away.

—I've been a bit busy lately, he said to her back.

—Understood, Yu Youyan said as she took a quick glance back.

28. Conversation

Time is different here, it is a more ancient time.
Time here is different from time in any other place in the world,
different from Paris, New York or Greenwich, different even from Beijing.
The conversation unfolded in analysis and logic, and it seemed as if outside of time.

It was late April. The Lhasa River was as tranquil as the sky. The river held the reflection of the city. One city against the sky, one city reflected in the water. Two Lhasas. Two Potala Palaces, two Barkhor Streets, two Jokhang Temples and two Norbu Lingkas, one above the other, like two halves of a shell. Everything was doubled. The upside-down reflection of the Potala on the water looked just as real as the real Potala against the sky. The Potala is the symbol of a city unlike any other, the symbol indeed of the entire Qinghai and Tibet plateau. Chomolungma isn't Tibet's only pinnacle, Tibet also reaches its apogee where the Potala rises into the sky. Tibet has a double zenith, one a mountain and one a palace. The mountain is the world's geographical peak, the Potala is the peak of spiritual attainment. Each peak is unsurpassed. The Potala and its river, its dream vision blue river. Because of the reflection in the water, everything is doubled, there is a doubled sky. At sunrise and at sunset, the city is a shining symmetrical mandala with the Potala at its centre. No Gothic structure anywhere in Europe can compare to the Potala, and while Egypt's pyramids may reach to the sky, their centre of gravity is deep underground. Only the Potala belongs wholly to the sky.

But none of this mattered to Robert, he scoffed at any suggestion that a philosophy can be shaped by geography. Religious beliefs might be shaped by our response to the natural environment, but in his opinion, philosophy was not, at least not directly. Drepung Monastery is an enormous sprawl of buildings scattered across a mountain slope with a maze of hundreds of alleyways through shadows and light, but it didn't impress Robert. To him it might as well have been a mirage, the product of an illusion.

—I have spent three days in the company of mirages, but now finally we meet officially.

Robert was indifferent to the sights of Lhasa, which is what he meant by "mirages". His son had met him at the airport but only briefly before they rushed him off to the hotel, which is what he meant about them finally meeting "officially". He had been at the hotel for three days and was not happy about it.

—Your friends offered to show me around Lhasa but that will be unnecessary, I have already seen it. I spent three days standing on the eleventh-floor terrace of the hotel admiring the view of the city. I think I can say that Lhasa is unique, it is very beautiful, full of illusions, but I am more interested in cities that are full of philosophy. But yes, Lhasa is also a city of philosophers, Buddhism is a philosophy, and philosophy is what we shall discuss.

Robert's tone was serious, without a trace of humour.

—I must admit that I am here because I had no choice but to come, which in part is because of the increasing interest in Buddhism in the West, which I am inclined to think is due to a crisis of Western philosophy. Does Buddhism have an answer to Western philosophy's ancient question, "How should I live?" You have made a deep study of Buddhism for years, and so I want to hear your views on it. In what ways may Buddhism be considered a philosophy? Is Buddhism a philosophy? Or is it a religion? Or is it both?

Most days they sat down to talk at nine in the morning and kept at it until five in the afternoon. Each day they broke for a simple lunch that they ate at the monastery, something Ukyi Lhamo made in the morning or the night before and brought up with her. They talked in Ma Dingge's low-ceilinged quarters in the morning, and in the afternoon, when the sun was high and the light brilliant, they moved outside to a small courtyard with a peach tree. Petals from the flowers floated down to the stone table now and again. Steam from their hot drinks curled up into the sunlight. Coffee, green tea, butter tea and sweet tea. Four different tastes, distinct, separate, not to be mixed, even the steam seemed to rise differently from each. And the four people were, of course, even more dissimilar: Ma Dingge, Ukyi Lhamo, Jean-Philippe Robert and Wang Mojie, all different.

The four of us together must have made quite a picture, Wang Mojie recalled. It was very peaceful, so peaceful in fact that I found it easy to forget what era we were in. Ma Dingge transcended time, time didn't touch him, and his father seemed like some eighteenth-century philosopher. Ukyi Lhamo looked modern. Or futuristic. She liked to wear a silvery-grey trench coat. It made her look like she just stepped off a spaceship or like she was a tour guide in some museum of post-modernity. I am not sure how to describe my own appearance. I wore a Chinese-style shirt, which was deliberate, I wanted to emphasise my culture. It made me look like a Daoist priest or maybe a 1930s Beijing shop owner, but probably more like an old-fashioned scholar. Not my usual dress at any rate. And in a break from my habit, I was not wearing my grey checked scarf. I'm not sure why. Did I think giving up the scarf would help me relax? Had I decided I no longer needed it tied around my neck like a rope? I really don't know. Ma Dingge and I were a lot alike but very different too. Ma Dingge had become very Tibetan, while I had held on to my ethnic identity. Sometimes sparrows flew up into the trees, where they sat and chattered away like they were curious about the smell of the coffee, Robert's white hair and his pipe. We were in our time, the birds were in their time, a more ancient time. Without a doubt, time for us was different from time in any other place in the world, different from Paris, New York or Greenwich, different even from Beijing.

Ma Dingge responded to his father's questions, speaking deliberately, his voice deep and powerful and filling the courtyard. He was every bit as serious as his father. Ukyi Lhamo poured him more butter tea, he took two sips and then, bowl in hand, he went on speaking, his voice rising with the aroma of the tea. Robert, pipe in his mouth, shrugged every so often and jotted something down in his notebook. Robert had been taking careful notes since the first day of their conversations, but it wasn't that he wrote down only those things about which he was sceptical. He would sometimes make it clear that he rejected some argument his son made, but this time his shrug wasn't dismissive, it was light-hearted, even happy. They might have taken things deeper in discussion at that point, but Robert felt there was no need, and he tried a different approach. Robert acknowledged that Buddhism had features of both philosophy and religion, which was a reason Buddhism was regarded so highly by many in the West.

Wang Mojie poured more coffee for Robert, and Robert nodded in thanks, seeming to recognise Wang Mojie for the gesture of solidarity. At the same time, Ukyi Lhamo filled Ma Dingge's wooden bowl with butter tea. She held it out to him with both hands, which was a gesture of respect, and he took it with both hands. She filled a bowl for herself with the same butter tea that Ma Dingge drank. Wang Mojie didn't drink butter tea, he drank coffee, always coffee. And so they had fallen into the habit of Wang Mojie making sure Robert had coffee and Ukyi Lhamo pouring tea for Ma Dingge. Occasionally Wang Mojie switched things around, and he poured tea for Ma Dingge and let Ukyi Lhamo take care of Robert's coffee. When he did this, he noticed that Ukyi Lhamo handed the coffee cup to Robert with only one hand, but Robert, copying his son, took it with both hands.

29. Cohabitation

A bedside lamp. Books. Just two people in bed reading, nothing sexual was going on.
Ukyi Lhamo's pyjama blouse had a collar, it had a high neckline.
She could just about wear it out in public.
He had no reason to feel afraid. What was it that was making him afraid?
Her beauty? Was it a fear of happiness? Of tenderness? Of the chance of a caress?

Robert moved out of the hotel and into Wang Mojie's house on Friday 28 April. On the trip from the hotel to the school, Robert surprised Wang Mojie and Ukyi Lhamo by going on about how wonderful the scenery was. He said the snow peaks reminded him of the Alps, as he had a home in the Alps where he spent some time every year. Wang Mojie's one-room, stone house couldn't compare to Robert's grand home, of course, but Wang Mojie's book-filled shelves were a comforting sight to Robert, and he settled in quickly. He said, with obvious hyperbole, that he felt like he was in his study in the Alps. This remark was out of keeping with his usual dour, intimidating demeanour, and what he meant to imply was that he had been right to insist that he move out of the hotel earlier than they had planned.

Ukyi Lhamo's first impression of Robert was negative, he didn't look like a philosopher to her, he looked like a detective. His eyes were deep-set among wrinkles and his gaze was keen. He seemed to look right into you. He didn't just look at you, he studied you. It was quite scary. After three days in the hotel, he said he had to get out of Lhasa, it was a fantasy land, he couldn't stand the quiet for another moment. He rapped the table with his pipe and demanded to move to the village immediately so that he could go to see his son at that other fantasy land, at the monastery palace (Robert referred to all monasteries as "palaces"). Ukyi Lhamo and Wang Mojie had come to the hotel with a gift of some fruit for Robert and to see how he was doing. The plan was for him to stay at the hotel for a few more days, but as soon as they walked into the room Robert started roaring at them like a caged animal. He was very worked up. He waved his pipe around as he yelled at them, his hair fell down over his forehead and one eye. Wang Mojie thought he looked younger with his hair tousled. It helped soften the effect of all the wrinkles. In his current unhinged state not only did he not look like a philosopher, he didn't even look like a detective any more, he looked like a man behind bars and unhappy about it.

—Think it's the altitude getting to him? Ukyi Lhamo asked Wang Mojie in Mandarin. Her tone was nonchalant.

Wang Mojie said no as he regarded Ukyi Lhamo sternly, he didn't find it funny. The plan was for Robert to relax at the hotel for two more days, then early on 1 May they would move him to the school and later that same day they would take him up to Drepung for his first conversation with his son. They wanted to give him plenty of time to adjust to the altitude, and they also had to work around the school's timetable. The 1 May Labour Day holiday fell on a Monday and to make up for it, lessons were to be held over the weekend of 29 and 30 April. Ukyi Lhamo and Wang Mojie had to work that weekend. Ukyi Lhamo explained all this to Robert in her very good French, and Wang Mojie added some words of appeasement in English and in his very limited French. But Robert did not budge. They were with him, they were free now, and lessons wouldn't occupy them for the entire day on either Saturday or Sunday. He insisted that they move him to the school promptly. He said he needed only one of them to take some time on Saturday to take him up to the monastery. His proposal made sense and, as he said, the Everest was expensive. Robert said he would rather give the money to them. Ukyi Lhamo answered bluntly that they had no plans to ask him for as much as a penny in rent.

—But it's only right that I pay you.

—We should stick to our plan, Ukyi Lhamo said, ignoring him. In France people don't change plans on a whim. We're not travel agents. We're all friends, aren't we?

Robert insisted that he pay. Ukyi Lhamo said that when she lived in

France, her friends told her that in French culture it just wasn't done to go back on an agreement at the last minute, friends didn't do that to one another. She stressed the word "friends". Ukyi Lhamo had dispensed with politeness. Wang Mojie intervened and, speaking for both of them, told Robert he could move out of the hotel immediately. Robert packed, they got in the lift, went down to the lobby, and Robert checked out. Wang Mojie got a taxi, he let Robert get in, and then, like a gentleman, held the door for Ukyi Lhamo. But Ukyi Lhamo did not get in. She took keys from her bag and gave them to Wang Mojie. She said they were the keys to her house, and she turned and walked down the street. The Everest was not far from Barkhor Street, and Wang Mojie realised Ukyi Lhamo was walking to her mother's house. Wang Mojie got in the taxi. Apparently, we are not going to cohabit after all, Wang Mojie thought to himself with relief. In English, he explained to Robert where Ukyi Lhamo was going. He said that Robert was moving into his house, he was moving into Ukyi Lhamo's house, and Ukyi Lhamo was moving in with her mother. Robert didn't entirely follow. Wang Mojie explained again.

—So you mean you move out of your house, she moves out of her house, I stay in your house, you stay in her house, and she has a different house in Lhasa? Robert said half in English half in French with a lot of gesturing.

Wang Mojie said yes, that was right. Robert didn't say anything else, but his face and upturned palms indicated his incomprehension, perhaps with all of Eastern culture. He looked at Wang Mojie.

—She's pretty. She has character, Robert said.

—Yes, she's very pretty.

—She studied in France, yes? She is like a French girl.

—She's half Tibetan by blood.

—Truly? She is half Tibetan?

—She thinks you are here to debunk Buddhism, which is why...

—Oh? This is so? You are a scholar of philosophy. You can explain to her.

—I have tried to, but it's complicated, there's a lot going on.

—Indeed. The truth never takes a simple form.

They arrived at the school, Wang Mojie got Robert's luggage and showed him to the house. Robert found Wang Mojie's home novel and said he would be fine there, his only regret was there was no telephone and therefore no dial-up connection to the internet. He wanted to be able to email, he needed to be connected to the world. Wang Mojie said that there was a telephone at Ukyi Lhamo's. Robert got his laptop, they went over, he connected, and the world appeared on his screen. Robert, pleased, asked why he couldn't just move into Ukyi Lhamo's place. He admitted that it might not be proper of him to ask, and he didn't mean to insist, but given that she had a telephone line, he just thought it would be simpler, especially as Ukyi Lhamo was at her mother's, and it would mean Wang Mojie wouldn't have to move out of his house. Wang Mojie reminded Robert that he had explained everything in the taxi.

—She knows you are a philosophical sceptic, which she takes to mean you are an enemy of Buddhism, so she does not want you living here.

Robert shrugged in incomprehension.

—Besides, Wang Mojie said, it's the custom in China that men do not enter an unmarried lady's boudoir.

—You're a man. Why is it OK for you but not me?

—I know there's no logic to it, but still there is a difference between you staying here and me staying here, and one of us has to, so that has to be me. Better the devil she knows than the devil she doesn't, we might say.

—We are devils? I am a devil?

—Of course. She's a feminist. To a feminist, all men are devils.

—Ha. Wang, you are amusing.

They walked back to Wang Mojie's house. Robert decided he liked Wang Mojie, and he liked that even in such a remote place Wang Mojie surrounded himself with books. He did not understand, however, why Wang Mojie had given up his job at the university to teach in a village school. Wang Mojie explained what had happened in his life, and he mentioned the example of Wittgenstein, who had been at Cambridge, where he studied under Bertrand Russell, but after fighting in the war and writing a book that he said solved all the problems of philosophy (but also said was nonsense to be thrown away), he took a job as a teacher in a primary school in the Austrian mountains.

—You know the villagers didn't like Wittgenstein, right? Robert asked. They thought he was mad, he added with a wave of his pipe.

—But his students liked him. He got them to build a model steam engine, and he took them on field trips. Working with children obviously influenced his ordinary language philosophy.

—The linguistic turn in philosophy. Wittgenstein helped cause that. Philosophy has become a language game, a mechanical exercise in metaphysics. Even if we hold that philosophy is imprisoned, its prison house is not language.

—Wittgenstein had his reasons for rejecting the doctrines of traditional philosophy.

—His ideas only made our fragmented world even more fragmented. His ideas made the world lose coherence. We must try to make the world coherent, even if we can never succeed. The attempt to make the world coherent is one of the fundamental tasks of philosophy, and if we abandon that effort, philosophy regresses into gibberish. If you rip up the dance floor, there can be no dance. If you don't believe the world can be made coherent, then it doesn't matter to you if your world is in fragments.

Robert and Wang Mojie were both enjoying the conversation. Robert asked Wang Mojie what his name meant. Wang Mojie joked that it was a name he had used during his past life. He had been a Tang dynasty poet and painter who was a Buddhist, everybody knew him as Wang Wei, but he had another name, Mojie. Robert said he had read a bit about the Tang dynasty. He wanted to hear more about this idea of a "past life". Wang Mojie said it was an Eastern thing, everybody believed that each of us has lived a past life. You can understand it as an expression of the idea that we are our ancestors, he said. Wang Mojie did not tell Robert that he didn't like his name, which had been given to him by his paternal grandfather, who revered Wang Wei.

His grandfather worked in the Imperial Palace Museum as an art restorer, working primarily with paintings. His entire life he had idolised Wang Wei, he didn't think somebody like Li Bai even came close. When he was a boy, Wang Mojie often visited his grandfather in the museum offices, there were a few years that he spent almost every day there, but these were unhappy memories for him. As a boy, he was overawed by the high walls and enormous palaces of the Forbidden City, and he wondered if the experience hadn't affected him psychologically. He didn't make too much of it, the experience hadn't shaped his entire childhood, but when he thought back on it, he felt physically uncomfortable, almost emasculated. He didn't feel like a palace eunuch but he had dreams along those lines. More than once he dreamed he was that performance artist who had cut off his penis, but he always woke up before he could complete the act. No one understood how that artist had done what he had done, but Wang Mojie thought he could understand, as he often felt an impulse to self-harm.

Wang Mojie never really knew why his grandfather loved Wang Wei so much or why he had named his grandson after him. He found it odd that his grandfather didn't like Li Bai. Who didn't like Li Bai? He was a national treasure. But then again Li Bai is not popular among scholars.

This is because Li Bai was larger than life and so he makes a painful mirror for characterless men. Li Bai makes them feel uncomfortable, he makes them feel ashamed and inadequate. Du Fu is another mirror, but Du Fu makes anyone, including Wang Mojie, feel good because you can tell yourself you share Du Fu's moral righteousness, you can tell yourself that like Du Fu you are unstained by the world. Li Bai is different, none of that applies to him, which makes Li Bai an outlier among the figures of traditional Chinese culture. But Wang Mojie didn't try to explain any of this to Robert. Robert didn't know much about today's China, much less did he understand Chinese history or the vast complexity of its cultural tradition. He knew about Confucius, of course, but was surprised to find that when he brought up Confucius, Wang Mojie was quick to say that Confucian teachings had done a lot of harm.

—But Confucius was a man of the Axial Age, Robert said. He cannot be held responsible for what was done later in the name of his philosophy. There is no point in reproaching someone who lived more than two thousand years ago.

—True, there is the historical Confucius, and there is the Confucius who is a later construct, but it is the invented Confucius who matters in China. All sorts of stuff has been loaded onto him that has nothing to do with the real Confucius. It is the invented Confucius who has influence. I think, however, that one day we will return to the historical Confucius and his actual philosophy. That does seem to be where we are heading, and as you say, the historical Confucius is not to blame for Confucianism.

Robert looked at Wang Mojie carefully and then spoke.

—Confucius means different things to different people, but be that as it may, let me ask you a different question. Philosophy speaks to contemporary realities, yes, but more often its purpose is to try to think beyond contemporary reality and address timeless questions. Are you able to get beyond current reality, beyond China's current reality?

Robert's gaze was piercing but had some of the benevolence that comes with age.

—I don't know, Wang Mojie said.

—You are young, Wang, but you are a deep thinker. I can't say the same about young people in France.

—In some ways, I think I am quite old.

—Wang, there is something to you, I like you.

Wang Mojie told Robert he should rest, but Robert wanted to keep talking. He hadn't had anyone to talk to in three days, he didn't want to let Wang Mojie go, and Wang Mojie was more than happy to keep chatting. They continued talking for more than an hour before Wang Mojie said goodnight and went to Ukyi Lhamo's. Wang Mojie was in the bathroom when there was a knock on the door. Wang Mojie didn't know what Robert could want unless it was to get online to check his email. He finished peeing as quickly as he could and came out and opened the door. It was Ukyi Lhamo. It took him a second to process that it wasn't Robert standing in front of him but Ukyi Lhamo. He had been so wrapped up in conversation with Robert that he had forgotten all about her. Even as he was putting some of her things away, she never tidied up after herself, his mind was on his conversation with Robert.

—What are you staring at? Don't recognise me? Ukyi Lhamo said, then she brushed by Wang Mojie and walked into the house.

—I thought...

—What did you think? You thought you were going to get your way?

—Yes, I did, and I was starting to feel really happy about it.

—I could tell you were when I gave you the keys.

—No, when you gave me the keys, I wasn't feeling happy yet.

—Oh no?

—I just folded up your quilt. Want me to lay it out for you again?

—Yes, she said, hands in her windbreaker's pockets.

Wang Mojie spread the quilt on the bed. Ukyi Lhamo took off her jacket and hung it up, put the food she had brought into the refrigerator, then went into the bathroom, taking her handbag with her. Her house was a little bigger than Wang Mojie's, and she had added a bathroom with a toilet and shower. Robert and Wang Mojie had both used the toilet, and when Wang Mojie was in the bathroom, he was thinking that Ukyi Lhamo's stubborn refusal to let Robert stay in her house was an inconvenience to Robert. Wang Mojie didn't have a toilet in his house, so if Robert needed it in the middle of the night, he would have to walk across the uneven ground of the playground to the public toilet. Wang Mojie knew that old men have to pee a lot, it was unkind to make a seventy-something-year-old get up and go outside again and again when he needed to pee. But Ukyi Lhamo simply refused to let Robert sleep in her house. Wang Mojie had a chamber pot that he used every winter, so Robert could use that, or he could buy Robert his own, but he didn't know what Robert would think of this and didn't know how to bring it up, and so he didn't mention it. He just showed Robert the public toilet. Robert was quite taken aback to see it was just a pit latrine in a stone building. Wang Mojie told Robert he was looking at one of the nicer public toilets in all of Lhasa, and better than you would find at some of Lhasa's tourist sites. Wang Mojie pointed up and said, They don't put any glass on the windows to help with ventilation. Sorry about this.

Wang Mojie could hear Ukyi Lhamo's shower running, and through the frosted glass on the bathroom door, he could see the blurred contour of her body, which made him think back to the bewitching spectacle she had made of herself that night in the river during Karma Rishi. Wang Mojie suffered no impediment when it came to his ability to appreciate female beauty, indeed he could give a precise account of each of the aesthetically pleasing features of Ukyi Lhamo's form, but for this, he had to have some distance. The object of his aesthetic enjoyment could not be too close to him. That night by the river he had had the distance he needed, and so he had felt safe, which allowed him to relax and think clearly. Now, however, even though there was frosted glass between him and Ukyi Lhamo, she was too close and he felt nervous.

Wang Mojie set up the camp bed, but the room wasn't large, so the only place for it was next to Ukyi Lhamo's bed. Fortunately the camp bed was only half as high as her bed, otherwise it would be as if they were in bed together. Wang Mojie had thought about moving the sofa and tea table over by the bed so he could put the camp bed under the window away from her bed, but that would involve rearranging the entire room and besides, he planned to fold the camp bed up every morning. Wang Mojie could see no solution. If they had to be side by side, so be it. Ukyi Lhamo came out of the bathroom. She told Wang Mojie to shower, not as a suggestion but as an order. Wang Mojie put it off as long as he could, he poured a cup of tea for Ukyi Lhamo and washed the dishes, just to delay, and then finally went into the bathroom. When he came out (he was in the shower for a long time) Ukyi Lhamo was in bed, her hair was down and her pyjama top buttoned up tight at her neck. The quilt was pulled up to her chest, her head was on the pillow, and a book was in her hands. The ceiling light was off, the only light came from the bedside lamp.

—What are you reading? Wang Mojie asked, trying to sound relaxed. Ukyi Lhamo raised the book for him to see, then lowered it and went back to reading. Wang Mojie moved closer to get a better look at the book.

—Alexandra David-Néel, *Voyage d'une Parisienne à Lhassa*, he read aloud slowly, then said, Of course! There's a Chinese translation, Eastern Publishing Company, 1987, I think. I read it. She was nearly fifty when she came to Tibet for the first time, she lived until she was a hundred and two. She walked to Lhasa when she was fifty-six. It took her seven or eight months, and she went all over.

Wang Mojie was still trying to sound casual, but his words rushed out in staccato bursts. Ukyi Lhamo put her book down and interrupted Wang Mojie, gently saying, You're uneasy, aren't you?

—Yes, I am, Wang Mojie said, deciding to be honest.

—There's no reason to be nervous, just be yourself.

—I can't just decide not to be nervous.

—OK, then be nervous, just stop talking.

—Hey, you know that tension rod and curtain we bought? I was going to put it up while you were in the shower, but this is your home, so I thought I should ask first. Can I put it up?

—No, I won't permit it.

—But I might have trouble sleeping... probably... definitely.

—Maybe so, but tomorrow you'll start to adjust.

—Why not let me have the curtain?

—Hey, what do you think about when you can't sleep? You know what, I think you should keep a body journal, you should write about your body, that would be better than taking notes on zero or whatever it is.

—Now you're my therapist? You're going to fix all my problems?

—Me? I wish I was. I wish I could.

Wang Mojie got onto the camp bed, right next to Ukyi Lhamo's bed, but lower by one big step, so to speak, which felt awkward to Wang Mojie. He wondered if he would be more comfortable if he was just a bit higher and she was just a bit lower, but he realised that wouldn't be good either because that way he would be able to see her too clearly. Still he wondered if everything would feel less out of whack if their beds were on the same level. Wang Mojie picked up a book but he couldn't concentrate. He was unaccustomed to lying next to a woman at night the way ordinary people do, and he felt jumpy, he kept twitching all over, and it got worse and worse. He felt sweat on his face, his hands got damp. It wasn't because he wanted sex with Ukyi Lhamo, it was something quite different. He needed Yu Youyan and what she gave him. He was hot, his skin was on fire, he fantasised about his ex-wife's leather belt, about Yu Youyan's leather belt, he wanted to hear the sound of belt on body, he was really sweating now... At the very same time, however, all he had to do was open his eyes and take a look around and his rational self would tell him how nice everything was, the bedside lamp, their books, the two of them reading in bed, nothing sexual going on. Ukyi Lhamo's pyjama top even had a collar, she could just about wear it out in public. There was no reason for him to feel afraid. What was he so afraid of? How beautiful she was? Was he afraid of happiness? Was he afraid of tenderness? The chance of a caress? All that sort of thing and more? If he ever did write a body journal, he would start by writing about his fear of happiness. She had told him to keep a body journal, she understood him too well.

—Go and wipe that sweat off, splash some cold water on yourself, Ukyi Lhamo said without looking up from her book.

—I never beg anybody for anything, but tonight I'm begging you, let's hang up the curtain, please? Wang Mojie said. He was looking not at Ukyi Lhamo but at the frosted glass on the bathroom door, and in his mind's eye he saw her beautiful body through the glass. After a moment, Wang Mojie continued to plead with her.

—I've been sleeping alone for years, I'm not used to this. Plus, tomorrow after school we're taking Robert to see Ma Dingge, we're going to be up at the monastery most of the day, how am I going to hold up if I don't get any sleep? I thought you were staying at your mother's. I'm not blaming you, I'm sorry, I don't mean to say it's your fault, what I want to say is I haven't had time to prepare myself mentally. I've been completely preoccupied with Ma Dingge, his father and the conversation they are going to have, I can't wait to listen. Robert is a big-deal public intellectual in the West, and his son is a custodian of the ancient Buddhist culture of the East. It's inconceivable how fantastic their talks are going to be. Could there be a more important conversation for the end of the century? Contemporary philosophy and ancient philosophy up against each other, in dialogue, it had to be. I don't think it's going to produce any sort of resolution, but this kind of collision of ideas is a chance for the most productive type of intellectual exercise, so I feel really lucky. I have to get some sleep so I can go all in.

—What good is it if you just think, think, think and don't have a life? Ukyi Lhamo asked, putting down her book.

—Who says I don't have a life? I have a life of the mind, an active one.

—You call that a life?

—Yes, for me the life of the mind is life, Wang Mojie said with utter sincerity. Besides, Ukyi Lhamo, you should know, you're a Buddhist, Buddhism regards human life with contempt, Buddhism teaches that we are not our bodies, the body is just skin and bones, it is of no importance.

—That's a complete distortion of what Buddhism teaches!

Buddhism is about release from the endless cycle of rebirth, but more importantly it's about the study and meditation that lead to the insight that makes this release possible. Khanor Rinpoche says it is a blessing to be born as a human being. All life is precious. But all life is impermanent, rebirth is determined by *karma*, and we can be reborn into any of the six realms of existence. This is a cycle of suffering, and Buddhism is the path to liberation from it, but it is so much more than that. Ma Dingge says there are eighty-four thousand gates to the Dharma, people are different and so there is a path to enlightenment to suit everybody, and this choice we are given shows the understanding and compassion the Buddha has for every single precious human life. Do you see contempt for human life in the eyes of the Buddha? In the eyes of Avalokitesvara? Do you see the slightest trace of anything like that? Have you ever actually looked? What you see is mercy and compassion for all forms of life. The light of the Buddha shines on all living things, it even shines on somebody like you, but you just don't know it.

—It shines on me?

—It shines on everything.

—How come it seems to me that it's you who's shining on me?

—The Buddha is omnipresent.

—I think you are a bit confused there, Ukyi Lhamo. That sounds like something a Christian would say. Christians say, "God is omnipresent", but I have never heard anybody say the Buddha is omnipresent. If you want to preach to me, you have to get your facts right.

—You are incorrigible, you have no faith and you are mean to those of us who do, but I've known that for a long time.

—No, no, I'm serious. You get things wrong, sometimes you mix up the two religions. Did you go to Catholic church a lot when you were in France? You must have gone to Notre Dame. I've seen that movie, *Notre Dame de Paris*.

—Enough! Ukyi Lhamo yelled at Wang Mojie.

—May I hang up the curtain?

—Yes!

Wang Mojie's strategy had worked. He quickly secured the tension rod against the walls on either side and hung the curtain on the rod. The curtain was dark blue, with an image of a crescent moon and waves. It was a heavy curtain that was intended for use outdoors, during a summer celebration for example.

—I hung it so the moon faces you, Wang Mojie said, trying to be friendly.

He lay down and relaxed but a minute later the curtain fell down, startling him. He got up and hung it back up, but when he lay down, it fell again.

—That's weird. What's going on?

—Don't imagine for a minute that you are going to get your way, Ukyi Lhamo said and then went back to her book.

—Oh, you pulled it down! I thought it was odd.

—Yes, I pulled it down.

—Why be this way? What do you want?

—Just showing you that you aren't the only one who can be mean.

Wang Mojie gave up, he didn't try to put the curtain up again. Ukyi Lhamo was right next to him, he couldn't get used to it, sweat started to trickle down his body again until finally he had to get up and wash again. He took a cold shower, and a cold rush of air followed him when he came out of the bathroom. He kept having to go back in and splash more cold water on himself, and every time, the cold would follow him out of the bathroom. This continued until two o'clock. Ukyi Lhamo had stopped reading.

—You have to write about cold showers in your journal. That was number seven.

She turned out the light without asking Wang Mojie if he was ready to sleep. She was exhausted and she quickly fell asleep. When he heard her breathing deepen, Wang Mojie carefully and quietly hung up the curtain and carefully and quietly got back in bed, listening in case Ukyi Lhamo stirred. The curtain stayed up and he relaxed, he was safe. In the moonlight he could see that the curtain divided the room into two unequal halves. It took him a while to fall asleep, and he started to think about what she had said about the eighty-four thousand different paths to enlightenment. He had made fun of her, but some of the things she said made sense. Ukyi Lhamo might be mixed up about who she was, and some of what she said might not really be in line with what Buddhism was all about, but she was no phoney. She was who she was, there was something pure about her, and despite how mixed up she was and how paradoxical she could be, that pureness gave her a certain radiance, a certain glow. She had been born with it, it was in her blood, in her genes, it was something he would never have.

30. Karma mudra, inana mudra

One acchata, *the time of a snap of the fingers, contains 320 trillion* smrti.
One smrti, *the time of a thought, equals 90* ksana.
One ksana *contains 900 instances of formation and annihilation.*
The process of formation and annihilation is without beginning or end.
The inana mudra *appears through repeated contemplation and visualisation.*
She then becomes the woman within you, maha mudra.
She becomes the female principle within you, as eternal as the male principle.

The mornings in Lhasa were limpid and bright, the sun set everything ablaze, lifting the spirits and making everyone happy. Robert was sitting on a stone bench in the sun but seemed indifferent to the fine weather. As he did before every day's session, he set up his tape recorder, opened his leather-bound notebook, recorded the date in it, and then with sombre concentration he filled and lit his Sherlock Holmes pipe. His first bowl lasted half the day, he waited until the afternoon before he emptied it, refilled it and relit it. The rest of the time it was out, but he liked to chew it, suck on it or have it in his hand. His snow-white hair was always neatly combed.

Ma Dingge had made no changes to his room in preparation for his father's arrival, he didn't even dust it. Ukyi Lhamo asked Wang Mojie to help her give the room a clean, and they showed up with detergent, rags, a duster, a bucket and brushes, but Ma Dingge wouldn't let them touch anything, he didn't even let them wipe away the thick dust everywhere. He wanted everything left as it was. His room was simple and as peaceful as always, and to Wang Mojie this feeling of continuity was the feeling of history. Except for the fragrance of green tea, nothing about the room was changed, the butter lamps in front of the image of the Buddha burned as they always did, and despite Ukyi Lhamo's feminine energy and her attentiveness to everything, the room still gave you the feeling that you were directly connected to history and a living tradition. The conversation every day revolved around Buddhism, which also often served as a point of departure that allowed them to talk about many things. Inevitably Robert brought the talk around to Freud, the unconscious, sex, repression, Tibetan esoteric Buddhism and tantric sex, and the general relationship of religion and sex, things of that sort.

These were familiar topics to Wang Mojie, he had discussed Freud with Ma Dingge many times. He once asked about some things he was interested in but had never understood, for example, *karma mudra*, which in Mandarin is *shuangxiu*, double practice, or more directly put, tantric sex, which he had never been able to understand. Neither had Robert. Ma Dingge acknowledged that *karma mudra* was part of the Tibetan tantric Buddhist tradition but said it was not something for all tantric adepts. He stressed that *karma mudra* was a technique that required that both parties already be of advanced spiritual attainment, to the extent that "at the closing of their eyes, fruit falls from trees, at the opening of their eyes, fruit grows on trees". Robert could not accept this. He said it was impossible from the standpoint of both physics and botany. But Ma Dingge said that to a spiritually advanced monk, the physical world is free of the constraints it has in our common experience. Ma Dingge also said, however, that this level of attainment is extremely difficult to achieve, only after fifteen or more years of training and an examination can a monk receive permission to practice tantric sex.

—The practitioner must first be initiated into the tantric tradition, Ma Dingge said, and then he must become completely familiar with his chosen meditational deity and learn the associated incantations and mantras, and then as is fitting for the natural capacity of his body-mind – the direct product of his previous life – he studies the level of Vajrayana practice that is appropriate to him. Which is to say that only those disciples who have the keenest natural capacity may practice *karma mudra*, which itself is actually a set of yogic practices with some more advanced than others.

Ma Dingge explained that there are four levels of *tantra*. The first is *kriya-tantra* or ritual deity practice, which is relatively simple. It is an external practice comprised of rituals of purification and cleansing. It has been likened to the bliss of partners looking at each other. The second level is *carya-tantra* or behavioural deity practice, which is both an external and internal practice, putting an equal emphasis on action and speech and the inner cultivation of *samadhi*. It has been likened to the bliss of smiling at each other. The higher level is *yoga-tantra* or integrated deity practice, which is built on the foundation of the first two levels and is an internal practice that unites method and wisdom. It is based on knowledge and understanding of the ultimate truth and the relative truth, and it emphasises contemplation that unites these truths. It has been likened to the bliss of hugging. *Yoga-tantra* is for the relatively few practitioners of sufficiently high ability, and there is one more yet higher level, *anuttara-yoga-tantra* or highest yoga deity practice, in which the practitioner and his consort experience the bliss of sexual union. This allows for the attainment of the subtle clear light of the luminous mind as the practitioner realises the emptiness of all things and lets go of all attachment. *Anuttara-yoga-tantra* is further divided into Father Tantras and Mother Tantras. Father Tantras are used in meditation that emphasises visualisation for personal transformation. Father Tantras focus on the generation phase of visualisation, Mother Tantras emphasise the completion phase of visualisation. Mother Tantras focus on a particular deity and his consort, and utilise desire as the path of practice.

—Oh, so you have to progress all the way up to Mother Tantras before you can do *karma mudra*? Robert asked with a sigh.

—Yes, the practice of sexual yoga is highly regulated, there is a strict logic to the rules.

—I thought, Robert said, that Buddhism was about freeing yourself from sexual desire. Why is that turned on its head when you get to the level of what you say is the "highest" practice?

—Tantric Buddhism includes antinomian beliefs and practices. If we accept the illusory nature of all things, then it follows that all ethical or moral laws and rules are illusory. When the practitioner reaches the level of the Mother Tantras, it is logical that the greatest taboo will be overthrown. The realisation of the emptiness of the greatest of taboos allows us to perceive the emptiness of all things. Tantric Buddhism emphasises the importance of the feminine, and it teaches that the origin of all energy in the universe is sexual union. The tantric practitioner must access *shakti*, the energy of the female, through sexual union, in which he and his consort become one, if he is to transcend sexual difference and perceive the illusory nature of sex and perceive the emptiness of all things.

—So the practitioner requires a "wisdom consort", he needs some extraordinary woman as a partner in sex? Robert asked, sucking on his unlit pipe.

—Yes, to transcend gender, the practitioner needs a consort, specifically he needs three types of consort, a flesh and blood real woman, known as *karma mudra*, the same term I used before but with a different meaning. The second is a consort visualised by the practitioner, an imaginary woman, if you will, called *inana mudra*, and the third is the *maha mudra*, the "inner woman", which is the feminine principle that is within the practitioner.

—Imaginary woman? Inner woman? This is all new to me. It all sounds incredible. By what process do you come up with your imaginary woman? Can it be anybody you want?

—No, it cannot, Ma Dingge said, as calmly as ever. The practitioner may not simply visualise as he wishes, he must visualise a consort who is described in the Kalacakra tantra. It takes a long course of training and meditation before the eye of wisdom opens in his mind allowing him to see his *inana mudra*. Through union with the *inana mudra,* the practitioner takes her feminine energy within him, which becomes his inner woman, at which point the female and male principles are both within the practitioner and are one, allowing him to perceive the illusory nature of sex and perceive the emptiness of all things, as I have said.

—But, if I follow you, the real woman is still part of it, Robert said, waving his pipe.

—That is true, Ma Dingge said.

—Since you have an imaginary woman, why do you need a real woman?

—Both the real woman and the woman visualised by the practitioner serve to awaken him to the illusory nature of the world, freeing his mind so that nothing will trouble him. The practitioner who attains this level of enlightenment can shape his universe with his mind. It is more difficult to grasp the illusory nature of all things when with a *karma mudra* than when one is visualising an *inana mudra*, and the more difficult the test, the greater the chance for enlightenment, that is why the real woman is necessary.

—But are there practitioners who engage in tantric sex with a real consort before they have completed the necessary training? To put it plainly, are there practitioners who just use all this as an excuse to satisfy their lust? Robert asked doubtfully.

—I can't say no, Ma Dingge said and paused before resuming. Speaking slowly, he continued, That is why the Gelug school has essentially eliminated real women from this practice. Tsongkhapa himself made use of only *inana mudra* and *maha mudra*, and Tsongkhapa founded the Ganden monastery, which later led to the establishment of the Gelug school, what the less informed call the "Yellow Hat" school. His example teaches us that engaging in tantric sex without having received the necessary training is harmful to Buddhism.

—I don't pretend to understand all the subtleties of sexual yoga, but am I right to say that it is a sexual practice and also a spiritual practice at the same time?

—Yes, Ma Dingge said.

—OK, if it is both then it must require some special sexual technique and special spiritual abilities, which to your way of thinking can't be separated, I get that. But what I want to ask is if the use of that special spiritual ability makes the sex better as just sex? Also, as far as I know, none of the world's other major religions incorporate sex in their rituals, Christianity doesn't and Islam doesn't. But Buddhism, or at least esoteric Buddhism at any rate, has made sex part of what you say is its "highest" spiritual practice and has done so in great detail and with much elaboration, which to my way of thinking is a unique contribution of Buddhism. For me, religion shouldn't only be about showing people the way to heaven or enlightenment or Buddhahood, it should help people in their ordinary lives, and here I mean sex lives. So can we say that the Buddhist practice of *karma mudra* has lessons that can help us in our lives, in our sex lives?

—Anyone who wishes to try that may try it, but that has nothing to do with Buddhism, Ma Dingge said and then fell silent.

—I understand that the purpose of sexual yoga is to help the practitioner perceive the illusory nature of everything and advance on the path to enlightenment, Robert said, conceding the point so as to sound less argumentative. Nevertheless there would be nothing wrong with lay people taking something from the Buddhist practice to help them in their sex lives, right? I mean, if Buddhism can't reduce our suffering, at least it can bring us more pleasure. It could help make sex something that is spiritual, not just physical.

—Maybe it could, but that is not a road to liberation, it is not a path to *moksa*.

—Obviously, but what I'm saying is the vast majority of people aren't ever going to achieve real liberation, so can't Buddhism provide them with a way to get something at least close to it? Lovers who are both believers, for example, through "double practice" could gain some insight into things.

—What things?

—Love, for example, everlasting.

Ma Dingge remained as calm as he always was, but he did not answer.

—What I'm saying is, shouldn't religion be concerned with helping people be happier in their ordinary lives? Robert asked.

—Buddhism has always been concerned with helping people, it has always tried to enlighten people and reduce their afflictions, but this does not bring them more happiness in the ordinary sense. The bliss that Buddhism brings us is spiritual, not physical, Ma Dingge said.

Wang Mojie broke in and asked Ma Dingge a question in English.

—Let me ask you something else, can physical pain be a path to spiritual bliss?

—The body isn't an instrument to be used in such a way, and the body isn't our ultimate concern, but of course, the body is one of the things that make us who we are.

—The idea is that the body can be used as an aid to enlightenment but also is an obstacle to enlightenment, right? Robert asked.

—That is right.

Smiling, Robert handed his empty coffee cup not to Wang Mojie but to Ukyi Lhamo, even though it was always Wang Mojie who took care of his coffee. Handing the cup to Ukyi Lhamo seemed to be, in Freud's terms, an "unconscious act" that betrayed a "latent tendency" that had been quite naturally building in him over time. Ukyi Lhamo did, of course, sometimes pour coffee for Robert, but this was usually during meals. Robert's "unconscious" had been influenced by this and had developed a "latent tendency" towards expecting coffee from Ukyi Lhamo. If so, it was understandable because she was the sole woman in the group, she was his translator, she brought a little spirit of the contemporary age to a conversation that otherwise might as well have been taking place in the Middle Ages, and she was attractive. All this combined was the reason for Robert's "latent tendency" or we might say the "layers of a mental state" he found himself experiencing.

In any case, Robert liked Ukyi Lhamo, and he was finding the Westernised Tibetan food she had been making surprisingly satisfying. She fried steak, made salad and baked bread, she made beef soup and bought Tibetan cheese. All this made Robert look on Ukyi Lhamo with greater and greater favour. Robert held old-fashioned beliefs about women, and so the way she was looking after their meals with such care and treating him with such subdued hospitality pleased him, and he made a point of expressing his pleasure whenever he got the chance. But for Ukyi Lhamo, keeping quiet and being polite wasn't a way of showing feminine deference, it was a way of expressing her distaste for Robert and keeping her distance from him. Robert seemed to understand this, he even seemed to admire it. Ukyi Lhamo took the cup and poured more coffee for Robert, continuing to translate for Wang Mojie as she did. His French was good enough for him to understand some of what was being said, and with Ukyi Lhamo translating and explaining, he was able to keep up with everything for the most part. If he still had questions, he had the recordings he made every day (both Robert and Wang Mojie recorded the talks). Each evening, he played back his recording from the day, and Ukyi Lhamo helped him clear up any remaining questions. When they ran into technical terms that Ukyi Lhamo didn't know, they turned to her French-Chinese Dictionary.

During the day's conversation, it became apparent that Robert didn't understand that Tibetan Buddhist monasteries were institutes of higher learning, that a monastery was much like a university. Drepung, for example, was a monastic university with "colleges," much like Oxford University has colleges. He asked for more details. Ma Dingge told him that Drepung's four great colleges, or Dratsang in Tibetan, are Loseling, Gomang, Deyang and Ngakpa. Each has its own academic administrative structure and tradition, each occupies its own buildings. Within the individual colleges, the monks study esoteric Buddhism, astrology, medicine, poetics, rhetoric, grammar, music, drawing and more. The course of study that the monks undertake is long and rigorous. On most days, the morning is for recitation, the middle of the day is for revision, and the afternoon is for debate.

—Can you give me a few examples? Of things the monks might debate, I mean, Robert said to his son.

—There is no end to possible topics of debate but to give you an example, the monks often discuss and debate our conception of time, they discuss and debate the concepts of *ksana*, *acchata* and *smrti*. Buddhism teaches that one *acchata*, the time of a snap of the fingers, contains three hundred and twenty trillion *smrti*; one *smrti,* the time of a thought, equals ninety *ksana*; one *ksana* contains nine hundred instances of formation and annihilation. Buddhism teaches that everything is always undergoing a process of ceaseless change through the cycle of birth, existence, change and cessation, this process is without beginning and without end. Time is a ceaseless flow, and we exist in space inside that flow.

—Oh! That idea has something in common with Heraclitus's argument that one never steps into the same river twice, Robert said, sucking on his empty pipe. Or maybe it's better to say it resembles the philosophy of Heraclitus's student Cratylus. Cratylus went a lot further than his teacher did. He said you cannot step in the same river even once. But then again Zeno, a rough contemporary of Heraclitus, made an opposite argument with his paradox of the arrow. A flying arrow does not move. Why? Because time can be divided into infinite instants and at every instant the arrow is motionless in the space it occupies at that instant. In this paradox, there is a deviation between time and space, the paradox denies that there is a flow of time in which motion may occur. Does Buddhism have any answer to this paradox?

—The Buddhist concepts of *kalpa* and *nirodha,* cessation, refute the idea that time may be divided into segments.

31. Silence

Ukyi Lhamo was all in white, and her quilt was white.
Her pyjama blouse was buttoned all the way up.
There was no skin showing, she looked like a nurse at a convalescent hot spring.
He loved that everything was white because white was the colour of reason.
White was the colour of marble, the colour of his heart.

It was noon. The sunlight was streaming straight down. All the shadows were gone, even the typically shadow-strewn recesses of the monastery were sunny, shot through with light, their white walls showered in sun that shimmered beautifully. The sky was clear, the monastery was bright, but slivers of shadows were starting to seep out on the edges of the stone steps, almost imperceptibly. This is the nature of things, time never stops, any end is a beginning. Their midday meal might come a little earlier or a little later, a small shift in time, time enough for the shadows to creep unnoticeably. Lunch was always simpler than their dinners, they either had leftovers from the night before or something made in the morning. They brought lunch up to the monastery each day with plates and utensils. Ma Dingge never cooked as he didn't have a kitchen, just a simple, small metal brazier for heating tea over a yak dung fire, but that served their needs, and they reheated their lunch on the brazier. On the first day of conversation with his father, Ma Dingge ate what they brought, but after that, he insisted on eating the even plainer lunch provided by the monastery of *tsampa*, butter tea, potatoes or radishes, sometimes milk-skin cheese and a piece of fruit. Ma Dingge lived an ascetic life, he was used to a simple diet. Every once in a while, he would have some of the green vegetables that Wang Mojie contributed to lunch but otherwise he ate as he normally did.

Ma Dingge had no special status in the monastery, he was just another monk, part of the day-to-day life of the monastery. If there was anything that made him different, it was that his background gave him a broad perspective on spiritual matters, which brought him great tranquillity. Wang Mojie lived a very simple life too, much like Ma Dingge, except of course for his involvement with Yu Youyan and Ukyi Lhamo. You could almost say they were the same, as Wang Mojie sat in his stone house and read, while Ma Dingge sat in his stone room and read. Ma Dingge read from the Tibetan Buddhist canon, texts from the Kangyur and the Tengyur. How is that any different from Wang Mojie reading *The Archaeology of Knowledge* (that's Foucault) and *Of Grammatology* (Derrida)? How much difference is there between the Heart Sutra and the *Dao De Jing*, or between the *Dhammasangani*, the *Dhatukatha* and the *Vibhanga* on the one hand and *Being and Time* (Heidegger) and *The Perfect Crime* (Jean Baudrillard) on the other? For those of us who seldom or never read texts such as these, there is no meaningful difference. Moreover, in his philosophising, his practice of taking long walks, and indulgence in introspection and inner calm, Wang Mojie was a lot like the contemplative Ma Dingge. But of course, any similarity between them was more than outweighed by the enormous difference between them: Wang Mojie was a masochist, which alone made him utterly unlike Ma Dingge in the final analysis.

By routine, the day's conversation ended at twilight. Things changed at twilight. The intricate labyrinth of the monastery was filled with the lustrous golden light of sunset – the light of the Buddha – and an intricate labyrinth of shadows. The contrast of light and shadow seemed to add a fourth dimension to the space. They walked through a flickering alternation of light and shadow, a stop motion effect, stopping and starting. As they broke through walls of light and shadow, they traversed past light and future light. Ukyi Lhamo walked between Wang Mojie and Robert. They went out of Ma Dingge's courtyard and its lattice of light and shadow and down a narrow passageway that took them through the monastery's web of corridors, pathways and alleys, and out of the front entrance. They passed through the grove of trees amid shafts of light. They walked through the village and the smoke from kitchen fires. By the time they reached the school, the sun was down and it was growing dark. They made the journey every day. Every day the three of them walked together, always just before sunset, punctually, like farmers rising with the sun to work and returning at sunset to rest.

Once, as they reached the edge of the woods above the village, Robert stopped. He said he needed to sit down for a while and then, out of nowhere and unusually for him, he said he found the sunsets at the monastery and in the village special. He said that there on the mountain he had the sense that the flow of time was uninterrupted, he felt connected to the past. The tourist sites he had visited seemed to have been wrenched out of that flow of time, they weren't connected to anything. He liked the village and the monastery because in these places ancient customs lived on in a natural state, they weren't cut off from the past. He said Tibet was special, unlike any other place. It wasn't just the highest of places, it was the most complete. Robert stated that all of humanity is driven by a feeling of nostalgia for home. It is in the unconscious of us all, regardless of our nationality, or ethnicity. Robert said there were a few places in the world that soothed our unconscious nostalgia and Tibet was one of them. They sat there until it grew dark and then they walked out of the woods, appearing at the edge of the village like beings from some other world.

In the afterword to his book A Trip to Tibet, *Robert described in detail these walks back from the monastery at sunset and summed up, with great introspection and insight, I think, what the trip to Tibet had meant to him.*

The sunsets in Tibet enchanted Robert but didn't turn him into a romantic. Tibet made Robert think harder and deeper, Buddhism earned his admiration but also confirmed his doubts. Nothing deterred Robert from unceasing, determined, probing intellectual inquiry, which was inspiring to Wang Mojie.

The daily conversation was stimulating but exhausting, and by the time they got home they could barely move, but this was when Ukyi Lhamo rose to the occasion, making Wang Mojie see her in a new light. She impressed him, she completely lived up to her promise to look after Robert's day-to-day needs and made no attempt to pass responsibility off to Wang Mojie. Indeed, they had agreed in advance to a division of labour, but she didn't let Wang Mojie do anything, she wouldn't even let him help with the cooking. She said if they were both busy, Robert would be left on his own, and so Wang Mojie's sole task was to keep the old man company. Wang Mojie had planned on doing at least half the cooking if Ukyi Lhamo wanted a break. She was translating for him, which was tiring, and listening to the recording and correcting the transcription, so Wang Mojie was prepared to do all the cooking if she wanted him to. He was surprised at how unyielding Ukyi Lhamo turned out to be when she had set her mind on something.

This Ukyi Lhamo seemed like an entirely different person, she took on all of the housework, and no matter how late they got back, she made a dinner that satisfied Robert. Every other day or so she made Western food: pork chops or steak, a salad, sometimes fried fish, always a soup. And always sausage, bread, honey, butter, milk and red wine. She did the shopping and made sure they had what they needed. The day Robert demanded to move out of the hotel, she went off alone and spent a long time buying food. If Robert was going to eat that day and the next, she had no choice. This hadn't occurred to Wang Mojie, of course. She first went to her mother's house in Lhasa and chatted with her mother about Wang Mojie and Robert's arrival. She said hello to her uncle and borrowed his silver tableware, including a long-handled serving spoon and three very Tibetan-looking tall wine cups that were beautifully decorated with auspicious symbols. The tableware and cups made the table she set for Robert more impressive and created the atmosphere she wanted.

The dinner table was always set neatly with cutlery, napkins, cups and glasses. There was a *thangka* on the wall and a niche for the image of the Buddha with butter lamps. It was like a Western restaurant with Tibetan decor or a bar with a Tibetan theme. The room looked like it had a history and would stay as it was into the future. When it was time to eat, Ukyi Lhamo took off her apron, changed into Tibetan dress and came to the table like a newly arrived guest. The first night, Wang Mojie and Robert were surprised by how wonderful everything was. Emerging from their involved discussion of abstract, abstruse questions, they were struck dumb by the restaurant-like ambience. Robert said, Oh, it's beautiful, I can't believe it. Despite the lines of age on his face and his interrogative Holmesian stare, Robert was a gentleman. He opened his arms to hug Ukyi Lhamo, but she simply stood where she was, so Robert put his hands on her shoulders and gave them a squeeze. She moved away and showed Robert where the bathroom was so he could wash his hands before dinner. Her coolness did not bother Robert, and he praised her and kept saying "OK" in the

American way. Even as she led him to the bathroom he kept saying "OK".

Ukyi Lhamo was a good hostess. Robert and Wang Mojie kept complimenting her. This was heartfelt but also their way of apologising to her. They had been so caught up in conversation – about Wittgenstein, about the linguistic turn in philosophy, about Emmanuel Levinas, about the metaphysics of Alfred North Whitehead, about contemporary readings of the *Dao De Jing* – that they had been oblivious to Ukyi Lhamo as she prepared their meal. They felt guilty and so praised her all the more earnestly.

Ukyi Lhamo served them and poured the wine. Wang Mojie didn't normally drink and wasn't sure how to pour wine properly. He fumbled with the bottle when he picked it up, so she took it from him. Wang Mojie was unaccustomed to the formality and felt off balance. Ukyi Lhamo was gracious and thorough and had everything just so. Robert said the antique silver tableware and wine cups she had borrowed from her uncle gave the room an eighteenth-century ambience. He felt he had travelled back in time. If Wang Mojie had not been so terrified of what lay ahead later that night, he might have fallen in love with Ukyi Lhamo, whatever "love" meant to him. She was so beautiful and handled everything so perfectly that Wang Mojie grew more and more nervous and afraid when he thought about the night to come. Normally she didn't fuss over anything, she didn't even bother to make the bed in the morning, her house was always a mess. Wang Mojie didn't understand where her ability to put together such an elegant dinner party had come from. Also, Ukyi Lhamo was being polite but very cool and distant with Robert, so the extravagance of the dinner made Wang Mojie wonder if she was trying to kill him with kindness. Maybe it wasn't only for Robert? Maybe she was trying to demonstrate something to Wang Mojie? Maybe it was a way for her to exert control over Wang Mojie? Wang Mojie realised that since Robert's arrival, Ukyi Lhamo's utterly changed behaviour had put him thoroughly under her sway.

When he had finished his first cup of wine, Robert, moved either by gratitude, embarrassment at the trouble he was causing or just an old man's appreciation of a young woman, tried to express his feelings to Ukyi Lhamo.

—Ukyi Lhamo, I have taken over his house, he has taken over yours, and I feel bad about that. We, by which I mean Mr Wang and myself, we can share a house, we have much to discuss and so that would be convenient. You would not have to keep going back and forth every day, that is too tiring for you. Move back into your house, no more going back to Lhasa. Wang Mojie and I will share his house.

Ukyi Lhamo was thrown by what Robert said, and she answered without thinking.

—I haven't been going back to Lhasa, I've been staying here.

—What's that? You two are living together? Robert asked, looking at Wang Mojie in confusion.

—Yes, yes, Wang Mojie said, rushing to explain. She was going to go back every night, but we decided that was unnecessary.

—Unnecessary?

Robert still looked confused, an expression not often seen on a philosopher's face. Robert had been observing Wang Mojie and Ukyi Lhamo but had noticed nothing to lead him to think they might be involved, so now he was rather befuddled, even a little embarrassed, in part because now he felt like a third wheel. He raised his cup of wine to toast them but neither Wang Mojie nor Ukyi Lhamo responded. She did not understand at all what Robert meant by the toast. Finally, Wang Mojie raised his cup and then Ukyi Lhamo did, and the three of them touched their cups together.

—Wang, you're a lucky man, Robert said and took a sip of wine. I am almost jealous.

Jealous, at your age? French men certainly are overly gallant, Wang Mojie thought to himself.

—I think we have you to thank, Wang Mojie said to Robert, with a glance at Ukyi Lhamo.

—We definitely have you to thank, Ukyi Lhamo said to Robert. He is afraid of me, and if you weren't here, we would never be living together.

Robert shrugged to indicate he did not know what to say. After dinner, Wang Mojie and Ukyi Lhamo cleared the table and started doing the washing up. Wang Mojie told Ukyi Lhamo she should take a break and leave it to him.

—You took care of everything else tonight, Wang Mojie said. You're tired, Robert is concerned about you. He's concerned about the fair maiden, leave it, go and have a rest. We still have the recording to go through.

Ukyi Lhamo was not to be deterred. She took each plate from Wang Mojie after he washed it, dried it and put it away.

—You're fretting about the recording. Don't, we will get to it. Everything I promised to do, I will do, she said.

—You're exactly right, that's what I'm fretting about. I'm worried you'll be too tired to listen to the recording.

—Get out of here, go and talk to him.

—I haven't finished the washing up.

—Don't worry about it.

—But he's just left.

—He was only being polite.

Wang Mojie went to check on Robert. He stood in front of his house, and it seemed unfamiliar to him. He felt he had been evicted, and Robert had taken over his house, but then again because he was starting to feel comfortable about the new "cohabitation" arrangement with Ukyi Lhamo, his house didn't feel like home any more. Caught between these different emotions, Wang Mojie stood looking at his garden, which somehow didn't seem like his any more either. Everything felt unfamiliar, the wine was having an effect, he walked over and leaned on the garden fence, and his thoughts suddenly turned to Ukyi Lhamo's grandmother. He had never met her nor seen a photograph of her. All he knew was what Ukyi Lhamo had told him, but he had a dreamlike sensation that the beautiful woman next door tidying up after their meal was the Madame Ukyi Lhamo who had lived in London. He could see her vividly in his mind's eye.

Was Ukyi Lhamo actually Madame Ukyi Lhamo? Wang Mojie hung onto the fence feeling as if he were rushing backwards in time and then spinning forwards again as history doubled back on itself. He felt an urge to hurry back to see if the woman he had left washing up was actually the remarkable Madame Ukyi Lhamo. She would turn from the sink and speak perfect English to him. Madame Ukyi Lhamo. She had left Lungshar, turned her back on that great revolutionary, never wrote a word to him and taken herself directly to Yuthok. Her granddaughter was actually proud of her for doing that. Then there was Mrs Ukyi Lhamo, his Ukyi Lhamo's mother, and her life had been as remarkable as any *jataka* tale. She had gone far away to raise her family and then she surprised everyone by leaving her husband and returning to Tibet alone, as if her years in the interior hadn't really happened. She came back to live among the sounds of prayer and chanting that she had grown up with.

There was something special about all three women. The granddaughter, Ukyi Lhamo, was a lot more concerned with the latest fashion than her mother, Mrs Ukyi Lhamo, had been and she was more wilful, but still there was a strong tie between them. Indeed, a strong connection linked all three of them. Given the lives her mother and grandmother had lived, who knew what life still had in store for the youngest of the three Ukyi Lhamos? Or had something that would prove pivotal in her life already taken place? Was it happening right then? Was history repeating itself? Had his fate become entangled with hers? He had moved in with her. Did that mean he was now part of her family's secret history, part of that marvellous tale?

No one knew the history of her family, which is not surprising because most people seem to think that Tibet has no history. To most people Tibet is just monasteries, mountains and blue sky. Anyone who learns about Tibet's history is amazed at how rich it is, and Wang Mojie was one of those people. He was interested in the history of the three generations of Ukyi Lhamos and couldn't resist delving deeply into it. Over long nights of conversation with Ukyi Lhamo, as they talked themselves back into history, he found himself taking on the role of her confidant. He provided her with insight and analysis, which she appreciated because she could get the advice she needed from no one else, not from her mountaineer, the poet, nor any of her suitors. Only Wang Mojie could help her, and he didn't shirk the responsibility. For her, he was heaven sent, and she was for him as well. On all those days and nights, they sailed back through history, pulling miraculous stories up from its deep water, and their life together became like a fairy tale. Ukyi Lhamo shaped their time together into something of her own, it was unique, singular. She was tolerant and generous, incredibly so, and Wang Mojie didn't know how to deal with this, he had no idea what he should do.

He didn't know how long he stood in front of his house. He walked in only when he heard Ukyi Lhamo's door open and didn't know if she had been watching him. He looked at Robert. He was on his laptop, a diligent old fellow with a strong work ethic who never wasted a minute, never took it easy. Robert stood up, clapped him on the shoulder and congratulated him again for Ukyi Lhamo.

—She is very pretty, very mysterious. I have never met such an enchanting woman. A worthy subject for your philosophy. You, Wang, are even more mysterious and that's because you control your mystery.

Wang Mojie was never much affected by flattery. He made Robert some tea and told him again that green tea was good for you. As he let the tea steep, he forgot for a second that the tea was not for himself but for a guest. It was still his house, he reminded himself, it was his space, those were his books, it all was his. Robert was back on his laptop, online. The day before, after they had come down from the monastery, Wang Mojie had made a trip to the western suburbs and bought telephone cable, which he spliced into Ukyi Lhamo's line and then ran over to his own house. This was Ukyi Lhamo's idea, and it worked, which greatly pleased Robert. Wang Mojie said goodnight, but Robert had a request. He asked for a torch so he could see where he was going when he crossed the playground to the public toilet. Wang Mojie apologised for forgetting that Robert would need a torch and said he had one Robert could use. But Robert didn't really want a torch, it was just a way to broach the subject. He asked if there wasn't a way for him to avoid walking out to the toilet when he needed to urinate. He made a gesture of comic helplessness. Wang Mojie realised that Robert wanted a chamber pot, and he said, Yes, sorry, of course. Robert was quick to say that he was happy using the torch for the toilet if Wang Mojie preferred he didn't use a chamber pot in the house. Wang Mojie said it was absolutely fine, he used one himself and had one under the bed, the kind with a lid. Wang Mojie had always meant to suggest that Robert use the chamber pot but thought that maybe he would find the idea off-putting, so he didn't mention it. Human beings are adaptable, there is nothing we cannot adjust to, and that was as true of Robert as of anyone else, but the problem of the chamber pot was, however, not so simple, Wang Mojie thought to himself. The chamber pot was connected to a nexus of problems. It had to be emptied, for starters, and Wang Mojie could not picture a seventy-something-year-old "immortal" of the French Academy carrying his chamber pot across the playground to empty it at the public toilet. It wouldn't do, at all. Should he empty the pot for Robert? That didn't seem entirely right either. It was a problem. Ukyi Lhamo was too stubborn about certain things, Wang Mojie thought. She should have let Robert have her house simply so he would have a bathroom.

Wang Mojie said goodnight to Robert, then walked back and forth on the playground under the stars for a while. Solitude was his habit of years, and he didn't want to go back to Ukyi Lhamo. He felt he had nowhere he could go. When he did go back to Ukyi Lhamo's, he found she had cleaned everything and tidied up, and had already made lunch for the next day. She asked if Robert wanted to come over and use the shower. Wang Mojie had already asked Robert, and he said no, he had showered the day before. Wang Mojie told her about his concern over the chamber pot. She didn't think it was worth discussing, but he persisted and asked her a rhetorical question.

—But we can't have him walking across campus carrying a chamber pot first thing every day, can we?

—Then you do it. Get up, go and say good morning and empty his chamber pot.

Ukyi Lhamo lit a cigarette and sat down at the table on which her French-Chinese dictionary lay open. Wang Mojie got the tape recorder and his notebook and sat down next to her.

—It's a problem, either way, Wang Mojie said. Let's assume I'm willing to empty it for him, he might not want me to. A chamber pot is a rather personal thing, and he might not want to talk about it.

—So let him empty it, I don't see what the big deal is.

—You can be pretty uncompromising, I've discovered.

—And you just discovered this now?

—I had an inkling before, but it's more obvious now.

—Uncompromising when it comes to Robert or you?

—Robert too but mostly me. You have everything under control, I'm powerless to resist you.

—So the chamber pot is just an excuse to try to make me feel guilty?

—Of course not, I wouldn't dare. Me? To make you feel guilty? About what? Shall we get started?

—How have you been sleeping?

—Don't ask, nightmare after nightmare.

—Write your nightmares down in your body journal.

—I don't keep a body journal.

—Then tell them to me.

—I don't get it, how come you aren't at all sleepy?

—I sleep well every night, so I'm not as tired as you, she said, lifting her head to look at him.

Wang Mojie couldn't keep up with her changes in personality, now she was back to her old unreasonable ways. Wang Mojie had no retort, but he still tried to argue back.

—Every night I wait until you fall asleep and then I hang the curtain up. After that I don't sleep well, but at least I sleep.

—I've been allowing you to get away with hanging the curtain up.

—Thank you so much, that is so beneficent of you.

—But tonight, I think the curtain is not an option.

—Why?

—Look up.

Wang Mojie looked up at the ceiling and for a full minute he stared at the spot where the rod had been. The expandable tension rod that he hung the curtain on every night was gone. He didn't know how he had missed this, his heart started to pound, but he tried to seem nonchalant.

—I don't really need it, Wang Mojie said to the ceiling.

—You could get up and look for it, Ukyi Lhamo said, also to the ceiling.

—No, no, Wang Mojie said, looking at Ukyi Lhamo.

—If you can find it, you can put it back up.

—Why put me through this? Let's get started.

Ukyi Lhamo was a little disappointed. Whatever reaction she had hoped for, she did not get. Wang Mojie could search all he liked, but he would never find the rod. She had put him in a tough spot, but he wasn't going to give her the satisfaction of letting her know it. When they got down to work, Ukyi Lhamo put everything else aside and performed her duty as the resident French expert. She looked particularly impressive every time she consulted her big hardcover dictionary. She drank coffee, Wang Mojie drank tea, and they kept at it until late and were meticulous, their disagreement over the curtain apparently forgotten.

Ukyi Lhamo had no problem with Wang Mojie pursuing a "philosophical quest", as he put it, indeed she did much to help him. She was keenly interested in clearing up the problems of translation that they were running into, and that was because from day one the conversation between Ma Dingge and his father had captivated her, and she realised Wang Mojie had been right to say the talks were something rare, not to be missed. Something like a chaste platonic love developed between them as they sat working by lamplight, concentrating on the task at hand, cooperating wordlessly, pausing to slap hands in celebration when they solved a difficult problem in translation before writing the text in the notebook. They worked on tirelessly, with no jokes, no bickering, sometimes their bent heads almost touched but neither seemed to realise it.

It was almost midnight when they finished their work, and they sighed in relief. They exchanged glances, and had they been lovers, this was the moment they might hug, kiss or even make love, but they weren't lovers. For one brief moment, Wang Mojie seemed to turn towards her ever so slightly but as he did, his mind turned back to his own anxiety. Ukyi Lhamo, always perceptive, picked up on something as Wang Mojie moved, but the moment passed, and she didn't read anything into it or react. She stood up and stretched, and Wang Mojie's anxiety eased. She said she was going to wash, and she told Wang Mojie to tidy up the table and put everything away. Simple, straightforward, nothing was going on between them, the perfect state of affairs, Wang Mojie thought.

Wang Mojie put everything away, he was feeling more at ease, but then the sound of Ukyi Lhamo in the shower started to make him feel agitated because he associated showering with sex. After moving in with Ukyi Lhamo he had gradually begun to relax because she never flirted with him, and he had started to see her go in and out of the shower and in her pyjamas without his mind going straight to sex. She never did anything seductive, quite the opposite. She never wore a negligee or a low-cut nightgown, always just pyjamas with long sleeves and a collar, usually white, white like a doctor's coat. She buttoned the top all the way up, and any skin that might be visible above the last button was covered by her hair. She was buttoned up. Still, buttoned-up she might be, but Wang Mojie's eyes kept going to her full breasts under her pyjamas. No bra, he noticed. She was sexy, but she wasn't making a show of it, and so Wang Mojie wasn't too anxious. She looked beautiful to him. With her long hair, damp from the shower, falling over her shoulders to her chest, she was effortlessly sexy, but she was doing nothing to entice or seduce him.

In sum, during these days and nights, Ukyi Lhamo never did anything to try to seduce Wang Mojie. Even when she came out of the shower and dressed, she was demure. Everything between them was cool, she was detached, and her detachment and the way she seemed to regard everything with objectivity started to make Wang Mojie feel as if he no longer knew himself. Wang Mojie had always regarded his body as an object. His body was an "other", and often he could not control this "other". He found himself always doing the bidding of his body. Wang Mojie's "other" was not simply the sum of his animal instincts and not just his natural bodily desires. His "other" had emerged only after he had lost his "subjectivity". As I have said, Wang Mojie knew that what was typically called "subjectivity" in Chinese was usually referred to as "agency" in English. Only when he lost agency had his "other" emerged. Whoever Wang Mojie was in his innermost being, whether we call it a "subject" or an "agent", his "other" had replaced it. There was nothing Wang Mojie could do. Only by satisfying his "other" could Wang Mojie get anything like what we generally mean when we talk about sexual pleasure. But Ukyi Lhamo's coolness was making him wonder if this might change.

Wang Mojie's thoughts turned to the rod on which he had been hanging the curtain. It was gone. He didn't know what would happen now. By the time Ukyi Lhamo came out of the shower, he had set up the camp bed. She was wearing her white pyjamas as usual, but the top button was undone, just one button, enough to get Wang Mojie's imagination going but not so much that he couldn't keep it in check. Wang Mojie went into the bathroom to wash and brush his teeth. He hadn't planned to shower, as he had showered the day before, but for whatever reason he did. The shower didn't feel good, he felt as if he didn't want to be clean, it didn't feel right on his skin. When he came out of the bathroom, he was relieved to see that Ukyi Lhamo was in bed reading. She lay there, her book in her hand. Her pyjamas were white, the quilt was white, her top was buttoned up, and no décolletage to be seen. Her look made Wang Mojie think of a nurse, a nurse at a convalescent hot spring in the mountains. His quilt should be white too, Wang Mojie thought, like at one of those resorts. He had come to love white, white was the colour of reason.

—Still not sleepy? Wang Mojie asked to break the silence, and he picked up his own book.

They both liked to read before sleep, no matter how late they went to bed. They both lay quietly, as they did every night. Wang Mojie was still thinking it would be nice to have a white quilt, but he was quite happy with his blue-and-white check pyjamas, which he had worn for years. He thought the pattern looked a bit as if he were bound up in bondage ropes. They resembled the pyjamas they give you at a "sauna" – the type that sells sex. When he was still teaching at the university, he and a colleague had gone on a recruiting trip and shared a hotel room. His colleague saw his pyjamas and asked him with a leer if he went to saunas a lot, and ever since then, Wang Mojie associated his pyjamas with prostitution. It didn't bother him, he rather liked it.

The curtain wasn't up but nothing happened, soon Ukyi Lhamo put her book down and closed her eyes, the sound of her soft breathing making everything pure and calm. Wang Mojie read for a while longer, then turned off the light, and the room went dark but not black. The night in Tibet is almost blue - as your eyes grow accustomed to the darkness everything starts to turn a strange diaphanous blue colour. It's because of the moon. The moon in Tibet is special, different from in the interior, almost too bright to look at, and the moonlight that comes in through the windows turns everything blue, like everything is under shimmering sea water.

Wang Mojie's thoughts drifted. Robert had asked him for a torch, not because he needed one, it was easy to see in the bright moonlight, but because he was trying to hint that he wanted a chamber pot. Sometimes the old man wasn't direct about things, Wang Mojie mused, he was an interesting fellow. His thoughts went back to the missing curtain. He looked at Ukyi Lhamo's hands and wrists, which were blue in the moonlight, her white pyjamas and quilt were blue in the moonlight. Aeons ago what is now Tibet lay under an ancient sea, the Tethys Sea, and every night Tibet dreams of that sea. Wang Mojie looked at Ukyi Lhamo and then at his arms. He felt as if they were at the bottom of the ocean, the two of them chained there for a thousand years. He had to move, he had to set them free, so he put his hand lightly on Ukyi Lhamo's hand, but as gentle as he was, the second he touched her, his fingers burned and his body spasmed, his skin ran with a masochistic need for pain. It was the desire he lived with. He withdrew his hand but quickly reached out and tried again. He knew she was awake, she had to be, his hand was shaking and it was on hers, but she didn't move, her breathing remained even. If she had moved, he would have pulled his hand back instinctively, but she did not, which meant she was awake.

It was like they were at the bottom of an ancient deep sea, in a moment from *One Thousand and One Nights*, or a wall painting in an old temple. Ukyi Lhamo's hands were slender, cool, marble and anaesthetised. Wang Mojie felt sweat – he felt cold air on his wet skin. He hadn't noticed when he started to sweat, you never do. He slowly withdrew his hand, looked at it, and then put it back on Ukyi Lhamo's hand. He withdrew it, put it back, withdrew it, put it back again. Being able to do this meant something to him, it proved that for the moment he was getting beyond his neurosis. He gently stroked her hand, she was tranquil, composed, like an *inana mudra*, she did not move at all, and something warm, refreshing and new flowed through Wang Mojie's body...

Wang Mojie woke up in the middle of the night, and he felt something cold under his underwear, his lace-waist panties. It woke him up, and when he woke up he was still ejaculating from his wet dream, and as his head cleared, his pleasure turned to panic. He opened his eyes but could see nothing for the moment. He didn't know what time it was, the moon was down, no light of dawn in the sky yet, and it was as dark as it could get. In his dream, he and Ukyi Lhamo were having powerful sex. He was sensual, and she was bewitching, then everything changed and it was the night by the river during Karma Rishi, and Ukyi Lhamo was dancing with her mountaineer. Then she was making love to him by the river in front of everybody, and then he was the mountaineer, coming long and hard into her body, then he was embracing Ukyi Lhamo, coming and coming, the river turned white, the river was full of life, full of doll heads, severed limbs, and the dolls were shouting. He also dreamed he saw the mathematician-poet's dead body bobbing in the water like a bottle.

It was such a strange dream, it felt good but frightening at the same time. He felt his underwear, it was wet and feeling colder. He got out of bed quietly, and semen ran down his leg. In his dream he had come in a waterfall, a tide, a flood. He felt embarrassed for having a wet dream while right next to Ukyi Lhamo. He went into the bathroom, turned on the light, undressed, turned on the tap, washed himself and rinsed out his underwear. There was semen on his pyjama trousers. He rinsed them out. He hung the underwear and pyjama trousers on a round plastic clothes hanger. Ukyi Lhamo's black bra was hanging from it. He had seen it before, but now he studied it again. It was simple, like a bikini top, with little structure to it, no lace border or anything.

Wang Mojie turned off the light, and as quietly as he could, he came out of the bathroom and sat down on his bed. He slowly put on a clean pair of women's panties. He had looked at his watch in the bathroom, it wasn't yet four. He thought about his dream, his mind kept going back to Ukyi Lhamo's blue hands and the way she danced like having tantric sex. She turned over in bed, he held his breath and stayed still. He wondered if the sounds from the bathroom had woken her, and he started to worry because in the morning she was going to see his lace-waist panties on the hanger, but that was no longer a secret so he decided it was nothing to worry about.

32. Mirror Image

Gandhi burned the racist registration certificates and was beaten to the ground by police.
He stood up, no hatred on his face, no anger,
and he threw more of the certificates into the fire.
He was beaten to the ground again. He stood up again, he burned more certificates.
He ignored the police, he focused on burning the certificates.
No violence, no anger, no submission.

Typically they got up at seven, had breakfast at seven-thirty and went up to the monastery at eight, but the next morning Wang Mojie didn't wake up until almost eight-thirty. Ukyi Lhamo had let him sleep. He leapt out of bed, brushed his teeth, washed his face, put away the camp bed and went over to his house. He was surprised to discover the door was locked, as he had assumed Robert and Ukyi Lhamo would still be there, but they were gone. Wang Mojie was a light sleeper, but that morning he had slept soundly, like never before. He felt good when he woke, full of energy, which shows that good sex is good for you, even in a dream, or at least it helps you sleep. Wang Mojie was puzzled that Ukyi Lhamo hadn't woken him. He wondered if Robert's chamber pot had been emptied (his thoughts had started to go straight to the chamber pot whenever he thought about Robert).

He went back to Ukyi Lhamo's house and in the kitchen found a note from her. It was under the plate of food she had left for him. It just told him to eat his breakfast. He wolfed it down as quickly as he could, then set out for the monastery. Over the 1 May Labour Day holiday, the school was as quiet as the monastery. The sunlight was wonderful as he crossed through the village, through the grove of trees and past the silent heaps of weathered rock that looked like a landscape out of science fiction. Everything was sharp and clear, he could see forever, and the snow on the mountains was melting and rising in breaths of vapour, white as swans. This was unusual and normally seen only later in the morning when the sun was higher. An endless procession of tourists and pilgrims lined the stairs up into the monastery. Wang Mojie rushed through the slow-moving crowd, ducking and dodging his way to Ma Dingge's humble little courtyard. The courtyard was quiet, just as it had been the day before. It looked to Wang Mojie as timeless as a painting.

Ma Dingge, Robert and Ukyi Lhamo were sitting at the white stone table as they had been the day before. Their tea, coffee, notebooks and the tape recorder were set out on the table as they had been the day before. Robert was wearing a leather jacket, pipe in hand, as he needed to hold it to settle his mind. His son was in his crimson robe. He held nothing in his hands. Ukyi Lhamo was in a beige trench coat, with her long hair down over her collar, she looked like a museum guide. Imagine a painting of this. In the painting one of the stone stools is empty, which leaves room for the imagination: they must be waiting for somebody. This would be the crucial touch if it were a painting. In a painting, one of the stools would have to be unoccupied. Having Wang Mojie sit on it would be superfluous, it would ruin the suspense. This is what Wang Mojie was thinking when he saw the others, and he hesitated a moment before sitting down. The figures in the painting came to life. Ma Dingge was the first to notice Wang Mojie, he stopped in mid-sentence and nodded in greeting. Robert stood up and gave Wang Mojie a big, enthusiastic hug. Wang, he said, I was starting to think you were going to stay in bed until noon. Ukyi said you needed the rest, she takes good care of you, doesn't she, letting you sleep. Ah, you young people! He clapped Wang Mojie on the back, chuckling at what he was implying. Wang Mojie decided that Robert must not mind having to use the chamber pot, maybe he found it amusing. He had been worried for nothing, and Ukyi Lhamo had been right.

Ukyi Lhamo poured tea for Wang Mojie and summarised for him what Ma Dingge and his father had been talking about. She pointed at the tape recorder to mean that Wang Mojie could listen to catch up.

Wang Mojie sat down, becoming part of the painting, and the conversation resumed. They talked about violence, nonviolence and Gandhi. They talked about the similarities and differences in what Christianity and Buddhism had to say about violence.

Thoughts about love, compassion, pity, tolerance, lace-waist panties, blue-and-white check pyjamas, the metaphysical and the substantial, the public and the private and more also ran through Wang Mojie's head, a jumble of thoughts, but he was able to compartmentalise all this, he was able to keep each thing separate from the rest.

With all of these things running through his head, Wang Mojie looked at Ukyi Lhamo. He could see nothing on her face that was any different from usual. Her mind was on translating, her eyes going from Ma Dingge to Robert and back, she was focused, professional. She couldn't have slept well, he thought, not with his trembling hand on hers... for how long? But she hadn't stirred, and that touched him, which is maybe why he had the dream that felt so good but was so frightening. He didn't know why it frightened him, but his heart raced when he thought of it. He had taken her hand in his, which was hard for him, it wasn't natural for him, it took an effort of will, but she had remained so very still that it allowed him some space, and so his effort of will came to feel almost natural, and this feeling lasted and turned into a sexy but scary dream. Ukyi Lhamo didn't give any indication that she was aware of what he was doing when he got out of bed to clean himself up, but in the morning when she saw his panties hanging in the bathroom, she would have realised.

He watched Ukyi Lhamo's face and posture looking for a sign that there had been some change in her but saw none. If he had been forced to identify something new and different about her, it would be that she was becoming more and more professional as a translator. She was more and more focused and professional, that was the only word for it, and the difference from when she had started was enormous. She now did everything with a professional élan: translation, transcription, cooking and hosting. To this list of what she was doing so well, Wang Mojie thought he could add the way she had taken down the curtain and the way she had kept so still when he put his hand on hers. A saying, he couldn't remember by whom, came to Wang Mojie: Give a woman the chance and she will outdo a man every time. And you will no longer recognise her, he thought.

Robert and Ma Dingge were talking about Gandhi and nonviolence, which interested Wang Mojie. Their words registered only lightly in his head, but this didn't prevent him from following and understanding everything they said. He was able to divide his attention between several things at once and could do so with clarity and comprehension. As he listened to Robert and Ma Dingge, at the same time in one part of his head he was playing back scenes from *Gandhi* (the 1982 Oscar-winning film). Gandhi burned the racist registration certificates and was beaten to the ground by police. He stood up, no hatred on his face, no anger, and he threw more of the certificates into the fire. He was beaten to the ground again. He stood up again and burned more certificates. He ignored the police and focused on burning the certificates. He kept putting himself under their clubs again and again. He did not fight back and he did not back down. The resistance movement turned violent and many police were killed. Gandhi called for an end to the movement, but it could not be stopped, so he went on a hunger strike. As long as the movement continued, he refused to eat. The movement slowed but didn't stop. Gandhi's life was in danger, and his followers begged him to eat. Some of them went out onto the streets and put garlands of flowers around the necks of the military and the police, who were men with blood on their hands. When Wang Mojie saw *Gandhi*, which circulated underground in 1989, it moved him to tears, even though he didn't know who exactly he was crying for, but now everything from that time seemed so far away, so unfamiliar, despite how vivid it still was in his mind.

Ukyi Lhamo poured butter tea for Ma Dingge and green tea for Robert and Wang Mojie. Four people, four dimensions. Wang Mojie reached out for the tea through four-dimensional space-time, through an interlacing of different space-times.

Wang Mojie was thinking about infinite compassion, infinite love, love even for one's enemy, and he asked himself what sort of power this love had. What courage and faith did it express? It was rooted in metaphysics, of course. Robert was steadfastly sceptical of all metaphysics but given how out of joint the world was, you could argue that to be sceptical was just another retreat to metaphysics. We are all caught in the trap of our own metaphysics. Robert believed that philosophy should not be bound by its historical moment, philosophy must transcend its historical moment. Religion, he said, is a direct reaction to the conditions of one's life, but philosophy should be more than just that. Religious faith is a rock, it is solid and immovable, philos-

ophy must be able to adjust endlessly. Philosophy is a process of unending questioning. It may lead us into error, but this is not a problem because the philosophical quest for truth never ends. This is what Robert believed, and Wang Mojie agreed with him, unequivocally.

The conversation was rich, it was solid, it was real, just like the lamination of sunlight filling the courtyard, Wang Mojie thought as he looked at the sunlight falling on the trees, on the faces of his friends, on their hands, on Robert's pipe. The old man's pipe, Ma Dingge's robe, Ukyi Lhamo's hand as it gestured. Wang Mojie saw these things as superimposed upon one another in space. He heard Ukyi Lhamo's voice as she translated for him and her voice caught the sunlight, her low, husky voice was layered on top of the voices of Robert and Ma Dingge. Polyphony, like birdsong from the trees. He also heard the sound of running water coming from beyond the courtyard, from several directions at once. Everything was tinged with the mystical.

Ukyi Lhamo no longer seemed to be translating solely for Wang Mojie's benefit. He didn't always appear to be listening, and long stretches would pass when he didn't react to anything that was said, but Ukyi Lhamo still concentrated on the translation, indifferent as to whether anyone was listening. She needed no audience, she was apparently translating for her own sake. Wang Mojie noticed this despite his wandering mind. Ukyi Lhamo had discovered something in the conversation that belonged to her, and it was making her stronger and stronger. What she had heard had changed her understanding of Buddhism, and this in turn awakened something in her blood. What Ma Dingge said about Buddhism impressed even Wang Mojie, who had no faith, so Ukyi Lhamo's reaction can be imagined. Ukyi Lhamo had been a very reluctant if not hostile participant at first, but now her focused professionalism could be interpreted as the expression of a kind of pride. Perhaps this is why she seemed more relaxed in Robert's company, less aloof with him, more as if she was pleased to be his host.

Robert didn't like tea, he drank coffee, but Ukyi Lhamo had surprised him by cutting off his coffee. Robert couldn't imagine doing without coffee, he couldn't work without it, so he helplessly begged for coffee, but Ukyi Lhamo shook the small bag at him and told him no.

—There isn't much left, wait until the afternoon. You don't want to drink the last of it now, do you?

Ukyi Lhamo said coffee was bad for the heart and raised your blood pressure, and in Tibet that could kill you, especially if you were old. Chinese green tea was healthy, it lowered your blood pressure and was good for the heart. That was all well and good, but a habit is a habit, and Robert refused to change his. Robert turned to Wang Mojie and asked for coffee.

—Coffee costs more than tea, she wants to save you money, Wang Mojie said with exaggerated sincerity.

—Mademoiselle Ukyi Lhamo, is this true? Robert asked, picking up on Wang Mojie's joke and feigning incredulity.

—If I say you can't have coffee, then you can't have coffee, understand? Ukyi Lhamo said flatly, ignoring Wang Mojie.

Only a woman or a doctor could speak with such imperious authority, and the way she was treating Robert gave you an idea of her relationship with her Uncle Lhalu. When Ukyi Lhamo looked after someone, she did so with an authority that came naturally to her.

They broke for lunch at noon, and then Robert and Ma Dingge wanted a rest. Wang Mojie asked Ukyi Lhamo to go for a walk. It was midday, everything was lucent in the sun, the white-washed walls reflecting the strong light. Ukyi Lhamo was wearing sunglasses and standing against a white wall in her trench coat, which swayed in the sunny wind. She looked like she had stepped out of a Versace advertisement. Wang Mojie's lifestyle was as ascetic as any monk's, but he remained a student of the semiotics of commodity culture, and to him, the symbolic meaning of a commodity was of far greater significance than its utility. What a commodity signified became part of the very being of the person who possessed that commodity. As soon as Ukyi Lhamo put on her Versace sunglasses, they changed her and her relationship with her surroundings, the monastery moved into the background, and the sunglasses came to the fore. Her posture and gait changed when she put on the sunglasses, those sunglasses were about some entirely different... thing. Entirely. Wang Mojie thought back to the first time he went with Ukyi Lhamo to see Ma Dingge. That day she was dressed like a Tibetan, head to foot, with prayer beads around her neck and bracelets on her wrists. She was one with the monastery, part of it. But now? There were two Ukyi Lhamos, the sunglasses were enough to prove it.

They walked along a stream for a while, then sat on stone steps by the ruins of one of the monastery's colleges. The stream, fed by snowmelt from the mountain above, burbled by the steps. Snowmelt ran in many channels through the monastery, through the woods and the village. The streambed opened up to a vista that carried the eye beyond the woods to the village below, to the school and the road, its tarmac shining in the sun. On the far side of the road were wetlands, willows, farm fields, the blue Lhasa River and then the endless mountains.

They should have talked about what happened the night before but they didn't. It was as if it hadn't happened. Daytime was one reality, night was another. Everything was different in the daylight, everything was sunlit, academic, pious. In the daylight it was impossible to understand the night, impossible to talk about it. But the night was real, it impinged on every moment of their day, and they found themselves incapable of having an ordinary conversation about anything. They had nothing to say. There was nothing they could say. They sat in silence for a while, looking across the valley towards the river, neither saying a word, the stream burbling on. The stream flowed to the Lhasa River, and Wang Mojie found himself thinking back to Karma Rishi and the stunning sight of Ukyi Lhamo slowly lowering herself into the water. Wang Mojie spoke first, he turned and asked Ukyi Lhamo if she was going to participate in the ritual cleansing this year. It was a silly question, of course she was, and she didn't answer. Wang Mojie changed the subject to Ukyi Lhamo's mother, who had made a deep impression on him. Gazing at the ridgeline of the snow peaks on the far side of the river, Ukyi Lhamo said that her mother was fine and she had asked about Wang Mojie.

—She asked about me? Wang Mojie said, perking up.

—Just casually, in passing, the way you just asked about her.

—There was nothing casual about me asking about her. I think there's a special connection between your mother and me.

—You think everything to do with you is special, it's your best quality, Ukyi Lhamo said acidly, as she tore up some grass and tossed it into the stream.

—But there is. I'll never forget that night at your mother's house for Losar. It was incredible.

—It's only because she doesn't know the real you. You tricked her with who you pretend to be.

—It's not all pretend. If I didn't have something inside me, then she and I wouldn't have been able to communicate as we did.

—Wouldn't it be best if you didn't put it into words? Doesn't that ruin it? You always do this, she said. She stared at him, and he could see her eyes through her sunglasses.

—I'm trying to say that from your mother I learned something important about myself, something I hadn't been aware of before. At first, the only reason I was talking to her was because you wanted me to persuade her to make the trip with you, so I had an ulterior motive, but as I was talking to her, a whole new world opened to me. I had never experienced that sort of mental state or that sort of connection to another person. That was all because of your mother. I had never realised that we all have the divine within us, even somebody like me.

At first, Wang Mojie had been arguing for the sake of it, it was all just sophistry, but then he was surprised to hear himself articulate something he had never been conscious of before but that struck him as true when he said it. Wang Mojie was capricious, he did and thought as he wanted, he never worried about pleasing anybody else, but this kept him grounded in what is real.

—My mother said the same thing, that's amazing, Ukyi Lhamo said, persuaded by Wang Mojie's argument.

—So I don't think she asked about me just in passing. I know it in my heart, Wang Mojie said with self-satisfaction.

—She would like to see you again, she said so several times.

—Why didn't you tell me?

—It can wait, it can wait until we go to Dromo together.

—Dromo, right, when is that? Wang Mojie asked.

—I was going to leave on the first of May, but then Ma Dingge's father arrived. We'll have to wait until the summer.

—OK, I wouldn't mind a trip. I haven't been anywhere else in Tibet since I came here. Dromo's a long way away, right? How many days? Can you see Makalu along the way? Wang Mojie asked, knowing nothing about Tibet's geography.

—No. But you see Cho Oyu and Qomo Lhari.

—Oh, your mountain-climbing friend should be reaching the summit by now, right?

—No, he should be at Camp Two.

—Is the Buddha watching over him?

—Of course.

Ukyi Lhamo's faith on this point was unwavering. She told Wang Mojie that on the day her mountaineer set out on his expedition, she went to Nechung and made an offering of a butter lamp to Maitreya for him, and ever since she had recited the mantra of Padmasambhava for him three times each day, morning, noon and night. Each time she chanted the mantra hundreds of times, and altogether she had recited it almost ten thousand times. She intended to chant it fifty thousand times, it was a promise she had made to her mountaineer in her heart. They had been together all the time over the last few days, and Wang

Mojie hadn't noticed her reciting any such mantra. In the mornings before getting out of bed, he had seen her in front of her statue of the Buddha, which he supposed might be when she did her reciting. He was curious about it and had to ask.

—Have you really been reciting it? How come I've never heard you?

—You recite a mantra for yourself, not for other people to hear, especially not people like you.

—So when do you do it?

—I recite silently.

—Why am I not allowed to hear it?

—You are not Buddhist. You have yet to be subdued, just like all the demons that plague us.

—I'm a demon?

—All of us have our demonic side, but with you it's dominant.

—Did you ever think about reciting something for my benefit?

—For you? Yes, but I didn't know what to recite, she said. Then she smiled and stood up, it was time to go back.

—You could try reciting a little something for me, it might help, Wang Mojie said as they walked.

—No, you don't need it.

—I know Ma Dingge prays for me, Wang Mojie said earnestly.

—How do you know that?

—He prays for all sentient beings, so I'm included of course.

—You're a sophist, you don't believe anything you say.

—But am I right?

—OK, yes, you're right.

Ukyi Lhamo stopped and stared at Wang Mojie. They didn't seem like ordinary roommates, but they didn't seem like lovers either. Their relationship was something unique.

—You've changed a lot recently, it's like I don't know you any more, Wang Mojie said.

—Oh yeah? Well I don't think I've changed, Ukyi Lhamo said and walked on.

—I've had in mind all sorts of futures for you, but this was never one of them.

—What is "this"?

—You seem temporarily, I'm saying temporarily, stronger, in control of something.

—Of what? Ukyi Lhamo asked. She stopped walking.

—Of Robert in the daytime, me at night. You've handled everything beautifully since he got here, which has given you the authority to control things. You're strong now and you have authority, two things that couldn't be said of you in the past. You know, if all of a sudden we find ourselves controlling our own lives or find ourselves in control of somebody else, we are given an unfamiliar strength. Don't you feel like a stranger to yourself now?

—I don't know what you are talking about. I'm the same as I've always been.

—No, you definitely are not. But I like this new you, I just don't know if it's the new permanent real you or just a temporary you. I don't know what you'll be like after Robert leaves.

—No need to wait for Robert to leave, Ukyi Lhamo said.

—What do you mean?

—What do *you* mean?

—What I mean is, I think you are going to lose something when he leaves, Wang Mojie said.

—Then there's no need to wait for Robert to leave, Ukyi Lhamo said.

—I don't follow.

They reached the door to Ma Dingge's courtyard. Ukyi Lhamo took off her sunglasses.

—We can finish this tonight, she said, putting a little emphasis on "tonight".

All afternoon that word "tonight" kept echoing in Wang Mojie's head as he tried to concentrate on the conversation. "Tonight." The word had significance for Wang Mojie, it could mean many things, its meaning wasn't clear, but then again, its meaning was obvious.

33. Abhiseka in Blue

Moonlight. The ocean depths. Moonlight. The room was entirely blue.
Wang Mojie gently took the book from Ukyi Lhamo's hands. He looked at the book.
He looked at her pale hands as she slept. She looked at peace.
She was a perfect sleeping beauty, and with the book, she was all the more beautiful.
He took the book, like picking up a ritual implement, a bell, a vajra *sceptre.*

As they did every day at twilight, they took the path back to the school, walking over the layers of shadows, heads full of thoughts from the day's talk. The day's conversation had left them excited but exhausted, and as soon as they got back Wang Mojie lay down on Ukyi Lhamo's bed as if it were his own. It was too early to set up the camp bed, so he settled himself on her bed. It didn't give him a thrill or anything like that, it was no different from lying on his own bed. Her quilt was folded up and placed at the foot of the bed. Wang Mojie had done that, as he did every morning. He was now entirely comfortable in Ukyi Lhamo's house. It felt like a home. It felt as if he had a family, he and Ukyi Lhamo and an elderly relative for them to look after. Robert didn't seem exactly like a father or a father-in-law, but when the three of them sat down to dinner it was quite like a traditional Chinese family unit.

When Ukyi Lhamo came out of the bathroom, Wang Mojie said the day had been so tiring that rather than her cooking they should go to eat at the little restaurant on the main road run by a couple from Sichuan. He said that over the past few days, the cooking had been too much of a burden on her. Ukyi Lhamo was quiet for a moment, she took a sip of cold tea, then shook her head. She said Robert was old, the restaurant was dirty, and they couldn't risk him falling ill. Wang Mojie said they could go into Lhasa for dinner. His treat, he said. Ukyi Lhamo needed a break. Wang Mojie was genuinely concerned about her.

—Or we can go into Lhasa for dinner but let Robert pay for it. It's time he took us out to dinner. We can take a cab into Lhasa, Wang Mojie said.

—Make up your mind, who's paying, you or him? Ukyi Lhamo asked with a look of stern impatience.

—I'll pay, my treat, Wang Mojie said hastily.

—Just drop it, you might be ready for that but Robert is tired, and we shouldn't be dragging him all over the place.

Ukyi Lhamo was focused on doing what was best for Robert and would not be swayed, which rather surprised Wang Mojie. He went into the bathroom, and his eyes immediately fell on his panties. He had been so intent on Ukyi Lhamo all day that he had completely forgotten about them. He was flustered at the sight of them, they looked bizarre, and he could no longer pretend there was nothing wrong with them. It was the very first time his habit of wearing women's underwear made him uncomfortable. He blushed. Ukyi Lhamo's bra, which was black like his panties, had been hanging next to them. No, he revised the thought, his panties had been next to her bra, but the bra was gone. Had she changed her bra and put the black one on? Normally she wouldn't have done this until after she had showered. Had she just taken it to put it away? He looked around, he opened one of the drawers in a plastic container unit and in it found the bra. There were two other bras, both placed neatly in the drawer, but the black one had just been tossed in. She had grabbed the bra in a hurry, she didn't want it near his panties probably. He thought he should put the panties away, but he didn't know where. He supposed he shouldn't put them in with her bra. He thought about putting them in the rubbish or throwing them out of the window, but then he told himself that would be ridiculous. He decided he would leave them where they were. They had been there all day, and what did it matter? But then he realised that Robert might want to use the bathroom during dinner. He couldn't let Robert see the panties, but what if he did? Robert would just assume they were

Ukyi Lhamo's. As all this went through Wang Mojie's mind, he started to feel happy. He wasn't sure why but the feeling just came over him, and it was nothing like he had ever felt before.

He came out of the bathroom, went into the kitchen, said he wanted to help with dinner and asked for a job. He said he needn't keep Robert company all the time because Robert was used to everything by now. Besides, after a day's work, he might want time to himself. Ukyi Lhamo said OK, but she still forced him out of the kitchen.

—If you have nothing else to do, go to the supermarket. We are running low on a few things, Ukyi Lhamo said, her back to Wang Mojie as she closed the microwave door.

—Go into town now? Wang Mojie said in protest, as he didn't want to leave her side.

—If not now, when? When else are you going to have time?

He realised she was right and reluctantly agreed to go. But he still felt happy, which gave him plenty of energy for the bike ride into Lhasa. He might have taken a taxi, but it was a bit late in the evening and cabs on the outskirts of Lhasa were rare to begin with. He rode to the supermarket and got what they needed. He wasted no time, but the trip still took him almost two hours. Ukyi Lhamo had prepared an ample dinner, the cutlery gleamed against the red tablecloth, the plates were arranged neatly, and the napkins were white. Ukyi Lhamo had already been waiting for a while and so as they were putting Wang Mojie's purchases away, she told him to call Robert to dinner. Wang Mojie had felt a little put out earlier, and now he was feeling pleased with himself for having made the shopping run, and so in answer to Ukyi Lhamo he said the bike ride had left him all sweaty and that he would go to get Robert in a moment, after he had a drink of water. He went into the bathroom to wash and looked at himself in the mirror. His face had a healthy glow, as was natural, given he had just biked about a dozen kilometres. He came out of the bathroom, had a drink of water and headed for the door to get Robert.

—Hold on, Ukyi Lhamo said. Put them away.

—Put what away? Wang Mojie asked, not understanding.

—In the bathroom, Ukyi Lhamo said sternly.

It was hard to read the expression on her face, but Wang Mojie suddenly realised what she meant.

—Oh, those, I um, I just bought new ones, cotton. The others I can get rid of.

—So why are they still hanging there then? Throw them away.

—Why? Robert won't think they're mine.

—Throw them away!

—OK, OK.

Wang Mojie hurried into the bathroom, took the panties off the hanger and stuffed them into his pocket. He was going to put them in the wastepaper basket but decided to take them out to a public rubbish bin. He got a thrill out of the look on Ukyi Lhamo's face. He loved the way she sneered at him, and he loved it when she ordered him around. It made him feel good down to his bones.

Robert was at work; while in Tibet, he maintained the same focus and discipline that was his habit at his quiet home in the Alps. Robert was seventy-something. He had a surreal cloud of white hair, he had vitality and there was something transcendent about him, he lived life fully. Wang Mojie wondered if he could say the same of himself, and the thought left him feeling deeply shaken.

Wang Mojie gave Robert the package of coffee he had bought at the supermarket and told him to keep it a secret from Ukyi Lhamo. Robert promised he would. Wang Mojie told Robert he should cut down on coffee because of the altitude. Tibet isn't just high points, he said in a bantering tone, it's a high plane. Robert said he liked this insight, and he elaborated on it in the same bantering tone. Mont Blanc is 4,807 metres, he said, but living in the Alps you don't feel the lack of oxygen, because it is all high points, with no high plane. He asked Wang Mojie how he knew this. Wang Mojie said he had intuited it. But, he added, one finds the principle of relativity working within all phenomena.

—It was an intuitive deduction, then, but still very impressive, Robert said.

Robert liked Wang Mojie, and he returned to his idea of inviting Wang Mojie to come to France as a visiting scholar. He had mentioned this the day before and the day before that as well. As we get on in years, we tend to repeat ourselves, and even with his intellect, Robert was no exception. Robert believed Paris was the intellectual capital of the world, and he thought Wang Mojie needed experience in the global academic arena, most importantly he needed exposure to a broader community of contemporary scholars. Robert talked about all this with undiminished excitement right up until they sat down to eat. As always, Robert expressed delight at the bountiful spread and gave Ukyi Lhamo a hug, but this time it seemed a little perfunctory, his thoughts still on matters of the mind.

—Eastern asceticism has its value, of course, Robert said, referring to the way Wang Mojie lived his life in Tibet. It heightens awareness, clears your mind and is a path to wisdom, but it tends to make one intellectually conservative, it is not conducive to original thought. Intellectual history teaches us that a monastic life, a reclusive life, is not a precondition for philosophy, quite the contrary, having a philosophy is a precondition for living a monastic life. As myriad examples prove, the only worthwhile way to live as a recluse is to live as one in the middle of the clamour of the world. What I'm talking about is creative, independent thought that nevertheless bears the traces of an engagement with all sorts of competing ideas. Ukyi, I say, Mademoiselle Ukyi Lhamo, do you agree with me?

—You said the same thing yesterday, I believe, Ukyi Lhamo said in a friendly but exasperated tone.

—Oh? Really? I'm sorry. It's my age.

—It's not your age, it's the altitude. Everybody is like that when they first arrive, they forget what they've said. That's why I tell you to drink more tea.

—Am I that bad?

—You've been repeating yourself all day long.

—Have I, Wang?

—If Ukyi Lhamo says you have, you have. But that's OK, here in Tibet there's nothing wrong with repetition. Many phenomena in Tibet are reiterated. Each monastery is a reiteration of other monasteries, and of course, each image of the Buddha is a reiteration of other images. There is nothing wrong with reiteration. As for the altitude, I think my own adjustment is still ongoing, but I like the feeling. Go on with what you were saying. It's all right if the speaker repeats himself but doesn't notice, and if his listener doesn't notice either, then you have a unique and quite wonderful state of affairs.

—If the speaker doesn't notice, that's one thing, but if the listener doesn't notice, it's because he's feeble-minded, Ukyi Lhamo said, and Wang Mojie and Robert both laughed out loud.

—Ukyi Lhamo is half Tibetan, Wang Mojie said, so the altitude doesn't bother her. But Ukyi Lhamo, might you be a little too clear-headed? Sometimes seeing things too clearly just makes you suffer.

—It doesn't make me suffer. Being with you two is what makes me suffer.

—Both of us? Me too? Robert asked with mock surprise. He picked up his wine cup and touched it to Wang Mojie's.

Wang Mojie gestured to Robert that they should drain their wine cups in toast. Wang Mojie did so first, and Robert hesitated but followed suit to be polite. Robert was not accustomed to Chinese drinking etiquette, and he obviously did not understand why Wang

Mojie tonight was knocking back the wine after repeatedly saying he did not drink. Robert was puzzled and he asked Ukyi Lhamo about it.

—Gosh, he can hold his wine. I thought he said he doesn't drink.

—He'll be drunk soon, Ukyi Lhamo said and refilled Wang Mojie's cup.

—Really? Then don't give him any more.

—He wants to get drunk, Ukyi Lhamo said with a charming smile, and then she filled Robert's cup.

There seemed to be something unspoken going on between Wang Mojie and Ukyi Lhamo that left Robert in the dark. For all his genius, he couldn't quite figure out the nature of this tense and nuanced relationship between the two of them. Wang Mojie did want to get drunk, Ukyi Lhamo knew it as soon as they sat down. Wang Mojie usually had tea, but tonight after Ukyi Lhamo had poured red wine for Robert and herself, Wang Mojie held his cup out. Ukyi Lhamo said something to herself under her breath, and she seemed surprised. She filled his cup, they exchanged a look, and a trace of a smile crossed her lips, only for a second, but it flustered Wang Mojie. Had she smiled because she saw through him? Because she found him ridiculous? Because she had some secret? Or was it a smile that recognised the rapport between them? It was all of these things combined.

The wine relaxed Wang Mojie, everything shifted a little, and the world grew more accommodating. They made quick work of the bottle, and Wang Mojie surprised them by suggesting they open a second bottle. He wasn't at all drunk, he said, which proved he was drunk. Ukyi Lhamo opened another bottle and poured a cup for Wang Mojie. Wang Mojie seemed drunk, but he believed he was more sober than ever. He felt split in two, one of his two selves was watching the other, his inner self was watching his outer self reeling around. He watched himself make Robert clink cups with him, and he watched the three of them toast to the success of the conversation between Robert and his son, which had been even more successful than they had hoped, and toast to a safe trip home for Robert, who had mentioned his impending departure. He watched himself unsteadily clink cups with Robert again and once again. He thought his drunken behaviour seemed foolish. He was aware that he had just clinked cups with Robert, and this awareness made him think he was sober, but he wasn't sober enough to stop himself from doing it again. He watched himself as he stood up; he realised what his body was doing only after it did it. The connection between his body and mind had come apart, but it felt good, it relaxed him. He felt free, which was precisely what he had hoped for when he held his cup out to Ukyi Lhamo for his first drink.

The dinner lasted until late, and when they finished Robert took a shower in Ukyi Lhamo's bathroom. Wang Mojie was unsteady on his feet but insisted on helping Ukyi Lhamo clean up. He helped with the washing up and even flirted with her. Wang Mojie heard himself tell her that Robert was like their father. Robert was like Ukyi Lhamo's father and his father-in-law, they were like his daughter and son-in-law. This was the wine talking, of course. He heard himself tell her they had no children, they were DINKs, and he asked her if she knew what DINK meant.

When everything was cleaned up and put away, Robert went back to Wang Mojie's house. Then, as they did every evening, Wang Mojie and Ukyi Lhamo started on the day's transcription, going through it all and clearing up any remaining questions of translation. Wang Mojie was still drunk, his head lolled and his attention wandered, and as he watched Ukyi Lhamo working away like some machine, he felt an emotion well up that he couldn't name. She should have been exhausted, but she was a rock, there was no fatigue on her face, he didn't know where she got her strength, she was perfection, she was fabulous, literally.

Ukyi Lhamo was extraordinary, no mistake, with her big French-Chinese dictionary, listening carefully to the recording, assiduous, tireless, looking everything up, translating every last nuance, a real expert. Had he not been so captivated by Ukyi Lhamo and were he not holding out hope that something might yet happen, Wang Mojie would have passed out from all the wine. He was drunk but awake and excited. He moved slowly and unsteadily, he was well and truly drunk, but his mind was alert. He was thinking clearly and was just as able as usual to help Ukyi Lhamo with the translation of philosophical terminology. You could call both of them workaholics, they worked every day from morning until late at night, but this was also because they seemed to be caught by something that left them hanging between hope and dread, and work was their way of putting off whatever was going to happen next. When they had cleared up the last question, Ukyi Lhamo sighed and closed the dictionary.

—The way you are swaying around, I thought you were going to pass out. I'm amazed you were able to keep going. Your body is drunk but your head is sober. That's strange.

—It's not strange. It's because I'm with you of course. Were you hoping I would pass out?

—No, but I was worried you were going to, she said, with what resembled praise for his stamina.

She told Wang Mojie he could have the bathroom first. Wang Mojie was confused because each night after they finished, Ukyi Lhamo was always the first to shower. She told Wang Mojie it was a day of *upavasatha* and she had a ritual she must do. Wang Mojie asked what sort of day, and Ukyi Lhamo explained that it was a day of observance for Buddhists. Ordinarily it was OK if she had to miss a day of prayer, but on days of *upavasatha,* she could not. She told Wang Mojie to take his time in the shower, it would sober him up. Wang Mojie wanted to know more about days of observance, he asked if today had a special name, and he asked why he hadn't heard about it. Ukyi Lhamo said there were many such days but only Buddhists knew them, outsiders rarely did, and Wang Mojie wasn't a Buddhist.

—So tell me, I'll learn something, what day is today? What is today called?

The wine had made him talkative, and he wouldn't let it go, but Ukyi Lhamo had stopped paying attention to him. She turned and walked up to the colourful niche where she kept her image of the Buddha. She stood silently for a moment, then put her hands together, lowered her head and entered some private mental realm. Wang Mojie felt as if she had splashed his face with sobering cold water and much of the effect of the alcohol seemed to vanish. He knew she must have prayed in the morning before he had woken up, and he thought about her finishing her prayers and then going into the bathroom and seeing his women's underwear hanging there. What would that have done to whatever feeling her prayers had left her with? But then he wondered if maybe her practice was to first brush her teeth and wash her face and then pray. But why would it matter whether she saw his lace-waist panties before or after her prayers? All these disordered thoughts ran through Wang Mojie's mind as he showered. Drunk, even his internal monologue was verbose. The hot water seemed to make his thoughts fly faster and faster, the shower wasn't sobering him up, it was making him drunker. Had seeing his underwear cancelled whatever it was that Ukyi Lhamo got from prayer? Or had it confirmed for her what she took from prayer? Wang Mojie decided he had noticed things that indicated that it was the latter. But it could be the former, he said out loud to the showerhead.

Wang Mojie heard a knock on the bathroom door. It startled him, he hadn't expected Ukyi Lhamo to finish her prayers so quickly. He had been in there a long time but hadn't realised it. He dried himself and put on the pyjamas that had been hanging in the bathroom all day. Steam billowed out of the bathroom when he opened the door.

—Finally. You were in there long enough.

—Was I in there a long time? Wang Mojie asked, turning red.

—Were you in there a long time? I thought you'd drowned.

Ukyi Lhamo went into the bathroom. Feeling energetic, Wang Mojie walked up to the statue of the Buddha, he felt nothing. Had he not seen Ukyi Lhamo standing in the same place, he wouldn't have even glanced at the statue. He was not unfamiliar with Buddhist philosophy, but the idea of praying to a statue was completely foreign to him. He was certainly not about to put his hands together in prayer or bow or prostrate himself, not even for Ukyi Lhamo's sake. This did not mean he did not respect Buddhism, he did, but he showed his respect not by ritual behaviour but by taking Buddhist metaphysics seriously. He believed that no one needs religion but we all need the spiritual. We all need a feeling of awe and reverence before the mystery of existence. We don't need religion, we need faith. This wasn't Wang Mojie's idea, it was Kierkegaard's. Husserl, Nietzsche, Levinas, Alfred North Whitehead and even Einstein all had a similar belief. In other words, even people who reject metaphysics can't avoid sometimes asking the very questions that metaphysics asks. This is why Wang Mojie could accept – or at least not reject out of hand – Ukyi Lhamo's faith in Buddhism. He wondered if he was in her prayers that day. He tried to remember what deity was worshipped on the day. Palden Lhamo? He knew something about her, she was a wrathful protectress. He felt thirsty. He picked up the bowl of offering water from in front of the statue of the Buddha and drank out of it, just a mouthful at first. It was very refreshing, very nice, he needed it, so he drank all of it. He drank it with an affected expression of piety on his face, but it was a disrespectful thing to do, only a heretic would do such a thing. Any assertion of the existence of the supernatural always made Wang Mojie want to do something childish in response.

He walked away from the Buddha, dragged the camp bed out from underneath Ukyi Lhamo's bed and set it up. He made up the camp bed and spread out Ukyi Lhamo's quilt. The quilt cover was a clean white, like the white dots on her pyjamas, as white as a doctor's coat. Ukyi Lhamo always wore something with white on it after her shower, and she looked beautiful in the blue light of the night. Wang Mojie turned out the bright ceiling light, turned on the bedside lamp, picked up a book, lay down and flipped through it. Wang Mojie didn't read a single word. It was just his habit to pick up a book after getting in bed.

The sound of the shower stopped. The room was silent. He listened carefully for any noise coming from the bathroom and took in nothing from the book. He expected the bathroom door to open at any minute, and he stared at it and waited.

We might as well be on the same bed, Wang Mojie thought, his eyes on the bathroom door. He was thinking that he had touched her blue hand, and he was hoping that tonight would be like the night before. He trusted she would remain passive. They understood each other so well that he was certain she would do nothing to take the initiative. It had been nice. She was still, like marble. He needed that feeling that came over him like a sedative. He imagined the feel of her skin, its marble coolness, he needed that sensation of his fingers on skin as cool as marble. Only it could stop him from wanting pain, the prick of a needle, the drip of hot wax, the sting of a belt, the pressure of rope. Only it could stop him from wanting the pleasure given by the pain from all those filthy practices. His book was open, but he didn't see it, his eyes were on the bathroom door.

Ukyi Lhamo came out of the bathroom. White. Warmth. A white that made him tremble harder than the white of his imagination. The white went all the way through him. She was wearing blue pyjamas with white polka dots. The polka dots popped against the blue and traced the motion of her body under the pyjamas. Her neckline was low, and he could see the valley of her breasts, but the blue light on everything kept the feeling cool and serious. Wang Mojie noticed something else. When Ukyi Lhamo came out of the bathroom, something made her walk over to the niche with the image of the Buddha, which was odd. It was as if she somehow knew he had drunk the water. She reached the niche, stopped combing her hair and stood in silence for a moment, then she picked up the jug of water for offerings and filled the offering bowl. Wang Mojie waited for her reproach, he had a rejoinder ready, but she didn't say anything. She got in bed and worked on her wet hair, wringing it out in a towel and then combing it. When she was finished, she lay down to read.

—That offering water is pretty good, tastes sort of like marble, Wang Mojie said.

—It had been sitting there for a few days, Ukyi Lhamo said, her eyes on her book, not taking the bait.

—Yeah, but it's holy, Wang Mojie said.

—You still haven't sobered up?

—Why would I want to sober up?

—Don't think booze is going to solve your problems, that's foolish.

Wang Mojie had been put in his place, but it didn't dampen his mood. Then what is going to solve my problems? he thought. The bedside lamp was too bright, Wang Mojie was waiting for the moonlight. They lay in bed and read, as they had the night before. They were quiet, acting as if everything was normal. They were like an old married couple who knew that today was not a day for making love, so there was no hint of anything sexual from either of them. By habit, they would read for a while and then just fall asleep. Wang Mojie couldn't wait to turn the light out, he longed for yesterday, yesterday's moonlight, yesterday's night made of marble.

Wang Mojie, of course, would make the first move, but not quite yet. This moment of anticipation had to happen first. The two of them, not lovers, lying side by side reading, almost touching. A wonderful thing, it could go on forever. Wang Mojie was lost in his beautiful reverie about this world they had to themselves, just the two of them reading when he noticed that things had changed – Ukyi Lhamo was snoring softly. He turned and looked, the book was in her hands, but she was asleep. He felt like a spurned lover, like he had been yanked from a dream, but he also felt relieved, and he relaxed. He had been uneasy to a degree, nervous. Only when he felt his body relax did he realise he had been tense. He let out a long breath and turned out the bedside lamp.

Moonlight. Blue moonlight. It was nice. The whole room was blue. Wang Mojie gently took the book from Ukyi Lhamo's hands. He studied her face in the deep sea of moonlight, he looked at the book, and he looked at her pale hands. He felt relieved, and a very unfamiliar feeling of tenderness overtook him. A sleeping beauty was exactly the right woman for him, especially a sleeping beauty with a book in her hands. If she wasn't a gift from heaven, who could be? Wang Mojie looked at her for a long time, he couldn't look away. It could have been an illustration of something from a tale in *One Thousand and One Nights*: the two of them, Wang Mojie and Ukyi Lhamo, two people imprisoned at the bottom of the sea, a *dakini* and her consort surrounded by swaying blades of kelp and the stylised clouds that symbolise beneficent fortune as painted in *thangka*.

Taking her book was like picking up a ritual implement during an *abhiseka* rite, a rite of empowerment, performed in blue light, like picking up a bell or a *vajra* sceptre.

She didn't mean to fall asleep, he thought. She was still holding her book, but she was too tired, and she fell asleep.

He gently put the book down, he took her hand, but he recoiled and pulled back.

He tried again and this time kept his hand on hers, which was warm.

Her hand moved as if reaching out from her dream.

A nervous twitch in his back slowly went away.

He held her hand in his, their two hands slowly rose as if making a *mudra*.

He put both hands on her hand. He gathered his courage and started to caress her hand.

Then suddenly he heard her say she was too tired and wanted to sleep.

This confused him, he didn't understand.

He had felt her squeeze his hand while she was dreaming, but now that she was awake she was turning him down?

He didn't move away and went on caressing her. He didn't know if she had been awake or still asleep when she spoke.

She opened her eyes, she was awake.

They looked at each other. She sighed lightly.

He liked the sound of her sigh, it emboldened him.

He took her head in his hands and pulled her to him, slowly, a slow-motion film. Her eyes were beautiful but there was no desire in them, her eyes were alert, and there was no seduction in them at all. She looked at him dispassionately, if not coldly. Her detached gaze felt to him like the cool surface of marble. Was this love? Some sort of medical cure for him? Or, he wondered, some form of tantric sex of her creation? Did she have some power to control his thoughts? Was her falling asleep or her pretending to be asleep, a way to exert that power? That she had fallen asleep was quite clearly her way of preventing anything from happening between them, but then again it was precisely her passivity that had given him the courage to act. You could say it had given him agency. For years he had no agency in sex, but now in these extraordinary circumstances he had regained some, and he felt a new sense of agency over his need. It didn't matter if this was some sort of tantric practice of Ukyi Lhamo's or if she really was just cool towards him, the effect on him was the same.

He slowly pulled her tight. She said nothing, she made no sound, it was as if she wasn't there. He liked this. His sense of having agency grew stronger and more distinct. He could feel her breath, her hair was spread like kelp across the pillow, her arms were cool, and her face glowed like moonlight. He kissed her face, he kissed the moonlight on her face, she gently turned away but allowed him to kiss her cheek. She brushed his lips with hers and turned her neck to him. As his lips touched her neck, he grew aroused, he felt pulled to her. Her coolness to him, her initial rejection of him, was a challenge to his ego, and that stirred up his sense of agency, his sense of self, a common reaction to rejection. And this was exactly what he needed. She understood something deep within him, together they were the equal for any tantric practitioner and his consort embracing in *karma mudra*. The ancient Buddhist practice of tantric sex did indeed have lessons for the modern bedroom, Ukyi Lhamo was proof of that.

There was nothing simple about Ukyi Lhamo as either a believer in Buddhism or as a Tibetan returned home. She was biracial and bicultural, and although she didn't completely understand herself, although it was impossible to know what she might become (Wang Mojie was thinking this as he kissed her neck, it was a sickness with him, he could not stop thinking, no matter what else was going on, he was always thinking, even the last time he had sex with his ex-wife the police officer he had never stopped thinking the entire time), Ukyi Lhamo nevertheless had a great chance of finally finding herself one day.

Wang Mojie had got her long hair in disarray. He put his lips on the hair across her lips, her beautiful, barely lipsticked lips, but she turned away, she would not kiss him, she kept moving her lips away from his. This was seduction, she was goading him on. He suddenly pulled her to him and kissed her hard on the mouth. He was decisive, it was instinctive.

It had been years since he had kissed a woman's parted lips with such real desire. Her hair was in his mouth, then he felt her tongue in his mouth, he could feel her arms and legs suddenly wrapping around him tightly. He felt the heat of blind desire between her legs, he could smell the tang of her. At the same time, his hands found her bare breasts, which she had freed from her pyjama top, and this inflamed him all the more. He grew intensely excited, his body went rigid, his fists clenched, and his eyes bulged. He started to sweat, it ran down his back, his muscles twitched, and he spasmed uncontrollably. He sucked desperately at her breasts, he put his mouth on her nipple and immediately he felt a shock through his body as if he had been electrocuted, it knocked him back, but he didn't let her go, he rolled over and pulled her on top of him. He heard himself yelling in a crazed, warped voice.

—Hurry, hurry, Ukyi Lhamo, rape me, rape me, rape me!

Despite Wang Mojie's utter loss of control, Ukyi Lhamo remained calm. Her hair fell over his face, which was contorted as he yelled. She remained still.

—Now, Ukyi Lhamo, rape me now, rape me now!

—You drank all that wine for nothing, she said as she looked down at him through her hair. She glanced at his erection, it was covered in purple scars, the scars vivid on his erect penis, like a pattern on a snake's skin.

—It's good, Ukyi Lhamo, just a different position, you on top, come on!

—No, she said. Raping someone is not something I ever want to do.

—It doesn't mean anything, it's just a word, come on, Ukyi Lhamo!

—Listen to me, Wang Mojie, she said as she pulled her hair back from her eyes, don't force yourself to do what you really don't want to do, don't ever do that.

—I'm not. I can tell you need it, come on, Ukyi Lhamo!

—It was not a real need, it was a mistake, she said. She was very calm and cool.

After she said this, she pushed Wang Mojie's hands, which were still shaking hard, away from her, climbed off Wang Mojie's body and walked straight to the bathroom. She was in there a very long time, forty-five minutes if not an hour. Then Wang Mojie heard the shower running. By this time, Wang Mojie had calmed down. He lay naked on Ukyi Lhamo's bed, and the sound of the shower told him he should put on his pyjamas and go back to his bed. When she came out of the bathroom, he was flipping through a book.

—I probably should shower too, huh, what do you think? Wang Mojie said, making a joke at his own expense, but Ukyi Lhamo didn't react.

—I'm sorry, let's go to sleep, she said flatly as she dried her hair with a towel. She lay down, her back to Wang Mojie.

—I never thought you'd have a problem with it. The woman can be on top, you know that.

—Stop making me want to throw up, OK?

—Let me just say that despite everything, I'm grateful to you.

—Go to sleep.

—Yes, time to sleep.

34. No, No!

Night. Blue light at night. Like the other nights,
like something out of One Thousand and One Nights.
Like two people imprisoned at the bottom of the sea. Like an illustration.
Practitioners of the tantric arts. Clouds of beneficent fortune. Blades of kelp.
Ukyi Lhamo was blue too. Her arms were blue, her face was blue, even her gaze.
Slowly but resolutely, he reached out and felt for her blue hand.

The discussion between father and son was far from over, but the time for Robert's flight home was upon them, and he was to leave the next day. As the day for him to return to France had approached, Robert increasingly regretted not giving himself more time in Lhasa when he booked his flight. It was his last evening in Tibet, but they were all as engrossed as ever in the discussion, and they could have talked on forever. You would have never known that Robert was to get on a plane the next day and fly halfway around the world. Ukyi Lhamo kept telling him that it was late and they should be getting back, but Robert always had more he wanted to say and would not be rushed. Finally, Ukyi Lhamo got up to leave. She said she was going back to her house to start preparing their "last supper", but Robert wouldn't let her go. He said he didn't want her to cook, he wanted to take her, Wang Mojie and Ma Dingge out to dinner at the Everest Hotel. He said it would serve as his thank you to them. It was appropriate that he do this, of course, but the thought had occurred to him only because it was a way for him to prolong the day's conversation with Ma Dingge. He had said nothing about going out to eat when they all had agreed earlier that they would share a last supper at Ukyi Lhamo's. Wang Mojie accepted the invitation immediately, and because he was every bit as wrapped up in the conversation as Robert was and wanted it to continue, he almost blurted out, That's perfect! None of the three men were in any hurry to end things, and Ukyi Lhamo simply had to go along and give up on the idea of cooking. It was a little cruel of the men to simply call it off because Ma Dingge, her guru, was going to come down from the monastery and eat at her house, and therefore she had everything planned meticulously.

Robert and Ma Dingge went on with their discussion until the sky was full of stars. The four of them left the monastery together and walked across the moonlight down to the main road. It took a long time before they were able to hail a taxi but once they did, they were quickly delivered to the Everest Hotel. They ate in the hotel's Western restaurant, which Robert was very familiar with. Their dinner was simple, but the occasion still felt grand. The men all expressed their thanks to Ukyi Lhamo, but she didn't seem happy. Had she been able to put on her "last supper" perhaps it might have been different, but it was hard to say. Even Ma Dingge noticed that Ukyi Lhamo wasn't quite herself. Ma Dingge toasted her with his bottled water, and she held up her glass to him with both hands in a gesture of respect and reverence. Ma Dingge asked Ukyi Lhamo if she was feeling all right, or if the last few days had been too exhausting. She admitted she was a little tired but said it was nothing and told him not to worry, then she drained her glass of wine in a toast to him. Robert was the next to toast Ukyi Lhamo, his head of white hair, heavily lined face and sonorous speaking voice added a certain gravitas and sincerity to what he said in praise of Ukyi Lhamo. He said he hoped to see her in Paris one day, and then he drank to her. Ukyi Lhamo, who did not lift her glass to Robert, asked Robert if Wang Mojie might now be said to be his student. Robert's keen eyes opened wide, and he turned the question to Wang Mojie, who raised his glass and said he had been Robert's student ever since the day they met. He had been Robert's student even before then, Wang Mojie said, because he had read Robert's books in translation years ago. He said that there was a saying in Chinese to the effect that one can be the disciple of a master without ever having taken lessons from that master himself. The saying came from Mencius, who considered himself a disciple of Confucius even though he never knew him. In other words, reading a man's books, one comes to admire the man who wrote them, and one takes that man as one's teacher. Robert gave Wang Mojie a hug and raised his glass to him, then he put his arm around Ukyi Lhamo, and the three of them drank a toast to one another.

The dinner didn't last long, it was intended primarily just to mark the occasion and give Robert a chance to express his thanks, as he had to leave early the next day. The four of them walked out of the hotel together, Ukyi Lhamo said she was going to look in on her mother, she apologised to Ma Dingge for not accompanying him any farther, and she told Wang Mojie to be sure to see Ma Dingge back to Drepung before he went home himself. That went without saying, Wang Mojie thought, sensing something he couldn't quite put his finger on. As she turned to go, he asked her if she was coming back to campus that night, it wasn't a frivolous question. She didn't answer at first, she was quiet for a moment, then she said, Of course.

It was a quick trip by taxi back to Drepung. Wang Mojie, Ma Dingge and Robert got out of the car. Ma Dingge and his father said their goodbyes there by the steps to the monastery gate, as Ma Dingge would not be coming to the airport in the morning. They didn't hug, they never did. Ma Dingge presented his father with a *khata*, he put it around his father's neck, gave his father a blessing and wished him peace.

When they got back to the school grounds, Robert and Wang Mojie sat in Wang Mojie's house and talked over a cup of tea, then Wang Mojie helped Robert pack. Robert gave Wang Mojie an astute summary of what he learned during the trip. He talked about the aspects of Buddhism that made it unique among the world's religions, he talked about how Buddhist wisdom was an inspiration to many in the West, but he also spoke of the limitations of Buddhist metaphysics. Robert reminded Wang Mojie that a way of life is an expression of a philosophy. He said that a contemplative life was a valuable life, contemplation ensures that one's thinking is clear, but one should not live for too long in isolated contemplation because if we are cut off from the exchange of ideas, our thinking can become ossified. It is good to be the custodian of a civilisation, he said, it is good to pass on the culture one has inherited, but there is a great need for people who have new ideas and who create new things and who therefore help civilisation advance. Wang Mojie understood what Robert was getting at, and he offered his own thoughts on the matter, but his attention wasn't fully on what they were saying. He was wondering if the next day, with Robert gone, he would be moving back into his house. The house seemed unfamiliar to him now, it seemed to belong to Robert, and with all the books it could have been Robert's home. If I am moving back here tomorrow, he thought, that means tonight is the last night, the last chance. He had a choice to make. Since the disaster of that one night, he had been feeling very at peace, and the coming of each night had held no particular significance for him any more, it just meant the day's work was done and it was time for them to read in bed before sleep. Ukyi Lhamo always fell asleep first and quite quickly, the only change was that now she kept her back to him. He knew that by keeping her back to him, which he couldn't believe she was doing, she was making a statement.

When Robert was packed, Wang Mojie said good night and went back to Ukyi Lhamo's. Or was this back to his new home? He was used to it now. He looked at everything in her house, everything, the niche for the Buddha, the way the windows were decorated in the Tibetan way, the *thangka*, but as he studied the room he realised it contained things he hadn't noticed before. He wondered if he should try to commit it all to memory. He washed, brushed his teeth and got into his camp bed. Ukyi Lhamo was not back yet. He lay on his back, hands behind his head, his body still. No matter what, he thought, I should try again, even to just let her know I'm thinking about it, at least I will have tried. This was their last night, it grew very late, Ukyi Lhamo had not returned, and Wang Mojie began to think she wasn't coming back. That was possible. It wouldn't be hard for her to find some excuse to stay the night at her mother's and then take a taxi in the morning to come over to say goodbye to Robert. But a while later Wang Mojie changed his mind because if she wasn't coming back she would call, and she hadn't called, which meant she was probably on the way, and of course, the later she got back the better because he felt anxious, and when you are anxious you want everything to be delayed.

He was right, she came back. She looked happy, and she explained why she was late. She wanted to get a farewell gift for Robert but couldn't decide what to give him, so it took her a long time. She didn't need to explain but the fact that she wanted to seemed somehow significant to Wang Mojie. She showed him her gift for Robert, saying it was virtually impossible to find a gift that was uniquely Tibetan but not religious. Wang Mojie was trying to figure out what sort of mood Ukyi Lhamo was in, and he was thinking about it as he took a look at what she had got for Robert. Wang Mojie's attention was always directed in two or more directions at once. He told her to turn on more lights so he could have a good look, making a show of being interested in the gift. Fussing over some little thing is a good way to distract yourself when you are feeling anxious and uneasy, which were the emotions Wang Mojie was experiencing because it was their last night.

The gift was a small piece of fabric, nothing costly but woven by hand. And most importantly it was a piece of fabric woven by the hand of Ukyi Lhamo's mother. Wang Mojie said that the fabric was going to be the thing that gave Robert a connection to the secret history of Tibet. Ukyi Lhamo's mother carried with her a part of Tibet's history that very few people knew about. Fabric woven by her hand had true historical significance. Wang Mojie told Ukyi Lhamo he would make sure Robert understood this and would suggest that Robert hang the fabric in his house in the Alps. Wang Mojie was confident that Robert's visit had given him an affection for Tibet.

—Hey, can we say it's from both of us? I didn't get him anything, Wang Mojie said beseechingly.

—It isn't something I bought. How can we possibly claim it's from both of us? Ukyi Lhamo said, but she still looked and sounded happy.

—It wasn't purchased, true, but that doesn't mean it can't be presented to him as an expression of our mutual good wishes for his continued health and well-being.

—You give it to him, you tell him what it expresses. I wouldn't know what to say.

—OK, give it to me, Wang Mojie said and took the fabric from Ukyi Lhamo.

Ukyi Lhamo went into the bathroom and showered. She got into bed, and they talked about their general impression of the conversation between Ma Dingge and his father. Ukyi Lhamo put her hands behind her head. She said she had disliked the old man at first but slowly had come to find him quite agreeable, and she had grown fond of his old, deeply lined face. Wang Mojie said Robert had a strong personality and was a sceptic but wasn't closed-minded. He explained that in philosophy "scepticism" meant something other than what is ordinarily meant by the word. In philosophy, scepticism is a way of thinking about things. They lay there talking as if everything was normal. But things only seemed normal, they weren't of course. They had to think about the next day. Was their cohabitation to end? They needed to talk about it, but neither wanted to broach the subject. They were avoiding something, pretending it didn't matter, which is not what Wang Mojie had hoped would happen, but he too was doing all he could to avoid discussing the very thing he knew they had to discuss. People are like that, there are circumstances in which what we say is not what we want to say and what we do is not what we want to do, and we find ourselves racing in a direction that is exactly opposite of where we want to be going. We are good at hiding what we feel with pretence. Their conversation trailed off, and they picked up their books. There in the glow of the bedside lamp, the atmosphere in the room, right up to the ceiling, grew charged with something just a bit different from the feeling on previous nights. Ukyi Lhamo put her book down but didn't turn her back to Wang Mojie. Wang Mojie heard her put the book down, and he put his book down too. He asked her if he should turn out the light, but the answer was obvious. He turned off the light. Darkness enveloped everything, and the day had come to its conclusion.

He waited for her to turn her back to him. But she did not. They lay side by side. It was night, a night that was slowly turning blue, like all the other nights. Like something out of *One Thousand and One Nights*. They were like two people imprisoned at the bottom of the sea. It was like an illustration in a book. They were like practitioners of the tantric arts, surrounded by clouds of beneficent fortune and waving blades of kelp. Ukyi Lhamo was as blue as the night. Her arms were blue, her face was blue, and he imagined that her eyes were emitting blue light. Slowly but resolutely, he reached out and felt for her blue hand, but as he did, she spoke.

—No, no, Wang Mojie! she said firmly, with no hesitancy at all in her voice.

Wang Mojie's hand stopped, but he didn't draw it back right away, it was suspended in midair. After a moment he lowered it, but his hand did not find hers. He didn't know where her hand was, he heard her speak again.

—I don't know if I owe you an apology or not, Wang Mojie. This is hard for me to say, but I need to say it. When we were leaving the restaurant, you asked me if I was coming back here only because you knew I might not. You're sensitive and so you know as well as I do that even though we haven't said it, it's over, it's finished. We've just been going through the motions for the last two days. To be honest, I didn't plan to come back tonight, but when you asked me, I couldn't say no. At my mother's house, I thought for a long time about calling you to say I wasn't coming back tonight and that I'd come over first thing in the morning, but in the end I decided to come back. I decided I wanted to say this to your face. Sorry, I need a cigarette.

She got out of bed, found her cigarettes, lit one and inhaled deeply.

—Since I did come back, there are some things I have to say. I want to be honest. I can't stand you any more. You said to me, "Rape me." That's sickening. When you said that, it made me realise how completely shattered you are, I can't think of you in any other way now, that is you. It wasn't about who is on top, who cares about that? I'm never going to be able to forget what you said, it left too deep an impression. I'd rather think about you licking Yu Youyan's high heels or barking like a dog, that's easier for me to accept. It's disgusting what you said. Why did you say it? I wouldn't have known what you were thinking. I like being on top. But you just had to say it, yes? You had to say it, didn't you? You had to say it!

—Yes, I must say it, and I have to say it out loud. I have to yell it.

—It didn't even sound like you. I thought I could change you, I was confident I could. You've noticed that I've changed, and you might think I changed for Robert's sake, but actually I changed for you. I changed myself completely, changed who I am during the day, changed who I am at night, changed in body and soul. Every single moment I've been acting as if I could do anything at all. You are very sensitive, and there is danger there, I've experienced it, and it made me realise that there are things I cannot do. Because of you, I kept changing myself, I made myself as cold and unfeeling as marble. That was a new me, a new me I didn't even recognise. I've realised that I did it for your sake, everything was about you, it was all about your feelings, and it made me lose myself. I don't think any flesh and blood person can turn to stone like I was trying to do. I was cold and distant like that because you wanted me to be or you hinted that you did, but that way our physical relationship became entirely mechanical. If sex is just mechanical, then not only is there no love in it, there isn't even any real desire in it, and so it was just mechanical between us, it was like I was supposed to be some sort of automaton sex doctor for you.

Ukyi Lhamo said all this slowly, pausing to draw on her cigarette, a look of concern for Wang Mojie on her face.

—You're so afraid of being touched, it's like you'll break in half if somebody touches you. You know what you're like? Like some invertebrate, nothing but exposed, overly sensitive nerve endings. You've made me just as sensitive, just as fearful of things, and I've discovered that in trying to save you, I lost myself. I stopped feeling human, I felt like an object, like a stethoscope, an ultrasound machine, a spectrograph. But fine, I could put up with that, I was willing to wait, but I never expected you would say something so sickening. I've never before felt that combination of being both sickened and afraid, but because of you, now I have.

—A person shouldn't show his real self to anybody else, you know that, Wang Mojie said. But you've forced me to show you my real self.

And you're right, there are definitely things you cannot do. Surprisingly enough, I have come to believe in something, in the religious sense.

—What do you believe?

—I believe that you're like Tara or a "wisdom consort".

—You are so ridiculous.

—I am indeed.

—I saw who you really are, but I just didn't believe it at the time, Ukyi Lhamo said.

—You mean when I was with Yu Youyan?

—Yes, I saw some of the real you then.

—That was just me acting out my true self. When a truth is expressed through a performance, that truth is deconstructed, which is why even though you saw it with your own eyes, you didn't believe what you were seeing.

—When you say, "rape me", is that acting?

—If only it were.

—I don't understand.

—Listen, with me and you everything is too real, too sincere, too earnest, and there is too much faith in something. It wasn't that way at all when I was with Yu Youyan. It wasn't real. The truth is always destructive, and when we confront the truth, it's unbearable, it's painful. The truth cannot be expressed with the language of truth. If we can't keep the truth hidden, the next best thing to do is express it through performance.

—You are utterly inhuman.

—That is so, Wang Mojie said.

—You have something in you, something really powerful. It's like a black hole. Nothing can resist it. It's more powerful than any faith or any religion. It will destroy everything, and I think it's destroyed the things I believed in.

—Don't say that. I was sort of counting on you, Wang Mojie said.

—Counting on me for what?

—As you know, I don't believe in any religion, but sometimes I can't stop myself from daydreaming about a variety of mystical things. For example, every time I think about you, I end up deciding that you are like a Tibetan Buddhist *inana mudra*: you are my meditational deity. I had imagined that our "cohabitation" might turn into our own "double practice", which I thought might change me. That's what I had been counting on you for...

—Don't profane Tantric Buddhism. I think it's best you don't discuss religion with me.

—OK, let's talk about that black hole then, let's talk about that pitiless black hole. That was interesting what you said, and you are exactly right. For years it's been like I've had a black hole in me. It's part of me, I wouldn't say I was born with it, but it's been in me a long time. Whether I like it or not, I always have it in me, and in some sense, it is who I am. I want to get rid of it, but I'm afraid to because I don't know what I would be like without it. I might not be myself any more. I think we're all right now. You've found yourself again, and I don't have to worry about losing anything.

—You are so cold-blooded, beyond what I'd imagined. There's no hope for you, you are truly cold-blooded.

—Colder than cold-blooded, maybe. I can be cold as ice, if I want.

—I never want to see you again, if I can help it, starting now.

—Starting now would be quite tricky. You'll have to tough it out for a few hours, OK?

—Do me a favour and go into the bathroom, all right? Or would you rather I go?

—I'll go, that would be best. I am very sorry, Wang Mojie said.

He sat up and got off the bed without hesitating. He went into the bathroom and shut the door tightly. He stood there for a while, then sat down on the toilet, opened the book he had brought with him and started to read. Now and again he looked up from the book, lost in memories. It took him a long time to grow sleepy. He finally fell asleep sitting on the toilet as the sky was starting to grow light.

35. Travelling through the Same Space

He was lonely, no doubt about it. Next to that palette of colour,
his hue in contrast became the colour of solitude.
But this sort of loneliness is normal, even elemental.
It is when we come closest to knowing who we are.

The riverside. The airport. The clouds. The coffee shop. After they said goodbye to Robert, Wang Mojie asked Ukyi Lhamo to join him for a cup of coffee. Through the airport coffee shop window, they could see Robert's plane. The last of the passengers were boarding. They were looking out of the window, waiting for the plane to depart. The terminal was mostly glass. It was beside the broad, slowly moving waters of the Yarlung Tsangpo, and planes seemed to come and go from the surface of the river. There was no need for them to wait for the plane to take off, they just needed the coffee. Before he left, Robert had given them some money in US dollars. This was a matter of form, but it was absurd because when Robert gave it to them, his manner made it clear he was still assuming that Ukyi Lhamo and Wang Mojie, obviously so awkward together, were a couple, were lovers. It also made it seem that the entire visit had come down to an exchange of money.

—Let's split the money, Wang Mojie said as Robert's plane took off.

—You keep it, it's rent, Ukyi Lhamo said with a forced smile.

—You cooked, and you were his translator, and you also... I'll take one third of it.

—And I also what?

—Um, something else I can't put a price on.

Ukyi Lhamo drank what was left of her coffee, stood up and left. Wang Mojie paid and hurried after her. He caught up just in time to get into the taxi with her. When they got back to the school, they divided up the things they had acquired while they were "cohabitating". They didn't quarrel, as neither really wanted any of it. Wang Mojie gathered the things he was taking and was about to leave. He said he was like a prisoner who had served his time and was ready for release, but the joke fell flat. It was a Monday, and they both had early lessons, but they delayed them. They should have started preparing the lessons as soon as they got back from the airport and let other things wait, but each was impatient to get away from the other. They headed off to the school. Everything was back to how it had been, yet nothing was the same.

They seldom saw each other. Although they were faculty colleagues and neighbours, they rarely crossed paths under normal circumstances as it was, and so even the slightest effort to avoid each other meant they were unlikely to meet. Wang Mojie didn't notice at first that Ukyi Lhamo was avoiding him. Each time he realised he had not seen her for a couple of weeks, he made a point of sitting by his open front door waiting for her. When Ukyi Lhamo left the school and walked home across the playground to her house, he could see her, and she could not help but see him. She never said hello, but Wang Mojie always said a casual hello to her and made a comment about how she looked or what she was wearing. He never said anything of substance, and eventually Ukyi Lhamo started to walk right by him. She went straight to her house, unlocked the door and went in, without waiting for Wang Mojie to finish whatever he was saying.

Summer came. The campus emptied and fell silent. Ukyi Lhamo moved back to Lhasa.

Wang Mojie didn't know if Ukyi Lhamo had taken her mother to Dromo. They had once planned that Wang Mojie would make the trip with mother and daughter, but after everything that had happened, Ukyi Lhamo never brought it up again. One afternoon, Wang Mojie went for a stroll outside the village and saw Ukyi Lhamo walk out of the woods below Drepung. For that one instant when she first emerged from the woods, it was like seeing something in a dream. Someone once said that there is always something dreamy about a woman walking among trees. In any case, had it been a man walking out of the woods, it wouldn't have been the same at all. Wang Mojie didn't walk towards Ukyi Lhamo, instead he stood and waited for her by a crossroads that she had to pass on her way down the path back to the village. As she walked by, Wang Mojie suddenly stepped out from behind a wall, startling her. But she immediately regained her poise. There was a sense of spiritual tranquillity about her, perhaps because she was wearing a long Tibetan skirt and perhaps because she had just been to see her guru Ma Dingge. A few months had gone by and so some things were starting to fade into the past, and Ukyi Lhamo was largely unaffected by encountering Wang Mojie. He, however, couldn't entirely read Ukyi Lhamo, and when he spoke to ask her if she had been to Dromo, the question came out with his habitual aggressive tone.

—Hey, I haven't seen you in a long time. I assumed you'd left for Dromo. Did you?

—No, she said. Her tone was plain, simple, honest, just like the grey Tibetan skirt she was wearing.

—Have you forgotten that you invited me to go with you? I haven't forgotten. Do you still plan to go and find your grandmother?

—Of course I do, she said, raising her voice, her composure deserting her.

—I am still volunteering my services. I believe I once promised to accompany you and your mother on your trip to Dromo.

—No thanks. You aren't needed.

—Well, will your mother still be willing to go if I don't go?

—Wang Mo! Who do you think you are? You are so full of yourself!

Not only had Ukyi Lhamo's composure deserted her, but now she was about to lose control completely. What she was wearing wasn't going to keep her calm now.

—Get out of my life, just thinking about you makes me sick! Ukyi Lhamo said with venom.

—I would love to go on a trip with your mother. I really miss her.

—I'm realising that you're not just sick in the body, you're sick in the head.

This was a cruel thing to say, but it didn't bother Wang Mojie, he ignored it and stuck to what he was talking about.

—I'd like to call on your mother one day soon and have another talk with her.

—Go and talk to them! Ukyi Lhamo said as she pointed at the vultures circling in the sky. Say what you have to say to them!

Ukyi Lhamo seemed to be forgetting that the vultures were regarded as emissaries of heaven, she was taking them as nothing but symbols of death. She walked away briskly, disappearing down the crooked alleys of the village. Wang Mojie stood stock still for a long time after she was gone. The sun was hot, the village was quiet, the dogs were sleeping in the shadows of the walls, the tractors were like objects in a still life, the stacks of yak dung seemed ready to combust. It was the eternal, unchanging village. He was aware that he was standing out against the village in the background, particles of sunlight covering his body. Once again, he thought about Seurat, and he thought about himself.

Ukyi Lhamo left for Dromo. She had no obligation to tell Wang Mojie she was going, of course, but that she chose to set out on her trip from her house at the school rather than from Lhasa certainly seemed to be meant for him to see. Early one morning a big SUV came roaring onto the quiet summertime campus. Wang Mojie was out in the sun doing something in his garden, and he watched as Ukyi Lhamo, her mountain climbing friend and her mother got out of the car and went into her house. A short while later, Wang Mojie was surprised to see that the man he thought was the mountaineer was not, and it wasn't his SUV either. He looked again, she had a new driver. He was a handsome younger fellow with a very nice complexion. He didn't look like somebody who was used to being behind the wheel of an SUV. He was a pretty boy, far less impressive than Ukyi Lhamo's mountaineer.

Wang Mojie filled a bag with cucumbers and tomatoes for Ukyi Lhamo's mother, something for her to eat on the trip. When the SUV started up again with a roar and did a U-turn in front of the garden, Wang Mojie waved it to a stop. The driver rolled down his window, but Wang Mojie ignored both him and Ukyi Lhamo, who was in the front passenger seat. He reached for the handle on the back door, opened it and handed the bag of vegetables to Ukyi Lhamo's mother, Mrs Ukyi Lhamo. She didn't say anything, but she put her palms together in a gesture of gratitude and accepted the bag. She didn't invite Wang Mojie to join them on the trip. Clearly she didn't feel in a position to do so. Wang Mojie told Mrs Ukyi Lhamo that he wished her nothing but good fortune and that he wished the same for her mother, Madame Ukyi Lhamo. Again she put her hands together and bowed in gratitude.

Three days later Wang Mojie sat studying a map of Tibet. He was preparing for a trip to Dromo, but he hadn't imagined that it could be so far away. He read that Dromo was in the southern foothills of the Himalayas, the area was thickly forested, and the weather was temperate all year round. From the map, Wang Mojie saw that Dromo was close to Gangtok, the capital of Sikkim. It didn't look all that far from the Bay of Bengal and the Indian Ocean. Wang Mojie wasn't the travelling sort, and though he had spent a long time in Tibet, he never went anywhere, so to him, Tibet was the school, the village, a stretch of the Lhasa River and Drepung Monastery. If he had spent more time in the city of Lhasa, then he would have known what everybody else knew, that you could go to any hostel and find travelling companions with whom you could hire a car and head out together for the places your group wanted to visit. That is not what Wang Mojie did. He went the old-fashioned way: he took a long-distance bus.

Early in the morning, Wang Mojie went into the city to the long-distance bus station. He had learned that the trip to Dromo took four days and three nights, and there were no bunks on the bus, just old-fashioned hard seats. Passengers spent the three nights in roadside inns along the way. He sat in the waiting room, and at the stroke of eight o'clock, the few passengers making the trip started to board. Half an hour later, the bus slowly pulled out of the terminal. It was half empty, and Wang Mojie guessed that the empty seats were reserved for passengers who would get on at stops along the way. It was a battered old bus that had travelled Tibet's mountain roads for many years. It was certainly different from the sort of buses used by up-market travel agencies or hired by work units for group outings. The passengers were all ordinary Tibetan folk. Inside the bus, it was very bright and colourful, with all sorts of fragrances. People were eating a variety of snacks and had with them all manner of goods. It was like a genre painting, a painting of everyday life. Not everybody was wearing Tibetan clothing, some were in leather jackets or military green, but the ornaments in their hair and the hue of their skin marked them as people of the high plateau.

When we claim we belong to the everyday people, when we say we belong to the ordinary folk, what do we mean? Who are the folk? Wang Mojie was finally realising that you have to take a long-distance bus if you really want to be among the ordinary folk. They are set in their ways but always on the move. Wang Mojie was definitely the most unusual passenger on the bus, and he wasn't even a regular passenger, he was the sole tourist. It took him a while to adjust to the smell of butter tea and milk-skin cheese (eventually it didn't bother him at all), but apart from this he was comfortable, and he rather liked being the only tourist on the entire bus.

A tourist is an outsider. He was lonely, no doubt about it, because he was an outsider. He wasn't part of the genre painting, not one of its colours, and as a bystander next to that palette of colour, his hue in contrast became the colour of solitude. But it is when we are lonely that we come closest to knowing who we are. Besides, all that mattered was that he could think about what Ukyi Lhamo might be doing up ahead of him on the same trip. He looked out of the window at the landscape that Ukyi Lhamo had looked at just a few days before. Everything she had seen, he could see. The road ahead. The endless road. All roads are the same road. Ukyi Lhamo was ahead of him. It could be a primary school maths problem: if Wang Mojie is behind Ukyi Lhamo and travelling slower than her, can he catch her up? If so, how long will it take? The answer, of course, is no, he can never catch up. But they were heading for the same final destination, at which they would both stop their travelling, and she would stop first, which meant he could catch her up. Primary school maths didn't take that into account. He thought about the difference between his bus and her SUV. It was better to be in the bus. The SUV was too new, an interloper, and out of harmony with the natural environment, it was alien. The bus was for the masses, for the ordinary folk, it blended right in with the rest of the scenery on the plateau and was a natural part of it. Nothing mechanical seemed native to the plateau, except for something as old fashioned as the bus, the rest all seemed alien. Wang Mojie was an alien presence on the bus, but he was the sole alien among many natives on the bus, so it was OK, he mused.

The bus made its way along the Lhasa River, it passed Drepung Monastery, the school, the cement factory and the bridge over the Yarlung Tsangpo in Chushur County, where the Lhasa River disappeared into the Yarlung Tsangpo. On the far side of the broad Yarlung Tsangpo, Gambala Mountain soared into the clouds, the mountain seemed to rise straight up, and it seemed incredible that somehow there was a road that wound up its sheer face. The bus followed the other vehicles up, all seemingly clinging to the mountainside, committed to the climb but looking in danger of falling off at any time.

From the map and from what Ukyi Lhamo had said, Wang Mojie knew that up in the clouds on top of Gambala was Yamdrok Lake, one of Tibet's four sacred lakes. Ukyi Lhamo said that near the lake was a town called Nangartse, one of the highest towns in Tibet. Wang Mojie knew that the bus would stop at Nangartse for the first night, but he didn't have to stay at the roadside inn booked for him with his ticket, he was free to stay elsewhere, he just had to be back on the bus on time in the morning. The inns used by long-distance buses are cheap and uncomfortable, and while Wang Mojie was happy to be one with the people on the bus, he was not ready to be one with the people in a roadside inn. When he bought his ticket, he had asked a lot of questions about all the details of the trip, including specifics about the food and lodging. He didn't have any experience as a traveller, but he was meticulous in everything he did, in his philosophical research and in everything else too. Wang Mojie had another reason for not wanting to stay in the inn booked with his ticket, he was looking for signs of where Ukyi Lhamo had been before him.

The road was endless. It wound up and up. He had never seen a road like it. Everything was unfamiliar to him, the landscape was, and the people were. He had no companion, he went all day without speaking a word to anybody. It wasn't anything he couldn't adjust to, but looking out at the sheer mountainsides weighed Wang Mojie down with a feeling of despairing loneliness, especially when he looked down. The Yarlung Tsangpo looked ever deeper, ever broader, and layers of clouds were reflected on the water, a sky on the earth. It was dizzying if you looked down too long, it made Wang Mojie's heart catch in his throat. In the end, he couldn't look any more, and he just shut his eyes.

There is no need for an intellectual, a philosopher for example, to be fond of travel. He never has to leave home if he doesn't want to, but to be a novelist you have to love to travel. A novelist travels the same way he works out a plot, he goes wherever his imagination and his fancy take him. Many of my novels first took shape as I was staring out of a car or train window at the landscape going by. I have been to many places in Tibet, up and over Gambala Mountain three times, twice in summer and once in winter. From Lhasa through Chushur County to Gambala Mountain is one of the most magical, beautiful trips in Tibet. The blue Lhasa River flows into the Yarlung Tsangpo and three big mountain ranges come together. The Himalayas, the Kailash Range and the Nyenchen Tanglha Mountains all start here, or all end here, depending on your perspective. Gambala is the main peak in the area, and it rises to the clouds, the three ranges clustered around it. Gambala raises a glass to the heavens, raises it high, and the wine in the glass is Yamdrok Lake. The water is clear to the bottom and seems part of the sky above. I have been in the mountains many times, through their mists, among their clouds, and I have stood above the clouds with the peaks, feeling freed from the world as I took in the expansive skies of Tibet. I have seen the dark blue water of Yamdrok Lake. It looks like a sea, and you almost expect the rise and fall of tides. They say that when the mountains rose, Yamdrok Lake was left when the rest of the Tethys Sea receded. The herdsmen on their horses could be the most ancient of men riding towards that ancient sea. From a distance, the black yaks and white sheep look like pieces on a chess board, paused in an endless game. The herdsmen are the chess masters, unrivalled champions who live in seclusion, forever going where they will, when they will, like clouds or flowing water. And if you come across a herdsman and you and he exchange a glance, you will suddenly feel as if you have been carried away down a vast flow of water. You feel lifted, you feel yourself float, you feel light as a feather, as if you could take flight.

Wang Mojie had unreserved high praise for my description of Gambala Mountain. He and I were very different, but in some ways we were quite alike, and that was entirely because of Tibet. I knew Wang Mojie well, and he knew me well. Me, Wang Mojie, Ukyi Lhamo, the three of us, as well as the dear, dead mathematician-poet, and Ukyi Lhamo's mountaineer, and sweet Yu Youyan, all of us, we all had Tibet in common. We all identified with a line by our predecessor in Tibet, the poet Ma Lihua: Let what has lived live once again / Let what has died die once again / We are brothers and sisters riding together in a yak-hide raft.

The bus didn't reach Yamdrok Lake and Nangartse until after four in the afternoon. When Wang Mojie opened his eyes, he found himself in the clouds, mountains all around, the lake like a mirror, and he felt safer. A cool breeze blew in Nangartse, and the sunlight streamed down. The town has one crossroads and is surrounded by peaks, there isn't much to it. The buildings are of stone, with roofs of galvanised iron sheeting, and the stalls of street vendors are out in the high, bright and beautiful sun. Wang Mojie didn't check into the roadside inn where the rest of the passengers were staying. He walked to the crossroads and soon had covered every inch of the town. Nangartse is a busy stopping place, and on both sides of the street are several simple, largely identical inns. He went into an inn run by people from Sichuan. He could see they kept it neat and tidy, but apart from that it was no different from any of the other inns: two floors, rooms for rent upstairs and a restaurant downstairs. But it was clean, which made it unique. Wang Mojie decided he didn't need to look any further, he would stay here.

He stood on the first-floor balcony. He could see the mountain rising up behind the inn and almost feel the mass of crisp, cold air sitting on the peak. The mountainside was the colour of cyan and looked smooth. There wasn't a tree on it, no vegetation he could see, and if it weren't for all the colourful prayer flags flapping in the wind, it could have been the surface of the moon. See that colour, he thought, it's like the craters on the moon. Wang Mojie took a look around his room, then went down and asked to see the guest register. He flipped through it and, just as he expected to, found the names of Ukyi Lhamo and her mountaineer from their visit about six months earlier. They stayed in the same room he was in. It had been six months, but he could feel their presence in the room. Ukyi Lhamo had told him that even though she had been with her mountain climber, Wang Mojie had been more and more on her mind, she had thought about him, she had missed him, she had missed everything about him. He didn't know what that felt like for her, but right then and there he felt a longing he couldn't put into words. Standing in that room felt to Wang Mojie like visiting the home of some departed friend, it was like holding a memento of someone you miss, and he experienced deep grief, which felt good to him, unfamiliar, and he thought he was about to cry.

Well, OK, he said to himself, go ahead and cry. Tears, it has been so long since there were tears. It hurt so badly, it felt good to hurt. He studied himself in the mirror. Then he suddenly snorted with laughter and saw himself laughing as his tears fell. He relished the hurt, he wanted to wallow in it. It was real human hurt, the sort of thing he had once felt, the sort of heartache you feel when you are young. He wept. He saw himself as he was as a boy. He felt happy. How long had it been since he had last cried? It was a feeling he had not known for a very long time, he felt reborn. He was in love with Ukyi Lhamo. It was love he felt. He came to this realisation standing there in the room she had been in. He took off his grey checked scarf and hung it on the mirror. The scarf meant Wang Mojie was here.

Over the next few days, he found nothing in the guest register of any inn that proved that Ukyi Lhamo and her mother had stayed overnight when they passed through each town a few days before he did. Standing in the inn in Nangartse, he thought to himself that the SUV was faster than the bus and so Ukyi Lhamo and her mother wouldn't have needed to stop in Nangartse. They had probably made their first stop in Gyangtse, where the inns were nicer. He was looking at his scarf, but his mind was elsewhere. He didn't know much about Gyangtse, he didn't know much about anywhere in Tibet, but he was confident he could find out where Ukyi Lhamo had stayed, including during her winter trip with her mountaineer. He went downstairs to eat and lingered over the meal, even though he wasn't drinking. He had nothing to do, and since it was still light when he finished eating, he asked the inn owner how far Samding Monastery was and if it was possible to get out there to have a look. The man said that Samding was dozens of kilometres away on a peninsula out into the lake and there was no bus. Wang Mojie stood out on the street for a while, but he didn't know what he wanted to do, so he went back to his room.

He got out a book, read and eventually stopped thinking about Ukyi Lhamo. Books, landscape and Ukyi Lhamo, these were the three things on his mind during the trip. When he read, he was able to forget everything else, his sole focus was his book. Sometimes when he read, he forgot he wasn't at home in his study, and when he looked up from his book he didn't know where he was for a minute. Reading often allowed him to forget he was on the road. It didn't matter where he was, Karola Glacier, Pelkhor Monastery or Shigatse, it could be any of those places amid the incredible topography that had been created by tectonic plates in collision. As soon as he opened a book, all of it might as well not even exist. But Wang Mojie had to admit that Pakri was different. They got to Pakri after three days of travel. He knew that Pakri is one of the highest settlements in the world. It sits on the drainage divide of the Himalayas, and below Pakri to the south, the climate is influenced by the warm, damp air off the Indian Ocean. The altitude at Pakri was extreme, the world outside the bus windows was silver with a cold mist, and the snowmelt flowed away in two different directions. Heraclitus said that we cannot step into the same river twice, and this is true, but it is also true that in Pakri we can step into two rivers at one time. Actually, it is more than two, it is many rivers. When a man stands at the divide between two watersheds, how many rivers of time flowing in different directions can he encompass?

When Confucius looked at his river, he was already an old man.

Heraclitus was probably not young either.

Many of us feel time flowing away.

Few of us feel a surfeit of time. Wang Mojie felt very good.

It is beautiful coming down from Pakri. Rivers run in deep gorges, the ice turns to lichen, the grass turns to brush, and the evergreens become broadleaf trees. You experience all four seasons along a stretch of river of no more than fifty kilometres. Time feels different from anywhere else. It rushes by with startling speed but also seems to stand still. The rickety and dirty old long-distance bus seemed to fly along through the universe, swooping down. Wang Mojie had to hold the straps tightly to keep from rising weightless in his seat.

Wang Mojie was astounded. If nature could dream, it would dream of the landscape that unfolds as you come down from Pakri. It was verdant, pretty as a picture, and he could feel warm, moist ocean air rising to meet him. The wind from the far off ocean felt different from the wind coming down from the mountain. Wang Mojie saw farm women by the river, rice fields, villages at the edges of woods, and in the distance, he saw the town of Dromo. Where the river slowed just slightly, the town spread out peacefully along both banks.

Dromo is surrounded by subtropical forests and wrapped tightly in a dream. As you approach, it looks sealed off, impenetrable, connected to the world only by the fast-flowing river with its old wooden bridges. The landscape is reflected in the water. The town seems unchanged since antiquity. Apart from a few masonry structures housing the limited government presence, everything is wooden, and going into Dromo is like losing yourself in a memory of the colourful wooden structures of the past. Dromo has what all cities have, shops, taverns, teahouses, street vendors selling handicrafts and antiques, and it has its neighbourhood street life, a bus station, hotels and guesthouses, but in Dromo all these things seem somehow special. Everything is built of wood, which gives you a sense of history and a feeling of calm. Walking through Dromo is like walking down a street in the Song dynasty, through the scene depicted in the painting *Along the River During the Qingming Festival* or would be like that if the culture depicted in the painting was Tibetan.

It was raining in Dromo, a fine drizzle, so all the buildings were wet, the trees, the roofs, the storefronts, everything was wet. Wang Mojie went into a post office and bought some postcards from the young woman behind the counter. He thought for a moment and then addressed the postcards to Tenpa Nyima, Sangnyi, Kalsang Dekyi, Penpa Tsering, and then one to himself. On all of them he wrote, From Sharsingma, Dromo. He thought that maybe he should send a few more, to people who were farther away than Lhasa.

But who were those people? Who? The past was gone like water down a river, Beijing had disappeared like smoke. Who were those people he might write to? Who? Wang Mojie stood on the bridge and watched the river flow into the distance. He walked down the street and went into each inn he passed. He had heard that a traveller makes a home in each place he stays, but only now did he start to understand the feeling. While still on the way to Dromo, he had stopped caring so much about finding where Ukyi Lhamo and her mother had stayed. He started to search instead for a particular feeling, but now that he had reached his destination, he let this go too. He asked himself what the real reason was for his making the trip. Maybe Ukyi Lhamo and her mother had already left Dromo, maybe not, but what did it matter? He decided he was searching for the mark Ukyi Lhamo had left. The mark she had left, this was precisely how to put it, he thought.

He checked into a small inn that was removed from the busiest part of town. Of the inns he looked at, he chose the one farthest from the town centre. As always, even in unfamiliar surroundings, as soon as he picked up a book he was in his element, this was true no matter where he was. He spent much of the first few days reading in his first-floor room. From time to time, he took a look out at the street below. Often as he sat in his sunlit wooden room, time seemed to have gone backwards, and he felt he was living in the Song dynasty. Only after three days, when it seemed that the feel of the place had worked its way into him, did he decide to get up, go out and look around. It was morning and the town was not yet awake, he walked down the street and across an old wooden bridge that spanned the hurtling waters of the Drolma River. The morning fog had not yet lifted, a white mist floated around Wang Mojie, and he felt he could reach out and take a handful.

Having crossed the bridge, he walked upstream along a small tributary flowing down into the Drolma. It led him up into the trees, and he walked steadily on, over a low hill thick with vegetation, stepping across countless bends of the small, clear stream. Every so often he made a mark on a moss-covered tree trunk so he could find his way back. He started to wonder if maybe he had crossed the border and had left the country, probably not, but who cares, he thought, no borders in nature, nature shouldn't be divided up among countries. The landscape grew more and more beautiful, many streams ran through the trees, and there were waterfalls all around. He could see the bright scales of fish flashing over fallen trees that had dammed the stream. The birdsong was loud, a choir of many different voices, one louder than the rest, the choirmaster, and many finer softer voices in the ensemble singing harmony to the sound of the streams. The ensemble grew suddenly louder, but he didn't know if this was a song of welcome or unwelcome. The latter, he thought, it's a protest against my arrival. Humans are never welcome in nature. Still, no matter, conscience told him that the beauty around him was fragile, it was a place to treasure, and such places were vanishing fast. He took a few plants as specimens and a lot of photographs. He imagined the first day of school when his students would be thrilled to discover their classroom had been transformed into a mini museum. They would trill and chatter like the birds of the subtropical forest.

He was heading for the nunnery. He could see it in his mind's eye. It would be yellow, bright yellow ochre, and just visible through the trees. He expected the nunnery to be quiet, secluded, bathed in bright yellow, that sort of aesthetic, rather than grand and masculine like a monastery. It would match its peaceful, beautiful, pleasing environment. And to see a few graceful young nuns in their flowing crimson, to watch them glide by like clouds and hear them recite *om mani padme hum* would be perfection. Any monastery, no matter how quiet and secluded, seems old and worn in comparison to the verdancy of flora and the liveliness of gurgling waters. The architecture of nunneries is much simpler than that of male-dominated monasteries, which makes nunneries seem more part of the nature that surrounds them.

When he reached the nunnery, he found that it wasn't large, its walls were covered in moss, and the lintel over the door in the front gate was low. Stepping through he had to be careful not to hit his head. It was the only entrance, and when it was locked at night, the place was sealed up tight. Nunneries are unassuming, and this was especially true of the nunnery at Dromo, he thought. The main structure had a central prayer hall jutting out in front that connected to three assembly halls. As he entered, he saw a statue of Padmasambhava, and on the walls in the halls to the sides were paintings of Vajradhara, the four Lokapalas and Shri Devi. Ukyi Lhamo must have been here more than once, and she would have certainly come here on this trip with her mother, but they were no doubt gone already, he thought.

Wang Mojie stopped a nun as she drifted by like a rosy cloud and asked her if there was an older nun in residence by the name of Ukyi Lhamo, Madame Ukyi Lhamo. The nun, who looked young to Wang Mojie (she wasn't, actually), pointed to a wooden building painted yellow ochre up ahead through the trees. Before she could drift away, Wang Mojie asked her how old Ukyi Lhamo was. The nun shook her head to say she didn't know. Trying a different tack, Wang Mojie asked if Ukyi Lhamo was the oldest resident. The nun thought for a moment and said, No, she is not the oldest, we have other nuns who are older. Wang Mojie asked if Madame Ukyi Lhamo was still able to talk. The nun gave Wang Mojie a quizzical look, studied him for a moment, then slowly turned and walked away. The nun had obviously never met anybody like Wang Mojie before. Who knows, maybe the nunnery hadn't had a guest like him in a thousand years.

So she wasn't the oldest nun there. Wang Mojie didn't know what to make of this. Did it mean that Madame Ukyi Lhamo was not there or that she was? She should be the oldest, but could some nuns be even older? Many monasteries and nunneries in Tibet have the power to inspire visions, and when you are in them, the things in your imagination, including your unconscious imaginings, begin to seem real. This is how Wang Mojie had always thought about the search for Madame Ukyi Lhamo, which is why he hadn't taken it that seriously. But now, much to his surprise, Wang Mojie found himself believing some of what Ukyi Lhamo had said, because if there were many very old nuns still around, then why couldn't Madame Ukyi Lhamo still be alive? But how could he be sure that the place wasn't making him hallucinate? Wang Mojie decided to trust his intuition. He believed that if he saw her with his own eyes, he would be able to tell if it was Madame Ukyi Lhamo or not, he had complete confidence in this.

He was, however, wrong. He could not tell. The woman was simply too old. She was so old it shocked him. She was so very ancient that his intuition could tell him nothing, and his confidence deserted him. Except for a little light in her eyes, to him she looked no different from any of the statues of deities in the nunnery. She was wearing a crimson *kasaya* and a yellow nun's shawl, and all her exposed skin (her face, arms, hands and fingers) was covered in wrinkles. He couldn't tell if she was male or female. Her eyes, which bulged like the eyes of the elderly do, were lidded with wrinkles, and the network of wrinkles and lines that ran across her face was so thick and complex it would defeat any sculptor who tried to depict her. Is this what one hundred years of life does to a person? If Madame Ukyi Lhamo was still alive, she would look like this, Wang Mojie thought. Was this some other nun named Ukyi Lhamo or was it Madame Ukyi Lhamo herself? He couldn't see any trace of his own Ukyi Lhamo in the woman's face nor any trace of her mother, Mrs Ukyi Lhamo. But was that just because she was too old? So old she didn't look like a person any longer? Because there was no trace left on her face of her former self? Had the three generations of Ukyi Lhamos met right there?

The nuns' dormitory was splendid, timeless, pious. There was splendour in the statues of deities and the butter lamps. The statue of Sakyamuni, the lids of his eyes half closed, gave the place a sense of timelessness. There was piety in the wall paintings, the *khaden*, the sutras, the wooden bowls, the altar tables, the rush prayer mats and the incense. She was sitting cross-legged on a round yellow *khaden*, dark prayer beads in her hand, a crimson altar table before her. Wang Mojie had trouble carrying on the conversation with her, and he had to shout.

—Madam, are you Master Ukyi Lhamo? May I, may I disturb you for one moment? Wang Mojie said this in Tibetan, repeating it three times, but she didn't react.

—Madam, your granddaughter, I'm her friend, I'm a friend of Ukyi Lhamo.

—She and I, we teach at the same school. I'm aware, I know she has been here.

—Were you happy to see your daughter and granddaughter, Madam?

She stared straight ahead and did not seem to understand anything Wang Mojie said. Wang Mojie showed her a photograph of Ukyi Lhamo as a young woman. She studied it for a long time, then lifted her head towards Wang Mojie. Her lips moved slowly, and she whispered something, but Wang Mojie had no idea what it was. He could tell from her expression, however, that she recognised the woman in the photograph.

—Your granddaughter? Is that your granddaughter? Wang Mojie asked loudly.

She did not react. Wang Mojie put his palms together and bowed. It was hopeless, he decided, it was time for him to make his farewell. But as he walked away, she suddenly gestured to him, and he stopped. She gestured for him to give her his hand, and she took the string of dark, translucent prayer beads from her wrist and put it on Wang Mojie's wrist, then she indicated he could be on his way. Wang Mojie felt confused, he didn't know what she meant by this. He didn't think he could just take her prayer beads, so he took out some cash as an offering and put it on the table. She put her palms together, closed her eyes, and began to softly intone a mantra. For her, there was no more world, no more Wang Mojie. Wang Mojie watched her for quite some time before he departed.

36. The Museum

They were both silent, they said nothing.
But their heart-to-heart conversation continued.
You could tell from the far-off look in their eyes.
The light from the fountain in the middle of the street lit up their faces and fell on the table, the bar and all the empty chairs.

After two weeks on the road, a worn and weary Wang Mojie returned to the school. He didn't feel any different, he was the same person he had been when he left. Nothing had changed, nothing at all. The campus was as quiet as when he had left, his house was undisturbed. When he left, there was a lock on Ukyi Lhamo's door, and it was still there when he got back. He didn't know if Ukyi Lhamo was back, he assumed she should be, but many days went by, and he didn't see her. He kept checking the lock on her door, thinking he would see some sign if it had been touched, but because he couldn't remember how it was positioned when he left, he couldn't tell if it had been moved. He spent his time reading, going for walks and pondering various abstruse topics until one day, just before the start of the new term, and as he was thinking to himself that Ukyi Lhamo was sure to be back soon to prepare her lessons, he looked up and there she was. He was in his garden, and over his garden fence he saw Ukyi Lhamo walking through the campus gate. She was wearing a white trench coat and short boots, her long hair fell to her shoulders, and she was walking fast. Wang Mojie stayed where he was and went on watering the garden in the warm yellow light of twilight. No need to rush things, he thought, she's back now. He thought he would wait for a while then go to see Ukyi Lhamo and ask her about her trip to Dromo, and he would tell her about his, but he was surprised when just a moment later he saw Ukyi Lhamo come out of her house and start to walk quickly towards the gate. Wang Mojie, not wanting to miss his chance, hurried out of the garden and called out to Ukyi Lhamo in a loud voice. He walked up to her.

—I thought you saw me, I was working in the garden.

—I saw you, she said evenly.

—And you didn't even say hello?

—Did you?

—I was busy. Why are you leaving? You just got back. Trying to avoid me?

—I came back to get a few things.

—Are you in a rush?

—Yes.

—Why? If you don't mind me asking.

—I have paperwork to do, have to get my file transferred.

—You're taking another job?

—I'm out of here.

They looked at each other for a long moment. Wang Mojie had been taken completely by surprise.

—Let me guess, Wang Mojie said. It is either the District CPPCC office or the Research Institute of Culture and History, right?

—Close. The Tibet Museum.

—That's great. As an archivist?

—And guide.

—Fantastic, that's great, Wang Mojie said, for once happy for someone else and not thinking of himself.

—Sorry, I have to go.

—I want to be the first person to take one of your tours.

Ukyi Lhamo did not respond.

—I once suggested that you work in the Tibet Museum.

Ukyi Lhamo did not respond.

—It was almost inevitable, and it's for the best, Wang Mojie said.

—Inevitable? For the best?

—Yes. Among all your possible futures, some were more likely than others, and among those more likely futures, some would be for the better, and one would be for the best, namely museum work. I once thought through all the places where you might end up. I imagined you at some peaceful nunnery, Gari, Neuchungri or Tsamkhung, and that would be good for you but not as good as a museum. Museums and monasteries do sort of the same thing, the difference is monasteries do it in a traditional way and museums in a modern way. The modern way is best for you, and for me too.

—You too? What does any of this have to do with you?

—I mean I'm suited for museum work, but then I could work anywhere. It doesn't matter to me where I work, but you're different, you've always been looking for a place where you can apply all your skills, and now you've found it. Oh, and how was the trip to Dromo?

—Good, very good, thank you for asking.

—How about some details? How did everything turn out?

—Forgive me, I have to be going.

—I'll wait for your taxi with you. The Tibet Museum. It's just so perfect, you going to the museum.

Wang Mojie walked with Ukyi Lhamo out of the gate to the road, all the while talking about how good it was that Ukyi Lhamo was transferring to the museum. Ukyi Lhamo was focused on looking for a taxi and didn't seem to be paying attention to Wang Mojie. She flagged down a taxi, got in, rolled the window down and turned to Wang Mojie.

—Look after yourself, she said.

—Thank you. Don't worry about me.

Ukyi Lhamo moved into the apartment the museum provided for her, and her new place of work welcomed her with enthusiasm. The museum had an increasing number of overseas visitors and needed staff who could speak foreign languages. Ukyi Lhamo was a graduate of the Beijing Foreign Languages Institute, where she had studied French, she had an advanced degree from a French university, and her English was very good too. This made her valuable. Also, and even more importantly, she was the granddaughter of the Tibetan early modern reformer Lungsharwa Dorje Tsegyal. She carried this history with her, she was the child of this history, and so she was the perfect person to explain the history to others. And her uncle was a vice chairman of the Tibetan Committee of the Chinese People's Political Consultative Conference, which of course worked in her favour. The museum job was Ukyi Lhamo's for the asking.

You could say it started with something Wang Mojie once said half-jokingly. It was after Ukyi Lhamo had talked about her faith and the history of her family, and they were discussing what she might do with her life. Half joking, Wang Mojie had said she had two choices, she could put on a red robe and move into Neuchungri Nunnery (she would make a pretty picture in the robe, he had said, like something out of *World Photography* magazine), or she could go to work at the Research Institute of Culture and History. But neither of those two choices would be as good as if she went to work at The Tibet Museum and walked around with a laser pointer leading tours. Wang Mojie was serious about this but not entirely. He did believe that working in a museum would be good for Ukyi Lhamo, but for the most part, he was just saying it, putting it into the discourse, speculating and trying out a narrative, it wasn't to be taken seriously. That is how language worked, Wang Mojie believed. More often than not language does not correspond to reality, language functions apart from reality, it must, because metaphysics depends upon it doing so. It hadn't occurred to Wang Mojie that Ukyi Lhamo would turn his words into a reality, she was such a mystery. They were perfect for each other, it was in the stars... or at least they would know it was in the stars if he too ended up working at the museum. Wang Mojie knew that a big reason Ukyi Lhamo had taken the job at the museum was to get away from him. She was trying to keep her distance from him, it couldn't be more obvious.

After Ukyi Lhamo started her job, Wang Mojie kept calling her to say the museum was his idea, and so she should take him out to eat to thank him. She had given him her apartment phone number, and he had made a joke about setting up a hotline between them. And he did pester her with calls, and finally she agreed to the dinner. He could tell from her voice that she was in a good mood. Over the phone, she told him that she had just led her first real tour, a group from Switzerland.

They met at a fancy Western restaurant on Yuthok Road, which runs through the centre of Lhasa. It is a modern commercial street, with the Potala Palace and the Lhasa Department Store at one end, and Barkhor Square and Jokhang Temple at the other end. Both sides of the street are lined with large planters with trees and flowers, and the whole street is colourful and brightly lit. There are fountains that play music and electronic billboards, and along both sides of the street are restaurants, bars and shops. The street is beautiful at night. The restaurant where they met, bathed in neon light from the street, was much the same as any high-end restaurant anywhere, Paris, New York, Beijing, Shanghai, but this was Lhasa and the restaurant was on Yuthok Road. It hadn't surrendered entirely to globalisation, which was a good thing. The atmosphere was somehow different, even if you couldn't say exactly how.

Ukyi Lhamo had her reasons for asking Wang Mojie out to this particular restaurant. The Western ambience would help them reminisce about their time together looking after Ma Dingge's father, and in so doing they could put those days behind them. She had cooked Western food for Robert every day, which had been a feat of perseverance. Both the days and the nights had been difficult but in different ways. During the day, Ma Dingge and his father talked of religion and philosophy, and at night she and Wang Mojie said mystifying things to one another with their bodies. Thinking back on it now, it all seemed incredible, none of it had been easy. But it was in the past now, it was over, completely, and now they weren't living near each other, they didn't see each other all the time as they once had, and so she could be more tolerant of Wang Mojie. They could have a relaxed conversation and share their memories. And Wang Mojie was an exceptional person in many ways, he was difficult to like, but still she wished him well.

A second reason she picked the restaurant was that it was on Yuthok Road. There aren't too many places in Lhasa named after old aristocratic families, but like the Lhalu Wetlands, Yuthok Road was named after a family Ukyi Lhamo had a connection to. The Lhalu and Yuthok families were also connected to each other of course. Ukyi Lhamo's grandmother was grateful to Yuthok, and Ukyi Lhamo's mother remembered him and his family fondly. All of this made Yuthok Road meaningful to Ukyi Lhamo, and even if it hadn't been for this personal connection, just the name Yuthok was enough to make her think about what Lhasa must have been like in the past. Yuthok Road was the perfect place to talk about her mother and their trip to Dromo and finding her grandmother. Even though Yuthok Road bore no resemblance to the old Lhasa, its name still connected it to history, and precisely because it had an old name but was a bustling, modern street with flowers, fountains, advertisements and music, it gave you a strong sense of time gone by. You thought about the past, with all its joys and sorrows, and you started to think you saw Ukyi Lhamo's grandmother, Madame Ukyi Lhamo, come walking up through the light and shadow. Her daughter, still a child, was walking with her and also Lhalu, who for a time was a frequent caller at the Yuthok home. What we go to museums to see can be found all around us at every moment, and we are perfectly capable of seeing everything around us in our daily lives as fit for display in a museum, it is just a matter of changing how we think about the past, and the present for that matter. This is what Wang Mojie said to Ukyi Lhamo. At certain moments, Wang Mojie could be counted on to come out with some clever remark that was surprising but apropos. Ukyi Lhamo knew of no one who was his match in this.

They had a nice, simple meal, with coffee for him and orange juice for her. Wang Mojie as a rule didn't drink, and at first he didn't notice that Ukyi Lhamo wasn't having her usual red wine. He didn't notice until he realised that not only was she not drinking, but she also hadn't had a cigarette, and he expressed surprise at the discovery. She said she had stopped smoking and drinking. Her giving up alcohol didn't seem like much to Wang Mojie, as he never understood the appeal of alcohol, but her giving up cigarettes was impressive. When they had been living together, she seemed always to have a cigarette in her hand. The way she held her cigarette was part of what gave her an air of sophistication. He had got used to her second-hand smoke. Sometimes she blew it straight into his face on purpose, but he could put up with it.

—Why give up cigarettes too? There is something sublime about you when you have a cigarette in your hand, especially when you are wearing jeans and a big sweater.

—Well, I'm not wearing jeans and maybe I never will again.

—Yes, you are dressed differently, and it's all nicely coordinated. It's like a museum guide's uniform.

—I came up with it myself.

—Yeah, it's retro, and it's feminine. But I'm going to miss the way you used to look. It used to be like you were posing for a series of paintings: *Ukyi Lhamo with a Cigarette*, *Ukyi Lhamo in Jeans*, *Ukyi Lhamo with a Glass of Red Wine*. What kind of paintings would those have been? Oil paintings? Maybe not paintings. Photographs? For advertisements?... But of course! You're not allowed to smoke in the museum.

—That is not why I stopped.

—OK. But you stopped drinking too?

They chatted casually. It felt to them that years had passed since they had last seen each other. In the past, Ukyi Lhamo always wore a little lipstick and make-up, but Wang Mojie noticed she wasn't that day. She looked natural, and he could see a few freckles on her face and some downy hair. It wasn't a big deal that she had forgone make-up, but it left him feeling something he couldn't quite name. She looked honest and a little older. Wang Mojie thought about the exhibits of unearthed artefacts at the museum, objects that represented the essence of the culture, and he guessed Ukyi Lhamo was feeling in touch with the deep past, connected to times when women wore no make-up. Connecting with history strips away all ornamentation and puts us in touch with what is essential. Or at least that's what we think history does. It's how history is depicted in museums.

Giving up cigarettes and alcohol, Ukyi Lhamo told Wang Mojie, hadn't been on her mind at all on the way to Dromo or even during the week she spent with her grandmother. But coming back home she had a sudden, strong sense of emptiness inside, and she had felt a powerful urge to take monastic vows and enter a nunnery, and she thought she would go to the nunnery at Dromo. She said that as she was having these thoughts, she lit a cigarette but before she could bring it to her lips, she watched herself throw it out of the car window. It was amazing, it was as if she weren't controlling her own movements. It was like someone else was guiding her hands and stopping her from smoking. That was how remarkable her giving up cigarettes had been. After that, it made sense to stop drinking. She had no desire for a drink. She had many memories tied up with drinking but they didn't mean anything to her.

—I don't need cigarettes or alcohol any more, or make-up or jeans either.

—It is hard to imagine meeting Madame Ukyi Lhamo could change you so completely that you would give up cigarettes, Wang Mojie said. He still liked to tease Ukyi Lhamo. That wasn't the first time you met your grandmother. The first time, you didn't seem to have such a strong reaction.

—It was different the second time. The first time I couldn't prove it was her and nobody believed me, and I ended up wondering if maybe I had just imagined it, and for a long time I felt blocked, I couldn't get beyond it. And of all the people who didn't believe me, it was you who made me feel the most lost and unsure.

—I don't recall ever saying that I didn't believe you, in fact, I always encouraged you.

—You might not have said it out loud but it was just your whole attitude. You are the sort of person who never believes anything.

—True, I have that shortcoming, Wang Mojie admitted.

—There is something I need to tell you, Ukyi Lhamo said, then she stopped for a moment and sighed before continuing. The day we left for Dromo I was feeling in despair, utterly lost. I don't know why, but every time I looked at my mother, it made me think of you. I really don't want to admit this to you, but every time I looked at her, I saw you, and it made me feel lost and empty but also calm somehow. It made me feel cold all over. The whole way there I was feeling depressed, and I started to ask myself why I had dragged my mother off on some fool's errand looking for someone who existed only in my imagination. You know, I had just about dropped the idea of continuing my search but then you asked me about it, and you were so sarcastic that I felt a sudden renewed determination. My mother didn't believe my grandmother was still alive and so she wasn't happy about making such a long trip for nothing, but she didn't bring it up, she just asked if you were coming. Which surprised me. You've got that special whatever it is, I'm well aware of that, and it's why I asked you to help persuade my mother to go. Still, I didn't expect that she would have so much trust in you.

—We have something in common, she and I, Wang Mojie said with self-satisfaction.

—Something in common, the two of you?

—Yes, Wang Mojie said with a tone of sincerity. I don't know why, but she and I can communicate. It's like I get some sort of energy from her, it's like she's my own mother. She and I experience the world in a similar way, I mean in an abstract sense. I get this feeling that she and I can see something deep inside each other.

—Yes, but she doesn't know the real you!

—What is the real me? Oh, that. You can't call that the real me. And anyway I think she can sense the "that".

—Enough, Wang Mojie, I don't want to keep talking about the past.

Ukyi Lhamo took a sip of her orange juice, she stared at her glass, and her expression gradually softened.

—To tell you the truth, Ukyi Lhamo said, I've always felt grateful to you. If it weren't for you, I don't know if I would've gone back to Dromo. I was ready to give it up and devote myself to Buddhist practice. So, thank you, Wang Mojie, you deserve the credit for my mother getting to see her mother again. It was so moving, I'll never forget it. It fulfilled my dream. They didn't seem to recognise each other at first, they stood still and looked at each other like strangers for a very long time, and just when I started to think I'd made a mistake, just when I had decided that that ancient old woman, her face was like a walnut, was not my grandmother, just when I started to feel miserable for having come all the way there on some preposterous quest, they suddenly embraced. I had this feeling of sorrow and joy all mixed together, but, Wang Mojie, mostly I was so happy! My mother started to cry with this wrenching sound, I didn't know she could cry like that. She was sobbing and moaning, years of pent-up tears were just gushing out of her like from a well, and then she stopped moaning, and her crying got softer and softer, she started to cry like a little girl...

—Wait a minute, Wang Mojie said, interrupting Ukyi Lhamo. Let me think, let me think. Your grandmother, did she cry too? I'm guessing no, I'm guessing she didn't cry, I bet she was composed.

—She was. She didn't cry, that's exactly right. She was very still. How did you know?

—It's her advanced age, she's almost already gone to the other side. What do they call it, *paramita*? She's looking back at this world from the other side.

—You're right, yes, it was like that!

—She's so old, she's in sort of a vegetative state, she's like a fossil.

—Wait, Wang Mojie, are you telling me you saw her? Did you find my grandmother too?

—Yes, I did.

—You did?

—Three days after you left, I took the bus all the way to Dromo.

—Really! Tell me the truth, did you really?

—I really did. I stayed at a little hotel called the Gentian, you probably don't know it.

—I know it, I know it.

Ukyi Lhamo seemed excited, but suddenly, as if realising something, she checked her emotion. Her expression darkened, and she looked at Wang Mojie with suspicion. She didn't doubt he had been to Dromo, but she wanted to know why he had gone. Wang Mojie was sensitive enough to pick up on this, and he paused and looked at Ukyi Lhamo. They both were quiet for a moment.

—Long-distance buses are rough, they're slow. How long did the trip take? Ukyi Lhamo asked, as casually as she could.

—It wasn't so bad, Wang Mojie said. I was among the folk, the people who take those buses are part of this place, at one with it.

—Why did you go to Dromo? Ukyi Lhamo asked, getting to the point.

—I felt some things hadn't been resolved or maybe were just beginning.

Ukyi Lhamo finished what was left of her orange juice and looked at Wang Mojie.

—I'm going to have a glass of wine, OK?

—Why are you asking me? It wasn't me who told you to stop drinking. You can smoke too.

—I need a glass of wine, she said, turning to look towards the bar.

—Think about why you gave it up, Wang Mojie said. Why did you?

—Fine, forget it, I won't have the wine.

Ukyi Lhamo waved a waiter over and asked for another glass of orange juice. She and Wang Mojie fell quiet. They let the conversation drop. They didn't speak for a long time. But in their hearts, their conversation continued, which brought a certain serenity to their faces, washed in light from a fountain outside on the street. The light also fell on the bar and the dozens of glasses hanging upside down above it, and on the tables and the empty chairs neatly arranged by them. Looking out of the window through the fountain they could see one end of the Potala at the far end of Yuthok Road. They could make out only part of the palace but it still looked imposing. They might have been in any city in the world, were it not for that view of the Potala.

—Wang Mojie, it's over between you and me, Ukyi Lhamo said.

—Sometimes an end is a beginning... You didn't fail you know.

—The thought of seeing you again scares me, really, the thought makes me very afraid.

—I followed you the whole way to Dromo. I was looking for the mark you left, I was looking for the hotels you stayed in, the rooms you stayed in. I checked all the guest registers, and I found your name, I even found the places you stayed a year ago on your trip with your mountaineer, and the feeling it gave me was very unusual. More than once I stood looking into a mirror that you had looked into, and I found myself starting to cry. Sometimes I was smiling at myself at the same time, it made me so very happy.

—I'm sorry, I have to go, Ukyi Lhamo said. She stood up.

—You made me who I am now. And I think it's great that you're at the museum.

—Wang Mojie, I'm not the same as I was, you know that. I didn't want to see you again, but I thought the past was the past, I thought it wouldn't stand between us. But I was wrong. We can't see each other again. This is goodbye.

Ukyi Lhamo asked for the bill, but Wang Mojie didn't let her go quite yet.

—Not see each other again? That's a little unrealistic. The museum is open to everybody, I can always come and take one of your tours.

—I'll ignore you if you do.

—I'll turn up when no one else is there. The tour might be just you and me.

—That won't matter to me because you'll be just another visitor, Ukyi Lhamo said. She didn't look emotional, but there was a despairing tone in her voice. She walked out of the restaurant.

Wang Mojie sat in the neon glow coming in the window and watched Ukyi Lhamo walk away. It seemed unreal, he felt he was watching her walk into history. She wasn't walking towards the Potala, which was in the same direction as the museum, she was walking towards Barkhor Square and Jokhang Temple, and he felt he was watching the young Madame Ukyi Lhamo. No matter which direction she might have walked in, either towards the museum or towards the square and the temple, to Wang Mojie it would have looked as if he was watching her walk back into history, into the depths of time.

37. The Museum Guide

When she spoke to groups of tourists, Ukyi Lhamo was professional.
She looked at each guest in turn, exchanging a glance.
She was poised and engaged with what she was saying.
She looked radiant and strong.
But now, in front of Wang Mojie, she was stiff and did not deign to even look at him.
Indeed, it was impossible to read her eyes, they were empty, as empty as the sky.

The Tibet Museum, the Potala Palace and the Norbu Lingka together comprise a magnificent vista that is emblematic of the sun-drenched city of Lhasa. The design of the Tibet Museum recalls the Potala. The museum's walls are built of granite and topped with a tamarisk parapet, and its roof is covered in glazed tile. It is a grand structure, distinctly Tibetan. Inside it is a thoroughly modern museum with a rich collection of artefacts from Tibetan culture and history. There are many relics of Tibetan prehistory, statues and images of the Buddha and bodhisattvas, ancient Tibetan-language manuscripts written in ink made from gold, silver and coral, seals made of gold that were used by the Living Buddhas over the ages, the golden urn and ivory slips used in the ceremony to select the reincarnations of lamas, colourful *thangka*, and all sorts of musical instruments, Buddhist ritual implements and distinctive pottery. There is a souvenir shop on the ground floor, and on the first floor is an exhibit on Tibetan history. The second floor houses the exhibits of Tibetan cultural artefacts, a display about Tibet's flora and fauna, and special temporary exhibits.

The museum offered tours in Tibetan, Mandarin, Japanese, English and after Ukyi Lhamo's arrival, French. She was capable of leading tours in all these languages with the exception of Japanese. Many foreign tourists visited the museum, mostly older, and they liked Ukyi Lhamo's open, friendly manner as a guide. She talked to them about Tibetan history, Buddhism and art; she talked to them about Padmasambhava, Atisa Dipamkara Srijnana, Tsongkhapa and Drogon Chogyal Phagpa; she talked to them about the Sixth Dalai Lama Tsangyang Gyatso; she talked to them about the modernisation and reform movement of the Thirteenth Dalai Lama; and she talked to them about the remarkable Lungshar Dorje Tsegyal. She told them that early in the twentieth century, the Thirteenth Dalai Lama dispatched Lungshar, along with his seventeen-year-old wife, Ukyi Lhamo, as chaperone to the seven young men the Dalai Lama sent to England to study. Lungshar and his wife stayed in England with their charges for four years, they attended dinners and soirees given by the king, and the British papers printed stories about them. She told her tours about Tibet's first hydropower station, the Dode Power Station, and how after it came online the government was ready to bring electric light to the homes of officials, but some conservative officials were frightened by this strange new thing, electricity. They begged for the project to be abandoned, but the Thirteenth Dalai Lama intervened and overruled the conservatives, saying the power station was the product of "boundless and miraculous intelligence".

Wang Mojie stood among the blonde and white-haired foreigners and listened attentively and with great appreciation as Ukyi Lhamo lectured. He was less interested in the content of what she was saying than in the way she said it. He appreciated it as a sort of ritual performance, and he was enjoying the self-satisfaction of knowing that he was the one who had suggested the job to her in the first place. Most of Ukyi Lhamo's tours were in English, which Wang Mojie understood with no problem. There were relatively few visitors from French-speaking countries. Over a few months, Wang Mojie encountered French-speaking tourists only twice, and each time there were only two or three in the group.

Ukyi Lhamo always saw Wang Mojie, of course, but just as she had vowed, she paid him no attention, treating him as just another tourist. Looking at Ukyi Lhamo working as a guide, Wang Mojie thought it undeniable that it was like seeing her grandmother when she was Ukyi

Lhamo's age. Indeed, he observed that whether consciously or not, Ukyi Lhamo sometimes dressed herself in a similar style to Madame Ukyi Lhamo when she was young, as confirmed by looking at the photograph hanging on the museum wall. It was of Madame Ukyi Lhamo in London, published in *The Times*. But who else besides Wang Mojie was going to notice that Ukyi Lhamo looked more and more like her grandmother in that photograph? And this meant, he told himself, that she was dressing that way especially for him. He never said hello to her. He listened to her, watched her and left when the tour was over.

On most days Wang Mojie had just two lessons to teach, and he was no longer a class adviser. Without that responsibility his job became much simpler, which left him with more time for philosophy and his notes on zero. As a writer, Wang Mojie was very articulate, his prose was logical and analytical. He wrote about mathematics, philosophy, Buddhism and Daoism and read prolifically. Now that Ukyi Lhamo was gone from the school, he lived a very quiet, almost monastic life. He maintained his habit of taking a walk every day at noon or in the early evening. On his walks, he was sure to bump into his students or their parents. The students he had supervised as class adviser were warmer and more friendly to him now that he no longer had authority over them. They would be loafing about by a river or sitting on a wall in the village or hanging out in the big shed where the tractors were parked, chewing on milk-skin cheese, and they would see him passing by and yell out in greeting. Sometimes the girls would come up and enquire why he was always looking down as he walked, then, giggling, they would ask, Are you thinking about someone you miss? He would gravely nod his head, and this made them laugh, and their laughter was as bright as the sound of water flowing in a stream. They knew about Wang Mojie and Ukyi Lhamo, and the two of them were a frequent topic of gossip on campus. The girls knew everything about Wang Mojie and Ukyi Lhamo's relationship, even a few things that didn't make sense to them. They knew things they had seen and heard, and they knew things they had imagined, and what they imagined became true in their minds, and so the girls knew some things about Wang Mojie and Ukyi Lhamo that would have surprised Wang Mojie and Ukyi Lhamo. But of course, there was a lot about their relationship that was well beyond anything the girls could have possibly imagined.

From time to time, Wang Mojie dropped in on Ma Dingge, and the two of them would sit in Ma Dingge's small room and get deep into conversation.

Ma Dingge spent his days in religious contemplation, but he was not cut off from the world, he was informed and had an active intellectual life. His talks with his father had of necessity been rushed, they had not had time to discuss everything at the length it warranted. Often they only had time to prepare the ground for a future, fuller discussion, which was, in fact, now taking place, but the participants in it were Ma Dingge and, not Robert, but Wang Mojie. Listening to Ma Dingge speak in detail about the Buddhist analysis of noumena and phenomena, Wang Mojie more and more began to perceive a similarity between Buddhist ideas and the cryptic notions of "différance", "trace", "presence" and so on. Wang Mojie took instruction from Guo Yancheng. In "Buddhist Philosophy and Derrida's Deconstruction," which was mentioned in Chapter 21, Guo wrote, "But Derrida also said that 'différance' is the origin of differences, the production of differences, the play of differences, the difference of differences... It is evident that Derrida negated neither the 'existence' of 'différance' nor the 'non-existence' of 'différance', which happens to coincide with the Buddhist idea of 'Non-complete Emptiness'." Wang Mojie wrote this down in his notes on zero. Zero, he wrote, is not absent and it is not present, it has no form but is not empty, and any theory of differences must account for zero, which is a beginning and an end... This sort of mental exercise is exhausting, and to recover from it a switch to an entirely different form of mental engagement is needed, which was not the most important reason for Wang Mojie's trips to the museum but was one of the reasons.

Wang Mojie was purposeful and regimented in everything he did, including visiting the museum, and over time he established the practice of going to the museum once every weekend, rather like the way Ukyi Lhamo went to a temple once a week. It was Wang Mojie's form of spiritual practice. One doesn't go to a temple in search of some reward, and the same was true of Wang Mojie when he went to the museum. He went as a form of self-cultivation, it gave him strength, and it made him feel there was a light shining upon him.

Wang Mojie hoped to see Ukyi Lhamo every time he went to the museum but sometimes he did not. Sometimes he waited all morning or even all day but did not catch a glimpse of her. Sometimes Ukyi Lhamo had tasks to attend to and sometimes, not often but every once in a while, no foreign tour group would turn up at the museum the entire day, which meant she stayed out of sight. Once or twice Wang Mojie thought about going to her office to look for her, but he always dropped the idea. The feeling of disappointment at not seeing Ukyi Lhamo made him acutely aware of something, and he knew exactly what it was. It was like a feeling of love, it felt good, and to keep this feeling he could not confront her, he could not, not ever. Every month he could count on having a few chances to listen to Ukyi Lhamo as she led her tours, and if his luck held, he could see her every weekend. Sometimes there were too many foreigners, a whole crowd of them, and he couldn't work his way to the front. It was possible that on these occasions Ukyi Lhamo didn't know he was there, but then he didn't necessarily always want her to know.

When there weren't many people in the tour group, Wang Mojie was always able to get close to Ukyi Lhamo and exchange a glance with her, and every time Wang Mojie watched with fascination as the professional smile disappeared from her face the instant her eyes met his and then reappeared as soon as her gaze moved from him to the next person in the crowd. If she knew Wang Mojie was in the crowd, as soon as she concluded the tour she walked away, head high, eyes averted, and he could hear her heels clacking across the red marble floor of the museum. He never called out to her, he simply stood and watched her disappear into the recesses of the museum, heading for her office where she did her research.

It would not be accurate, however, to say Wang Mojie never spoke to Ukyi Lhamo. Sometimes, standing at the back of the group, he would ask a question as if he were just another tourist, and he always said he was asking on behalf of some young blonde woman or white-haired gentleman standing next to him. This was not a lie, he often fell into whispered conversation with the people near him, and sometimes they had questions he could not answer, so when the opportunity arose, he would politely put those questions to their tour guide, Ms Ukyi Lhamo. Typically, just as they were finishing with a particular exhibit, Wang Mojie would ask a question, which always caught Ukyi Lhamo by surprise, and so she would have to ask him to repeat it (Wang Mojie told himself that this counted as conversation). Wang Mojie would see a look of vexation cross her face, but then she would quickly compose herself and answer the question, and her tone declared she was simply a tour guide speaking to just another tourist. But she looked at him when she spoke, and it was at these moments that Wang Mojie felt he was standing in light that flowed over him like water from a fountain, and the light spoke to him, no less, and all the darkness in his world disappeared as everything became clear and bright. Robert had said it was crucial for a philosopher to have a sense of internal clarity. He said that because Ukyi Lhamo brought this clarity to Wang Mojie, she could be his philosophy, and while this was an exaggerated way of putting it, it turned out to be prophetic. When Robert had said this, Wang Mojie and Ukyi Lhamo were working through their enigmatic "philosophy of the body". The old man seemed to have an intuitive understanding of Wang Mojie. You could never tell with Robert, he was not a man to be underestimated, as it turned out he knew something about what was going on between the two of them.

On days when few people came to the museum, Ukyi Lhamo might have only three or four people in a group and sometimes only two, one tourist and Wang Mojie. When this happened, Wang Mojie didn't ask any questions of Ukyi Lhamo, they were standing too close together, and he was too exposed. Nevertheless on one such occasion, he saw a look of distress come over Ukyi Lhamo. She suddenly looked tired, she paused, clutched her chest as if it pained her and laboured to catch her breath. Wang Mojie feared she might faint, but she was stronger than most people, and after a brief moment she recovered and continued her lecture. Wang Mojie pondered over what might have happened and concluded that if over an extended period one is forced to pretend that one does not know someone with whom one is very familiar, the mental strain will become exhausting. Therefore, from that day on, when he joined one of Ukyi Lhamo's smaller tours, he stayed at the back and also kept a distance from the person directly in front of him, as if he were that person's shadow. Wang Mojie couldn't imagine what might happen if he hired Ukyi Lhamo to give him a private tour of the museum. It would be expensive, but Wang Mojie didn't care about the money, he was worried that it would be stressful for Ukyi Lhamo, and he didn't know if she could take it. He couldn't decide whether or not to give it a go, but he became obsessed with the idea, he couldn't stop thinking about it, he kept putting it off, but he loved the suspense of not knowing if this gratification delayed might ever be fulfilled. And that is how things stood right up until the day he received a letter from Robert.

It had been almost a year since Robert had left Tibet, and this was the first time he had communicated with Wang Mojie. Robert had been corresponding with Ukyi Lhamo, Wang Mojie realised after reading the letter. Along with the personal letter from Robert was a formal letter inviting Wang Mojie to come to Paris-Sorbonne University as a visiting scholar for a term of eight to ten months. While in Paris, he would have the opportunity to attend a course of lectures on philosophy and he would be asked to lecture on Daoist philosophy. He would be free to pursue research, and the term of his stay in Paris could be extended as necessary. In the personal letter, Robert wrote that to his incomprehension and disappointment, Ukyi Lhamo had remained steadfast in rejecting the similar formal invitation that he had extended to her. Robert wrote that he still wanted to bring the two of them over together as visiting scholars but realised he was powerless to make this happen. Wang Mojie knew that by this Robert meant that he wanted him to persuade Ukyi Lhamo to go to Paris. Wang Mojie inferred that when writing to Ukyi Lhamo, Robert must have indicated that he planned to bring her and Wang Mojie to Paris together. He assumed they were a couple. If Ukyi Lhamo was refusing to go to Paris because of him, which he was certain was the case, what could he possibly say to her that was going to change her mind? She would never change her mind. Wang Mojie also knew he would never be able to explain to Robert the nature of the Eastern riddle that was his relationship with Ukyi Lhamo.

Robert wrote that his conversation with his son had been published to a very good reception, and it spent weeks on the list of bestselling non-fiction books in France. Robert wrote that readers seemed to be particularly taken by his afterword, which he had written in the form of a long excerpt from his diary describing his daily routine in Tibet and his friendship with the young Chinese intellectual Wang Mojie and the lay Buddhist Ms Ukyi Lhamo. He even wrote about the Western food they ate almost every day. Robert said he had put a copy of the book in the post to Wang Mojie, and in his letter he included a photocopy of a page of the afterword in which he wrote:

> Ukyi Lhamo, who is half Han and half Tibetan, was born in Beijing and has studied in Paris. She is the descendant of an aristocratic family and speaks several languages. She currently studies Buddhism under the tutelage of my son Matthias. Wang Mojie was a lecturer in philosophy at a Beijing university. He came to Tibet as a volunteer teacher. He is erudite and has a keen intellect. The two of them teach at a middle school on the outskirts of Lhasa in a quiet little village. Wittgenstein left academia to teach in a remote school, and a young Chinese philosopher has done the same.

To Robert, Wang Mojie and Ukyi Lhamo were like characters in a charming, uniquely Asian story. He misunderstood their relationship, of course, and didn't realise that Ukyi Lhamo had ended it completely.

It was morning and the museum had just opened. Wang Mojie walked up the tall flight of granite steps to the front door. It was quiet in the museum, you could almost hear the rush of sunlight flooding in. Wang Mojie noticed that he was one of the first visitors of the day, and then he realised that the person who had walked in ahead of him worked there, and so Wang Mojie was the very first visitor, which he needed to be to get a private tour from Ukyi Lhamo. Recently, every time he thought of Ukyi Lhamo, he thought of her in the company of her mother and grandmother, because over the past year, she had proved herself worthy of their company. Her work in the museum had proved something about her character. The museum was a perfect setting for her, she stood out there. Any work of art needs to be placed against the proper background. Ukyi Lhamo and the museum were inseparable in Wang Mojie's mind.

As was his custom on each of his visits to the museum, Wang Mojie was wearing a Western suit jacket, a tie with a tie pin and leather shoes. He looked nothing like he did at school, where he was indifferent to what he wore. The suit jacket made him look serious, he stood straighter in it, but the big difference was that the boxy shape of the suit jacket somehow made the features of his ordinarily lopsided face look a little stronger. Given what Wang Mojie's face looked like, you wouldn't think Western attire would suit him, but the more you looked at him, the more you realised that in a jacket and tie Wang Mojie looked good, his face seemed almost attractive, he appeared very well put together, head to toe, in a way he otherwise never did. It is often the case that when things that are in opposition become unified, the union is strong, and we approve of it. Wang Mojie in Western dress was an example of this dialectical unity of opposites.

Wang Mojie looked handsome, he looked suave. But he wasn't dressed nicely for Ukyi Lhamo's sake, it was simply his habit, formed over many years, to look smart for a formal occasion. He had great respect for museums and considered a visit to a museum to be a formal occasion. Because he was the first person there, he was able to secure Ukyi Lhamo for a private tour. It was shockingly expensive, but he had always toured for free, he always slipped into group tours that somebody else paid for, and so he decided it wouldn't be fair to complain about the price. Wang Mojie knew Ukyi Lhamo's schedule, he knew which days she gave tours and which days she stayed in her office to do research. He knew she was doing tours that day, so he was confident his scheme would work.

Ukyi Lhamo was dressed in her museum uniform skirt and blouse. The uniform was modern with Tibetan touches, including the colour: it was black and red, the red of a monk's robe. A laser pointer in her hand, she came walking down the corridor at a brisk pace. She stopped short when she saw Wang Mojie. She was poised to retreat, as this was the first time she had run into him so near her office. She looked at him, and it dawned on her that the private tour she had been called out to lead was for Wang Mojie. Then she slowly removed from her face all traces of the shock and aversion that had quickly come over her. Wang Mojie looked at her calmly, saying nothing, watching the fascinating way her expression changed. Ukyi Lhamo did not speak either, she walked right by Wang Mojie, head high, back straight, and stepped to the spot at which she began all her tours. She began and moved quickly, not caring if Wang Mojie was keeping up. He thought she looked beautiful from behind, even more beautiful than from the front. The crimson-and-black skirt accentuated all the lines and curves of her body in a way that he found very, very pleasing. He watched her walk, he thought she looked good as a museum guide. Of course, Wang Mojie simply enjoyed seeing a woman out before the public in a uniform, it brought him a secret, private thrill, which had nothing at all to do with any ideological meaning of the particular uniform, and besides, a museum guide's uniform was like a stewardess's, intended to look both official and attractive.

Wang Mojie walked slowly after Ukyi Lhamo, but when she stopped and turned, he sped up and hurried to where she stood waiting for him. Wang Mojie was not interested in having a tour, he just wanted a chance to talk to her, but before he could reach her, she began to lecture. Wang Mojie could just about recite her entire tour from memory. He was very familiar with the entire lecture, he almost had it memorised. She began with a brief overview of what they would see, then she covered plate tectonics, the Tethys Sea, the uplifting of the Tibetan Plateau, the emergence of the Himalayas, the Kailash Range and the Yarlung Tsangpo, the excavation of the Karub Ruins, the building of the first palace on the site of the Potala in the seventh century... Wang Mojie had heard all this many times before, but standing there alone with Ukyi Lhamo made it feel very different. When she spoke to groups of tourists, Ukyi Lhamo was professional, she smiled, and she looked at each guest in turn, exchanging a glance. She was poised and engaged with what she was saying, she looked radiant and strong. Now, however, in front of Wang Mojie, she was stiff, and she did not deign to even look at him. Indeed, it was impossible to read her eyes, they were empty, as empty as the sky. Her laser pointer moved over the exhibits as she talked about Tibet's first king Nyatri Tsenpo, Songtsen Gampo, Langdarma, about the *Sakya Lekshe*, Drogon Chogyal Phagpa... each piece of the tour in turn... Wang Mojie knew it all well but now it seemed very unfamiliar.

Wang Mojie did not interrupt, he had no thought to. He had been worried the private tour would exhaust Ukyi Lhamo, but he realised he needn't have. To some degree, he could take credit for Ukyi Lhamo being in her current position, and now she was free of him. She had tried hard to change him, and she hadn't failed completely. But what was it that was making her put more and more distance between them?

What was it? He asked himself again, What was it?

She had tried being a doctor to him, his "wisdom consort", his *dakini*, but he had frightened her.

She was not anyone's "wisdom consort", she was not a *dakini*, he had almost destroyed her. He had overpowered her and her faith, which terrified him, but it terrified her more and more profoundly. The reason she wouldn't look at him was because he terrified her, and she was sick of feeling terrified.

What she is probably most afraid of, Wang Mojie thought to himself, is that I will tell her that I love her.

Nothing could be more terrifying to her.

He knew she had changed something deep within him.

She hadn't failed completely in her effort to change him, but this effort became too much for her and she had to stop. Which was a shame.

Wang Mojie loved museums, he loved Ukyi Lhamo, and he loved seeing Ukyi Lhamo in the museum.

It was so wonderful that Ukyi Lhamo had come to the museum. She began to tell the story of Lungshar Dorje Tsegyal, and she did so as if she were telling it to him for the very first time, as if those long conversations between them about Lungshar had never even happened. She certainly meant business when she had severed relations with him. She was worthy of being Madame Ukyi Lhamo's granddaughter. It was impressive how thorough and resolute she was, she was able to act as if they were strangers, and he sincerely admired her ability to do so. But he had to interrupt her, now, right away, because the tour was almost over.

—Sorry, one second, Wang Mojie said as he cupped one hand in the other before his chest in salute. For the story of Lungshar, shouldn't you have a recent photograph of Madame Ukyi Lhamo, the great Buddhist? It could go right here, yes, right here would be good. It wouldn't have to be too large. I think this would be a pretty good spot for it.

Ukyi Lhamo stopped, and she breathed deeply.

—And there should be some wall text that identifies her as both Madame Ukyi Lhamo and Buddhist Master Ukyi Lhamo. That would unite history and religion here at this spot. They are often united as it is, and your grandmother's life as both an important historical figure and a great Buddhist is the perfect example of this. The study of history should be more than the study of the dead. When in our study of history we consider the living, history comes alive for us, it becomes real, we feel connected to it, and we realise we can find the past in the present. So why not put up a photograph? If you didn't get a photo of her when you were in Dromo, you can use one of the ones I took. They're not bad, actually they're really good. I think it is fair to say that she, I mean Buddhist Master Ukyi Lhamo, is Tibet.

There was something about Wang Mojie that made him difficult to resist, and Ukyi Lhamo's stern expression slowly softened.

—Do you want to see my photographs? Wang Mojie asked.

—Did you bring them? Ukyi Lhamo replied, trying to sound indifferent.

—Of course. I noticed a while ago that you didn't have one displayed, I just never had the chance to bring it up.

Wang Mojie handed Ukyi Lhamo three photographs. She looked for a long time at each of the first two and stared at the third one even longer, seemingly lost in her thoughts about history. Wang Mojie was now ready to accept that even if it didn't conform to our conventional idea of what was real and unreal, there were times when things were just as Ma Dingge had said: phenomena cannot be separated into the past, the present and the future, all phenomena are present simultaneously, all past and present lives rise before us in the moment. Ukyi Lhamo's tears were included in this.

Ukyi Lhamo took out a very beautiful handkerchief, looked away and wiped her eyes. As she did, her left sleeve slipped down and Wang Mojie saw a bracelet of dark, translucent prayer beads on her wrist. Wang Mojie had been feeling quite satisfied with himself for being so broad-minded, but seeing the prayer beads made him suddenly dizzy. He almost took out his own prayer beads but did not. Their prayer beads were exactly alike. He told himself to be rational, but he could not stop himself from imagining that there was a lotus flower above him and he was bathed in the light of the Buddha. Was the old woman really Madame Ukyi Lhamo? She could not be, he told himself, she could not be.

—Yours are better than mine, Ukyi Lhamo said. She still wouldn't look at him. She kept her eyes on the photographs.

—What are you sad about? Look how dignified she is. She is history itself.

—When do you leave? Ukyi Lhamo asked, recovering her air of indifference. She meant leave for France.

—Soon, otherwise I wouldn't have paid such an extravagant amount for the private tour.

—You need to get out of Tibet, you need broader horizons.

—And you should go abroad too, for graduate study, in museum studies I mean.

—If there is ever a need, I'll be in touch. I'm sorry, the tour's over, my next group will be here soon.

—Wait, come back, we haven't talked about the most important thing, give me two more minutes. Just two minutes.

She stopped, he looked at her.

—I have two favours to ask, and you have to say yes. I'm going over as a visiting scholar, it's not permanent, I'm definitely coming back, but the school probably won't let me keep my house. They'll make me move out, but I don't want to have to go back to the interior just because of that. Everything I own is here, it's not much, just all my books. Can you keep my books for me? If you don't want to have to see them because they are mine, can you store them at your mother's place? I don't think she'd say no to my books, but, still, it would be best if you kept them in your new apartment. The museum owns the apartment, so it would be like the books were in the museum, and that's a good place for them. I'm joking of course about the museum, but I really don't have anywhere to leave my books. I don't have friends here, you know that. You are the only one I can ask. When I come back, at least I'll have my books to welcome me home.

Ukyi Lhamo was silent for a long moment before she spoke.

—I know of someone else. You can give your books to him, she said.

—Who? Who do you mean?

—Ma Dingge.

—Ukyi Lhamo, don't be that way, OK?

Ukyi Lhamo, her voice flat, said she would take the books.

—And the second favour I have to ask is, will you come to see me off at the airport? I'm leaving next Sunday.

—No.

Her answer was quick and categorical.

—Come to see me off, you can endure just a bit more of me. As soon as that plane takes off, maybe it's goodbye forever.

—Nice way to put it, but I shouldn't expect more from you. What can you expect from a dog but barking? she said, using an idiom and putting emphasis on the word "dog".

—You love me, right? Wang Mojie said with a smile.

—No. I pity you.

—Coming to the airport?

—No.

Ukyi Lhamo started to walk away. Wang Mojie took a few quick steps and stopped her.

—When will you come for the books? You'll have to find a van. I have a lot of books.

—Patience. I'll find somebody to do it and he will contact you.

—Is this goodbye?

—Have a good trip.

—Shake hands. Let's shake hands. Shake hands.

Wang Mojie stood with his hand out. Ukyi Lhamo did not move. Wang Mojie reached over, took her hand and shook it. Wang Mojie hugged Ukyi Lhamo, but she did not hug back, she waited for him to release her.

—When I come back, then. I'm coming back.

—Safe travels.

Wang Mojie walked away, he turned and looked back once. Ukyi Lhamo's back. The depths of the museum. The eternal...

In either May or August 1998, not that the month matters, J. Hillis Miller published Reading Narrative, *in which he makes an intriguing assertion about the ending of any fictional narrative. In the chapter titled "The End of the Line", Miller writes, "Endings in narrative are difficult to pin down, whether 'theoretically', or for a given novel... The impasses of closure in narrative are present already in the terms commonly used to describe endings." Miller argues that if we study narrative endings with sufficient attention to detail, we will discover that it is "impossible ever to tell whether a given narrative is complete", as he put it in his 1978 journal article "The Problematic of Ending in Narrative".*

Miller argues that we can't identify one point in narrative time as the ending because we can always project a second point that comes later in time, therefore unless time itself stops, no narrative can end. In Reading Narrative, *Miller takes Virginia Woolf's* The Voyage Out *as an example. In this novel, Woolf seems to wrap up the story of the Dalloways, but years later she resumed the story in* Mrs Dalloway. *There are many examples of novels that are sequels to earlier novels (and even more examples among those interminable serial dramas on television, a form that is derivative of the novel), and this proves that any novel can, theoretically, go on forever. But this novel of mine is slightly different. On the one hand, the story of Ukyi Lhamo and Wang Mojie might develop in all sorts of ways from the point at which I have left it, and there is plenty of room for the exercise of the imagination. On the other hand, however, one could argue that this book really ended at the conclusion of Chapter 34. We are in Chapter 37 now, which means I have already written three extra chapters, and I could keep writing, I could do so endlessly, but I also need to make it clear to you, dear reader, that after Robert left Tibet, Wang Mojie and Ukyi Lhamo stopped living together and their, shall we say, experimental physical relationship ended.*

The philosophical conversation they had participated in was a success, their cohabitation was a failure, which just about sums up the whole novel. On their last night living together, the night that is the subject of Chapter 34, Wang Mojie wanted to make one more attempt at physical intimacy, but Ukyi Lhamo rejected him. She said she never wanted to see his face again, not even for a minute, and he spent the night in the bathroom. That is in Chapter 34. But contrary to what I wrote in Chapter 35, the next day she did not go with Wang Mojie to the airport to say goodbye to Robert. The scene out there by the Yarlung Tsangpo in the airport coffee shop never actually took place.

I once asked Wang Mojie if he thought that what I wrote in the last three chapters could possibly have happened. Ukyi Lhamo did go to work for the museum, and so I asked him if his going to see her at the museum was within the realm of possibility. He said it was the prerogative of fiction to make anything at all happen, but we do not have the same prerogative in life. That's true enough, but I would argue that what happens in life happens because of choices made by individuals, nothing happens by chance, and we have the prerogative to make those choices. I often said to Wang Mojie that life starts in the head, we first imagine something and then later it becomes part of our actual life. I told him there is no such thing as a life that just happens. All "normal lives" unfold as they do at least to some small degree according to someone's design. What I meant by this is that while fiction is, of course, made up, we should think of it as the art form of the exploration of the possible, fiction imagines different possible lives. Wang Mojie understood what I was saying, and he didn't deny that it would be possible for him to do what he does in the novel and walk into the museum and join a group of strangers in one of Ukyi Lhamo's tour groups. He admitted that he had this prerogative, it was not just my prerogative when writing the story, but he said that conceding it was one thing, but acting on it was quite another, and rather than exercise his prerogative, he preferred to leave things hanging, and maybe he would leave it hanging there forever.

—Better to leave it hanging, right? Better for me, better for Ukyi Lhamo and better for your novel.

—On this question, discussion of my novel is irrelevant, it doesn't matter about my novel, I said.

—You're wrong, your novel matters a lot, it shows us a possible future, which is why we can say that in a way novels teach us more than life does, we learn more from texts than we do from life. Don't you find that having some suspense in real life is just as fascinating as suspense in fiction?

Wang Mojie is stubborn and skilled at debate. He can't be fully understood, and he can't be changed. Indeed, I doubt that his deep-seated sexual proclivity actually shifted much for the better, and if not, then what I imagine in my last three chapters isn't very realistic. But I can't accept and don't believe that Wang Mojie didn't change for the better at least a bit. How could it be possible for him not to change at all? Ukyi Lhamo tried so very hard! She made efforts worthy of White Tara or a "wisdom consort", it was like she climbed down from a temple wall painting of a goddess and came into Wang Mojie's life. But because of him, she failed, and no sort of faith-based intervention, even tantric, was going to be of much use with Wang Mojie. Looking at things objectively, however, we can't say she failed completely, because on that last night, didn't Wang Mojie put himself through the pain of giving it one last try? Also, to be honest, it appeared to me that in comparison with the past there was a different look in Wang Mojie's eyes. His eyes were still calm, still full of intellect, still cold, but before they were dark and guarded and hard to see into, but now there was just a little bit of light in them, like distant starlight. I thought that given he had that little bit of light in his eyes, he should make a trip to the museum, he should go to make obeisance, he should go for redemption. But what I imagined happening is not what happened in reality. Wang Mojie didn't go to the museum, not once. Never before he left Tibet, before he left China, did he set foot inside the dreamlike world of the museum.

Wang Mojie, of course, was not out to deliberately discredit my novel, he wasn't deliberately contradicting what I wrote, he was just more complicated than the character of my imagination, much more difficult to understand. After Wang Mojie left, he didn't forget Lhasa, not for a moment. He wasn't done with the place, quite the contrary, every year he returned once or twice. While in Paris as a visiting scholar, he began work towards his PhD under Robert's supervision, the only Asian graduate student Robert had in that late stage of his career. His life was just what Robert had hoped for and promised, and he met many well-known European intellectuals of the older generation and also scholars closer to his own age. He attended the annual meetings of a variety of academic organisations, and even before he had finished his PhD, he was hired to teach in the University of Paris's Centre for Asian Studies. He offered courses in Asian philosophy and one on the future for philosophy in modern Asia. Not long after securing his teaching job in Paris, he became an affiliated scholar at Tibet University, where he taught his course on East-West comparative philosophy (the course was also popular at the University of Paris). He flew back and forth from Paris, spending part of each year at Tibet University, where he had an office reserved for his use and an apartment that was just like Ukyi Lhamo's.

That's how connected to Tibet Wang Mojie remained. He loved Tibet, he loved the Tibetan sky and the philosophy that the sky inspired. There was Ukyi Lhamo as well and the way things had been left hanging between them, there was that "suspense". Ukyi Lhamo was everything to Wang Mojie that Robert had once said she was. Robert had said that for Wang Mojie, Ukyi Lhamo was eternal, she was transcendent, she was like the sun (French men are prone to hyperbole when they talk of women, but they mean everything they say). What surprised me was that for about five years Wang Mojie and Ukyi Lhamo didn't have a single one-to-one meeting, and if they ran into each other at parties given by mutual friends, they took it perfectly in their stride and exchanged pleasantries. It was as if everything between them in the past had never happened.

Long after I had finished the last three chapters, I was still waiting for the day when Wang Mojie would leave his apartment on the Tibet University campus and, as I had imagined him doing, walk into the museum and quietly slip into one of Ukyi Lhamo's tour groups. I believed this might happen, I thought sooner or later it was bound to, I was sure of it. But very regrettably it never did, not once.

When I considered things objectively, I accepted that there might be very practical reasons Wang Mojie did not return to the museum. For starters, Ukyi Lhamo was married, she had a family, and so it wouldn't do for Wang Mojie to just drop in on her. But then I realised I was being naive, because, come on, when has a connection between two lovers' hearts been broken just because they marry other people? Besides, Ukyi Lhamo had married her mountaineer. She had fallen for Wang Mojie while she was in the middle of a passionate affair with her mountaineer, and so why would she refuse to see Wang Mojie simply because she was now married to the man? No, the mountaineer wasn't the reason, at least not the main reason. Wang Mojie never married, he didn't have a girlfriend, he stayed single. He flew back and forth through the vast space between East and West, a possessor of infinite possibilities, endlessly deferring the exercise of his prerogative, endlessly leaving it in "suspense", and this "suspense" seemed to have become something spiritual for Wang Mojie, it was part of his history. It is also true, however, that if we consider everything that might be possible for Wang Mojie, we can't say there has been no turn for the better in his life, even though this turn for the better was unfortunate for someone else. Recently friends in Lhasa told me that Ukyi Lhamo's mountaineer died this past spring in a climbing accident and now like so many of his friends he lies forever in the snow – this was bound to happen, my novel was anticipating it all along – and any way you want to look at it, his death is a turning point, because with the mountaineer gone, nothing stands between Wang Mojie and Ukyi Lhamo. But everything is up to Wang Mojie, of course. He's not young any more. All his memories, of his garden, of the violence, of history, all those memories are likely fading as his hair turns prematurely grey. Even if he is no longer looking for love and redemption, as long as he turns up in the museum one day, I think there will be a new beginning.

Maybe Wang Mojie will find romance, find love, get redemption... and get that hug from Ukyi Lhamo, who knows?

Beijing, 2006 to 2010

About the Author

Ning Ken (1959 -), born and raised in Beijing, began his writing career as a poet, first publishing in 1982. From 1984 to 1986 he taught at a village school outside of Lhasa, Tibet. Beginning in 1987, Ning Ken's lyric essays about Tibet contributed to the revitalising of the contemporary nonfiction prose essay, a literary genre of great importance in China. Ning Ken was a pioneer of online publication, and he posted his first novel, *The City of Masks*, serially on Sina.com. It was named the best internet novel of 2000; its 2001 printed version won a Lao She Literature Award in 2002 and was nominated for the 2009 Newman Prize for Chinese Literature. Ning Ken has since published the novels *The Gate of Silence* (2004), *The Ringed Mountain* (first published as *The Ringed Woman* in 2006), *Tibetan Sky* (2010) and *Three Trios* (2014), which was named as one of the best novels of its year by *Asia Weekly*. *Tibetan Sky* won several awards, including a Lao She Literature Award, and was nominated for the prestigious Mao Dun Literature Prize for best novel. Ning Ken's short fiction has been collected in his books *The Order of Things* (2014) and *Ukyi Lhamo* (2015). For many years, Ning Ken was the executive deputy editor of the literary magazine *October*. Ning Ken continues to live in Beijing, where he is affiliated with the Lao She Literary Institute and is an honorary member of the faculty of Beijing International Studies University. His works have been translated into Czech, English, French and Italian.

About the Translator

Thomas Moran (1957 -) studied English and American literature as an undergraduate at Syracuse University. He taught at the International School of Beijing from 1981 to 1983. He studied at Peking University in 1984 to 1985 and did research there and at Suzhou University from 1989 to 1991. He received his PhD in East Asian Literature from Cornell University in 1994, and since that year he has been on the faculty of the Chinese Department at Middlebury College, where he teaches modern and contemporary Chinese literature and film, as well as Modern Standard Chinese (Mandarin). He directed Middlebury's CV Starr School Abroad in Beijing in 2011 and in 2012 did research there as a Fulbright Scholar. He has edited or co-edited and contributed to three volumes on Chinese writers for the *Dictionary of Literary Biography* series and has published translations of Chinese short stories, plays, poems and essays. He lives in the Green Mountains of Vermont, USA with his wife, the painter Rebecca Purdum.

ABOUT **SINO**IST BOOKS

We hope you enjoyed this story about the philosophical and spiritual journeys of Wang Mojie and Ukyi Lhamo.

SINOIST BOOKS brings the best of Chinese fiction to English-speaking readers. We aim to create a greater understanding of Chinese culture and society, and provide an outlet for the ideas and creativity of the country's most talented authors.

To let us know what you thought of this book, or to learn more about the diverse range of exciting Chinese fiction in translation we publish, find us online. If you're as passionate about Chinese literature as we are, then we'd love to hear your thoughts!